Abou [...]

A fifth generation Cali [...]
in San Diego within m [...]
knows with their help [...]
She takes particular j [...]
nephews who are all [...]
future. If she's not at a family event, you'll usually find
her at home reading or writing her next grand romance.

Shirley Hailstock likes to explore new worlds and visit
exotic places. As an author, she can visit those places,
and be the heroine of her own stories. The author of over
thirty novels and novellas, Shirley has received numerous
awards. Her books have appeared on *BlackBoard*,
Essence and *Library Journal* bestseller lists. She is a
past president of Romance Writers of America.

New York Times and *USA Today* bestselling author
Shirley Jump spends her days writing romance to
feed her shoe addiction and avoid cleaning the toilets.
She cleverly finds writing time by feeding her kids
junk food, allowing them to dress in the clothes they
find on the floor and encouraging the dogs to double
as vacuum cleaners. Chat with her via Facebook:
www.facebook.com/shirleyjump.author or her website:
www.shirleyjump.com

Ever After

COLLECTION

December 2020
Dreaming Ever After

January 2021
Imagining Ever After

February 2021
Passionately Ever After

March 2021
Enchanted Ever After

April 2021
Royally Ever After

May 2021
Happily Ever After

Happily Ever After

TERESA CARPENTER

SHIRLEY HAILSTOCK

SHIRLEY JUMP

MILLS & BOON

First Published in Great Britain 2021
by Mills & Boon, an imprint of HarperCollins*Publishers* Ltd,
1 London Bridge Street, London, SE1 9GF

www.harpercollins.co.uk

HarperCollins*Publishers*
1st Floor, Watermarque Building,
Ringsend Road, Dublin 4, Ireland

HAPPILY EVER AFTER © 2021 Harlequin Books S.A.

The Best Man & The Wedding Planner © 2015 Harlequin Books S.A.
All He Needs © 2017 Shirley Hailstock
The Firefighter's Family Secret © 2016 Shirley Kawa-Jump

Special thanks and acknowledgement are given to Teresa Carpenter for her contribution to *The Vineyards of Calanetti* series.

ISBN: 978-0-263-30028-4

MIX
Paper from
responsible sources
FSC™ C007454

This book is produced from independently certified FSC™ paper to ensure responsible forest management.

For more information visit: www.harpercollins.co.uk/green

Printed and bound in Spain
by CPI, Barcelona

THE BEST MAN & THE WEDDING PLANNER

TERESA CARPENTER

This book is dedicated to my editor Carly Byrne for her patience, understanding, speed and good cheer. I never see her sweat. Even when I do. Thank you for everything.

CHAPTER ONE

"Now boarding, first-class passengers for Flight 510 to Florence."

Lindsay Reeves's ears perked up. She glanced at her watch; time had gotten away from her. She closed her tablet folio, tucked it into her satchel and then reached for the precious cargo she was personally escorting across the ocean. She hooked the garment bag holding the couture wedding dress for the future Queen of Halencia over her shoulder and began to move as the attendant made a second announcement. "First-class passengers now boarding."

"Welcome aboard." The attendant looked from the second ticket to Lindsay. "I'm sorry, both passengers will need to be present to board."

"We're both here. I bought a seat for this." She held up the garment bag.

The woman smiled but her eyes questioned Lindsay's sanity. "You bought a first-class ticket for your luggage?"

"Yes." She kept it at that, not wanting to draw any further attention. With the wedding only a month away, the world was alive with wedding dress fever.

"We have a storage closet in first class that can hold it if you want to refund the ticket before takeoff," the attendant offered.

"No, thank you." Lindsay pressed the second ticket into the woman's hand. "I'm not letting this bag out of my sight."

On the plane she passed a nice-looking older couple already seated in the first row and moved on to the last row where she spied her seats. She draped the garment bag over the aisle seat and frowned when it immediately slumped into a scrunched heap on the seat.

That wouldn't do. She pulled it back into place and tried to anchor it but when she let go, it drooped again. The weight of the dress, easily thirty pounds, made it too heavy to lie nicely. She needed something to hold it in place. After using her satchel to counter the weight temporarily, she slid past a young couple and their two children to speak to the flight attendant.

"We have a closet we can hang the dress in," the male attendant stated upon hearing her request.

"I've been paid not to let it out of my sight," she responded. True enough. Her reputation as a wedding planner to the rich and famous depended on her getting this dress to the wedding in pristine condition without anyone seeing it but her, the bride and her attendants.

"Hmm," the man—his name tag read Dan—tapped his lips while he thought.

"Welcome aboard, sir." Behind Lindsay another attendant, a blonde woman, greeted a fellow passenger.

Out of the corner of her eye Lindsay got the impression of a very tall, very broad, dark-haired man. She stepped into the galley to give them more room.

"You're the last of our first-class passengers," the attendant advised the man. "Once you're seated, please let me know if you need anything."

"Check," the man said in a deep, bass voice and moved down the aisle.

Goodness. Just the one word sent a tingle down Lindsay's spine. She sure hoped he intended to sleep during the long, red-eye flight. She wanted to get some work done and his voice might prove quite distracting.

"I've got it." Dan waved a triumphant hand. "We'll just put the seat in sleep mode and lay the bag across it."

He poured a glass of champagne and then another. "Will that work?"

"Yes, that will be perfect. Thank you."

"Seats aren't allowed to be reclined during takeoff. Once we reach cruising altitude I'll be along to put the seat down. And I'll look for something to secure it in case the flight gets bumpy."

"Great. You've been very helpful."

Lindsay headed back to her seat. Halfway through first class she caught sight of the newcomer and her breath caught in the back of her throat. He was beautiful. There was no other word for it. Long, lean features with high cheekbones, dark, slanted eyebrows and long, black eyelashes. Dark stubble decorated his square jaw.

Suddenly her eyes popped wide and she let out a shriek. "Get up!" she demanded. "Get up right now!"

He was sitting on the dress!

A frown furrowed his brow. He slowly opened lambent brown eyes so stunning she almost forgot why she was yelling. Almost.

"Are you talking to me?" he asked in a deep, rasping voice.

"Yes." She confronted the man, hands on hips. "You're in my seat. Sitting on my dress. Get up!"

"What's the problem here?" The other attendant appeared next to her.

"He's in my seat." She pointed an accusing finger. "Sitting on my garment bag. Make him move."

Behind her a young child began to cry. Lindsay cringed but held her ground.

The beading on this dress was intricate, all hand-sewn. If it had to be repaired it would cost a fortune. And she'd already paid a pretty penny to make sure nothing happened to it. How could someone sit on a garment bag without noticing it?

"Let's all calm down." The blonde attendant squeezed by Lindsay. "Sir, can I ask you to stand, please?"

The man slowly rose. He had to duck to the side to avoid hitting the overhead compartment. He must be six-four, maybe six-five; a long way to glare up from five feet four. She managed.

"I'm not sitting on anything." He gestured across the aisle. "I moved it there because it was in my seat."

Lindsay looked to her left. The garment bag rested in a heap on the seat with her heavy satchel dumped on top. She jumped on it, removing her bag and smoothing the fabric. It was all mushed as though it had been sat on.

"May I see your tickets, please?" Dan requested.

Lindsay pulled hers from the front pocket of her satchel and waited to be vindicated.

"Actually, you're both in wrong seats. My fault, I'm afraid. I'm used to a different plane. I do apologize. Ms. Reeves, you are on the left and, Mr. Sullivan, you need to move forward a row."

Lovely. She couldn't even blame the beast. Except she did.

At least he'd be in the row ahead of her so she wouldn't have to have him next to her the entire flight.

His brown gaze went to the toddlers in the row in front of the one the attendant indicated. "I'd prefer the back row." He pasted on a charming smile. "Is it possible to trade seats?"

No. No. No.

"Of course." The blonde gushed, swayed, no doubt, by his dimples. "There was a cancellation so no one else is boarding in first class. Is there anything I can get you before we continue boarding?"

"A pillow would be nice."

"My pleasure, Mr. Sullivan." She turned to Lindsay. "Anything for you, ma'am?"

Ma'am? Seriously? "I'd like a pillow. And a blanket, please."

"We'll do a full turndown service after the flight gets started." She gave Sullivan a smile and disappeared behind the curtain to the coach area.

Lindsay stared after her. Did that mean she didn't get a pillow or a blanket? This was her first time flying first-class. So far she had mixed feelings. She liked the extra room and the thought of stretching out for the long flight. But Blondie wasn't earning any points.

Lindsay draped the garment bag over the window seat as best she could until the seat could be reclined. Unfortunately that put her in the aisle seat directly across from Mr. Tall, Dark and Inconsiderate.

Nothing for it. She'd just have to ignore him and focus on her work. It would take the entire flight to configure the seating arrangement for the reception. She had the list of guests from the bride and the list of guests from the groom. And a three-page list of political notes from the palace of who couldn't be seated next to whom and who should be seated closer to the royal couple. What had started as a private country wedding had grown to include more than a hundred guests as political factors came into play.

It was a wedding planner's nightmare. But she took it as an opportunity to excel.

Before she knew it she was being pushed back in her chair as the plane lifted into the air. Soon after, Dan appeared to fold down the window seat. He carefully laid the heavy garment bag in place and secured it with the seat belt and a bungee cord. She thanked him as she resumed her seat.

She glanced out of the corner of her eye to see Sullivan had his pillow—a nice, big, fluffy one. Ignore him.

Easier thought than done. He smelled great; a spicy musk with a touch of soap.

Eyes back on her tablet, she shuffled some names into table seats and then started to run them against her lists to see if they were all compatible. Of course, they weren't. Two people needed to be moved forward and two people couldn't be seated together. That left four people at the table. She moved people to new tables and highlighted them as a reminder to check out the politics on them. And repeated the process.

A soft snore came from across the way—much less annoying than the shrill cry of one of the toddlers demanding a bandage for his boo-boo. Blondie rushed to the rescue and the boy settled down. Except for loud outbursts like that, the two boys were actually well behaved. There'd been no need for Sullivan to move seats.

"Would you care for a meal, Ms. Reeves?" Dan appeared beside her.

She glanced at the time on her tablet. Eight o'clock. They'd been in the air an hour. "Yes, please."

"You have a choice of chicken Cordon bleu or beef Stroganoff."

"I'll have the beef. With a cola."

He nodded and turned to the other side of the aisle. Before he could ask, Sullivan said he'd have the beef and water.

Her gaze collided with his. Brown eyes with specks of gold surveyed her, interest and appreciation sparkled in the whiskey-brown depths, warm and potent.

Heat flooded her, followed by a shiver.

"What's in the bag?" he asked, his voice even deeper and raspier from sleep. Way too sexy for her peace of mind.

"None of your business." She turned back to her table plan.

"Must be pretty important for you to get so upset. Let

me guess, a special dress for a special occasion?" He didn't give up.

"Yes. If you must know. And it's my job to protect it."

"Protect it? Interesting. So it's not your dress."

She rolled her eyes and sent him a droll stare. "I liked you better when you were snoring."

He grinned, making his dimples pop. "I deserve that. Listen, I'm sorry for my attitude earlier and for sitting on the dress. I had wine with dinner and wine always gives me a headache."

Lindsay glared at Sullivan. "So you did sit on the dress." She knew it. That had definitely been a butt print on the bag.

He blinked, all innocence. "I meant I'm sorry for dumping it over there."

"Uh-huh."

His grin never wavered.

"Why did you have wine with dinner if it gives you a headache?"

The smile faded. "Because dinner with my folks always goes better with a little wine. And I'm going to have a headache at the end either way."

"Okay, I get that." Lindsay adored her flighty, dependent mother but, yeah, dinners were easier with a little wine. Sometimes, like between husbands, a lot of wine was required.

A corner of his rather nice mouth kicked up. "You surprise me, Ms. Reeves. I'd have thought you'd be appalled."

"Parents aren't always easy." She closed her tablet to get ready for her meal. "It doesn't mean we don't love them."

"Amen. Respect is another matter."

That brought her attention around. He wore a grim expression and turmoil churned in his distracted gaze. The situation with his parents must be complicated. It was a sad day when you lost respect for the person you loved most in the world. She understood his pain only too well.

Thankfully, Dan arrived with a small cart, disrupting old memories. He activated a tray on the side of her seat and placed a covered plate in front of her along with a glass of soda. Real china, real crystal, real silverware. Nice. And then he lifted the cover and the luscious scent of braised meat and rich sauce reached her.

"Mmm." She hummed her approval. "This looks fantastic."

"I can promise you it is," Dan assured her. "Chef LaSalle is the pride of the skies."

She took her first bite as he served Sullivan and moaned again. She couldn't help it, the flavors burst in her mouth, seducing her taste buds.

"Careful, Ms. Reeves," Sullivan cautioned. "You sound like you're having a good time over there."

"Eat. You'll understand." She took a sip of her drink, watching him take a bite. "Or maybe not. After all, you've already eaten."

"I wasn't hungry earlier. Damn, this is good." He pointed to the video screen. "Shall we watch a movie with our meal?"

She was tempted. Surprising. After the disaster of last year, work had been her major consolation. She rarely took the time to relax with a movie. She was too busy handling events for the stars of those movies. A girl had to work hard to make the stars happy in Hollywood. And she had to work harder than the rest after allowing an old flame to distract her to the point of putting her career at risk. But she'd learned her lesson.

Luckily she'd already signed the contract for this gig. And she planned to make the royal wedding of the Crown Prince of Halencia, Antonio de l'Accardi, to the commoner, Christina Rose, the wedding of the century.

Thirty days from now no one would be able to question her dedication—which meant returning to the puzzle of the table seating.

"You go on," she told Sullivan. "I have to get back to my work."

"What are you doing over there? Those earlier moans weren't as pleasant as your dinner noises."

"It's a creative new form of torture called a seating arrangement."

"Ah. It sounds excruciating."

"Oh, believe me. It's for a political dinner and there are all these levels of protocols of who can sit with whom. And then there's the added element of personal likes and dislikes. It's two steps back for every one step forward. And it's a lot of manual double-checking…talk about a headache."

"Politics usually are." The grimness in his tone told her there was something more there. Before she had time to wonder about it, he went on. "The information isn't on spreadsheets?"

"It is, but there are more than a hundred names here. I have to seat a table and then check each name to see if they're compatible."

"You know you can set up a program that can look at the information and tell you whether the table mates are compatible at the time you put the name in."

She blinked at him. "That would be wonderful. How do I do that exactly?"

He laughed, a deep, friendly sound, then rattled off a string of commands that had her eyes glazing over. "The setup will take a few minutes but will likely save you hours overall."

"Yeah, but you lost me at the word 'algorithm.'" She wiped her mouth with the cloth napkin. "You really had my hopes up for a minute there."

"Sorry, tech talk. I own a company that provides software for cyber security. A program like this really isn't that difficult. Let me see your computer after dinner and I'll do it for you. It'll take me less than an hour."

This man was tempting her left and right. She weighed the hours she'd save against the confidentiality agreement she'd signed and sadly shook her head.

"Thank you for offering but I can't. This is a special event. I'm not allowed to share information with anyone except my staff, designated officials and pre-approved vendors."

"This is for the royal wedding of Prince Antonio of Halencia, right?"

Her eyes popped wide. How could he know that?

"Come on, it's not hard to guess. The wedding dress, the seating chart. We're on a flight to Florence. And I know they have an American event planner. Hang on, I'll take care of this."

He pulled out his cell phone and hit a couple of buttons.

"What?" she challenged. "You're calling the palace in Halencia? Uh, huh. I don't think so. You can hang up now."

"Hey, Tony." He raised a dark eyebrow as he spoke into the phone.

Tony? As in Antonio? Yeah, right.

"I got your text. Don't worry about it. I'm here for a month. I'll see you next week." He listened for a moment. "Yes, I had dinner with them. They were thrilled with the invitation. Hey, listen, the wedding planner is on my flight and she needs some programming to help her with the seating chart. She's bound by the confidentiality agreement from letting me help her. Can you give her authorization? Great, I'm going to put her on."

He held the phone out to Lindsay. "It's Prince Antonio."

CHAPTER TWO

LINDSAY ROLLED HER eyes at the man across the way, wondering how far he meant to take this joke and what he hoped to achieve.

"Hello?"

"*Buona sera*, Ms. Reeves. I hope you are having a nice flight."

"Uh, yes, I am." The voice was male, pleasant and slightly accented. And could be anyone. Except how had he known her name? Sullivan hadn't mentioned it.

"Christina is thrilled to have your services for the wedding. You have my full support to make this *il matrimonio dei suoi sogni*—the wedding of her dreams."

"I'll do my best." Could this actually be the prince?

"Duty demands my presence at the palace but I look forward to meeting you at the rehearsal. Zach is my best man. He will be my advocate in Monte Calanetti for the next month. He is available to assist you in any way necessary."

She turned to look at the man across the aisle and quirked a brow at his evil smirk. "Zach…Sullivan?"

"Yes. We went to college together. He's like a brother to me. If he can assist with the meal plan—"

"The seating chart." She squeezed her eyes closed. *OMG, I just interrupted the royal prince.*

"Of course. The seating chart. If Zach can help, you must allow him to be of service. He is quite handy with a computer."

"Yes. I will. Thank you."

"It is I who thanks you. You do us an honor by coming to Halencia. If I can be of further assistance, you have access to me through Zach. *Buona notte*, Ms. Reeves."

"Good night." Instead of giving the phone back to Sullivan she checked the call history and saw she'd spoken to Tony de l'Accardi. She slowly turned her head to meet chocolate-brown eyes. "You know the Prince of Halencia."

"I wouldn't take on the best man gig for anyone else."

The flight attendant appeared with the cart to collect his meal and sweetly inquire if he'd like dessert.

Lindsay rolled her eyes, barely completing the action before the blonde turned to her.

"Are you done, ma'am?"

Ma'am again? Lindsay's eyes narrowed in a bland stare.

Her displeasure must have registered because the woman rushed on. "For dessert we have crème brûlée, strawberry cheesecake or a chocolate mousse."

Lindsay handed off her empty plate and, looking the woman straight in the eye, declared, "I'll have one of each."

"Of course, ma… Ms. Reeves." She hurriedly stashed the plate and rolled the cart away.

Lindsay slowly turned her head until Sullivan's intent regard came into view. Okay, first things first. "I'm only twenty-nine. Way too young to be ma'am."

He cocked his head.

She handed him his phone. "Why didn't you tell me you were the best man?"

He lifted one dark eyebrow. "Would you have believed me?"

She contemplated him. "Probably. I have a file on you."

His slanted eyebrow seemed to dip even further. "Then I'm surprised you didn't recognize me. You probably have profiles on the entire wedding party in that tablet of yours."

She lifted one shoulder in a half shrug of acknowledgment. "I've learned it's wise to know who I'll be working with. I didn't recognize you because it's out of context.

Plus, you don't have an eight-o'clock shadow in your company photo in which you're wearing glasses."

"Huh." He ran the backs of his fingers over his jaw. "I'll have to get that picture updated. I had Lasik eye surgery over a year ago. Regardless, I didn't know you were involved in the wedding until you started talking about the meal arrangements."

"Seating arrangements," she corrected automatically.

"Right."

The flight attendant arrived with dessert. She handed Zach a crystal dish of chocolate mousse and set a small tray with all three desserts artfully displayed in front of Lindsay.

"Enjoy," she said and retreated down the aisle.

"Mmm." Lindsay picked up a spoon and broke into the hard shell of crystalized sugar topping the crème brûlée. "Mmm." This time it was a moan. "Oh, that's good."

"Careful, Ms. Reeves, you're going to get me worked up if you continue." Zach gestured at her loaded tray with his spoon. "I see you like your sweets."

"It's a long night." She defended her stash.

"I guess you don't plan on sleeping."

"I have a lot of work." She gave her usual excuse then, for some unknown reason, confessed, "I don't sleep well on planes."

"It may help if you relaxed and watched the movie instead of working."

No doubt he was right. But work soothed her, usually. Over the past year she'd found it increasingly more difficult to believe in the magic of her process. She blamed her breakup with Kevin last year. But she hoped to change that soon. If a royal wedding couldn't bring back the magic in what she did, she needed to rethink her career path.

"Thank you for that insightful bit of advice. What don't you like about being best man? The role or the exposure?"

"Either. Both. Seems like I've been dodging the lime-light since I was two."

"Well, you did grow up in a political family." That brought his earlier comment and reaction into context. Her research revealed he was related to the political pow-erhouse Sullivans from Connecticut. "Never had any as-piration in that direction?"

The curse he uttered made her glance worriedly toward the toddlers. Luckily the lack of sound or movement in that direction indicated they were probably asleep.

"I'll take that as a no."

"I wished my father understood me so well."

She empathized with his pain. She felt the same way about her mother. Perhaps empathy was why she found him so easy to talk to. "I've found parents often see what they want to see. That addresses the exposure…what do you have against the role of best man?"

"I hate weddings. The fancier the event, the more I de-test them. There's something about the pomp and circum-stance that just screams fake to me." He licked his spoon and set the crystal dish aside. "No offense."

No offense? He'd just slammed everything she stood for. Why should she be offended?

And he wasn't done. "It's like the couple needs to dis-tract the crowd from the fact they're marrying for some-thing other than love."

"You don't believe in love?" It was one thing for her to question her belief in what she was doing and another for someone else to take shots at it.

"I believe in lust and companionship. Love is a myth best left to romance novels."

"Wow. That's harsh." And came way too close to how she felt these days.

The way his features hardened when he voiced his feel-ings told her strong emotion backed his comment. Kind of at odds with his family dynamic. The Sullivans were touted as one of the All-American families going back for generations. Long marriages and one or two kids who were all upstanding citizens. They ranked right up there with the Kennedys and Rockefellers.

The attendants came through the cabin collecting trash and dirty dishes. They offered turndown service, which Lindsay turned down. She still had work to do.

"Just let us know when you're ready."

Across the way Zach also delayed his bed service and got the same response. Once the attendants moved on, he leaned her way.

"Now you know you can trust me, are you ready for me to work on your spreadsheet? I'd like to do it before I start my movie."

"Oh. Sure." Could she trust him? Lindsay wondered as she pulled out her tablet. Just because she knew who he was didn't mean he was trustworthy. Too charming for her peace of mind. And a total flirt. "Do you want to do it on mine or should I send it to you?"

"Little Pixie, I'd like to do yours." His gaze ran over her, growing hotter as it rolled up her body. Her blood was steaming by the time his gaze met hers. "But since I have to work, you should send it to me."

"It'll do you no good to flirt with me." She tapped in her password and opened her spreadsheet. "What's your email?" She keyed in the address and sent it. "This wedding is too important to my career for me to risk getting involved with the best man."

"Oh, come on. The best man is harmless." Zach had his laptop open. "Got it. He's shackled for the whole event."

"The best man is a beast. His mind is all wrapped up in the bachelor party and strippers. He feels it's his duty to show the groom what he'll be giving up. And more than half the time he's on the prowl for some action just to re-mind himself he's still free, whether he is or not."

Zach flinched. "Wow. That's harsh."

Oh, clever man. "With good cause. I have a strict 'no fraternizing with the wedding party—including guests'—policy for my company and the vendors I work with. But, yeah, I've had to bolster a few bridesmaids who took it too far and expected too much and went home alone. Or refer them back to the bride or groom for contact info that wasn't shared."

"That's a lot of blame heaped on the best man."

"Of course, it's not just the best man, but in my expe-rience he can be a bad, bad boy."

"It's been a long time since I was bad."

"Define long."

He laughed.

"Seriously, I just want you to rewind the conversation a few sentences and then say that again with a straight face."

His gaze shifted from his laptop to make another slow stroll over her. Jacking up her pulse yet again.

He needed to stop doing that!

Unremorseful, he cocked an eyebrow. "I'm not saying I don't go after what I want. But I'm always up front about my intentions. No illusions, no damages."

Sounded like a bad boy to her.

"Well, you have fun, now. I'm here to work."

He shook his head as he went back to keying com-mands into his computer. "All work and no play makes Ms. Reeves a dull girl."

"I'm not being paid to have fun." And that was the problem right there—the one she'd been struggling with for nearly a year.

Her work wasn't fun anymore.

And the cause wasn't just the disillusionment she suf-fered in her love life. Though that ranked high on the

motive list. She'd started feeling this way before Kevin
had come back into her life. Instead of being excited by
the creative endeavor, she'd gotten bogged down in the
details.

Maybe it was Hollywood. Believing in the magic of
happily-ever-after got a little harder to do with each repeat customer. Not to mention the three-peats. And the
fact her mother was her best customer. Hopefully, husband number six would be the charm for her.

Seriously, Lindsay crossed her fingers in the folds of
her skirt. She truly wished this marriage lasted. She liked
Matt and he seemed to get her mom, who had the attention
span and sense of responsibility of a fourteen-year-old.
There was nothing mentally wrong with Darlene Reeves.
She could do for herself. She just didn't want to. Darlene's
dad had treated her like a princess, giving her most everything she wanted and taking care of all the little details
in life. He'd died when she was seventeen and she'd been
chasing his replacement all her life.

She'd had Lindsay when she was eighteen and then she
learned to get the wedding ring on her finger before they
lost interest. In between love interests, Lindsay was expected to pick up the slack.

She loved her mother dearly. But she loved her a little
easier when she was in a committed relationship.

"Did you fall asleep on me over there?"

His question called her attention to his profile. Such
strong features—square jaw dusted with stubble-defined
cheekbones, straight nose. He really was beautiful in a totally masculine way. Too much temptation. Good thing
her policy put him off limits.

"No. Just going over what I need to do."

"Perfect timing then." He swirled his finger and hit
a single key. "Because I just sent your file back to you."

"So soon?" She reached for her tablet, excited to try the

new program. The file opened onto a picture of circles in the form of a rectangle. Each circle was numbered. She'd refine the shape once she viewed the venue. She ran her finger across the page and as it moved over a circle names popped up showing who was seated at the table.

"Cool. How do I see everybody?"

"You hit this icon here." He hung over his chair, reaching across the aisle to show her. He tried showing her the other features, but his actions were awkward. Being left-handed, he had to use his right hand to aid her because of the distance between the seats.

"This is ridiculous." Unsnapping her seat belt, she stood. "Do you mind if I come over there for a few minutes while we go over this?"

"Sure." He stood, as well, and stepped aside.

Standing next to him she came face to loosened tie with him. She bent her head back to see him and then bent it back again to meet his gaze. "My goodness. How tall are you?"

"Six-four."

"And the prince?"

"Six-one." Long fingers tugged on a short dark tendril. "Does this brain never stop working?"

"Not when I get a visual of a tall drink of water standing next to a shot glass."

"I'm not quite sure what that means, but I think there was a compliment in there somewhere."

"Don't start imagining things at fifty thousand feet, Sullivan. We're a long way from help." She tugged on his blue-pinstriped tie. "You can ditch this now. Was dinner a formal affair?"

The light went out of his eyes. He yanked the tie off and stuffed it in his pants' pocket. "It's always formal with my parents."

She patted his chest. "You did your duty, now move on."

"Good advice." He gestured for her to take the window seat.

She hesitated for a beat. Being trapped in the inside seat, surrounded by his potent masculinity, might be pushing her self-control a little thin. But his computer program blew her mind. From the tiny bit she'd seen, it had the potential to save her hours, if not days, of work.

"Ms. Reeves?" His breath wafted over her ear, sending a shiver racing down her spine. "Are you okay?"

"Of course." She realized he'd been talking while she fought off her panic attack. "Ah...hmm." She cleared her throat to give herself a moment to calm down. "Why do you keep calling me by my last name?"

"Because I don't know your first name," he stated simply.

Oh, right. The flight attendants had used their last names. The prince had given her Zach's name and then she'd read it on her spreadsheet.

"It's Lindsay."

A slow grin formed, crinkling the corners of his eyes. "Pretty. A pretty name for a pretty girl."

So obvious, yet the words still gave her a bit of a thrill. She pressed her lips together to hide her reaction. "You can't help yourself, can you?"

"What?" All innocence.

"Please. That line is so old I think I heard it in kindergarten."

She expected to see his dimple flash but got an intent stare instead. "It's not a line when it's true."

A little thrill chased goose bumps across her skin. Oh, my, he was good.

She almost believed him.

Shaking her head at him, at herself, she slid past him and dropped into the window seat.

He slid into his seat, his big body filling up the small

space. Thankfully they were in first class and a ten-inch console separated their seats, giving her some breathing space. Until he flicked some buttons and the console dropped down.

"That's better."

For who? She leaned away as he leaned closer. Just as she feared, she felt pinned in, crowded. When he dropped the tray down in front of her, the sense of being squeezed from all sides grew stronger. Not by claustrophobia but by awareness. His scent—man and chocolate—made her mouth water.

"So is it easy for you?" He half laughed, going back to their previous conversation. "To move on?"

"It's not, actually. My mom problems are probably just as bad as or worse than your parent problems. Yet, here I am, jetting off to Italy."

Mom's words, not hers. Darlene couldn't understand how Lindsay could leave and be gone for a month when Darlene's next wedding was fast approaching. It didn't matter that Lindsay had booked this event well before Darlene got engaged or that it was the wedding of the year—perhaps the decade—and a huge honor for Lindsay to be asked to handle it.

"I doubt it."

"Really? My mother is my best customer."

"Oh-hh." He dragged the word out.

"Exactly. Soon I'll be walking her down the aisle to husband number six."

"Ouch. Is she a glutton for punishment?"

"Quite the opposite. My mother loves to be in love. The minute a marriage becomes work, it's the beginning of the end. What I can't get her to understand is that you have to work on your marriage from day one. Love needs to be fostered and nourished through respect and compromise."

"Honesty, communication and loyalty are key."

"Yes!" She nudged him in the arm. "You get it. Maybe you won't be such a bad best man, after all."

He lifted one dark eyebrow. "Thanks."

"Anyway. I can waste a lot of time worrying about Mom or I can accept that it's her life to live. Just as my life is mine to live." She didn't know why she was sharing this with him. Her mother's love life wasn't a secret. Far from it. But Lindsay rarely talked about her mother. "Until the next time she comes crying on my shoulder, I choose the latter."

"At least she lets her suckers off the line."

"What does that mean?"

"Nothing." He ran a hand around the back of his neck, loosening tight muscles. "It's hard to let my parents just be when they keep harping on me to join the campaign trail."

"They want you to run for office?"

"Oh, yeah. I'm to stop messing around with my little hobby and turn my mind to upholding the family name by running for the next open seat in congress."

"Hobby? Didn't I read an article that your company just landed a hundred-million-dollar government contract to upgrade electronic security for the military?"

"You did." While he talked he opened the seating arrangement program. "And between that contract and Antonio selling me his share of the business, I've met a goal I set the day I opened my business."

Clearly, resignation overshadowed pride, so she ventured, "You exceeded your father's net worth?"

He shifted to study her. "So you're psychic as well as a wedding planner?"

"When you work with people as closely as I do, you get to know how they think."

"Hmm."

"It's an impressive accomplishment."

The Sullivans came from old money made from banking and transportation. Their political dynasty went back several generations. "Your parents must be proud of you."

"They didn't even mention it. Too focused on when I'd leave it all behind and fall in line with my family obligations." He tapped a few keys and her seating arrangement popped up on the screen. "Feels kind of hollow now."

"I'm sorry."

He didn't look up. "It doesn't matter."

"You mean it didn't matter to them."

He gave a negligent shrug. "I'm a big boy. I can handle it."

"Well, I officially call the parent battle a draw. I know it's not the same but…congratulations."

That earned her a half smile and a nod. Then he started to run her through the features of the computer program.

"This is fabulous." All she had to do was type a name into a seat slot and all the notes associated with that name appeared sorted by category and importance. "You have saved me hours of work."

His eyes gleamed as he went on to show her a few additional options. "And if you do this—" he punched a couple of keys "—it will auto-fill based on a selected category." He clicked social standing and then pressed Enter. Names popped into assigned seats.

She blinked. "Wow. What do the colors mean?" Many of the names were in red and blue.

"Blue means there's a conflict with someone else at the table. Red means there are two or more conflicts."

While he showed her how to access the conflicts, she impulsively pressed the button to call the attendant. The blonde appeared with impressive speed, her smile dimming slightly when she saw Lindsay seated with Zach.

"How can I help you?"

"We'd like two glasses of champagne, please. And some strawberries if you have them."

"I think I can find some. Be right back."

"Champagne?" He cocked his head. "You turned it down earlier."

"That was before. Now we have things to celebrate. I have this to help me finish my seating plan and you met a career-long goal."

The attendant arrived with a tray, setting it down between them. "*Buon appetito!* Ms. Reeves, would you like us to do your turndown service now?"

"Sure." Maybe the champagne would help her sleep. The woman turned away and Lindsay lifted a flute of bubbling gold wine. "To you. Congratulations and thank you."

Zach lifted his flute and tapped it against Lindsay's. "To you." A crystal chime rang out as pretty as the sound of her laughter. Her simple gesture almost undid the butcher job his parent's self-absorption had done to his pride. He didn't get them, probably never would. They couldn't spare the smallest show of affection. But this prickly little pixie put her animosity aside to toast his success.

She didn't know him except as a helpful jerk and a few dry facts on paper. Heck, she hugged the window in an attempt to maintain her distance yet she still celebrated his accomplishment.

It almost made him feel bad about sabotaging the wedding.

CHAPTER THREE

IT WAS A drastic plan. One Zach took no pleasure in. But he'd do whatever necessary to ensure his friend didn't suffer the frigid existence his parents called marriage. Antonio was already sacrificing his life for his country; selling off his business interests in America to Zach. He shouldn't have to give up all chance of happiness, too.

Zach reluctantly agreed to be best man. He didn't believe in big, lavish weddings. And he didn't approve of Tony's insane sacrifice. So why would he agree? Because Tony was the closest thing he had to a brother. Of course, he had to support him.

And of course he felt compelled to talk him out of throwing his future away.

Zach knew the circumstances of Antonio's marriage and it made him sick to think of his honorable, big-hearted friend locked into a miserable existence like his parents had shared.

He wasn't thinking of doing anything overt. Certainly nothing that would embarrass the royal family, especially his best friend. But he could cause a few delays. And earn enough time to talk his friend out of making the biggest mistake of his life.

Tony had a lot on his plate taking on the leadership of his country. Halencia had reached a state of crisis. Antonio's parents were gregarious, bigger-than-life characters madly in love with each other one moment and viciously in hate the next. There'd been public affairs and passionate reconciliations.

The country languished under their inattention. The

king and queen lived big and spent big, costing the country much-needed funds.

The citizens of Halencia loved the drama, hated the politics. Demands for a change had started years ago but had become more persistent in the past five years. Until a year ago when the king was threatened with a paternity suit. It turned out Antonio wasn't getting a new sibling. It was just a scare tactic gone wrong.

But it was the last straw for the citizens of Halencia.

The chancellor of the high counsel had gone to Antonio and demanded action be taken.

Antonio had flown home to advise his father the time had come. The king must abdicate and let Antonio rule or risk the monarchy being overthrown completely.

The citizens of Halencia cheered in the streets. Antonio was well loved in his home country. He lived and worked in California, but he took his duty as prince seriously. He returned home two or three times a year, maintaining a residence in Halencia and supporting many businesses and charities.

Everyone was happy. Except Tony, who had to leave everything he'd worked to achieve and go home to marry a woman he barely knew.

Zach knew the truth behind Tony's impromptu engagement four years ago. He was one of a handful of people who did. And though it was motivated by love, it wasn't for the woman he'd planned to marry.

Tony was a smart man. Zach just needed a little time to convince him that marriage was drastic and unnecessary.

Lindsay seemed like a nice person. She'd understand when this all played out. Surely she wouldn't want to bring together two people who were not meant to be a couple. Plus, she'd get paid either way. And have a nice trip to Italy for her troubles.

Once he was in Halencia and had access to Tony and

Christina, he'd subtly hound them until one or the other caved to the pressure. And maybe cause a snag or two along the way so the whole thing just seemed like a bad idea.

Of course he'd have to distract the pretty wedding planner with a faux flirtation to keep her from noticing his shenanigans. No hardship there. He was attracted enough to the feisty pixie to make it fun, but she was way too picket-fence for him so there was no danger of taking it too far.

He saw it as win, win, win. Especially for those not stuck in a loveless marriage.

She lifted her glass again. "And thanks again for this program."

"I hope you like puzzles, because there's still a lot of work there."

"Not near what there was." She picked up a strawberry, dipped it in her flute and sank dainty white teeth into the fruit. The ripe juice stained her lips red and he had the keenest urge to taste the sweetness left behind. "In fact, I may actually watch the movie."

"Excellent." He all but had her eating out of his hand with that act of kindness. And he'd needed something after stumbling onto the plane half blind with a migraine and sitting on the blasted dress. He'd popped some over-the-counter meds just before boarding. Thank the flight gods the headache had finally eased off.

He needed to stick close to her if this sabotage was going to work. He'd do his best to protect her as he went forward, but if it came down to a choice between her job and the happiness of the man who meant more to him than family, he'd choose Tony every time. No matter how pretty the wedding planner.

He'd revealed more about himself than he meant to, than he ever did really. But her attitude toward parental problems appealed to him: do what you can and move on. How refreshing to find someone who understood and accepted that not all parents were perfect. Many people didn't get along with their parents but most loved and respected them.

He tolerated his parents, but he wasn't willing to make a total break, which probably meant he harvested hope for a better relationship at some point. He couldn't imagine what might bring it about so he pretty much ignored them except when he was on the east coast or at a family function requiring his presence.

Next to him Lindsay sipped champagne and flipped through the movie choices. The dim lights caught the gold in her light brown hair. She had the thick mass rolled up and pinned in place but soft wisps had broken free to frame her face. He wondered how long the confined tresses would flow down her back. Her creamy complexion reminded him of the porcelain dolls his mother collected, complete with a touch of red in the cheeks though Lindsay's was compliments of the champagne.

She shot him a sideways glance, a question in her pretty baby blue eyes.

He realized she'd asked a question. "Sorry. I got lost in looking at you."

A flush added to the red in her cheeks and a hand pushed at the pins in her hair. "I asked if you preferred the comedy or the World War One drama." She turned back to the screen, fidgeted with the buttons. "But maybe I should just go back to my seat."

"No. Stay. This is my celebration, after all."

She glanced at him through lush lashes. "Okay, but you'll have to behave."

"I'll have you know my mother raised me to be a gentleman."

"Uh-huh." She made the decision for them with the push of a button. "That might be reassuring, except I doubt you've been under your mother's influence for quite some time."

He grinned and reached up to turn off the overhead light. "Very astute, Ms. Reeves."

Lindsay came awake to the rare sense of being wrapped in warm, male arms. She shot straight up in her seat, startling the man she cuddled against. His whiskey-brown eyes opened and blinked at her, the heat in his slumberous gaze rolling through her like liquid fire.

Escape. Now. The words were like a beeping alarm going off in her head.

"Can you let me out?" She pushed away from him, gaining a few inches and hopefully reinforcing the message to move. Now.

"Is the movie over?" He reined her in with an easy strength. His broad chest lifted under her as he inhaled a huge breath and then let it go in a yawn.

"Yes. This was fun." Too much fun. Time to get back to the real world. "But I need to get past you." He tucked a piece of her hair behind her ear instead of moving. The heat of his touch called for desperate measures. "I've got to pee."

He blinked. Then the corner of his mouth tipped up and he stood. "Me, too." He helped her up and gestured for her to go first.

"You go ahead," she urged him. "I want to grab a few things to freshen up with."

"Good idea." He opened the overhead compartment and grabbed a small bag. "Can I help you get anything?"

"Thank you, no." She waited until he wandered off to gather what she needed from her tote.

The attendants had performed her turndown service so both beds were down for the night. She automatically checked the garment bag holding the royal wedding dress.

It lay nicely in place, undisturbed since the last time she checked. She bent to retrieve her tote from under the seat in front of hers and decided to take the bag with her. Strap looped over her shoulder, she hurried down the aisle.

It was after one and the people she passed appeared to be out for the count. Even the attendants were strapped in and resting. Good. Lindsay intended to take her time. She wanted Zach to be back in his seat and sound asleep when she returned.

He was too charming, too hot, too available for her peace of mind. She hadn't needed to hear his views on marriage to know he was single. From her research she'd already gathered he had commitment issues. The only hint of an engagement had been back in his college days.

She'd found that snippet of information because she'd been researching his history with the prince. They'd both been going to Harvard's school of business but they'd met on the swim team. They both broke records for the school, Zach edging out Antonio with a few more wins. Antonio explained those extra wins came from Zach's longer reach. In the picture accompanying the article it was clear that Zach had at least three inches on all his teammates.

Tall, dark and handsome. Tick, tick, tick. The stereotype fit him to a tee, but did little to actually describe him. He was brilliant yet a terrible flirt. Could apologize when he was wrong and laugh at himself. But it was the touch of vulnerability surrounding his desire for his parents' approval that really got to her. She understood all too well the struggle between respect and love when it came to parents.

Bottom line: the man was dangerous. Way out of her league. And a distraction she couldn't afford. She may be headed for one of the most beautiful places on earth, but this was so not a vacation. She needed to stay sharp and focused to pull off the wedding of the century.

Face washed, teeth brushed, changed into yoga pants and a long-sleeved T-shirt, she glanced at her watch. Twenty minutes had passed. That should be enough time. She gathered her clothes and toiletries and tucked them neatly into her tote before making her way quietly back to her seat.

Zach lay sprawled on his bed. He was so tall he barely fit; in fact, one leg was off the bed braced against the floor. No doubt he had a restless night ahead of him. For once she'd sleep. Or pretend to. Because engaging in middle-of-the-night intimacies with Zach Sullivan could only result in trouble. Trouble she couldn't afford.

Climbing into her bed, she pulled the covers around her shoulders and determinedly closed her eyes.

She had this under control. She'd just ignore the man. If she needed something from the groom, she'd get it from the palace representative or Christina. There was no need for her to deal with Zach Sullivan at all. That suited her fine. She'd learned her lesson.

No more falling into the trap of self-delusion because a man paid a little attention to her. But more important—work and play did not go together.

"There must be some mistake." Lindsay advised the car-rental clerk. "I made my reservation over two months ago."

"*Scusa.* No mistake. My records show the reservation was canceled."

"That's impossible," Lindsay protested. Exhaustion tugged at her frayed nerves. This couldn't be happening. With everything she needed to do for the wedding, she absolutely required a vehicle to get around. "I had my assistant confirm all my reservations a week ago."

The clerk, a harried young man, glanced at the line behind her before asking with exaggerated patience, "Perhaps it is under a different name?"

"No, it is under my name." She gritted her teeth. "Please look again."

"Of course." He hit a few keys. "It says here the reservation was canceled last night."

"Last night? That doesn't make any sense at all. I was in the middle of a transatlantic flight." Enough. Arguing did her no good. She just wanted a car and to get on the road. "You know it doesn't matter. Let's just start over."

"*Scusa*, Ms. Reeves. We have no other vehicles available. Usually we would, but many have started to arrive for the royal wedding. The press especially. And they are keeping the vehicles. We have requested more autos from other sites but they won't be here for several days."

"There you are." A deep male voice sounded from behind her.

She glanced over her shoulder to find Zach towering over her. Dang, so much for losing him at the luggage carousel. Assuming her professional demeanor, she sent him a polite smile. "Have a good trip to Monte Calanetti. I'll keep you posted with updates on the arrangements. I'm going to be here for a bit." She smiled even brighter. "They've lost my car reservation."

"They didn't lose it. I canceled it."

"What?" All pretense of politeness dropped away. "Why would you do that?"

He held up a set of keys. "Because we're going to drive to Monte Calanetti together. Don't you remember? We talked about this during the movie last night."

She shook her head. She remembered him asking her what car-rental company she'd used and comparing their accommodation plans; he'd rented a villa while she had a room at a boutique hotel. Nowhere in her memory lurked a discussion about driving to Monte Calanetti together. There was no way she would have agreed to that. Not only did it go against her new decree to avoid him whenever possible, but she needed a vehicle to properly do her job.

"No," she declared, "I don't remember."

"Hmm. Must be champagne brain. No problem. I've got a Land Rover. Plenty of room for you, me and the dress." He grabbed up the garment bag, caught the handle of her larger suitcase and headed off. "Let's roll."

"Wait. No." Feeling panicked as the dress got further out of her reach, she glared at the clerk. "I want my reservation reinstated and as soon as a car is available, I want it delivered." She snatched up a card. "I'll call you with the address."

Dragging her smaller suitcase, Lindsay weaved her way through the crowd, following in Zach's wake. Luckily his height made him easy to spot. She was right on his heels when he exited the airport.

Humidity smacked her in the face as soon as she stepped outside; making her happy she'd paired her beige linen pants with a navy-and-beige asymmetrical short-sleeved tunic.

Champagne brain, her tush. What possible motive could he have for canceling her reservation if she hadn't agreed?

This just proved his potent appeal spelled danger.

Okay, no harm done. She handed him her smaller case and watched as he carefully placed the garment bag across the backseat. It should only take a couple of hours to reach Monte Calanetti. Then she could cut ties with the guy and concentrate on doing her job.

"How long to Monte Calanetti from here?" she asked as he held the door while she slid into the passenger seat.

"I've never driven it, but I can't imagine it's more than a few hours." He closed her in, rounded the front of the Land Rover and climbed into the driver's seat. A few minutes later they were in the thick of Florence traffic.

The old world elegance of the city charmed her, but the stop and go of the early evening traffic proclaimed work-force congestion was the same worldwide. She could admit, if only to herself, that she was glad not to be driving in it.

"Have you've been to Tuscany before?" she asked Zach.

"I've been several times. A couple of times with Antonio and once with my parents when I was twelve."

"So you know your way around?" She smothered a yawn.

"I do." He shot her an amused glance. "Enough to get us where we're going."

"I was just going to offer to navigate if you needed me to."

He stopped at a traffic light, taking the time to study her. "Thanks." He reached out and swept a thumb under her left eye in a soft caress. "You're tired. I guess relaxing didn't help you sleep."

She turned her head away from his touch. "I slept a little, off and on."

"Disrupted sleep can be less restful than staying awake." He sympathized. "Are you better at sleeping in a car?"

"Who can't sleep in a car? But I'm fine. I don't want to miss the sights. The city is so beautiful."

He drove with confidence and skill and a patience she lacked. He'd shaved on the plane; his sexy scruff gone when she woke this morning. The hard, square lines of his clean-cut jaw were just as compelling as the wicked shadow. The man couldn't look bad in a bag, not with a body like that.

Unlike her, he hadn't changed clothes, he still wore his black suit pants and white long-sleeved shirt, but the top two buttons were open and the sleeves were rolled up to his elbows. The suit jacket had been tossed onto the backseat.

"Florence is beautiful. The depth of history just draws me in. Halencia is the same. Since I'll be here for a month, I'm really hoping to get a chance to play tourist."

"Oh, absolutely. They have some really fantastic tours. I plan to stay after the wedding and take one. I'm torn between a chef and wine-tasting tour or a hiking tour."

"Wow, there's quite a difference there."

"I'm not going to lie to you. I'm leaning toward the pasta and wine tour. It goes to Venice. I've always wanted to go to Venice."

"Oh, yeah," he mocked, "it's all about Venice and nothing about the walking."

"Hey, I'm a walker. I love to hike. I'll share some of my brochures with you. There are some really great tours. If you like history, there's a Tuscan Renaissance tour that sounds wonderful."

"Sounds interesting. I'd like to see the brochures."

"Since technology is your thing, I'm surprised you're so into history."

"I minored in history. What can I say? I'm from New England. You can't throw a rock without hitting a historical marker. In my studies I was always amazed at how progressive our founding fathers were. Benjamin Franklin truly inspired me."

"You're kidding."

"I'm not." He sent her a chiding sidelong look. "I did my thesis on the sustainability of Franklin's inventions and observations in today's world. He was a brilliant man."

"And a great politician," she pointed out.

"I can't deny that, but he didn't let his political views define or confine him. I respect him for that. For him it wasn't about power but about proper representation."

"I feel that way about most of our founding fathers. So tell me something I probably don't know about big Ben."

"He was an avid swimmer."

"Like you and Antonio. Aha. No wonder you like him—" A huge yawn distorted the last word. "Oh." She smothered it behind a hand. "Sorry."

"No need to apologize." He squeezed her hand. "Don't feel you have to keep me company. Rest if you can. Jet lag can be a killer."

"Thanks." He'd just given her the perfect out from having to make conversation for the next hour. She'd snap the offer up if she weren't wide-eyed over the sights. Nothing in California rivaled the history and grandeur of the buildings still standing tall on virtually every street.

Zach turned a corner and the breath caught in the back of Lindsay's throat. Brunelleschi's Dome filled the skyline in all its Gothic glory. She truly was in Italy. Oh, she wanted to play tourist. But it would have to wait. Work first.

Riding across a beautiful, sculpted old bridge, she imagined the people who once crossed on foot. Soon rural views replaced urban views and in the distance clouds darkened the sky, creating a false twilight.

Lindsay shivered. She hoped they reached Monte Calanetti before the storm hit. She didn't care for storms, certainly didn't want to get caught out in one. The turbulence reminded her of anger, the thunder of shouting. As a kid, she'd hated them.

She didn't bury her head under the covers anymore. But there were times she wanted to.

Lightning flickered in the distance. Rather than watch the storm escalate, she closed her eyes as sleep claimed her. Her last thoughts were of Zach.

Lack of motion woke Lindsay. She opened her eyes to a dark car and an eerie silence. Zach was nowhere in view. Stretching, she turned around, looking for him. No sign. She squinted out the front windshield.

Good gracious, was the hood open?

She pushed her door open and stepped out, her feet crunching on gravel as a cool wind whipped around her. Hugging herself she walked to the front of the Land Rover. Zach was bent over the engine using a flashlight to ineffectually examine the vehicle innards. "What's going on?"

"A broken belt is my best guess." He straightened and directed the light toward the ground between them. "I've already called the rental company. They're sending a service truck."

She glanced around at the unrelenting darkness. Not a single light sparkled to show a sign of civilization. "Sending a truck where? We're in the middle of nowhere."

"They'll find us. The vehicle has a GPS."

Relief rushed through her. "Oh. That's good." She'd had visions of spending the night on the side of the road in a storm-tossed tin can. "Did they say how long before they got here? *Eee!*" She started and yelped when thunder boomed overhead. The accompanying flash of lightening had her biting back a whimper to the metallic taste of blood.

"As soon as they can." He took her elbow and escorted her to the passenger's-side door. "Let's stay in the car. The storm looks like it's about to break."

His big body blocked the wind, his closeness bringing warmth and rock-solid strength. For a moment she wanted to throw herself into his arms. Before she could give in to the urge, he helped her into her seat and slammed the door. A moment later he slid in next to her. He immediately turned the light off. She swallowed hard in a mouth suddenly dry.

"Can we keep the light on?" The question came out in a harsh rasp.

"I think we should conserve it, just in case."

"Just in case what?" It took a huge effort to keep any squeak out of her voice. "The truck doesn't come?"

"Just in case. Here—" He reached across the center console and took her hand, warming it in his. "You're shaking. Are you cold?" He dropped her hand to reach behind him. "Take my jacket."

She leaned forward and the heavy weight of his suit jacket wrapped around her shoulders. The satin lining slid coolly over her skin but quickly heated up. The scent of Zach clung to the material and she found it oddly comforting.

"Thank you. You won't be cold?"

She heard the rustle of movement and pictured him shrugging. "I'm okay right now. Hopefully the tow truck will get here before the cold seeps in. Worst case, we can move into the backseat and cuddle together under the jacket."

Okay, that option was way too tempting.

"Or you could get another one out of your luggage."

His chuckle preceded another crash of thunder. "Pixie girl, I don't know if my ego can survive you."

Maybe the dark wasn't so bad since he hadn't seen her flinch. Then his words struck her. "Pixie girl? That's the second time you called me that."

"Yes. Short and feisty. You remind me of a pixie."

"I am average," she stated with great dignity. "You're a giant."

"You barely reach my shoulder."

"Again, I refer you to the term 'giant.'" She checked her phone, welcoming the flare of light, but they were in the Italian version of Timbuktu so of course there was no service.

"Uh-huh. Feisty, pretty and short. Pixie it is."

Pretty? He'd called her that before, too. Pleasure bolstered her drooping spirits. She almost didn't care when the light faded again. Not that his admission changed her feelings toward him. He was a dangerous, charming man but she didn't have to like him just because he thought she was pretty. He was still off limits.

Hopefully he took her silence as disdain.

Right. On the positive side, the bit of vanity served to distract her for a few minutes. Long enough for headlights to appear on the horizon. No other vehicles had passed them in the twenty minutes she'd been awake so she said a little prayer that the approaching headlights belonged to their repair truck.

"Is the repair service coming from Monte Calanetti? How far away do you think we are?" She feared the thought of walking, but she didn't want to stay in the car all night, either.

"We're nowhere near Monte Calanetti," Zach announced. "By my guess we're about ten miles outside Caprese."

"Caprese?" Lindsay yelped in outrage. Caprese was the small village where the artist Michelangelo was born. "That's the other direction from Monte Calanetti from Florence. What are we doing here?"

"I told you last night. I have an errand to run for Antonio before I go to Monte Calanetti. It's just a quick stop to check on his groomsmen gifts and do a fitting."

"You so did not tell me."

"I'm pretty sure I did. You really can't hold your champagne, can you?"

"Stop saying 'champagne brain.' When did we have this conversation? Did I actually participate or was I sleeping?"

"You were talking, but I suppose you might have dozed off. You got quiet toward the end. I thought you were just involved in the movie. And then I fell asleep."

"Well, I don't remember half of what you've told me.

You should have reminded me of the plans we supposedly made this morning. I need to get to Monte Calanetti and I need my own car. I know you're trying to be helpful but..."

"But I got you stuck out in the middle of nowhere. And you're already tired from the flight. I'm sorry."

Lindsay clenched her teeth in frustration watching as the headlights slowly moved closer. Sorry didn't fix the situation. She appreciated the apology—many men wouldn't have bothered—but it didn't get her closer to Monte Calanetti. She had planned to hit the road running tomorrow with a visit to the wedding venue, the Palazzo di Comparino and restored chapel, before meeting with Christina in the afternoon.

Now she'd have to reschedule, move the interview back.

"Lindsay?" Zach prompted. "Are you okay?"

"I'm trying to rearrange my schedule in my head." She glanced at her watch, which she'd already adjusted to local time. Seven-fifteen. It felt much later. "What do you think our chances are of getting to Monte Calanetti tonight?"

"Slim. I doubt we'll find a mechanic willing to work on the Land Rover tonight. We'll probably have to stay over and head out tomorrow after it's fixed."

"If they have the necessary part."

"That will be a factor, yes. Here's our help." A small pickup honked as it drove past them then made a big U-turn and pulled up in front of them.

Zach hopped out to meet the driver.

Lindsay slid her arms into Zach's jacket and went to join them.

"Think it's the timing belt." Zach aimed his flashlight at the engine as he explained the problem to the man next to him. Their savior had gray-streaked black hair and wore blue coveralls. The name on his pocket read Luigi.

"Ciao, signora," the man greeted her.

She didn't bother to correct him, more eager to have

him locate the problem than worried about his assumption that she and Zach were married.

The driver carried a much bigger flashlight. The power of it allowed the men a much better view of the internal workings of the Land Rover. The man spoke pretty good English and he and Zach discussed the timing belt and a few other engine parts, none of which Lindsay followed but she understood clearly when he said he'd have to tow them into Caprese.

Wonderful.

Luigi invited her to sit in his truck while he got the Land Rover hooked up to be towed. She nodded and retrieved her purse. Zach walked her to the truck and held the door for her. The interior smelled like grease and cleanser, but it was neat and tidy.

"From what I remember from my research of Italy, small is a generous adjective when describing Caprese. At just over a thousand residents, 'tiny' would be more accurate. I'm not sure it has a hotel if we need to stay over."

"I'm sure there'll be someplace. I'll ask Luigi. It's starting to rain. I'm going to see if I can help him to make things go faster." He closed the door and darkness enveloped her.

The splat of rain on the windshield made her realize her ire at the situation had served to distract her from the looming storm. With its arrival, she forgot her schedule and just longed for sturdy shelter and a warm place to spend the night.

A few minutes later the men joined her. Squeezed between them on the small bench seat, she leaned toward Zach to give Luigi room to drive. The first right curve almost put her in Zach's lap.

"There's a bed-and-breakfast in town. Luigi's going to see about a room for us there." Zach spoke directly into her ear, his warm breath blowing over her skin.

She shivered. That moment couldn't come soon enough. The closer they got to town, the harder it rained. Obviously they were headed into the storm rather than away from it.

Fifteen minutes later they arrived at a small garage. Lindsay dashed through the rain to the door and then followed the men inside to an office that smelled like the truck and was just as tidy. Luigi immediately picked up the phone and dialed. He had a brief conversation in Italian before hanging up.

He beamed at Lindsay and Zach. "*Bene, bene,* my friends. The bed-and-breakfast is full with visitors. *Si,* the bad weather—they do not like to drive. But I have procured for you the last room. Is good, *si*?"

"*Si. Grazie,* Luigi." Zach expressed his appreciation then asked about the repairs.

For Lindsay only two words echoed through her head: one room.

CHAPTER FOUR

THE B AND B WAS a converted farmhouse with stone walls, long, narrow rooms and high ceilings. The furniture was sparse, solid and well worn.

Lindsay carried the heavy garment bag to the wardrobe and arranged it as best she could and then turned to face the room she'd share with Zach. Besides the oak wardrobe there was a queen bed with four posters, one nightstand, a dresser with a mirror above it and a hardback chair. Kindling rested in a fireplace with a simple wooden mantel, ready to be lit.

The bathroom was down the hall.

No sofa or chair to sleep on and below her feet was an unadorned hardwood floor. There was no recourse except to share the bed.

And the bedspread was a wedding ring quilt. Just perfect.

Her mother would say it was a sign. She'd actually have a lot more to say, as well, but Lindsay ruthlessly put a lock on those thoughts.

Lightening flashed outside the long, narrow window. Lindsay pulled the heavy drapes closed, grateful for the accommodation. She may have to share with a near stranger and the room may not be luxurious, but it was clean and authentic, and a strong, warm barrier against the elements.

Now why did that make her think of Zach?

The rain absorbed the humidity and dropped the temperature a good twenty degrees. The stone room was cool. Goose bumps chased across her skin.

She lit the kindling and once it caught added some wood. Warmth spread into the room. Unable to wait any longer, she made a quick trip down the hall. Zach was still gone when she got back. He'd dropped off her luggage and had gone back for his. She rolled the bigger case over next to the wardrobe. She didn't think she'd need anything out of it for one night.

The smaller one she set on the bed. She'd just unzipped it when a thud came at the door.

Zach surged into the room with three bags in tow.

"Oh, my goodness. You are soaked." She closed the door and rushed to the dresser. The towels were in the top drawer just as the innkeeper said.

Zach took it and scrubbed his face and head.

She tugged at his sopping jacket, glad now she'd thought to give it back to him. "Let's get this off you."

He allowed her to work it off. Under the jacket his shirt was so damp it clung to his skin in several places. He shivered and she led him over to the fireplace.

"Oh, yeah." He draped the towel around his neck and held his hands out to the heat.

"Take the shirt off, too," she urged him. She reached out with her free hand to help with the task, but when her fingers came skin to skin with his shoulder she decided it might be best if he handled the job himself.

To avoid looking at all the tanned, toned flesh revealed by the stripping off of his shirt, Lindsay held the dripping jacket aloft. What were they going to do with it? He handed her the shirt. With them?

A knock sounded at the door. Leaving Zach by the fire, Lindsay answered the knock. A plump woman in a purple jogging suit with more gray than black in her hair gave Lindsay a bright smile.

"*Si, signora.*" She pointed to the dripping clothes, "I take?"

"Oh. *Grazie.*" Lindsay handed the wet clothes through the door.

"And these, too." From behind the door Zach thrust his pants forward.

Okay, then. She just hoped he'd kept his underwear on.

"Si, si." The woman's smile grew broader. She took the pants while craning her head to try to see behind Lindsay. She rolled off something in Italian. Lindsay just blinked at her.

"She said the owner was sending up some food for us."

As if on cue, Lindsay's stomach gurgled. The mention of food made her realize how hungry she was. It had been hours since they'd eaten on the plane. *"Si."* She nodded. *"Grazie."*

The woman nodded and, with one last glance into the room, turned and walked down the hall.

"You have a fan." Lindsay told Zach when she closed the door. "Oh, my good dog." The man had his back to her as he leaned over the bed rummaging through his luggage. All he wore was a pair of black knit boxer briefs that clung to his butt like a lover. The soft cloth left little to the imagination and there was a lot to admire.

No wonder the maid had been so enthralled.

And Lindsay had to sleep next to that tonight.

"What about a dog?" He turned those whiskey-brown eyes on her over one broad, bare shoulder.

Her knees went weak, nearly giving out on her. She sank into the hard chair by the fire.

"Dog? Huh? Nothing." Her mother had taught her to turn the word around so she didn't take the Lord's name in vain. After all these years, the habit stuck.

He tugged on a gray T-shirt.

Thank the merciful angels in heaven.

"I'm going to take a quick shower. Don't eat all the food."

"No promises."

He grinned. "Then I'll just have to hurry."

He disappeared out the door with his shaving kit under one arm and the towel tossed over his shoulder.

Finally Lindsay felt as though she could breathe again.

He took up so much space. A room that seemed spacious one moment shrank by three sizes when he crossed the threshold. Even with him gone the room smelled of him.

She patted her pocket. Where was her phone? She needed it now, needed to call the rental agency that very moment and demand a car be delivered to her. They should never have allowed a party outside the reservation to cancel. They owed her.

The hunt proved futile. Her phone wasn't in her purse, her tote or either suitcase. She thought back to the last time she'd used it. In the Land Rover, where it had been pitch-black. It must still be in the vehicle.

That was at the garage.

There'd be no getting her phone tonight. Dang it.

Stymied from making the call she wanted to, she took advantage of Zach's absence to gather her own toiletries and yoga pants and long-sleeved tee she'd worn on the plane. And a pair of socks. Yep, she'd wear gloves to bed if she had any with her. And if she had any luck at all, he'd wear a three-piece suit.

There'd be no skin-to-skin contact if she could help it.

Loosen up, Lindsay. Her mom's voice broke through her blockade. *You're young and single and about to share a bed with one prime specimen. You should be thinking of ways to rock the bed not bulletproof yourself against an accidental touch.*

How sad was it that her mother was more sexually aggressive than she was?

Her mom was forever pushing Lindsay to date more, to take chances on meeting people. She'd been thrilled when Lindsay had started seeing Kevin again. She'd welcomed him; more, she'd invited him to family events and made a point of showing her pride in Lindsay and her success.

Right, and look how that turned out.

To be fair, Mom had been almost as devastated as Lindsay when Kevin showed his true colors. She may be self-absorbed but Lindsay never doubted her mom's love. She wanted Lindsay to be happy and in her mind that equated to love and marriage. Because for her it was—at least during the first flush of love.

Lindsay wanted to believe in love and happily ever after, but it was getting harder to do as she planned her mother's sixth wedding. And, okay, yeah, Mom was right; Lindsay really didn't make an effort to meet men. But that wasn't the problem. She actually met lots of interesting men. While she was working, when it was totally inappropriate to pursue the connection.

The problem was she was too closed off when she did meet a nice guy. After stepfather number two, she'd started putting up shields to keep from being hurt when they left. She and Kevin had been friends before they were a couple and when they'd split up, her shields just grew higher.

She hadn't given up on love. She just didn't know if she was brave enough to reach for it.

You're in Italy for a month with a millionaire hunk at your beck and call. It's the perfect recipe for a spicy summer fling. Every relationship doesn't have to end with a commitment.

Mom didn't always practice what she preached.

The food hadn't arrived when Zach returned smelling of freshly washed male. He wore the same T-shirt but now his knit boxers were gray. She could only thank the good Lord—full-on prayer, here—that the T-shirt hung to his thighs, hiding temptation from view.

"Bathroom is free," he advised her.

Her stomach gurgled, but he looked so relaxed after his

shower and the storm had her so on edge she decided to get comfortable. Grabbing up the cache she'd collected, she headed for the door.

"Don't eat all the food," she told him.

"Hey, you get the same promise I did."

She stared at him a moment trying to determine if he was joking as she'd been. His features were impassive and he cocked a dark brow at her. Hmm. She better hurry just in case.

The bathroom was still steamy from his visit. As she pulled the shower curtain closed on the tiny tub she envisioned his hard body occupying this same space. His hard, wet, naked body. Covered in soap bubbles.

Oh. My. Dog.

She forced her mind to the nearly completed seating chart to remove him from her head. But that, too, reminded her of him so she switched to the flowers. Christina had yet to decide between roses and calla lilies or a mix of the two. Both were beautiful and traditional for weddings.

It may well depend on the availability. Christina wanted to use local vendors and merchants. She'd said it was for the people so should be of the people. Lindsay still puzzled over the comment. *It* was obviously the wedding, but what did she mean "it was for the people"?

Was the royal wedding not a love match?

Lindsay could ask Zach. He'd know.

No. She didn't want to know. It was none of her business and may change how she approached the wedding. Every bride deserved a fantasy wedding, one that celebrated the bond between her and the groom and the promise of a better future together. It was Lindsay's job to bring the fantasy to life. The reality of the relationship was not in her hands.

Her musings took her through the shower, a quick attempt at drying her hair, brushing her teeth and dressing. Fifteen minutes after she left the room, she returned to find

Zach seated on the bed, his back against the headboard, a tray of food sitting beside him.

The savory aroma almost brought her to her knees.

"Oh, that smells good." She dropped her things into her open case, flipped the top closed and set it on the floor before climbing onto the bed to bend over the tray and the two big bowls it held. She inhaled deeply, moaned softly. "Soup?"

"Stew."

"Even better. And bread." She looked at him. "You waited."

He lifted one shoulder and let it drop. "Not for long. It just got here. Besides, we're partners."

Her eyebrows shot up then lowered as she scowled at him. "We are so not partners." She handed him a bowl and a spoon. Tossed a napkin in his lap. Then settled cross-legged on her pillow and picked up her own bowl. "In fact, I think I should arrange for my own car tomorrow. I need to get to Monte Calanetti and you have to wait for the Land Rover to be repaired, which could take a couple of days."

"Getting a car here could take longer yet. You heard the rental clerk. All the vehicles are being taken up by the media presence here for the wedding."

"Oh, this is good." No point in arguing with him. She was an adult and a professional. She didn't require his permission to do anything.

"Mmm." He hummed his approval. "Are you okay with sharing?"

"The room?" She shrugged. "We don't really have a choice, do we?"

"The bed," he clarified and licked his spoon. She watched, fascinated. "I can sleep on the floor if you're uncomfortable sharing the bed."

"It's hardwood." She pulled her gaze away from him. "And there isn't any extra bedding."

"I can sleep near the fireplace. It won't be comfortable, but I'll survive. We're still getting to know each other, so I'll understand."

Crack!

Thunder boomed, making Lindsay jump and spill the bite of stew aimed for her mouth.

"Dang it." She grabbed her napkin and scrubbed at the stain on her breast. "Are you uncomfortable?"

"No." He took her bowl so she could use both hands. "But I'm a man."

Oh, yeah, she'd noticed.

"If something happened between us, I'd be a happy man in the morning. You, on the other hand, would be satisfied but regretful."

She glared at him. "Nothing is going to happen."

He held up his hands, the sign of surrender blemished by the bowls he held. "Of course not."

"So there's no reason not to share."

"None at all."

"It's settled then."

"Yep." He handed her bowl back. "Now you want to tell me what your deal is with storms?"

Zach watched the color leech from Lindsay's cheeks, confirmation that his suspicions were right that her reaction to the thunderstorm exceeded the norm.

She was nervous and jumpy, which was totally unlike her.

Sure she'd gone ballistic when he'd sat on the wedding dress, but considering the cost of the gown she could be forgiven for hyperventilating.

Generally he found her to be calm and collected, giving as good as she got but not overreacting or jumping to conclusions. Efficient but friendly. The storm had her shaken and he wanted to know why.

"Nothing." She carefully placed her bowl on the tray. "I'm fine."

"You're jumpy as hell. And it started before we got to the room so it isn't the sleeping arrangements. It has to be the storm."

"Maybe it's you." She tossed the words at him as she slid from the bed. "Did you consider that?"

"Nope." His gaze followed her actions as she put the suitcase back on the bed and began to organize the things she'd dumped in. "We're practically lovers."

Ice burned cold in the blue glare she sent him. "You are insane."

"Oh, come on." He taunted her. "You know it's going to happen. Not tonight, but definitely before the month is up."

"In your dreams. But I live in reality."

"Tell me about the storms."

"There's nothing to tell." The jerkiness of her movements told a different story.

"Okay. Have it your way." He relaxed back against the wall and laced his arms behind his head. "I like storms myself."

"You like storms?" The astonishment in her voice belied her indifference. "As I said, insane. I'm going to take the tray downstairs."

Zach grabbed the bread and wine from the tray and let her escape. Pressing her would only antagonize her.

He'd had nothing to do with the engine failure, but he approved of the results. If he were a man who believed in signs, he'd take it as karma's righteous nod.

He'd been playing with her when he'd alluded to them being lovers. Or so he thought. As soon as the words had left his mouth, he'd known the truth in them. He generally preferred leggy blondes. But something about the pixie appealed to him.

Her feistiness certainly. At the very least it was refreshing. With his position, family connections and money, people rarely questioned his authority and never dismissed him. She'd done both. And still was.

He had no doubt she'd try to make a break for it tomorrow.

He sipped at the last of his wine, enjoyed the warmth as it rolled down his throat. The fire had burned down to embers and he stirred himself to get up and feed it. The thick stone walls and bare wood floors kept the room cool so the fire gave nice warmth to the room. Plus, he imagined Lindsay would find it a comforting offset to the storm.

She was more pretty than beautiful, her delicate features overshadowed by that lush mouth. His gut tightened as heat ignited his blood just as flame flared over the fresh fuel.

Oh, yeah, he wanted a bite of that plump lower lip.

He'd have to wait. He'd put her off limits when he concocted the sabotage plan. He couldn't use her and seduce her, too. That would be too much. But she didn't need to know of his restraint. Just the thought of him making a move on her would keep her on edge, making it easier for him to cause a little chaos.

A glance at his watch showed the time at just after nine. Early for him to go to bed most nights but tonight, fatigue from travel, the time change and the concentration needed to drive an unfamiliar vehicle on unfamiliar roads weighed on him.

The room held no TV so it was sleep or talk.

He wouldn't mind getting to know his companion better but somehow he knew she'd choose the escape that came with sleep. Whether she actually slept or not. His feisty little pixie had a bit of the ostrich in her.

The door opened and she slipped inside.

"You're still up?" She avoided his gaze as she crossed to the bed and zipped the case that still sat on her side.

"Just feeding the fire."

She lifted the case and he stepped forward to take it from her.

"I can do it," she protested, independent as always.

"So can I." He notched his chin toward the bed. "You're falling asleep on your feet. Go to bed."

"What about you?" Caution filled her voice and expression.

"I'm going to tend the fire for a bit. I'll come to bed soon."

Relief filled her blue eyes and he knew she thought she'd gotten a reprieve; that she hoped to be asleep before he joined her in the far too small bed.

Truthfully, he hoped she fell asleep, too. No point in both of them lying awake thinking about the other.

Lindsay pretended to be asleep when Zach came to bed. His presence kept her senses on edge. Between him and the storm that still raged outside her nerves were balanced on a fine-edged sword.

She tried to relax, to keep her breathing even so as not to disturb Zach. The last thing she wanted was another discussion on why storms bothered her. It was a weakness she preferred to ignore. She usually plugged in her earphones and let her playlist tune out the noise.

Tonight there was nothing in the still house to disguise the violence of the weather outside the window. Everything in her longed to press back into the strong male body occupying the other half of the bed. Instead she clung to the edge of the mattress determined to stay on her side.

Thunder boomed and lightening strobed at the edges of the closed drapes. Lindsay flinched then held herself very still.

"Oh, for the love of dog, come here." Long, muscular arms wrapped around her and tugged her against the hard planes of a male chest.

Shocked by both action and words, Lindsay chose to focus on the latter. She glanced over her shoulder into dark eyes. "What did you say?"

"Woof, woof." And his lips settled softly on her cheek, a simple human-to-human contact that left her wanting more.

She sighed and made a belated attempt to wiggle away. Her body and nerves might welcome his touch but her head shouted, *Danger!* "I know it's silly. It's something my mom taught me when I was little. It kind of stuck."

"I think it's cute."

She went still. "I'm not cute. I'm not a pixie. And we're not going to be lovers. You need to let me go." One of them needed to be smart about this.

His arms tightened, pulled her back the few inches she'd gained. "Tell me about the storms."

"There's nothing to tell!"

His silence was a patient demand.

"What's to like about them? They're angry and destructive."

"A storm is cleansing. It can be loud, yes, but it takes the old and washes it clean."

She thought about that. "Destruction is not cleansing."

"It can be. If something is rotten or breaking, it's better to come down in a storm than under a person's weight. You might have to finish the cleanup but life is fresher once you're done."

"I doubt people who have lost their homes to a hurricane or tornado would agree with you."

"Hurricanes and tornadoes are different. This is a simple summer thunderstorm. Nothing to get so worked up over."

"I know." She lay with her cheek pressed against her hand. She should move away, put space and distance between them. But she didn't. Couldn't. Having strong arms surrounding her gave her a sense of belonging she hadn't experienced in way too long. It didn't even matter that it was all in her head. Her body had control right now. With a soft sigh she surrendered to his will and her body's demand.

"It's not even my phobia. It's my mother's that she passed on to me." She blamed the kiss for loosening her resolve. Hard to keep her wits about her with the heat of his kiss on her cheek.

"How'd she do that?"

"She hates storms. They don't scare her, though, they make her cry."

"Why?"

"She was only seventeen when she got pregnant with me. My dad tried to step up and they got married, even though he was barely eighteen. My mom is very high maintenance. Her dad always gave her everything she wanted. Took care of things for her. She expected my dad to do the same. She was too demanding and he finally left. It was during a storm that he took off and never came back. She was left pregnant and alone."

"So she cries when it rains."

"Yes." Lindsay had pieced the story together through the years. She loved her mother; she was fun and free-spirited. But Lindsay also recognized her faults; it had been a matter of self-preservation.

"Her dislike of storms comes from sadness."

She nodded, her hair brushing over his chin. She'd never talked to anyone about this.

"But your jumpiness suggests a fear-based reaction."

A shiver racked her body and she curled in on herself. Everything in her tightened, shutting down on a dark memory. She wanted to tell him it was none of his business, but then he might let her go and she wasn't ready to give up the cocoon of his embrace.

His arms tightened around her and his lips slid over her cheek, giving her the courage to answer.

"It's a lingering unease leftover from childhood. It's distressing to hear your mother cry and know there's nothing you can do to help."

"It seems the mother should be comforting the child, not the other way around."

"She's more sensitive than I am."

A tender touch tucked her hair behind her ear, softly trailed down the side of her neck. "Just because you're tough doesn't mean you don't need reassurance now and again."

She relaxed under the gentle attention. Though she rejected the truth in his words.

"This storm caught me when I was tired. I'm sorry I disturbed you. I usually put my earbuds in but I left my phone in the Land Rover."

"Ah, a sensible solution. I should have known." He shifted behind her, leaving her feeling chilled and alone. And then his weight settled against her again and earbuds entered her ears. "You're stuck with my playlist, but maybe it'll help you sleep."

She smiled and wrapped her hand around his. "Thank you."

His fingers squeezed hers.

She felt the tension drain away. Now she had the music, she'd be okay. She no longer needed the comfort of his arms.

Her eyes closed. In a minute she'd pull away. There was danger in staying too close to him. Already her body recognized his, which made it all too easy for him to hold sway over her. She needed to stay strong, to stay distant…

The last thing she knew was the feel of his lips on her cheek.

CHAPTER FIVE

LINDSAY WOKE JUST before eight with the earbuds still in her ears. The tunes had stopped. She felt around for the phone but came up with the end of the earbuds instead. Her hand hadn't encountered a hard male body, but the stillness of the room had already told her Zach was out and about.

She threw back the covers and her feet hit the floor, her toes curling in her socks against the chill of the hardwood. Padding to the window, she pushed back the drapes to a world awash in sunshine. The ground was still wet but the greenery and rock fences had a just-scrubbed brightness to them.

Or was that Zach's influence on her?

A peek down the hall showed the bathroom was free so she quickly grabbed her things and made a mad dash to claim it. Aware others may be in need of the facilities she kept it short and soon returned to the room to dress and put on her makeup.

Before going downstairs, she packed her things so she'd be ready to leave when a car arrived. In spite of Zach's comfort and kindness last night, or maybe because of it, she fully intended to make her break from him today.

The heavenly scent of coffee greeted her in the dining room. Some fellow occupants of the B and B were seated at the long wooden table, including Zach. Cheerful greetings came her way as she moved through the room.

"Breakfast is buffet style this morning as there're so many of us." A gray-haired gentleman pointed with his fork toward the buffet she'd passed.

"Henry, don't use your utensils to point." An equally

gray-haired woman pushed his hand down. "They'll think we have no manners." She smiled at Lindsay with a mouth full of crooked teeth. "That handsome husband of yours made you a cup of coffee he was about to take upstairs. I'm glad you could join us. I'm happy to meet up with some fellow Americans. We're Wes and Viv Graham from Iowa and the folks there on the end are Frank and Diane Murphy from Oregon."

"Nice to meet you all." She sent Zach a questioning look at the husband comment and received a shrug in reply. Right. She'd get him for that. Hopefully they wouldn't be there long enough for it to be an issue. She backtracked to the buffet.

Croissants, sausage, bacon, quartered oranges and some cappuccino. No eggs. She took a couple of pieces of bacon, one sausage and a few orange wedges.

"I was just about to come wake you." Zach appeared beside her and took her plate. "I've arranged for alternate transportation and it'll be here in about half an hour. How'd you sleep?"

Huh. If he was leaving in half an hour maybe she'd stick with him, after all. It would take her longer than that to get her phone. "I slept well, thank you." Truly thanks to him.

"You're going to want one of these." He placed a croissant on her plate. "It's called a *cornetto*. There's a wonderful jam inside."

He took off for his seat, leaving her to follow. Their audience watched with avid curiosity. At their end of the table, Lindsay smoothed her hand across his shoulders. "Thank you, sweetie." She kissed him softly, lingering over his taste for a beat longer than she intended to, then slid into the chair around the corner to his right.

She pressed her lips together. Okay, that bit of payback totally backfired. But playing it through to the end, she glanced shyly down the table. "I'm sorry. We don't mean to be rude. Newlyweds." She rolled her eyes as if that explained everything.

A pleased smile bloomed on Diane's face. "Oh, my dear, don't mind us old folks. Congratulations. You two enjoy yourselves." She turned to her husband. "Frank do you remember on our honeymoon when we—"

"Well done." Zach pushed her coffee toward her. "But that's the first and last time you ever call me sweetie."

She flashed him a provocative look. "We'll see."

Let him stew on that. He was the one to say they'd be lovers, after all.

"Be nice to me or I'll take your *cornetto*."

"I don't think so." She picked up the horn-shaped pastry and bit in. Chewed. Savored. "Oh, my dog."

"I told you so." Satisfaction stamped his features as he leaned back in his straight-backed chair.

"This is wonderful." She pointed at the jam-filled roll. "We have to have these at the wedding."

"We're a long way from Monte Calanetti."

"Oh, I'm aware." Censure met unrepentance. "Tell me again why we're in Caprese and not Monte Calanetti?"

"An errand for the prince."

She waited for more. It didn't come.

"I took care of it this morning. I'm ready to go when the new transportation gets here."

That was a relief. She finished the last of her *cornetto* with a regretful sigh and a swipe of her tongue over her thumb. "Maybe not these exact rolls but definitely *cornettos*."

"I'm all for it, but I suggest you discuss that with Christina."

She nodded, eyeing him speculatively through another bite. "How well do you know Christina?"

"Not well." He glanced down, snagged one of her orange wedges. "I met her once. Theirs has been a long-distance relationship."

"She seems really nice. And she showed a lot of enthusiasm when we first started planning, but she's cooled off lately."

"Really?" That brought his head up. "Do you think she's having second thoughts?"

Lindsay gave a half shrug. "Very few brides make it to the altar without suffering a few nerves along the way. It's probably nothing. Or nothing to do with the wedding, anyway."

"Tony's been off, too. He got me to come all this way a month in advance of the wedding, but now it feels like he's avoiding me."

"I'm sure they both have a lot on their plates right now." So much for the reassurances she'd been hoping for. The fact Zach had noticed something off, too, gave her some concerns. "I'll know more after my appointment with Christina, which was supposed to be this afternoon. I'll have to reschedule. Oh, that reminds me. I need to get my phone out of the Land Rover."

"Sorry, I forgot." Zach reached around and pulled something from his back pocket. He set her phone on the table. "I had Luigi bring it by this morning."

"Thanks." She picked it up, felt the warmth of the glass and metal against her flesh and tried to disengage from the fact it had absorbed the heat from his hot bum.

A loud whopping sound overhead steadily got louder. Everyone looked up. Then, in an unchoreographed move, they all stood and rushed to the back terrace. Lindsay, with Zach on her heels, brought up the rear.

As she stepped out onto the cobblestone patio, a helicopter carefully maneuvered in the air, preparing to land in the large farmyard.

Zach watched Lindsay's face as the big bird neared the

ground, knew by the pop of her eyes exactly when she spied the royal insignia on the door. She turned to stare at him as the inn occupants wandered forward to examine the helicopter and talk to the pilot.

Zach surveyed the royal conveyance with a smirk. "Our new transportation."

"You have got to be kidding me."

He liked the look of awe in her eyes. Much better than the fear she'd tried so hard to hide the night before. There was something more to her dislike of storms than a leftover agitation from her mother's distress. Something she wasn't willing to share, or maybe something she didn't fully remember.

He wished he could have done more than just lend her his earbuds.

"It's good to have friends in high places. When I told Tony you were concerned about missing your appointment with Christina, he insisted on putting the helicopter at my disposal in assisting you for the duration."

Actually, Zach had suggested it; still Tony jumped at the chance to accommodate Christina. Forget bending over backward, Tony was doing flips to give Christina the wedding of her dreams. Because he knew their lives were going to suck.

For Zach's part, he figured the sooner he got to Christina, the sooner he could talk sense into her. They'd only met once, but Tony lauded her with being a sensible, caring person. Surely she saw the error in what they were about to do.

He could only hope she'd listen to reason and end things now. Then he and the wedding planner could spend the next month exploring the wonders of Tuscany.

Shock had her staring wide-eyed at the big machine. "I have a helicopter for the next month?"

"I have a helicopter until after the wedding. The pilot takes his orders from me."

"Ah. But you're here to help me." She rubbed her hands together. "So, I have my very own helicopter for the next month. Oh, this is going to make things so much easier."

"I'm glad you're happy." And glad he'd be able to keep tabs on her. Things were falling nicely into place. "I told him I had designs on his wedding planner and I needed something to impress her."

All wonder dropped away in a heartbeat.

His little pixie turned fierce, getting right up in his space.

"Listen to me, Mr. Sullivan." Her blue-diamond eyes pinned him to the spot. "You may not think much of what I do, but it's very important to me, to your friends and, in the case of this wedding, to this country. I was starting to like you, but mess with my business and you won't like me."

Dog, she was beautiful. She may be tiny but she worked that chin and those eyes. He'd never wanted to kiss a woman more in his life. Defensive, yes, but not just for herself. She honestly cared about Tony and Christina. And the blasted country.

He did like her. More than he should. He'd have to be careful not to damage her in his rescue mission.

"Tony is why I'm here. Ms. Reeves. I promise you, I'm going to do everything in my power to make sure this turns out right for him."

"Okay, then." Her posture relaxed slightly. "As long as we understand each other."

"Understand this." He wrapped his hands around her elbows, lifted her to her toes and slanted his mouth over hers.

She stiffened against him for the briefest moment, in the next all her luscious softness melted into him. She opened her mouth to his and the world dropped away. The sparkling-clean farmyard, chattering Midwest tourists and his majesty's royal helicopter disappeared from his radar.

He'd meant the kiss to be a distraction, to focus her on his mythical seduction and away from his actual plan to change Tony's mind about marrying Christina. And vice versa.

But all he knew in that moment, all he wanted to know, was the heated touch of the pixie coming apart in his arms. He wrapped her close, angling the kiss to a new depth. She tasted of berry jam and spicy woman. Her essence called to him, addled his senses until he craved nothing more than to sweep her into his arms and carry her up to their room.

Her arms were linked around his neck and he'd dragged her up his body so they were pressed together mouth to mouth, chest to chest, loins to loins. It wasn't enough. It was too much.

Someone patted him on the arm. "You young ones need to take that upstairs."

The world came crashing back. Zach slowly broke off the kiss. He lifted his head, opened his eyes. Passion-drenched pools of blue looked back at him. Her gaze moved to his mouth. A heavy sigh shifted her breasts against his chest. She looked back at him and blinked.

"You should put me down now."

Yes, he should. The kiss had gotten way out of control and he needed to rein it in. "I don't want to. Christina will understand if we're an hour late."

What was he saying? *Get a grip, Sullivan.*

"I won't." She pushed against him. "This was a mistake. And it won't happen again."

"Why not?" he demanded because that's what he'd want to know if he were seriously pursuing her, which he wasn't. She was too sweet, too genuine for him. He needed someone who knew the rules of non-commitment.

Still, when he set her on her feet, he took satisfaction in the fact he had to steady her for a moment.

"Because I'm a professional. Because you are the best man."

"And you have a policy. You're the boss, you can change policy."

"Not a good idea." She straightened her shirt, smoothing the fabric over her hips. "I have the policy for a reason. I'm the wedding planner. I'm not here to have fun. I'm here to work. You—" she swept him with a glance "—would be a distraction when I need all my wits about me."

"Signor..." The pilot approached. "If you desire to stick to your flight plan, we should leave within the next fifteen minutes."

"Thank you."

"May I assist with the luggage?"

Glad to have this scene wrapping to a close, Zach met her gaze. "Are you ready?"

"I am." She stepped back, composed herself. "I just need to grab my luggage and the wedding dress." She headed into the house. "Do you think they'd mind if I took a few *cornettos* to go?"

Grinning, he followed her inside. He best be careful or this woman was going to turn him inside out.

Lindsay loved traveling by helicopter. She'd been a little nervous to start out with, afraid the heights might get to her. Nope. Whizzing through the air above the scenic vista gave her a thrill.

The helicopter flew over a meadow that looked like gold velvet. She pointed. "It's beautiful. What crop is that?"

"No crop, *signorina*." The pilot's voice came over her headphones. "Sunflowers."

"Sunflowers," she breathed. She'd never seen a whole field of the big, cheerful flowers.

Zach tapped the pilot on the shoulder and he took them down and did a wide loop so she actually saw the flowers. She'd told Zach she wasn't there to have fun, but, oh, she was.

That didn't mean she could throw caution to the wind and jump into a summer fling. Her blood still thrummed from his embrace. It would have been so easy to let him seduce her. Except she couldn't. She needed to grow a spine, put him in his place. The problem was she melted as soon as he touched her.

If she was honest, the physical attraction wasn't what worried her. She liked him. Way too much for her peace of mind. That made the physical all the more tempting. She wanted love in her life but this was the wrong time, wrong place, wrong man.

Restraint came at a cost, but she wouldn't jeopardize everything she'd built on an overload of hormones. She just needed to resist him for a few weeks and then she'd be back in Hollywood and he'd be back in Silicon Valley.

Zach pointed out the palace as they flew over Voti, Halencia's capital city and Christina's home. The big, yellow palace presented a majestic silhouette with its square shape and the round battlement towers at the corners. The notched alternate crenels screamed castle. The building had a strong, regal presence set on a shallow cliff side overlooking the sea on one side and the sprawling city of Voti on the other.

One of the towers had been converted into a heliport.

"Are we landing at the palace?" She spoke into the microphone attached to the headphones.

"Yes." Zach nodded.

"So I'll get a chance to meet Prince Antonio?"

Now he shook his head. "Sorry, he's in meetings all day. We'll be going straight down and out to a car waiting for us. We'll be just in time for your one-thirty appointment with Christina."

The helicopter made a wide turn then started its descent. Lindsay experienced her first anxious moments, seeing the land rush up to meet her. Without thinking, she reached out and grabbed Zach's hand.

His warm grip wrapped around her fingers and gave a squeeze. She instantly relaxed, feeling grounded. Putting her stringent, no-fraternizing policy aside for a moment, she smiled at him. He'd been gentle and kind last night and was supportive now. No doubt he'd hate the description, but he was a genuinely good guy.

Even though she was essentially a stranger to him, Zach had gone over and beyond the call of duty.

She longed to see some of the interior of the palace, but a palace attendant met them and a very modern elevator took them straight down to the ground level. The attendant led them through a ten-foot portico, which he explained was the width of the castle walls.

Wow, Lindsay mouthed. Seriously, she felt like a little girl at Disneyland. She was so busy trying to see everything at once she nearly tripped over her own feet.

Zach grasped her elbow. Steadied her. "Careful, Tinkerbell."

Caught gawking. But she couldn't care. This was amazing. "We're in a castle. Couldn't I be Cinderella?"

He released her to tug on her straight ponytail. "No changing up now. Tinkerbell is a pixie, right?"

"She's a fairy. And you need to stop. I'm not that short."

"You're a little bitty thing. With lots of spunk. Nothing bad about that."

She rolled her eyes. "If you say so." They exited onto

a round driveway where a car and driver waited. She grabbed Zach's arm to stop him. "Listen, you don't need to come to my appointment with Christina. I can promise you'll be monumentally bored. If you stay here, you may get a few minutes to visit with Antonio."

"I want to come. It'll be good to see Christina again and to let her know Antonio isn't shirking his groom duties." He waved the driver off and held the door open for her himself. "Besides, I'm not hanging around hours just to get a few minutes of Tony's time. We'll connect soon enough."

She should go through her notes on the ride through Voti to be prepared for the appointment. Should, but wouldn't. The city was so charming, not a high-rise to be seen, and the buildings were bunched closely together, creating narrow lanes. The warmth of the earth tones and red-tiled roofs was like an architectural hug. She loved the bursts of color in hanging planters. And the odd little plazas they'd drive through that all had lovely little fountains.

Christina worked not far from the palace. All too soon the car pulled to a stop in front of a three-story building. Lovely, black, wrought-iron gates opened into a cobblestoned courtyard.

"Zach, Ms. Reeves, welcome." The driver must have called ahead because Christina stepped forward to greet them.

She was tall—Lindsay's notes read five nine and her subtle heels added a few inches to that—and stunning with creamy, olive skin and thick reddish-brown hair sleeked back in a French twist. She wore a fitted suit in cobalt blue.

Standing between her and Zach, Lindsay did feel short.

"Christina." Zach wrapped her hand in both of his. "You haven't changed a bit in four years."

"You flatter me," she said in perfect English, her accent charming. She led them through the courtyard and up a curving wrought-iron staircase to an office on the second floor. "We both know that's not true. Thank goodness. I was barely out of school and quite shy."

"And soon you'll be the Queen of Halencia."

Christina's eyelashes flickered and she looked down as she waved them into seats. "I prefer to focus on one thing at a time. First there is the wedding."

"Of course."

"Thank you, Ms. Reeves, for coming so early to assist in the preparations. I originally intended to continue with the foundation on a part-time basis in their offices here in Halencia, but the prince's advisors have convinced me I'll be quite busy. It would be unfair to the foundation to hold a position and not be here to help. It is such a worthy endeavor. I would not want to hamper it in any way."

"It's important work. I'm sure, as the queen, your interest will be quite beneficial, so you'll still be of help."

"That's kind of you to say." Christina inclined her head.

A regal gesture if Lindsay had ever seen one. Maybe she'd been practicing.

Lindsay waved toward the open window. "You have a lovely view of the palace from here. It must be amazing to sit here and see your future beckoning for you."

Christina's smile slipped a little. "Yes. Quite amazing."

"It's a lot to think about, isn't it?" Zach spoke softly. "All that you're giving up. All that you're taking on?"

Appalled at the questions that were sure to rattle the most confident of brides let alone one showing a slight nervousness, Lindsay sent him a quelling glance.

"I am at your disposal to assist in any way I can," she advised her bride.

"You have been wonderful. My mind is just everywhere these days. I hope you do not mind taking on the bulk of the arrangements?"

"Of course. If we can just make some final decisions, I

can take care of everything. Your attendants are all set, the dresses have been received and a first fitting completed. I just need to know your final thoughts on the flowers, the total head count and whether you want to do indoors or outdoors for the reception. I have some sketches for you to look at." She passed a slim portfolio across the desk. "The palace wants to use the royal photographer, but I know some truly gifted wedding photographers if you decide you want a specialist."

"I am sure the royal photographer will be fine. These are marvelous drawings, Ms. Reeves. Any of these settings will be wonderful."

"Lindsay." She gently corrected the soon-to-be princess, who seemed near tears as she looked at the reception scenes. Lindsay could tell she wasn't going to get much more from the woman. "Every wedding should be special. What can I do to make your day special?"

"You have done so much already. I like the outdoors. I remember playing in the palazzo courtyard, pretending it was a palace. It seems appropriate."

"Outdoors is a lovely choice. Regarding flowers, we passed a meadow of sunflowers on our way here today. Gold is one of the royal colors you listed. I wondered—"

"Sunflowers! Yes, I would love that. And roses, I think. You seem to know what I want better than I do."

"I've done this for a long time. I'll get the final head count from the palace contact. We've covered almost everything. But we never addressed if they do the traditional 'something old, something new, something borrowed, something blue' here in Halencia or if you even want to play along?"

"What is this tradition?" A frown furrowed her delicate brow.

"It's just a fun tradition that originated in England. It

represents continuity, promise of the future, borrowed happiness and love, purity and fidelity."

"It sounds quite lovely. But I do not have any of these things."

"The fun is in getting them. In America the items are often offered by friends and family. If you share you're doing this, you'll get everything you need and it will all have special meaning for you."

"I know of something old." She tapped a finger against her desk. "Yes, I would like to have it for the wedding. It is a brooch that has been in my father's family for many years. It is said that those who wore the brooch at their wedding enjoyed many happy years together. Yes. I must have the brooch."

"Sounds perfect." Pleased to get a positive reaction and some enthusiasm from the bride, Lindsay made a note in her tablet.

"But I do not know where the brooch is." Sadness drained the brief spark of light. "The women of my generation have not chosen to go with the old tradition. Do you think you can help me find it?" Christine's eyes pleaded with Lindsay. "My grandmother or Aunt Pia might know who had it last."

Goodness, Lindsay never liked to say no to a bride, but she couldn't see how her schedule would accommodate hours on the phone tracking down a lost family jewel.

"Sure, we'll be happy to locate it for you."

Zach stole her opportunity to respond. But, sure, it was a good way to keep him occupied and out of her hair.

"We're talking a few phone calls, right?"

Christina shook her head. "The older generation of women in my family are very traditional. They will not talk of such things to a stranger over the phone. And they will not talk to you alone, Zach." She reached for a pen and paper. "I will write a letter you can take with you. *Grazie*, both of you."

Oh, Zach, what had he got them into? The hope in Christina's eyes prevented Lindsay from protesting time constraints.

"I wish I could give you more time but with learning the workings of the palace, I am a bit overwhelmed." Christina handed Lindsay the letter she'd written. "With the two of you helping, I feel so much better."

"I'm glad." Lindsay tucked the letter into her tote.

"Lindsay, do you mind if I have a moment alone with Christina?" Zach made the quiet demand and tension instantly radiated from his companion.

"Of course." Lindsay stood and offered her hand to Christina. "I'll keep you apprised of the arrangements."

"Thank you." Christina used both hands to convey her urgency. "And the progress in locating the brooch."

"Absolutely." Lindsay smiled and turned away. With her back to Christina, Lindsay narrowed her eyes at him and mouthed the words, "Do not upset the bride."

He maintained an impassive demeanor. "I'll be along in a moment."

Though Christina watched him expectantly, he waited for the distinct click of the door closing before he addressed her.

"I hope you'll forgive my concern, but I noticed you seem unsettled."

"I have much on my mind."

"I understand. But I also know the circumstances of your…relationship with Antonio." The situation warranted discretion on so many levels. "And I wonder if you're having second thoughts?"

Her chin lifted in a defensive gesture. "No."

"Perhaps you should."

Surprise showed before she composed her features

into a calm facade. "I can assure you I have considered the matter thoroughly. Did Antonio send you here to test me?"

"No. Tony has asked me to be his advocate in all things wedding related. I take my responsibilities seriously and when I look at this situation, I have to wonder what the two of you are thinking. Marriage is a binding, hopefully lifelong, commitment. The two of you barely know each other. No one would blame you if you changed your mind. Least of all Tony. He knows how much you've already sacrificed for your country."

Her shoulders went back. "Has he changed his mind?"

It would be so easy to lie. To destroy the engagement with a bit of misdirection that resulted in an endless loop of he said, she said. But he had some honor. The decision to end it must be hers, Antonio's or theirs together.

"No. He's determined to see this through. He's very grateful to you."

She nodded as if his words affirmed something for her. "Thank you for your concern. There is much to adjust to, but I will honor my promise. In little over a month, I will marry Prince Antonio."

CHAPTER SIX

LINDSAY WAS STILL puzzling over what Zach felt compelled to talk to Christina about in private as she climbed to her room on the third floor of Hotel de la Calanetti, a lovely boutique hotel situated on a hillside overlooking Monte Calanetti's central courtyard.

Considering his opinion of lavish weddings and how unsettled Christina came across, leaving them alone together made Lindsay's left eyebrow tick. He better not have caused trouble.

In retrospect she wished she'd waited to say goodbye to Christina until after he'd spoken to her. Then Lindsay might have learned what the discussion had been about. Or maybe not. The other woman's natural poise hid a lot. Lindsay had been unable to tell if the woman was upset when she'd walked them out.

Holding the garment bag draped over her arm, Lindsay stepped aside so the hotel manager's teenage son, Mario, could unlock the door.

"Signorina." He ducked his head in a shy move and gestured for her to precede him.

She stepped in to a comfortable, refined room furnished with nice 1800s furniture. Thankfully there was a private bathroom. One large window allowed sunshine to flow in and provided a delightful view of the village and town center.

But it was tiny; smaller than the room at the farmhouse. Though this room included a desk, which she was happy to see, and a comfortable chair, she barely had space to walk around the double bed.

She tipped Mario—who'd lugged her suitcases up the three flights—with some change and a smile.

"*Grazie, signorina.*" He rewarded her with a bashful grin and raced away.

The garment bag took up the entire closet to the point she had to bump it shut with her hip. She'd hoped to leave the dress with Christina, but the bride had nixed that plan. The queen had made a reservation with a favorite *modiste* in Milan and Christina had asked Lindsay to hold on to the dress and bring it to the fitting.

So of course that was what she'd do. And apparently everything else.

When Christina had walked them out, she'd given Lindsay a brief hug and whispered, "I trust you to finish it. Please make the prince proud."

Lindsay got the message. She was on her own for the final push. Luckily her assistant would be arriving in a few days.

Hands on her hips Lindsay surveyed her room. It was lovely. And if she were here on vacation it would be perfect. But where was she going to work?

The desk for computer work was the least of her needs. She'd shipped five boxes of pre-wedding paraphernalia to the hotel. Upon check-in, Signora Eva had eagerly informed Lindsay the boxes had arrived and she'd be sending them up shortly.

Lindsay puffed out a breath that lifted her bangs. She thought longingly of the hillside villa Zach had pointed out as they'd flown over it. He had the whole place to himself. He probably had a room he could donate to the cause. Unfortunately he'd constantly be around. Talking to her. Distracting her. Tempting her.

Better to avoid that trap if she could.

She lifted her suitcase onto the bed and started unpacking. When she finished, she'd walk down to the town cen-

ter to get a feel for the small city. She may have to find
office space; possibly something off the town courtyard
would be pleasant and close. In the meantime, she'd ask
Signora Eva to hold on to the boxes.

Dressed in beige linen shorts and a cream, sleeveless tunic,
Lindsay strolled down the hill. There was no sidewalk,
just the ancient cobblestoned street. Charming but not the
easiest to walk on.

A young man zipped by her on a scooter, followed
closely by his female companion. Lindsay watched them
until they turned a corner and vanished from view. She
hadn't heard from the car-rental company yet. Monte Calanetti was a lovely little city, but not small enough she could
do all her business by foot.

The zippy little scooter looked promising. It wouldn't
hold anything, but she could have things delivered. But
where? Not the hotel. She'd get claustrophobic after a day.

She reached the city center; not a courtyard, but a plaza.
Oh, it was lovely. In the center an old fountain bubbled
merrily, drawing Lindsay forward. Businesses ringed the
plaza, many with hanging pots of flowers. It was bright
and colorful and had probably looked much the same a
hundred or even five hundred years ago.

Well, minus the cars, of course.

History in Tuscany wasn't something that needed to be
brought to mind. The past surrounded you wherever you
went, influenced your very thoughts. Already Lindsay was
contemplating how she could make it a part of the wedding.

"Buon giorno, signorina," a male voice greeted her.
"May I assist you in finding your way?"

She swung around to confront a large, barrel-chested
man with a full head of black hair dusted gray on the sides.
His bushy mustache was more gray than black. Friendly
brown eyes waited patiently for her assessment.

"Hello." She smiled. "I'm just wandering." She waved her hand around. "I'm spellbound by the beauty of Monte Calanetti. You must be so proud the royal wedding will be performed here."

"Indeed we are. I am Alonso Costa, mayor of this fair city. I can assure you we have much to offer those who stay here. Amatucci's is one of the best boutique vineyards in the world, and Mancini's restaurant is superb. I fully expect Raffaele to earn an Italian Good Food Award this year. What is your interest, *signorina*? I will direct you to the best."

Oh, she was sure he could. She liked him instantly. He'd be a great source to help her.

"It's nice to meet you, Alonso, I'm Lindsay Reeves and I'd like to learn more about your beautiful city. Would you like to join me for coffee?"

White teeth flashed under the heavy bush of his mustache. "I would be most delighted, *signorina*. The café has a lovely cappuccino."

"Sounds wonderful." She allowed him to escort her across the plaza to an outdoor table at the café. He went inside and returned with two cappuccinos and some biscotti. She began to wonder if they had a gym in town. All this wonderful food, she'd be needing one soon.

She introduced herself more fully to the mayor and he proved a font of information. As she'd expected the media, both print and electronic, had already landed heavily in Monte Calanetti.

Alonso rubbed his chin when she asked after office space. "I will ask around. But I must warn you most available space has already been rented or reserved. The wedding has proved quite prosperous for the townspeople. Many have rented out spare rooms to house the paparazzi or provide work space as you have requested."

He named a figure a family had asked for the rental of their one-car garage and her mouth dropped open.

"Si," He nodded at her reaction. "It is crazy. But the press, they bid against each other to get the space."

"Well, it's more than I can afford. I'll have to figure out something else."

The empty chair next to Lindsay scraped back and Zach joined them at the table. He laid one arm along the back of her chair while holding his other hand out to Alonso. "Zach Sullivan. I've rented the De Luca villa."

"Ah, the best man." Alonso shook hands. "A palace representative provided a list of VIPs who would be visiting the area for the wedding. Your name is on the top."

Zach grinned. "It's good to know Tony has his priorities straight."

The casual reference to the prince impressed the mayor. He puffed up a bit as he gave Zach the same rundown about the town he'd given her. Except he offered to arrange a tour of the vineyard and make reservations at the restaurant. With great effort she restrained an eye roll.

"Tell me about the fountain," she asked to redirect the conversation.

Alonso gave her a bright smile. "The legend is that if you toss a coin and it lands in the clamshell you will get your wish. We recently learned that the sculptor of the nymph was Alberto Burano. The fact that the nymph wore a cloak caught the attention of an art historian. She recognized Burano's style and researched the fountain and Burano until she linked the two."

"That's amazing. And brings more value to the fountain and the city. Do you know anything more about the legend?"

"Actually, Lucia's search inspired me to do one of my own and I found that nymphs are known to be sensual creatures of nature, capricious in spirit living among humans but distant from them so when one presents an offering, such as the clamshell, it means the nymph has found true love and the offering is a gift of equal love."

"It's a lovely legend of unselfishness and love." The romance of it appealed to Lindsay.

"But does it work?" Zach questioned.

"Before I did the research I would have said half the time. Now, when I think back to the stories I've heard, success always involved matters of the heart. I believe when the coin lands in the clamshell it activates the gift and the wish is granted when true love is involved."

Zach quirked one dark eyebrow. "You're a romantic, Mr. Mayor."

Alonso smiled and shrugged in a very Italian gesture. "This is what I have observed. Does it make me a romantic to believe in the legend? Maybe so. But the tourists like it."

"I'm sure they do," Lindsay agreed. "Who doesn't like the thought of true love? Wouldn't it be cool to have a replica of the fountain at the reception?"

"*Si*. There is a mason in town that makes small replicas he sells to tourists. I'll give you his number. He might be able to make something bigger."

"That would be great. Thanks."

The mayor's cell phone rang. "Excuse me." He checked the display. "I must take this call. It has been a pleasure to meet you both. *Il caffè* is my treat today."

"Oh, no," Lindsay protested. "I invited you."

"And I am pleased you did. Allow me to welcome you both to Monte Calanetti with this small offering. You can reward me by thinking of local resources when planning this illustrious wedding."

"I already planned to do so."

"Ah—" he made a show of bowing over her hand "—a woman who is both beautiful and clever. You are obviously the right person for the job."

"You flatter me, Alonso. But I must be truthful. The bride insists that I use local goods and people whenever I can."

"Molto bene." He nodded, his expression proud. "Already our princess looks after the people. But I think maybe you would do this anyway, *si*?"

"I've found that local talent is often the best."

"Si, si. As I say, a clever woman. *Buona giornata.* Good day to you both. Ms. Reeves, I will get back to you with a referral. *Ciao."* He made his exit, stopping to yell something inside the café. Then with a salute the mayor hurried across the square.

"I thought the French were supposed to be the flirts of Europe," Zach mused.

"I liked him."

"Of course. He was practically drooling over you. Clever woman."

She laughed and batted her lashes. "Don't forget beautiful."

His eyes locked on hers, the whiskey depths lit with heat. "How can I when you're sitting right next to me?"

Held captive by his gaze, by a quick and wicked fantasy, it took a beat to compose herself. She cleared her throat as she chased the tail of the topic. Oh, yeah, the mayor. "You can tell he cares about his town and his people. I respect that. Excuse me."

She grabbed her purse and made her escape. Whew, the man was potent.

"Where are we going?" He slid into stride next to her.

And apparently hard to shake.

"We are not going anywhere." She reached the fountain and began to circle the stone feature, making the second answer unnecessary.

"I thought I made it clear, I'm here to assist you."

She flashed him a "yeah, right" glance.

"I appreciate the offer, but my assistant will be arriving at the end of the week." She continued circling.

"What are you doing?"

"I'm checking out the fountain, choosing the best place to throw a coin." The fountain was round, about twelve feet wide with a rock formation rising from slightly off center to a height between seven and eight feet. The cloaked nymph, reclined across two rocks from which the water flowed, reached forward, displaying one nude breast as she offered the clamshell to the side of the rushing water so some of it ran over the stone dish. If you threw too far to the left, the flow of water would wash your chance away, too far to the right and an over-cropping of rock would block the coin.

"You're going to make a wish? For true love? I thought your schedule didn't allow for such things."

"It doesn't." He was right about that. "It's not for me."

"For who then? Your mother?"

"Now there's a thought. But…no." Unfortunately she didn't know if her mother would recognize true love if she found it. She was so focused on the high, she rarely made it past the first few bumps. Even true love required an effort to make it work. "I'm making a wish for Antonio and Christina."

He stopped following her and planted his hands on his hips. "Why? They're already headed for the altar. They don't need the nymph's help."

"Really?" she challenged him. "You're that sure of them?"

His expression remained set. "I think fate should be allowed to take its course."

"And I think it needs a little help." She dug out her coin purse. Hopefully American coins worked as well as euros. Choosing a spot a little to the left because she was right-handed, she tossed her coin. Too light. It fell well short of the clamshell. She tried again. This one went over the top. A third got swept away by the water. "Dang it. That one was in."

"You're not going to make it in. It's set up to defeat you."

"Hey, no advice from the galley." Maybe a nickel? Oh, yeah, that had a nice heft. "What did you talk to Christina about earlier?"

"If I'd wanted you to know, I wouldn't have asked you to leave."

"Tell me anyway." The nickel bounced off the rock.

"No. Try a little twist at the end."

"I'd share with you," she pointed out as she tossed her last nickel. And missed.

"It's none of your business."

She fisted the dime she was about to throw and faced him. "Wrong. I'm here to plan the royal wedding, which makes the bride very much my business. She was already unsettled. And I know you're not a big fan of lavish weddings. I need to know if you upset her."

"I didn't upset her," he said too easily.

"Good. Great. So, tell me, what did you talk about?"

He just lifted a dark eyebrow at her.

"Seriously, I need to know. Just because she didn't look upset doesn't mean she wasn't."

"You're being a nutcase."

"And it'll all go away if you just tell me."

"Okay." He shoved his hands into his pockets. "I picked up on her uneasiness, as well. I asked her if she was having second thoughts."

"Zach!"

"What? This is my best friend. If she's going to bolt, now would be the time to speak up. Not when he's standing at the altar."

"I told you, all brides go through a bit of nerves. Unless you're the M-O-B, pointing out their shakiness only makes it worse. Even then it can be iffy."

His features went blank. "M-O-B?"

"Mother of the bride."

"Oh. She's probably the last person Christina would confide in."

"Why do you say that?"

"My impression is the two aren't particularly close."

"Hmm. Good to know." Lindsay had already noted Christina's reluctance to include her mother in the planning.

Mrs. Rose made her displeasure quite well known, which brought Mr. Rose out to play. Lucky for Lindsay the palace official had taken over dealing with the Roses.

"All the more reason to show Christina support rather than undermine her confidence," Lindsay advised Zach.

"Rest easy. She assured me she would be marrying Tony."

"Okay." She read his eyes and nodded. "Good. Thanks." She turned back to the fountain. "My last coin. What kind of twist?"

"You're still going to make a wish? I just told you Christina's fine."

"I want more than fine. I want true love."

"You do know most political marriages aren't based on love." Something in his tone had her swinging back to him. The late-afternoon sun slanted across his face, casting his grim features into light and shadow.

"Yes," she said softly, "but is that what you want for your friend?"

He moved closer, brushing her ponytail behind her shoulder. "So what is your wish?"

"I'm wishing for true love and happiness for the bride and groom." With the words, she pulled her arm back. As it moved forward Zach cupped her hand and, as she released the coin, gave it a little twist.

The dime flew through the air and plopped with a splash right in the middle of the clamshell.

"We did it!" Lindsay clapped her hands then threw her arms around Zach's neck and kissed his cheek. "Thank you."

He claimed a quick kiss then set her aside. "Don't celebrate yet. We still need to see if it works. Which should only take—what?—the next fifty years."

"Nope." Flustered from the kiss, Lindsay stepped back shifting her attention from him to the fountain. What had he said? Oh, yeah. How did it work? "Now we have faith."

The first attempt to find the brooch was a bust.

Lindsay tried insisting she could handle finding the brooch herself. It was something she could do while she waited for her assistant to arrive and figured out her work space situation. And she needed a break from Zach, especially after the kiss at the fountain. His casual caresses were becoming too common and were definitely too distracting for her peace of mind.

A little distance between them would be a good thing.

Unfortunately, as he pointed out, Christina's grandmother lived in a tiny house in a village halfway between Monte Calanetti and Voti, and Lindsay didn't have transportation without him. A new rental hadn't showed up and the helicopter flew at his discretion. Plus, he'd offered to interpret for her. Since Mona didn't speak much English and Lindsay didn't speak much Italian, she was stuck.

Mona Rose was small with white hair, glasses and lots of pip. She greeted them warmly as Christina had called to say they would be coming. Lindsay sat on a floral-print couch with crocheted lace doilies on the arms while Zach lounged in a matching rocking chair.

Mona served them hibiscus tea and lemon cake while she chatted with Zach.

Lindsay smiled and sipped. After a few minutes of listening, she discreetly kicked Zach in the foot.

He promptly got the clue. "She's very pleased Christina wishes to wear the brooch. She wore the brooch for her wedding and had many happy years with her Benito. Her daughter, Cira, chose not to wear the brooch and now she's divorced with two children."

"I'm sorry to hear that." Lindsay accepted a plate of cake. "Does she know where the brooch is?"

Zach conveyed the question.

Mona tapped her chin as she stared out the window. After a moment she took a sip of her tea and spoke. "Sophia, my youngest sister, I think was last to wear *le broccia*." She shook her head and switched to Italian.

Zach translated. "Pia is her older sister. Her daughter was the last to get married. She didn't wear the brooch, either, but Mona thinks Pia may have it."

"Grazie." Lindsay directed her comments to Mona, smiling to hide her disappointment. She was hoping this chore could be done.

"Would you be willing to do a quick look through your things while we're here? Just to be on the safe side."

Zach translated both the question and Mona's answer.

"Si. I will look. Christina is a good girl. And Antonio, he is good for Halencia. But they will both need much luck."

The next morning Lindsay struggled to get ready while shuffling around five large boxes. When she'd returned to the hotel last night, all five boxes had been delivered to her room. As predicted, she'd had a hard time getting around the bed. She'd actually had to climb over it to get to the bathroom.

When she'd asked about it at the front desk, Signora Eva apologized but explained a delivery of provisions had forced her to reclaim the space she'd been using to store Lindsay's boxes. That had meant the boxes needed to be delivered to Lindsay's room. This morning she'd managed to arrange them so she had a small aisle around the bed, but she had to suck in a breath to get through.

The thought of unpacking everything in this limited space made her cringe. She'd be tripping over her samples every time she turned around.

Frustrated, she left the room for some breakfast. Later she wanted to view the palazzo and chapel where the wedding and reception would take place. But she hoped to rent a scooter before making the trip to the other side of town. If any were still available.

The press truly had descended. On her way to breakfast she fended off two requests for exclusive shots of the wedding dress. She informed them the dress was under lock and key at the palace and suffered no remorse for her lie.

When Signora Eva came by to refill her coffee, Lindsay asked if she knew of any place she might rent for a work space and received much the same response as she'd gotten from the mayor.

She was processing that news when her cell rang.

With a sinking heart she listened to her assistant advise her she wouldn't be joining her in Halencia, after all. While Mary gushed on about the part she'd landed in a situation comedy all Lindsay could think about was how she'd manage without an assistant.

Lindsay needed to be out in the field a lot. She counted on her assistant to keep track of all the details of a wedding, do follow up and advise Lindsay of any problems. She'd quickly become bogged down if she had to take on the extra work.

Because she cared about Mary, Lindsay mustered the enthusiasm to wish her well. But as soon as she hung up she had a mini meltdown. Stomping over to the sideboard, she plopped an oversize muffin onto her plate and returned to her seat, her mind churning over her lack of options…

As Lindsay made the hike up the hill to Zach's villa she contemplated the obvious answer to her space problem. Much as she preferred to avoid Zach, after two short days she seriously considered asking him for help.

Her hesitation wasn't worry over his answer. He'd been ordered to assist her and he genuinely seemed to take his duty seriously.

The problem would be in dealing with him.

From the air, the villa had looked vast enough to provide a small corner for her without causing her to trip over him at every turn. But she wouldn't know until she saw the inside, which is what had prompted this little trip.

She wiped her brow with the back of her hand. Only eight in the morning and already the day had some heat to it. The blue, cloudless sky offered little relief from the relentless sun. But it also meant no humidity.

"Good morning, partner." Zach's voice floated on the air.

She paused and shaded her eyes to seek him out. He stood on a terrace of his rented villa. The big, stone building rested right up against the old protective wall that ringed the city. From this vantage point it looked huge. Three stories high, the bottom floor created the terrace where Zach stood. The top floor was a pergola with windows on all sides.

"Good morning." She waved.

"You missed the street." He gestured for her to backtrack a bit. "It's a narrow drive right by the pink house."

She followed his directions, turning at the pink house, and there he was coming to greet her. He wore khaki shorts and a blue cotton shirt untucked. The sleeves were rolled to expose his muscular forearms. He looked cool, calm and competent.

How she envied him.

The trees thinned as they neared the villa. He took her

hand and led her down a steep set of steps and a walkway along the side of the house. When they rounded the corner, her breath caught in her throat.

The small city spread out below them, a backdrop to the green lawn that covered the hillside. Oak, olive and pine trees provided shade and privacy. To her right a table and chairs sat under a covered patio, the ivy-covered trellis lending it a grotto effect while a stone path led to a gazebo housing white wicker furniture.

To the far side rosebushes lined a path leading to an infinity pool.

Forget the palazzo. This would make a beautiful setting for a wedding. Well, if you weren't a royal prince.

She took pride in the large, lavish weddings she'd planned for hip and rising celebrities, but she took joy in putting together weddings that were cozy gatherings. Yup, give her intimate and tranquil over pomp and circumstance any day of the week.

"Come up with me." A spiral wrought-iron staircase took them to the terrace he'd been standing on when he'd hailed her. She followed his tight butt up the steps.

Good dog, he was fine. His body rivaled any sight she'd seen today. Even the view from the terrace that provided a panoramic vista of everything she'd seen.

"Impressed yet?" Zach asked behind her left ear.

"I passed impressed before I reached the pool."

"I had my coffee out here this morning. I don't think I've ever spent a more peaceful moment."

"I'm jealous." She stepped away from the heat of his body. She needed her wits about her when she presented her proposition. His assertion they'd be lovers haunted her thoughts. And dreams.

Oh, she was a weak, weak woman in her dreams.

As heat flooded her cheeks she focused on the view

rather than his features. "I'm afraid I'm about to disrupt your peace."

"Pixie, just looking at you disrupts my peace. In the best possible way." He punctuated the remark by tracing the armhole of her sleeveless peach-and-white polka dot shirt, the backs of his fingers feathering over sensitive flesh.

She shivered, shaking a finger at him as she created distance between them. "No touching."

He grinned, again unrepentant. "What brings you by today?"

"I wondered if you wanted to go to the cake tasting with me." She tossed out her excuse for the spy mission. Men liked cake, right?

As soon as the words left her mouth, she thought better of her desperate plan. If she worked here, it would be more of his charming flirtation and subtle caresses until she gave in and let him have his wicked way with her. Or she stopped the madness by seducing him on the double lounge down by the pool. Enticing as both scenarios were, neither was acceptable.

"You know…never mind. I've already taken advantage of your generosity. Enjoy your peace. I can handle this on my own." She turned for the stairs. "I'll catch you later."

The chemistry between them nearly struck sparks in the air. The force of the pull buzzed over her skin like a low-level electrical current. She had it banked at the moment, but the right word or look and it would flare to life in a heartbeat.

Her best bet was to walk away and find another solution to her problem. One that didn't tempt her to break her sensible rules and put her company at risk. She purposely brought Kevin to mind, remembered the pain and humiliation of his betrayal and recalled the looks of pity and disapproval on the faces of her friends and colleagues.

She'd never willingly put herself in that position ever again.

"Cake." Zach caught her gently by the elbow. "You can't tease me with cake and then walk away. It's one of the few chores regarding this wedding gig I'd actually enjoy."

She studied him for a moment before replying. He met her stare straight-on, no hint of flirting in his steady regard. She appreciated his sincerity but still she hesitated.

"Okay. You're in. But we have to go now. I have an appointment to view the palazzo this afternoon. Has the rental company replaced your car yet?"

"No. I have my assistant following up on it. Do we need the helicopter?"

She shook her head. "The bakery is in town." She supposed she'd have to follow up on her own rental now. Pulling out her phone, she made a note. "But it's hot out. My plan is to rent a scooter."

A big grin brought out a boyishness in his features. "You don't have to rent a scooter. There are a couple downstairs in the garage along with something else you might find useful."

"What?"

"Come see." He strode over to a French door and stepped inside.

Trailing behind him, she admired the interior almost as much as the exterior. The bedroom they moved through displayed the comfort and luxury of a five-star hotel. Downstairs it became apparent the villa had gone through a modern update. The lounge, dining room and gourmet kitchen opened onto each other via large archways, creating an open-concept format while exposed beams and stone floors retained the old world charm of a Tuscan villa.

Oh, yeah, she could work here. Too bad it was a no-go.

Off the kitchen Zach opened a door and went down a

half flight of stairs to the garage. He flipped a light and she grinned at what she saw. A sporty black golf cart with a large cargo box in the back filled half the space. On the far side were two red scooters.

"Sweet. This will work nicely."

"Dibs on the cart."

She lifted her eyebrows at him. "What are you, ten?"

"No, I'm six-four. I'd look foolish trying to ride the scooter."

Running her gaze over the full length of him, she admired the subtle muscles and sheer brawn of his wide shoulders. She saw his point. He'd look as though he were riding a child's toy.

He grunted. "Work with me here, Lindsay. You can't tell me no touching and then look at me like that."

"Sorry," she muttered. She claimed the passenger seat. Caught.

Turned out wedding planning could be quite tasty. Zach finished the last bite of his sample of the white amaretto cake with the vanilla bean buttercream icing. And way more complicated than it needed to be.

The baker, a reed-thin woman with a big smile and tired eyes, had six samples set out for them when they'd arrived at the quaint little shop on a cobblestoned street just off the plaza. She'd dusted her hands on her pink ruffled apron and explained what each sample was.

Lindsay explained Christina had already chosen the style and colors for the cake; their job was to pick out the flavors for the three different layers. It took him five minutes to pick his three favorites. Lindsay agreed with two but not the third. He was happy to let her have her preference, but…no. The baker brought out six more samples, which were all acceptable.

The fact was they couldn't go wrong whatever choice

they made. There was no reason this appointment needed to be an hour long. But Lindsay insisted the flavors be compatible.

They were finally done and he was finishing off the samples of his favorites while Lindsay completed the order with the baker up at the counter.

He'd be taking a back seat on the hands-on stuff from now on. He was a stickler for attention to detail, but efficiency had its place, too.

The little bell over the door rang as two men strolled in, one tall and bald, the other round and brown-haired. They eyed the goods on display and Zach heard a British slant to their accent.

He knew immediately when they realized who Lindsay was. They closed in on her, obviously trying to see the plans for the cake. Their interest marked them as two of the media horde invading the town.

Lindsay politely asked them to step back.

Baldy moved back a few inches but Brownie made no move to honor her request.

Zach's gaze narrowed on the two, waiting to see how Lindsay handled herself. His little pixie had a feisty side. She wouldn't appreciate his interference. And this may well blow over. All press weren't bad, but he knew money could make people do things they'd never usually contemplate.

Ignoring the looming goons, Lindsay wrapped up her business and turned toward him. The media brigade blocked her exit, demanding details about the cake, pestering her for pictures. She tried to push past them but they went shoulder to shoulder, hemming her in.

In an instant Zach crossed the room.

"You're going to want to let her by."

"Wait your turn." Brownie dismissed him. "Come on, sweetcakes, show us something."

Sweetcakes?

"It's always my turn." Zach placed a hand on either man's shoulder and shoved them apart.

They whirled on him like a mismatched tag team.

"Back up," Brownie snarled at Zach's chest. And then he slowly lifted his gaze to Zach's. Even Baldy had to look up.

Zach rolled his thick shoulders. That's all it usually took. Sure enough, both men took a large step back.

"Ms. Reeves is with me." He infused the quiet words with a bite of menace. "I won't be pleased if I see you bothering her again."

"Hey, no disrespect." Baldy quickly made his exit. Brownie clenched his jaw and slowly followed.

"Thank you." Lindsay appeared at his side. "Those two were more aggressive than most."

"Are you okay?" He pulled her into his arms. "Do you put up with that often?" He couldn't tolerate the thought of her being hassled by those media thugs on her own.

"All the time." For a moment she stood stiffly, but with a sigh she melted against him. "One of the guys at my hotel offered me a hundred-thousand dollars for a picture of the wedding dress, which means the tabloids are probably willing to pay a million for it."

"That explains why you've lugged it halfway across the world."

"I said it was locked up at the palace. But for a million dollars, I don't doubt someone might try to check out my room anyway."

That did it. He may not support this wedding, but he had his limits. He wouldn't put his plan, or Tony's happiness, before Lindsay's safety. The thought of her vulnerable on her own at the hotel and someone forcing their way into her room sent a primitive wave of rage blasting through him. He had to fix this.

"You should give up your room at the hotel and stay with me at the villa. It would be safer for you."

CHAPTER SEVEN

"Uh, no." Lindsay pushed away from the safety of his arms. Yes, she'd been spooked by the menacing media jerks, but was Zach totally insane? "That is not an option." She even thought better of asking for work space at the villa. "This—" she waved between the two of them, indicating the chemistry they shared "—makes it a bad idea."

"Even I'm picking up on what a big deal this is for the press." He led her back to their table. "It didn't really strike me at first. I'm used to photographers hanging around hawking at Antonio for a picture. Some of them can be unscrupulous in their bid for a shot." He sat back crossing his arms over his chest his gaze intent, focused on her, on the problem. She had a sudden, clear vision of what he'd look like sitting at his desk. "It's the only solution that makes sense."

She sent him a droll stare. "You're just saying that to get in my pants."

"Not so."

The bite in the denial sent embarrassed heat rushing through her.

"Yes, I want in your pants, but not at the expense of your safety."

She blinked at him, her emotions taking a moment to catch up with her hearing. Obviously she'd touched a nerve.

"Okay."

"Excellent." Satisfied, he leaned forward in his chair. "It's settled. You'll move into the villa. We'll find a secure spot for the dress and you can choose a room for yourself and one of the spare rooms for your office. Or you can use the sunroom if you prefer."

"No. Wait." Panicked, she made a sharp cut-off gesture with her hand. "I was acknowledging your comment not agreeing to move in. We need to talk about this."

"We just did."

"Yes, and I appreciate your putting my safety ahead of your libido, but what does that mean? I've told you how I feel about maintaining a professional distance with all members of the wedding party, especially the best man."

A raised eyebrow mocked her. "I remember."

She gritted her teeth. "Well, you're a touchy-feely guy and I can't deal with that in a professional relationship."

A stunned expression flashed across his well-defined features but was quickly replaced with a contemplative mask.

"You have my promise I'll try to keep my hands to myself."

"The problem with that sentence is the word *try.*"

He ran a hand over the back of his neck, kneading the muscles and nerves as if to relieve tension, studying her the whole time. Then he flexed his shoulders and faced her.

"Here's the deal. I'm not a touchy-feely guy. Not normally. I go after what I want, but I respect boundaries and I can handle being told no."

Yeah, like that happened.

"For some reason it's different with you. I like my hands on you, like the touch and taste of you to the degree it's instinctive to seek it."

OMD. That is so hot.

"So, yes. I promise to *try.*"

She gulped. "Okay."

His eyes flashed dark fire. "Is that okay you'll stay or—"

"Yes. Okay, I'll move in." It may be insane to move in

with him, but she would feel safer. Plus, it solved her work problem. "But I'm keeping my room at the hotel. Space is already at a premium here in Monte Calanetti and I need a place I can retr—uh…go to if things don't work out."

"Fair enough. And as a gesture of my commitment, I'll pay for the room since you won't be using it."

"That's not necessary."

"It is to me. I'll feel better with you at the villa, and I want you to know you can trust me."

She slowly nodded. "Okay. I'll go pack."

"I had your boxes delivered up here, but if you choose this space, you'll need a proper desk. It has a bar and a billiard table, but that's it."

"I don't need anything new," Lindsay protested.

"I doubt the owners will object to us leaving behind an extra piece of furniture."

"That's not the point." He'd warned her that the space lacked a desk or table for her laptop. But, seriously, she didn't see the problem; she sat with it in her lap half the time.

"Pixie." He stopped in the upper hallway and swung to face her. His hand lifted to touch but he caught himself and curled the fingers into a fist that he let drop to his side. "Didn't you look at the numbers? The government contract will lift me to billionaire status. I can afford a desk."

He opened a door she'd thought was a linen closet. It revealed a staircase of stone steps. His hand gestured for her go ahead of him.

"First of all—" she paused in front of him "—congratulations."

A pleased smile lit his eyes. The simple expression of joy made her glad she'd put that first.

She got the feeling he received very little positive reinforcement in his personal life. The business world recognized and respected his genius, and his employees obviously appreciated his success and most likely his work ethic. But as an only child whose parents ignored his personal business interests in favor of their own agenda for him to join his father in politics, who did he have that mattered to tell him job well done?

She shook the thought away. He was not a poor, unfortunate child, but an intelligent, successful man.

And he'd hate her pity.

"Second—" she started up the stairs "—it's not for you to buy me a desk."

"The duties of a best man are unlimited. But you could be right. Do you want me to call Tony and ask him? Because I can pretty much guarantee his response will be, 'If the wedding planner needs a desk then buy her a desk. And don't bother me with such trivial things.'"

Aggrieved, she rolled her eyes, making sure he saw as she rounded the bend in the stairs. "Please, even if he blew off the request that easily, he wouldn't add that last bit."

"Not only would he say it, Pixie, that was the clean version. Tony doesn't have a whole lot of patience these days."

"He must be dealing with a lot—oh, I love, love, *love* this."

She strolled into the middle of the bright room and did a slow turn. The room was a long octagon. Three walls were made of glass and windows, two others were of stone and one held a fireplace. The last was half stone, the other half was a stained-glass mural of a Tuscan hillside; a bar with brown-cushioned stools ran almost the full length of the wall. At the far end there was a door. She checked it out and found it opened onto another spiral staircase that led to the terrace below.

"A separate entrance."

"Yes, I'll give you a set of keys. When your assistant gets here, she can still have access if we're gone."

"That'd be great but my assistant won't be coming."

"What happened?"

"My practical, poised, ever-efficient assistant finally landed a part in a sitcom."

"Ah, the joy of proprietorship in Hollywood."

Still feeling deserted, Lindsay nodded. "It's the third time it's happened to me. Of course, I'm thrilled for her. But seriously? Worst timing ever."

"Hey, listen. I'm the first to admit this wedding stuff is not my thing, but I'll help where I can."

"Thanks, but you've done enough by offering me this space. I'll finally be able to put up my wedding board. And the help I need involves a hundred little things, well below your pay grade." She really couldn't see him playing secretary. And she may appreciate the space and assistance, but the last thing she needed was to have him constantly underfoot.

"There's no help for it. I'll have to hire someone local. Maybe Alonso knows someone he can recommend. On the plus side, it will be good to have someone who knows the area and the people, who speaks the language and knows the cost of things."

"Alonso will know someone. In the meantime, I'm sticking with you. I'll get a locksmith in to reinforce the locks on all the doors."

She wanted to protest the need for him to shadow her. Instead she nodded, knowing he was reacting out of concern for her. And she was happy to have the extra security for the dress. It might seem a bother for something they'd only have for another week, but she'd be more comfortable knowing the villa was secure.

She strolled further into the room. In soft beige and sage green, the furniture looked sturdy and comfortable. A U-shaped couch invited her to sit and enjoy the amazing view. The billiard table Zach had mentioned was on the right and her boxes were stacked on the green felt. Past it was the fireplace wall with a bookshelf that offered a wide selection of reading material. Another door hid a bathroom.

The ceiling was high, the beams exposed, and a large fan circulated the air in the room.

There were only two low-slung tables. One in front of the large couch and one between the swivel chairs near the fireplace.

"Oh, yeah, I can work here. No hardship at all."

She'd totally make do.

Hands on his hips, Zach surveyed the room. "You'll need a desk." He repeated his earlier decree. "And you mentioned a wedding board. Is that a whiteboard?"

"A whiteboard would be nice, too. My wedding board is usually a corkboard. I need to be able to tack things to it."

He had his phone in his hands and was making notes. She sighed, knowing there'd be no shaking him until she hired an assistant. In one sense it was reassuring to know she wasn't on her own, but it made her plan to avoid him a no-go. It was almost as if fate were working against her.

"I guess we have our shopping list, then. What do you want to do now? Unpack your boxes? You said earlier that you wanted to check out the palazzo."

"Yes. The boxes can wait." Better to have the boards when she went to do that, anyway. "But, honestly, there's no need for you to accompany me. Stay. Enjoy your day."

"I'm coming with you."

Of course he was. At this point, it was easier to agree than to argue. "Fine. Let me call Louisa and remind her I'm coming then we can go."

"Who's Louisa?"

"The owner of the palazzo. We've spoken a couple of times. She seems nice. Did you hear they discovered a fresco when they were restoring the chapel?"

"No. That's quite a discovery. It has to add to the property value."

"You are such a guy."

"Pixie, were you in any doubt?"

"Hello, Louisa, it's so nice to finally meet you. Thank you for allowing us to tour the property today." Lindsay greeted the owner of the palazzo.

It surprised Zach to see Louisa was an American. The two women were close to the same age but dissimilar in every other way. Louisa topped Lindsay by four or five inches and wore her white-blond hair in a messy knot on top of her head. Her willowy frame and restrained posture gave her a brittle appearance.

Funny, she held no attraction for him because she fit his type to a tee: long, lithe, and blond. Sure he recognized she was a beautiful woman, but she appeared almost fragile next Lindsay's vibrancy.

"Louisa, I have to say I'm a little concerned. I thought the renovation would be further along." Lindsay swept her hand out to indicate the overgrown vegetation and construction paraphernalia strewed through the courtyard and surrounding grounds.

"I can see why you'd be confused." Louisa's smile was composed. "But we're actually right on schedule. They've just completed the interior restoration. The construction crew will be back today to finish clearing out their equipment and trash. The next step is the landscapers, but I was actually thinking of hiring some men from town first, to just clear all this out."

"That might be a good idea," Lindsay agreed. "Just level it and start fresh."

"Exactly. I can see some rosebushes, lavender and a few wild sunflowers. But it's so overgrown it's hard to know if they'd be worth saving if we took the time and effort to clear the weeds around them."

Lindsay nodded as the other woman talked. "I think you have the right idea."

Zach enjoyed watching them interact. He liked how Lindsay's ponytail bobbed as she talked and the way the sunshine picked up golden highlights in her hair.

He almost forgot his purpose in shadowing her every move.

Mostly because it was against his nature to be covert, to be less than helpful. Case in point: this morning. When he saw Lindsay being intimidated by the press, he jumped right into fix-it mode and invited her to move into the spacious villa. And he'd provided her with a prime workspace. Hell, he fully intended to get her a desk.

All of which went against his prime objective of keeping Antonio from a life of misery. With that thought Zach took out his phone and texted his friend, tagging him for a meeting time.

Right now his biggest problem was the blurring line between his mock flirtation with Lindsay and his honest reactions. There'd been too much truth in his arguments to get her to stay at the villa. She was too comfortable to be around, too soft to the touch, too easy to imagine in his bed.

And too dangerous to succumb to.

He hadn't felt this way about a woman since…ever. And he wasn't going there.

From here on out he was back on his game.

"Thanks for talking it through with me." Louisa folded her arms in front of her. "I'm very grateful to the monarchy for doing the renovation of the palazzo and chapel. I certainly couldn't have afforded anything this elaborate all at once. Probably never, come to that. But it's been a pretty intense process. It's good to have someone to discuss a decision with."

"I bet." Lindsay grinned. "Call on me anytime. I'm great at discussion."

"I can see you are." A friendly sparkle entered Louisa's light blue eyes. "And probably pretty good at decisions, too."

Lindsay rocked on her heals. "Yeah, it's kind of part of the job description."

The composed smile held a little more warmth as Louisa gestured to the chapel. "Shall we do a walk-through? I'm afraid we'll have to make this fairly quick. I have an appointment in Florence tomorrow. I'm driving over tonight so I'll be there in the morning. I've booked passage on the two o'clock ferry."

"That's fine. Today I just want to get a feel for the place and take some pictures so I know what I'm working with. And—oh, this is beautiful." Lindsay surveyed the interior of the chapel with a mix of wonder and calculation on her face. "So charming with the arched windows and the dark wood pews. I can come back on another day to get actual measurements and check out the lighting. I love how the jewel colors flow over the stone tiles from the stained-glass windows. Christina has chosen an afternoon wedding and evening reception. She wants to have it outdoors, so the landscaping will be important."

"I won't be able to hire the workers to clear the grounds until I return from Florence," Louisa informed her, "but I'll make it a priority when I get back."

"Why don't I handle that for you?" Zach offered, seeing an opportunity to cause a few days' delay. He'd simply tell the workers to be careful to preserve any original flowers. "I'll talk to the mayor to get some referrals."

"Thank you. I appreciate it. They did a wonderful job with the restoration," Louisa stated. "It was quite a mess in here. Stones were missing, the stained-glass windows were broken and some of the walls had wood covering them. Here's the fresco that was uncovered." Louisa moved to a shallow alcove and Zach followed Lindsay over.

He understood her gasp. The ancient painting of Madonna and child took his breath away. The colors were vibrant, the detail exquisite. It was almost magnetic—the pull of the fresco, from the pinky tones of Jesus's skin and the color of Mary's dark blue robe, to the white and yellow of the brilliant beam of light encasing them and the greens of the surrounding countryside bright with orange and red flowers. The details were so exact, every brush stroke so evident, it seemed it could have been painted a week ago rather than five hundred years.

"Look at the love on their faces." Lindsay breathed. "The artist caught the perfect expression of Mary's unconditional love for her child and Baby Jesus's childlike wonder and awe for his mother. It shows the full bond between mother and child. This will certainly add to the ambience of the wedding."

With the beauty and love inherent in the fresco, Zach could see how she'd think so. But with his friend's future and happiness at risk, he couldn't take that chance.

Zach surprised Lindsay with his patience and insight the next day as they toured four nurseries. She had a whole list of requirements from bouquets and boutonnieres to centerpieces and garlands and more.

Lindsay planned to use roses for the groomsmen, sunflowers over linen chair covers for the reception and a combination of the two for everything else.

To bring about a sense of intimacy in the courtyard and to define the separate areas for eating and dancing, she planned to have rustic scaffolding erected. Lights, flowers and silk drapery would blend rustic with elegance to create a sense of old and new. She actually appreciated Zach's male point of view and his logistical input.

The helicopter came in handy as they buzzed around the countryside. Deciding on the second vendor she spoke with, Lindsay asked to return to the nursery to put in her order. Zach made no argument. He simply directed the pilot and helped her aboard.

Zach waited patiently in an anteroom of the magnificent palace. He stood at the terrace doors overlooking a section of the rose garden. Curved benches spaced several feet apart created a circle around a marble fountain of a Roman goddess.

Lindsay would love it. He had to hand it to her, that woman worked. He could practically hear her discourse on what a lovely venue the rose garden would be for a wedding, how the circle represented the ring and the ring represented the commitment made between bride and groom, who once joined together there became no beginning and no end, just the unity of their bond.

"Yeah, right."

"Talking to yourself, *amico mio*?" a gruff voice said before a hand clapped on his shoulder.

"Just keeping myself company waiting for you."

"I'm glad you came." Tony pulled Zach into the hug he'd learned to endure through the years. Tony was a demonstrative man, how could he not be with such passionate parents?

"Yeah, well, it became clear if I wanted to see you, I'd have to come to you."

"I only have thirty minutes. I wish I had more time to give you. Hell, I wish we were at Clancy's eating wings, drinking beer and catching a game."

"We could be there in fourteen hours," Zach said, hoping it would be that easy.

Tony laughed. "I'm tempted." He opened the terrace door and stepped outside. To the left stood a table with comfortable chairs. And a bucket of beers on ice.

"What, no chicken wings?"

"They are on the way."

Zach sat across from his friend and leaned back in his chair. Tony looked tired. And harassed. Zach knew Tony had to be busy for him to put Zach off. They were as close as brothers, too close for the other man to brush him aside.

"How are things going with the wedding?" Tony asked.

"Let's just say I could tell you in excruciating detail and leave it at that."

Tony grinned. "Thanks, bro. I mean that."

"Only for you," Zach assured him. "How are things going here?"

"Slowly." Tony grabbed a beer and opened it. "Everyone has a different opinion of how the monarchy should be run."

"And you have to learn the worst-case scenario for each before you'll make a determination," Zach stated, knowing that's how his friend operated. In working security protocols he liked to work backward to make sure the worst never happened.

"It doesn't help that I constantly have to address some question or concern about the wedding or coronation. It's a lot to juggle."

"So maybe you should put the wedding off." Zach took the opportunity presented to him. "Get the monarchy stabilized first and then revisit the idea of marriage when you can choose someone for yourself."

"Are you kidding me?" Tony laughed again. "Instead of cheering me, the people would be rioting in the streets. I think they want this wedding more than anything else."

"Because it's a Cinderella story?"

Tony shrugged. "Because I've made them wait so long."

"Because you never intended to marry Christina."

"Shush." Tony glanced around the terrace. "We won't speak of that here."

"Someone needs to speak of it before it's too late to stop it."

"That time is long gone, my friend. Christina will make a good queen. The people love her."

"They don't know her any better than you do. She's been off in Africa."

"Taking care of sick children. It plays well. Ah, the chicken wings. *Grazie*, Edmondo."

The servant bowed and retreated.

Zach quirked a brow at his friend. Tony shrugged and they both reached for a chicken wing.

After a moment Tony sighed. "Man, I needed this." He upended his beer, drinking the last. "I don't know anything about running a country, Zach."

"You know plenty. You've been training for this your whole life. Even while living in California," Zach reminded him.

"That's different. I always planned to hand over control to a republic, but I'm not sure that's what the people want. They are all behind this wedding and I can't let them down. I just need to do the opposite of what my dad would do and I'll be doing a better job than has been done."

"A little harsh, don't you think?"

"No." Tony shook his head and reached for another beer. "I love my parents, but their relationship is messed up. I don't ever want to love anyone so much it messes with my head. Better a business arrangement than a volatile, emotional mess."

Zach plucked a bottle of beer from the bucket, knowing he'd gotten as far as he was going to get tonight. He reached out and clicked bottles with Tony. "To the monarchy."

Tony's statement about a business arrangement only made Zach more determined to see him freed from a loveless marriage. Because his friend was wrong. At least a volatile, emotional mess inferred someone cared. You didn't get that guarantee with a business arrangement. What you got was a cold, lonely life.

CHAPTER EIGHT

WHAT A DIFFERENCE a week made. As she flew through the air on the way to Milan, Lindsay thought about all she'd accomplished since her last flight in the helicopter. She had her wedding board up and she'd made contact with all the local vendors she'd lined up before coming to Halencia, confirming plans and reevaluating as necessary.

She'd talked to the landscapers and she had an appointment at the end of the week to meet at the palazzo to go over her needs for the wedding and reception. On the mayor's recommendation, Zach had hired a crew to clean up the palazzo and chapel grounds. They should be well done by the time she met with the landscapers.

Yesterday she'd hired an assistant. Serena was twenty-two, fresh out of university and eager to assist in any way she could with the royal wedding. Lindsay worried a little over the girl's age, knowing she'd have to be strong enough to say no to outrageous offers for inside information about the wedding, and mature enough to know when she was being played. But Serena was Mayor Alonso's daughter and she had his glib tongue and a no-nonsense attitude that convinced Lindsay she could handle the job.

Plus, she just plain liked the young woman.

She'd gone a little googly-eyed over Zach but, seriously, who wouldn't? It was a fact of life she'd have to put up with.

"We are coming up on Milano," the pilot announced.

Lindsay leaned forward to get a view of the northern city. Two prominent pieces of architecture caught the eye. A very modern building of glass and metal that twisted well into the air and an ancient cathedral dramatically topped with a forest of spires. Both buildings were stunningly impressive.

She glanced at Zach and found his gaze on her. Smiling, she gestured at the view. "It's spectacular."

"It is, indeed," he agreed without looking away from her.

She turned her attention back to the view, pretending his focus on her didn't send the blood rushing through her veins.

He'd kept to his promise not to touch her. Well, mostly. He didn't play with her hair or take her hand, but he stayed bumping-elbows close wherever they went. And he still liked to put his hand in the small of her back whenever he directed her into or out of a building or room.

Serena had asked if they were together, so Lindsay knew the townspeople were speculating about their relationship. She'd given Serena a firm no in response and hoped the word got out about the true state of things.

They landed at a heliport on a mid-rise building not far from the Duomo di Milano. Downstairs a car was waiting to take them to a shop along Via Monte Napoleone. Lindsay checked her tablet to give Zach the address.

She looked forward to handing the dress over to Christina and the queen's seamstress. Providing security for the gown had proved more stressful than she'd anticipated. Having it off her shoulders would allow her to focus on the many other elements of the wedding demanding her attention.

"There it is. Signora Russo's. Christina and the queen are meeting us there. I already spoke to Signora Russo about the damage to the beading. She said she's a master seamstress and she would fix it."

"I'm glad to hear it."

A valet took the car and she and Zach were escorted inside. An attendant took the garment bag and led them to a plush fitting suite. A large, round couch in a soft ivory

with a high back topped by an extravagant flower arrangement graced the middle of the room.

The bride and queen stood speaking with a petite, age-
less woman in a stylish black suit. Lindsay walked across
the room with Zach to join them.

Christina made the introductions. It might have been
Lindsay's imagination, but the other woman seemed quite
relieved to see them.

"Zachary!" exclaimed Her Royal Highness Valentina
de l'Accardi, Queen of Halencia when she saw Zach. "As
handsome as ever." She glided forward and kissed him on
both cheeks. "*Mio caro*, thank you for helping Antonio.
He is so busy. Many, many meetings. We do not even see
him at the palace."

"Valentina." Zach bent over her hand. "You are ever
youthful. I thought for a moment Elena was here."

"Zachary!" Valentina swatted his forearm and giggled.
Yes, the matriarch of Halencia giggled. And flushed a
pretty rose. "Such a charming boy. Be careful, Ms. Reeves,
this one knows what a woman wants to hear, be alert that
he does not steal your heart."

"Yes. I've noticed he's a bit of a flirt."

"*Si*, a flirt." Warm brown eyes met hers with a seriousness her lighthearted greeting belied. The woman clasped
her hand and patted it. "I am so pleased you were able to
come to Halencia to plan Antonio and Christina's wedding. I wanted only the best for them."

"Now, you flatter me." Lindsay squeezed the queen's
hand before releasing her and stepping back. "It is I who
is privileged to be here. And to be here in Signora Russo's
shop. I may have to steal a moment to shop for my own
dress for the wedding."

"Oh, you must. My friend will take the best care of you.
Giana, Ms. Reeves needs a dress. Charge it to my account.
It shall be my treat for all her hard work."

Appalled, Lindsay protested. "Your Highness, I cannot—"

"I insist." The queen waved her objection aside. "I only wish I could stay and help you shop. And see Christina in her gown!" She sighed with much drama. "Regretfully, I must leave. One of Antonio's many meetings draws me away. Christina—" Valentina moved to the bride's side and Christina bowed to receive a kiss on the cheek. "Worry not. Giana has made many women look like a princess. She will do her *magia* and make you a *bella* bride."

For an instant Christina seemed to freeze, but in a blink it passed and she bowed her head. "*Grazie*, Your Highness."

"But you, Christina, will be a real princess. And that demands something special from a woman. The reward is something special in return." She picked up an ornate, medium-size box from the couch and slowly lifted the lid. A glimmering tiara rested on a bed of white velvet.

Christina put a hand to her throat. "Valentina."

"I wore this when I married Antonio's father. It must stay in my family, but you would honor me if you wore it when you marry my son."

Tears glistened in Christina's eyes. "It's beautiful." Diamonds and sapphires swirled together in gradually bigger scrolls until they overlapped in the front, creating a heart. "It's too much."

"Nonsense. A princess needs a tiara," Valentina insisted. "It would please me very much."

Christina sent Lindsay a pleading look. What should she do?

Lindsay gave a small shrug. "It's something borrowed and something blue."

"Oh, my." Christina gave a small laugh. "You said the items would come."

"I must go." Valentina handed the box to Christina.

"Try it on with your dress and veil, you will see. A security officer will stay behind to collect it until the wedding."

"Valentina." Christina gripped the other woman's hand. *"Grazie."*

"Ciao, my dears." With a wave of her fingers, the queen breezed out the door.

Immediately the room felt as if a switch had been flipped and the energy turned off.

Giana Russo excused herself and followed behind Valentina.

Christina sighed, her gaze clinging to Zach. "And I'm supposed to follow that?"

Lindsay's gut tightened. She'd soothed many a nervous bride. But a nervous queen-to-be? That was out of her league. She sent Zach a pleading look.

He didn't hesitate. He went to Christina and wrapped her in a warm hug. "She's a force of nature, no denying that. Everyone likes Valentina. She's fun and vivacious." He stepped back at the perfect moment. "But what Halencia needs now is warm and constant. And that's you."

"Grazie, Zach." Christina's shoulders relaxed with his words. "I am glad you came today."

"Of course. Hey, listen. I'm sorry for sitting on your dress. I'll pay for all the repairs and alterations."

"You sat on my dress?" Christina's surprise showed on her face. "Lindsay said some beading came loose during the travel."

"With a little help from my butt." He glanced at Lindsay over his shoulder, gratitude warming his whiskey eyes. "She seems to think Signora Russo can do *magia* and fix it."

"Si, si. I can fix." Giana blew back into the room. An attendant followed behind and carried Christina's beautiful gown into one of the dressing rooms. "I have looked

at the damage. It is not so bad. A little re-stitching will solve everything."

"Nonna!" A little girl ran into the room. Adorable, with big brown eyes and a cap of short, wild curls, she clutched a bright pink stuffed dog under arm. She came to a stop when she spotted three strangers with her grandmother.

"Ah, Lucette. *Scusa il bambina.*" Giana tried to pick up the toddler but she squealed and ducked behind Christina. "My apologies. We had a small emergency and I was re-cruited to babysit. My daughter should be here shortly to get her. Lucette, come to Nonna."

"Oh, she's no trouble. *Ciao*, Lucette." Christina bent at the knees so she was on the same level as the little girl, who stared at her with big, beautiful eyes. "What's your doggy's name?"

Lucette giggled and held out the dog. She jabbered a mouthful of words that made no sense to Lindsay at all. She looked at Zach but he shook his head, indicating he didn't understand the words, either.

"What a lovely name." Christina apparently made the dog's name out or pretended to. She chatted with the child for another few minutes, making the girl laugh. From her ease with the little one, it was obvious Christina loved children. Her gentleness and genuine interest delighted Giana's granddaughter until a harried assistant hurried into the room and swept the girl up.

"Scusa." The young assistant bobbed her head and left with the little girl.

Giana sighed. "Such excitement today. Are you ready, Signorina Rose, to try on your dress?"

Christina nodded. She and Giana disappeared into one of the dressing rooms.

Lindsay and Zach looked at each other.

"Do we stay or go?" Zach asked.

"I'm going to stay until she comes out." Lindsay sat

facing the occupied dressing room. "She may want company for the whole appointment. You can go if you want. I'm sure she'd understand."

"I'll wait to see how long you're going to be." He settled next to her. Way too close. His scent reached her, sensual and male, distracting her so she almost missed his question. "Have you ever come close to being the bride?"

"Not really." She smoothed the crease in her pale beige pants. "The one time I even contemplated it, I found out the relationship existed more in my imagination than in reality."

Interest sparked behind his intelligent gaze.

"How about you?" She tried to sidetrack him.

"Once," he admitted. "How do you get to marriage in your imagination? You're too levelheaded to make up what's not there."

"Thanks for that." She uncrossed and then re-crossed her legs, creating distance between them on the couch though her new position had her facing him. "He was my high school sweetheart. We got split up during our senior year when his parents moved away."

"That's tough."

She chanced a quick peek at him through her lashes to see if he truly understood or was simply saying what he thought she wanted to hear. The intensity in his regard showed an avid interest, encouraging her to go on.

"It was tough. We just understood each other. I lost my best friend as well as my boyfriend." The crease on her right leg got the same smoothing action as her left. "I always felt he was the one who got away."

"But you reconnected."

"We did. When the royal wedding was announced last year, he saw a piece where it mentioned I was the event planner, so he looked me up in Hollywood."

"And you had fonder memories of him than he had for you?"

"You could say that." The gentle way he delivered the comment made it safe to look at him as she answered. "I was so surprised and happy to see him. My mom, too. She's always on me to find a man. At first it was as though Kevin and I'd never been apart." Because of their past connection, he'd skipped right under her shields. "We were having lots of fun just hanging out and catching up. But I was so busy. Especially after word I'd been chosen to handle Antonio's wedding started to get around.

"Kevin was a freelance writer, so his schedule was flexible and he offered to help. I didn't want to take advantage, but I wanted to be with him. I let him tend bar at a few of the smaller events. That went well, so he started pushing to work the weddings."

"This is where the but comes in?"

Lindsay nodded, went back to plucking at her crease.

Zach's hand settled over hers, stilling the nervous motion.

She calmed under his touch. Under the sympathy in his eyes.

It still hurt to recall what a fool she'd been.

"First I got a warning from one of my vendors. He didn't know we were involved and he said I should keep an eye on the new bartender. He'd seen him outside with one of the guests."

"Bastard."

"It gets worse. And it's my own fault."

"How is it your fault when he's the one cheating?"

Good question. Too bad she didn't have a good answer.

"Because I let him charm me. When I asked him about what the vendor had seen, he didn't get defensive or act guilty. He had a story ready that the woman told him she was feeling sick so he'd walked her outside, hoping fresh air would help. I had no reason not to believe him. It explained what the vendor saw and…Kevin could be very solicitous."

"But it happened again."

Her head bobbed; perfect representation for the bobble-head she'd been.

"He tried to explain that one away, too. But I was starting to wise up. I should have ended it then." But that ideal from the past lingered in her heart, overriding the urging of her head. "Before things started going south, I'd been invited to a big wedding of a studio head and asked Kevin to go with me. I didn't want to go alone and I wasn't working so I thought it would be okay." She blinked back tears. "I should have known what he wanted. The clues were there."

"He was using you."

"Oh, yeah. He always wanted to know who everyone was. I thought he was just starstruck by the movers and shakers of Hollywood. The truth was he had a script he was shopping. I found him messing around with a well-known producer."

"Male or female?"

That surprised a bark of laughter from her; the moment of levity easing her rising tension. "Female. But thanks for that perspective. I guess it could have been worse."

"Bad enough. He hurt you."

"Yes. But only because I saw what I wanted to see."

"The possibility of a wedding for the wedding planner?"

"How is it you can see me so clearly?" she demanded.

It was uncanny how he saw straight to her soul. She hadn't been half as sad at losing Kevin as she had been to lose a boyfriend with marriage potential. She wanted what she gave to all her clients. A lovely wedding, in a spectacular venue, with friends and family surrounding her as she pledged her love. She longed for it with all her heart.

Kevin had stolen that from her. He'd given her hope, dangled the reality within her reach, only to yank it away. He was a user with no real affection or respect for her.

He'd seduced her for her contacts. And, yeah, that hurt. Her pride had taken a huge hit and the experience had left her more relationship-shy than ever. But it had taken less than a week for her to recognize it was more work-related than personal. He could have damaged her reputation. She'd worked twice as hard since the breakup to make sure it didn't happen again.

And she shored up her defenses to keep from letting anyone close enough to use her again. Or hurt her.

"Because it's all right here." Zach responded to the question about seeing her so clearly by stroking his thumb over her cheek. "There's no deception in you, Lindsay. You're open and giving and articulate."

"You're saying I'm an open book. How flattering." Not.

"I'm saying there's no artifice in you. When you interact with someone, they know they're getting the real you—straightforward good or bad. Do you know what a gift that is? To know you can trust what's being presented to you without having to weigh it for possible loopholes and hidden agendas?"

"Politics," she said dismissively.

"School. Business. Friends. Dates." He ran down a list. Then, too restless to sit, he rose to pace. "For as far back as I can remember I've known not to take anything at face value. My nannies used to praise me for being a good kid then lie about my behavior to get a raise."

"That's terrible." What a sad lesson for a child to learn. "You said you almost got close to a wedding. What happened? Is it what put you off big, fancy weddings?"

"It never got that far." He fell silent and fingered a wisp of lace edging a floor-length veil. Then he moved to one glittering with diamonds and, finally, to one of lace and the opalescence of pearls.

As the silence lengthened, she knew an answer wasn't coming. And then he surprised her.

"Luckily I learned before it was too late that it wasn't me she wanted but the Sullivan name." The lack of emotion in his reply spoke volumes.

He didn't add more. He didn't have to. After a childhood of indifference, he'd fallen for a woman only to learn she had more interest in his family name than in the man who carried that name.

Lindsay felt his pain. Shockingly so. Meaning he was getting under her skin. That shouldn't be happening; her shields were firmly in place. Zach just refused to acknowledge them. And he was getting to her.

She wanted to know more, to ask what happened, but she'd been wrong to get so personal. They weren't on a date. They were working. She had no right to dig into his past when she insisted theirs was a professional relationship.

Yet she was disappointed. She rarely talked about herself, never exposed her heart like that. And he'd responded, obviously reluctant to share but reciprocating just the same. How unfair that life should send her this man when all her attention needed to be focused on her job.

He lifted the lace-and-pearl veil and carried it to her.

"What are you doing?" she breathed.

Pulling her to her feet, he turned her and carefully inserted the combs of the veil in her hair. The exquisite lace flowed around her, making her feel like a bride even in a sleeveless beige-linen pant suit.

"Imaging you as a bride." His breath whispered over her temple. "What would you choose for yourself, Lindsay?"

"I'm like you," she said as he led her toward a three-way mirror. Why was she letting him do this? "I want small, intimate."

"But with all the trimmings?"

"Of course. Oh, my." The pearls on the lace gave it a glow. He'd placed the veil just under her upswept bun. The lace caressed her arms as it fell down her back in an elegant waterfall of tulle and lace and pearls. It had such presence it made her beige pantsuit appear bridal.

The picture in the mirror stole her breath. Made her longing for what eluded her come rushing back.

She'd hoped coming to Tuscany, managing the royal wedding, would help her get her wedding mojo back. Peering into the mirror she realized that would only happen when she opened herself to love again. Sweat broke out on her upper lip at the very notion of being that vulnerable.

"I love the pearls against your sunshine-brown hair." Zach brushed the veil behind her shoulder and met her gaze in the mirror. "You're going to make a beautiful bride."

With him standing beside her in his dress shirt and black pants the reflection came too close to that of a bride and groom. Her heels brought her up to his shoulder. They actually looked quite stunning together.

She swallowed hard and took a giant step backward, reaching up at the same time to remove the veil. She was in so much trouble.

"I'm the planner, not the bride," she declared. "I don't have time to play make-believe." Handing him the veil, she retreated to the couch and her purse. Time to put fanciful thoughts aside and call Christina's aunt to set up an appointment on their way home.

Because she'd liked the image in the mirror way too much for her peace of mind.

Just Lindsay's luck. Christina's aunt Pia couldn't meet with them until five in the evening. She ran through her current to-do list in her head, looking for something she could check off.

"Oh, no, you don't." Zach tugged on her ponytail. "You've worked nonstop this past week. We are due some rest and relaxation. We're in the lovely city of Milan. I say we play tourist."

Okay, there were worse ways to spend the afternoon than wandering the streets with a handsome man on her arm.

Lunch at an open café on the Naviglio Grande—a narrow canal with origins in the 1100s used to transport the heavy marble to the middle of the city where the Duomo di Milano was being built—was a true delight. As was strolling along the canal afterward and checking out the antique stores and open-air vendors.

A lovely candleholder at a glassblower's stall caught her eye. How perfect for the reception tables. They had a flat bottom and five-inch glass petals spiked all the way around to create a floral look. The piece had presence but was short enough to converse over without being in the way. And she loved that it came in so many colors. She wanted the one with spiking gold petals. It reminded her of sunflowers.

"I'd like to order two hundred, but I need them within two weeks. Can you do that?" The young artist's eyes popped wide.

"Si. Si," he eagerly assured her. "I have ready."

"Why so many?" Zach asked. "And don't you already have candleholders with the royal crest on them?"

"Yes, but I think the clear glass bowls etched with the royal crest will sit nicely right in the middle of these and be absolutely gorgeous with a candle inside. A win-win." She got a beautiful, unique presentation that was both fragile and bold, and the palace got their staid, boring candleholders used.

"That's pretty genius." He applauded her.

"It's my job to mix the styles and needs of the bride and groom into a beautiful event that's appealing to them individually and as a couple."

"I'm learning there's more to this wedding planning stuff than I ever would have believed."

"Yeah. I'll convert you yet."

"Now, that's just crazy talk."

She sent him a chiding glance. "I want two hundred because I want plenty for my reception tables, but I also think the candleholders will make good gifts for the guests. What do you think, best man? Christina has pretty much left the decisions up to me and you're Antonio's stand-in. Do you think this would make a good gift for the guests to take away?"

He blinked at her for a moment, clearly surprised to have his opinion sought. He rubbed his chin as he contemplated the candleholder she held. "It's a pretty sophisticated crowd, but, yeah. Each piece is unique. That will appeal to the guests while the piece will also act as a reminder of the event."

"Then it will have served its purpose."

She turned back to the vendor. "In two weeks," she repeated, needing to know his excitement wasn't overriding his capabilities.

"*Si, si…due* weeks. I work night and day."

Given he would be working with heat and glass, she wasn't sure that was a good idea. She made a note in her tablet to check on his progress in a week. If he wasn't going to make it, she'd adjust her order to cover the tables only. And just give the royal crest candleholders away as a gift. But she really hoped he could pull it off.

She gave him her card with her email, asked him to send her a purchase order and advised him he'd have to sign a confidentiality agreement. His hand shook as he took the card, but he nodded frantically and handed Zach the package containing the sample she'd bought.

Zach made the next purchase. A Ferrari California T convertible. She thought they were just window shopping when he dragged her to the dealership. There was no denying the cars were sexy beasts. And it seemed the height of luxury to have the showroom on the fifth floor.

Even when Zach started talking stats and amenities, she blew it off. Nobody walked into a Ferrari dealership and walked out with a car. Or they shouldn't. It was a serious investment and required serious thought.

But Zach stood, hands on hips, surveying the slick car and nodding his head to whatever the salesman was saying. The portly man spoke English with such a thick accent she didn't know how Zach understood him.

"What color?" Zach asked her.

Her turn to blink at him in surprise at having her opinion sought. "What?"

"What color do you like better? The red or the black?"

"Are you insane? You can't just walk in here and buy a car."

"I'm pretty sure I can."

"But—"

"I've been thinking of buying one," he confessed. "I'm stoked at the idea of buying it here in Italy, from the original dealership. And it'll be nice to have a car since the rental company hasn't replaced the Land Rover yet."

She eyed the beautiful, sleek cars. "They'll probably have it replaced before they can deliver one of these."

"Pixie, they could have a car ready in an hour. But they have one downstairs with all the amenities I want. I could drive it back to Monte Calanetti if I wanted."

"Oh, my dog. You're serious about this."

He grinned, flashing his dimple and looking younger and as satisfied as a teenaged boy getting his first car.

"It's the California T series. I have to have one, right? I deserve something for closing the government deal. What color?" he demanded again.

Okay, she got it. He sought a physical treat for recent accomplishments because he wasn't getting any emotional accolades. Who could blame him? Not her.

"Indeed you do." Adjusting her mood to his, she glanced around the show room. "You don't want red or black. Too cliché."

"I'd use the word classic."

"I like that pretty blue. It reminds me of the sea around Halencia. If you're taking a souvenir home, it should represent where you've been."

"The blue." His inclined his head, his brown eyes reflecting his appreciation of her comeback. "Hmm." He strolled over to look it over better. "I'm not really looking for pretty."

"Is rockin' a better adjective? More masculine? We can use that if you prefer, because it's a rockin' pretty blue."

"I like rockin'."

"But do you like the blue?"

"I do. Though the classics are nice, too."

"They're cliché for a reason."

"*Signora.*" The salesman flinched, unable to stay silent any longer. "*Per favore*, not say cliché."

"*Scusa,*" she apologized, sending Zach an unrepentant smirk.

He said something in Italian to the salesman, who nodded and stepped away.

"I have to do this," he said, lifting her chin on his finger and lowering his mouth to cover hers as if he couldn't wait another moment to taste her.

CHAPTER NINE

THE FLAVOR OF him filled her senses. Oh. Just, oh.

She should protest, step away, remind him of their professional status. She did none of those things. Instead she melted against him, lifting her arms around his neck.

How she'd missed his touch. She thrilled at his hands on her waist pulling her closer, at his body pressed to hers from mouth to knees, the two of them fitting together like cogs and grooves. This was more dangerous than watching their reflection in the mirror at Signora Russo's. By far.

Didn't matter. She sank into sensation as she opened to him. More than she should in a Ferrari dealership. Or maybe not. They were hot cars, after all.

A throat clearing loudly announced the return of the salesman.

Zach lifted his head, nipped her lower lip.

"Hold on." She ducked her head against him, turning away from the salesman.

"What are you doing?" He spoke gently and cradled her head. Perfect.

"Saving you some money. Tell our friend over there that you're sorry, but I'm totally embarrassed and want to leave."

He rattled off a few words of Italian. Predictably the salesman protested.

She pushed at Zach, making a show of wanting to leave. "Tell him you'll have to buy the car when you get back to the States because we're leaving Milan tonight and probably won't make it back here."

While he conveyed her message, she grabbed his hand

and began pulling him toward the exit, carefully avoiding the salesman's gaze.

The salesman responded in a conciliatory tone, his voice growing closer as he spoke.

"He just dropped the price by ten thousand dollars," Zach advised her.

She frantically shook her head and, holding his hand in both of hers, she bracketed his arm and buried her face in his shoulder. "Let's see if we can get him to twenty. Shake your head sadly, put your arm around me and head for the elevator."

"You know I can afford the car."

"So not the point."

"What was the point again?"

"Trust me. He's not going to let you walk away."

He sighed, then she felt the movement of his head and his arm came around her. She leaned into him as they walked toward the elevator.

"I can't believe I'm leaving here without a car."

"You can always order it online and have them deliver it. If he lets you walk away."

"You owe me dinner for this."

They got all the way to the elevator before the salesman hailed Zach. He rushed over, all jovial and solicitous, giving his spiel as he approached. The elevator doors opened just as he arrived next to them. The man opened his arms wide in a gesture that welcomed Zach to consider what a good deal was being offered.

Zach nodded. *"Si, avete un affare."*

"You took the offer?"

"I have. And you're invited to visit the gift shop and pick out a gift while I finalize things here."

"Oh. Nice touch. Okay, you can buy the car." She stepped into the elevator. "Don't be long."

Thirty minutes later he collected her from the gift shop

and they headed out. On the street he pulled her into his arms and gave her a long, hard kiss. Then he draped his arm around her shoulders and started walking.

"That's the most fun I've had in a long time."

"How much?"

"For twenty-five thousand less than quoted."

"Aha! So you owe me dinner."

"You have skills, Pixie."

"I have a few tricks. I'm always working with a budget whether it's five hundred dollars or five million, so I've learned to negotiate for my job. I enjoy the challenge. You have money. You're used to buying what you want without worrying about the cost."

"I've negotiated for my business."

"But that's different, isn't it? You're on the sales side then, demanding value for services. When it comes to buying—"

"I want the best regardless of price. It's how I was raised."

"You were fortunate." As soon as the words left her mouth she remembered what he'd said about people in his life always having an agenda even when he was a young child and how his parents brushed aside his success to make demands of him. Money didn't make up for everything. She quickly changed the subject.

"So, are you driving home? Am I visiting Christina's aunt on my own?"

"I'm going with you. I went with the blue car, which needed modified for some of the upgrades I wanted. They'll be delivering the car in a couple of days. We have an hour before we need to meet the helicopter. Do you want to go see the cathedral?"

He was right. Today had been fun. She couldn't remember when she'd last let go and played for a day. She liked playing tourist. Wanted it to continue.

She sighed, knowing she needed to rein them in. A bell kept pinging in her brain, warning her to stop the foolishness, reminding her of the danger of surrendering to his charm. Hadn't she already rehashed all this with herself at the fitting?

Yes, and she knew what she risked if she continued to let her emotions rule her actions.

Yet she still reached up and tangled her fingers with his at her shoulder.

"It'll be rushed, but it sounds like fun."

"Okay, let's go." He stepped to the curb and waved down a taxi. "At least we'll get to see it. And if we really want to see more, we can plan a day when we can come back and do a full tour."

Her heart soared at the way he linked them into the future.

She deserved this time. Work always came first and because the nature of it was so party central she experienced a faux sense of having an active social life. For too long she'd suppressed her loneliness. Just this once she'd let loose and enjoy the history and charm of an ancient city in the company of a gorgeous man totally focused on her.

Sliding into the back of the cab, she smiled when Zach linked their hands. And sighed when he leaned in for a kiss.

Tomorrow could take care of itself.

Zach in a Speedo was a piece of art.

He swam once or twice a day. She remembered from her research that he'd met Antonio on the Harvard swim team. Obviously he still enjoyed the water. And she enjoyed him.

Funny how his swims always seemed to coincide with her need for a break. Uh-huh, a girl was allowed her illusions.

And she could look as long as she didn't touch.

The man was grace in motion. Watching that long, tanned, toned body move through the water gave her a jolt that rivaled caffeine. It was one fine view in a villa full of spectacular views and it made Lindsay's mouth water with want.

Now that she knew how it felt to brush up against that fine body, she longed for more. But she was back in the real world so she turned away from the sight of Zach striding confident and wet from the pool.

She took a sip from her soda, needing the wet and the cool. And drained it before she was through. Leaving the empty can on the bar she joined her assistant at the lovely oak table Zach had purchased for her use.

She pulled up her email and sent Christina a message to let her know they were still on the hunt for the brooch. As Christina had warned her Aunt Pia had been leery about talking to them, but with Christina's note she'd finally softened. She'd given the brooch to her daughter, but the younger woman hadn't worn it for her wedding, either. Pia had called her daughter while they were there and she couldn't recall what had happened to the brooch. Pia suggested Sophia might know.

Lindsay would be meeting with Sophia tomorrow, two weeks from the wedding.

"Serena, can you call and remind Louisa that Zach and I will be meeting the landscapers at the palazzo this morning."

The two of them were set to leave in a few minutes and she needed work to help her get the visual of his nearly nude body out of her head.

"Already done. And I sent the information to the glass-blower as you requested. He already confirmed delivery for a week before the wedding."

"Excellent."

Serena turned out to be a godsend. She looked cool and competent in blue jeans and a crisp white tee, her long black hair slicked back in a ponytail that nearly reached her waist. And she was every bit as efficient as she appeared.

"Let's put it on the calendar to check with him in a few days to be sure he's on schedule. If I have to find another gift, I'd rather know sooner than later."

"*Si*, I put a note on your calendar."

"Perfect."

They went over a few other items, scratching off two on the to-do list and adding three. "The palace rep is supposed to take care of ordering the table and chairs, but can you call to make sure they have and confirm what they've ordered."

Her brown eyes rounded. "You want me to check the palace's work?"

"Yes. There's no room for misunderstandings. I need to know every detail is covered."

The girl nodded. "*Si*, I will call them."

"Good. I know this may be a hard concept for you, Serena, but until this wedding is over, your first loyalty is to me. It's my job to give the prince and Christina a beautiful wedding that will represent the house of L'Accardi well. You have no idea how many errors I've found by following up on details handled by other people. Some have been innocent mistakes, but others were outright sabotage."

"That's terrible!"

Lindsay nodded. "If I hadn't caught the mistakes, intentional or otherwise, not only would the bride and groom have been disappointed and possibly embarrassed, but my reputation would have suffered badly."

"*Si*. I will check every detail."

"*Grazie*. And don't forget to find a nice, understated dress for the occasion. Something in light blue."

Serena's brown eyes rounded even bigger than before. "I am to attend the royal wedding?" It was a near squeak.

"You'll be working it with me, yes."

"Oh, my goodness! I have to shop!"

Lindsay smiled. "After you check on the table and chairs."

"*Si.*" Serena nodded, her eagerness offset by a desperate look in her eyes.

"And bring me the receipt. It's a work expense."

Relief flooded the girl's features. "*Grazie.*"

"Are you ready to go?" A deep male voice filled the room.

Zach stood in the doorway to the house, thankfully fully dressed in jeans and a brown T-shirt that matched his eyes.

"Ready." Lindsay grabbed her purse and dropped her tablet inside. "Let's go."

The wind whipped through her hair as Zach drove them across town in the golf cart. He pulled straight into the drive.

Two things struck her right away. Louisa was in the middle of a heated discussion on her doorstep. Her opponent towered over her smaller frame. He had dark hair, broad shoulders and a wicked-fine profile.

And second, construction paraphernalia had been cleared away but the grounds were only a quarter cleared.

"What the heck, Zach?" Lindsay demanded as she climbed out of the golf cart. "I thought you hired someone to clean this all out."

"I did and I take full responsibility for the mess-up. I hired the crew the mayor recommended and I told them to clear out all the weeds but to save the original plants."

"No, no, no. Everything was supposed to be cleared out."

He grimaced. "I'm hearing that now, at the time I was answering a text from my office. I got it wrong. I'm sorry."

"They didn't even do what you asked." She stomped forward, scanning the dry brush and overgrown ground cover. "The landscaping team is going to be here any minute. The construction team is scheduled to start the day after they're done. This needed to be done already."

This couldn't be happening. She'd had everything planned down to the last minute. There were acres to clear. The whole property needed to be in shape, not just the area around the chapel and palazzo.

"Lindsay, I'm sorry."

Lindsay swung around to Louisa. The other woman stood huddled into herself, the tall man she'd been arguing with at her side.

"This is my fault," Louisa said. "I've been distracted the past few days. I should have noticed the grounds weren't being cleared out like they should be."

"No. It's mine. I should have been checking on the progress." Follow up on every detail. Hadn't she just pressed that fact home with Serena? She'd been the one to drop the ball.

"Placing blame does no good." Zach refused to play the role of dunce. He'd made this mess. It was up to him to clean it up. "We need to focus on a solution."

"He's right." Hands on his hips, the tall man Louisa had been arguing with surveyed the grounds. "You must be Lindsay Reeves, the wedding planner. Nico Amatucci." He held out his hand as he introduced himself. "I own the vineyard next door."

"Right." She shook his hand, appreciated the firm grip. "We're serving your wine at the reception. I've sampled some. It's very good."

"Zach Sullivan, best man." Zach inserted his hand between the two of them, not caring for the admiration in

Amatucci's gaze as it ran over Lindsay. Some distance between the two suited Zach fine.

No way was Zach letting the other man play hero while he chafed under the restraint of his plan. It didn't help that his gut roiled with guilt at seeing Lindsay so upset.

He was making her work harder than she needed to on the most important event of her career. Watching her blame herself for something he'd done didn't sit well, no matter how well-intentioned his plan had been.

Especially when he had nothing to show for it.

Neither Tony nor Christina showed any signs of backing out of the wedding. The two of them had managed to distance themselves from what went on in Monte Calanetti so any delays Lindsay suffered were mere blips on their radars.

Zach had only managed one meeting with Tony, but whenever he broached the topic on their hurried calls, Tony shut him down. Christina did the same when Zach got a few minutes alone with her at the fitting, though he had to give her points for being much more polite about it.

"I'm not sure how this happened." Zach gritted his teeth as he played his part for his audience of three. "I was telling Lindsay I hired the crew Mayor Alonso recommended. He mentioned the owner had just broken up with his girl, but I didn't figure that signified."

"Are you talking about Fabio?" Nico ran his hand through his dark hair. "He gets *molto* messed up when he and Terre are fighting, and he is no good for anything."

"I need to call him, get him out here." Lindsay took out her tablet. "This needs to be finished today. If he can't get it done, I need to get someone who can."

"Let me talk to him, *signorina*," Nico offered, his tone grim. "His girl is *incinta*. Fabio needs the work. I will make sure it gets done."

Lindsay hesitated then slowly nodded.

Seeing the despair in her indomitable blue eyes shred-ded Zach. He decided right then to stop messing with her. Why should she suffer for Tony and Christine's stub-bornness?

She shouldn't.

No more than he should be forced to play the fool.

The trip to Milan rated as one of the best days of his life. He'd enjoyed spending time with Lindsay, more than anyone he could remember in a long time. She was smart and fun, and too restrained, which challenged him to loosen her up. And she constantly surprised him. He marveled at her performance at the Ferrari dealership.

Her ex had given her enough grief. Zach wouldn't add to it.

He'd still try talking sense into the couple. For all the good it would do him. But no more messing with the wedding.

"Fabio's going to need help getting this all done," Zach announced, feeling the need to fix the problem. "Who else can we get to help?"

"I can call my men over to lend a hand for a few hours," Nico offered.

"Thanks, that's a start. I'm going to call the mayor."

"I'll help," Louisa stated. "It'll feel good to get outside and do some physical labor for a change."

Zach lifted his brow at that. The temperature topped eighty and the palazzo was in a valley. There was little in the way of a breeze to offset the mugginess from the clouds overhead.

"It is too hot for you," Nico told her bluntly. "You will stay inside."

Wrong move, buddy. Zach watched the storm brew in the palazzo owner's light blue eyes. She was almost guar-anteed to work harder and longer than she would have if the other man had kept his mouth shut. But her offer gave him an idea.

"No," Louisa informed Nico, her chin notched up, "I will not. I'm partially responsible for this situation and I want to help."

"Me, too," Lindsay piped in. "Louisa, do you have an extra pair of gloves? We can get started while Nico contacts Fabio."

"I do. I have a scarf, too. You'll want to put your hair up."

The women wandered off. Nico glared after them. "She never listens."

Zach cleared his throat and clapped Nico on the shoulder. "My man, let me give you some advice. Rather than order a woman about, it's better to make her think it's her idea to start with."

Nico grimaced. "I know this. But she drives me... *pazzo*."

"Crazy? I know the feeling. Perhaps when she starts to weary you can casually mention how thirsty the workers look and she'll go inside to provide refreshments."

"You misunderstand. There is nothing between us," Nico clarified with more emphasis than necessary. "As there is between you and Ms. Reeves."

"If you asked her, she would say there is nothing between us, either."

Nico scowled.

Zach laughed. "You should call me Zach, as we'll be working together." And they got to work.

The whole town came out to help. Or so it seemed. The mayor arrived shortly after a remorseful Fabio. Alonso didn't ask what needed to be done. He wore khaki pants and an old denim shirt with the sleeves rolled up to his elbows. He picked up a shovel and got to work.

Lindsay called Serena and she showed up with a few

friends, four of Nico's men arrived in a pickup, including his brother Angelo. Eva's son, Mario, and a pack of early teens pitched in. The barber closed his shop to help. And on and on it went. Even the landscaping crew joined in, helping to haul debris and refuse away.

Everyone was happy and laughing.

At some point Lindsay was introduced to Vincenzo Alberti, the director of tourism. When she expressed her gratitude, he explained that the whole town was proud the royal wedding was happening there. That they wanted their city to be represented well and that they were all excited to be a part of it in some way.

Lindsay wiped at the sweat on forehead with a towel she'd tucked into her waistband and surveyed their progress. Another hour should see it done. A good thing as it would be dark not long after.

She was hot and sticky, tired and sore. And hungry.

She imagined everyone else was, too. But no one was leaving. They all meant to see it finished. Nico and Louisa had put their animosity aside to coordinate the workers' efforts.

"Almost done." Zach appeared beside her, his tanned and muscular chest on full display. As had many of the men, he'd ditched his shirt somewhere along the way.

She resisted the urge to run her palm down his sweaty abs. More than once she'd caught herself admiring the flex and flow of muscle and tendon under smooth flesh. Dark and tanned, he fit right in with the Halencians. Fit and toned, he matched the laborers pace for pace.

He was poetry in motion and she had a hard time keeping her attention fixed on her chore. Especially with him standing in front of her.

"I'm amazed by the support we got from everyone." Rather than look at him she watched the landscapers fill their truck with bags of weeds. "I wish there was something we could do for them."

"I was thinking the same thing." He took her towel and wiped the back of her neck, sending tingles down her spine where his fingers trailed over her skin. "I thought about hosting a party at the villa, but I prefer to reward everyone now, so I asked Alonso for a suggestion. He mentioned Mancini's. I called and talked to the owner. Raffaele Mancini said he'd open up the patio for us and put a nice meal together."

"'Nice' is the operative word there, champ. Mancini's is catering the wedding. Eva also told me about Mancini's as an option for an upscale meal. I'm not sure I can afford that."

"I'm covering it."

"You don't have to do that."

"I insist. I feel this is mostly my fault. Paying for dinner is a small enough thing to do. Plus, Mancini heard about what happened and apologized for not making it over here to help out. So he's giving us a discount."

The spirit of this town just kept amazing her.

"Shall we start passing the word? Mancini's at eight. That'll give Raffaele time to cook. And the rest of us time to clean up."

Dinner turned into a party. When Lindsay stepped inside, assisted by Zach's hand at the small of her back, she got pulled into a big hug by the maître d', who was a curvy blonde with bright gray eyes and a smile so big she beamed.

"Hello. Welcome to Mancini's." Surprisingly the bubbly blonde was American. Then she announced why she was so excited, "Winner of the Italian Good Food Award!"

"Wow." Lindsay knew the award was on par with the

Michelin Star in France. "Congratulations. That's fantastic."

Zach echoed her. "Raffaele didn't mention it when I spoke to him earlier."

"We just heard an hour ago. You must be Lindsay Reeves and Zach Sullivan, the wedding planner and best man. I'm Daniella, Rafe's fiancée. We have the patio all set up for you. Some people have already started to arrive. You'll have to excuse us if we're a little giddy tonight. We're over the top about the award."

"As you should be," Zach said easily. "I hope you, Raffaele and the staff can join us later for a congratulatory toast."

That smile flashed again. "I'm sure that can be arranged. I'll tell Rafe."

The patio was enclosed but the large windows were wide open, letting in the cool evening air. Wine bottles hung from the overhead beams along with green ivy. Red-checked tablecloths covered two large picnic tables that seated twenty each and three round tables at the far end.

A couple of extra chairs were needed, but everyone shuffled around so everyone got seated. Alonso arranged it so he and Vincenzo sat with Lindsay and Zach along with Nico and Louisa.

Raffaele had "thrown together" a steak Florentine for them that melted in Lindsay's mouth. She was definitely putting it on the wedding menu.

She wondered if Raffaele knew how to make *cornettos*.

"I'm exhausted," Louisa told Lindsay toward the end of the delicious meal when they had the table to themselves. "But it's a good tired."

"It's the same for me." Lindsay sipped her wine. "We accomplished a lot today. The landscapers will start tomorrow and the owner assured me they would make up the lost time."

"That's great. I'm glad we were able to get it done for you."

"I'm so impressed with the townspeople. How they rallied together to help out and were so cheerful even working in the heat and mugginess."

"Well, they're all enjoying dinner. This was a nice gesture."

"Zach's the one to thank. But we were happy to do it. Everyone worked so hard. I can tell you I've decided to order some big fans for the wedding and reception. I want the guests to be comfortable."

Louisa clinked her wineglass against Lindsay's. "I like the way you think. I'm sorry I dropped the ball."

"Don't sweat it. You worked as hard as anyone today." Lindsay eyed Zach talking with Nico, Alonso and a couple of other men near the bar. "And I know how easy it is to get distracted."

"Are the two of you involved?" Louisa asked.

Lindsay's gaze whipped back to her fellow American.

"There's a…tension between the two of you," the woman explained.

"He'd like there to be." Lindsay rolled the stem of her wineglass between her fingers, watched the liquid swirl as her thoughts ran over the past two weeks. "But I need to stay focused on the job. As today clearly proved."

"He can't take his eyes off you."

"And Nico keeps you in his sights. Is there something between the two of you? You seemed to be arguing this morning."

"We're always arguing." Louisa's gaze flicked over the man in question. Her expression remained as composed as always, but there was no hiding the yearning in her pale eyes. "That is why it's good there's nothing between us."

A loud cheer went through the patio. Lindsay glanced around to see Rafe and Danielle had joined the party. Another round of cheers sounded as waiters flowed through the room with trays of champagne glasses.

Alonso grabbed a flute and held it high. "*Primo*, a huge *grazie* to Raffaele and Mancini's for hosting us tonight on such short notice. And for the wonderful meal he provided." More cheers. "*Secondo*, we are all excited to be here to share in the joyous news of Mancini's receiving the Good Food Award!" He held his glass high. "We had no doubts, *amico mio*, none at all. *Complimenti!*"

"*Complimenti!*" The crowd clapped and cheered, lifting their glasses and sipping.

Rafe stood on a chair. "*Grazie, grazie.* I am happy so many of my friends could be here to share this with me tonight. Business picked up when Mancini's was chosen to feed the royal wedding guests. Now, we have the Good Food Award the tourists will come even more. Monte Calanetti is on the map!"

A roar of approval rose to the roof.

"Nice touch, sharing his success with the citizens." Zach slid into his seat. "Classy."

"Raffaele is good people," Louisa affirmed. "I'm going to congratulate him on my way out. Good night. Zach, thank you for dinner."

"My pleasure."

Louisa walked away, leaving Lindsay and Zach alone together. He picked up her hand. "You look tired."

"I am." Too tired to fight over possession of her hand. She really needed to tell him the day in Milan had been a mistake and they needed to regroup to where they'd been before the trip. But every touch weakened her resolve.

"I'm sorry I messed up." There was a quality to his voice she couldn't quite pinpoint. She dismissed it as fatigue and the fact he probably didn't have to apologize for his work effort very often. Like never.

"You thought you were hiring the best crew," she reminded him. "And, you know, I really enjoyed today, getting to know more of the local people, seeing how they all rallied around each other to help. It was an inspiring experience. As you said before, too often people are all about their own agendas. Today reinforced my view of humanity."

"Sometimes those agendas can be well-meaning." Again his tone was off.

"You mean like Fabio obsessing over his girl and their baby? I get that, but look at how many lives he impacted by not honoring his contract. Yes, I enjoyed the day, but the landscaper is still going to have to make up lost time, and I lost a whole day. Life is so much easier when people are up front with each other."

He brought her hand to his mouth and kissed her knuckles. "Let's go home and soak our aches away in the Jacuzzi."

Oh, goodness, that sounded wonderful.

And dangerous.

She'd promised herself she'd get her head on straight today, put her infatuation aside and focus on the job. It was the smart thing to do. All he wanted was a summer fling. She had only to recall how he'd clammed up after she'd shared her humiliating history with Kevin to realize his interest was strictly physical.

And still she tangled her fingers with his. "Let's go."

CHAPTER TEN

AFTER THE INTENSE heat of the day, the balmy softness of the night air caressed Lindsay's shoulders with the perfect touch of cool. The rest of her, submerged in the hot, roiling water of the spa, thanked her for her foolish decision.

"I really did need this." She rolled her neck, stretching the tendons.

Strong hands turned her and began to work at the tightness in her shoulders. "So much stress."

The low timbre of Zach's voice made her whole body clench in need. She tried to shift away, but he easily held her in place.

"I never would have thought a wedding would be so much work."

She bit her bottom lip to suppress a moan, not wanting to encourage him. "Why, because it's just a big party? It's more than that, you know. It's two people creating a life together. That requires the meshing of many moving parts. The bride and groom, family members, attendants and, in this case, palace representatives and dignitaries. And that's just on the day. Before that there's flowers, food, wine, cake, photographers, seating in the chapel, setting up for the reception. Seating arrangements. Thank you, once again, for your help with that. I got the final approval from the palace today."

"My pleasure."

There was that tone again. She glanced at him over her shoulder. "You stopped listening after family members, didn't you?"

"You caught me." He let her float away a bit before turning her so she faced him.

"What's up with you?" She brushed the damp hair off his furrowed brow. "You've been slightly off all night."

"Today was my fault."

So that was it. Zach was so laid-back with her she sometimes forgot he ran a multibillion-dollar company. He was used to being in control and being right.

"We already talked about this. Stop feeling guilty."

"You know how I feel about large weddings."

"So what? You deliberately hired someone you knew couldn't do the job? You're just feeling bad because you're a problem solver and today it took a lot of people to fix the problem. It's okay. You repaid them all with a very nice dinner. And they all got to celebrate Mancini's award with Raffaele. I didn't hear a single gripe from anyone today, so cut yourself some slack."

"It's not that. I can't help but think Tony and Christina are making a mistake."

"So you subconsciously sabotaged the cleanup?"

He looked away, staring out at the lights of Monte Calanetti. "Something like that. They barely know each other."

"They've been engaged for four years."

"And he's lived in America the whole time."

This was really tearing him up. So often since they'd met he'd been there for her when she'd needed him. She wished she had the magic words that would ease his concerns.

"They have no business getting married."

"Zach—" she rubbed his arm, hoping to soothe "—that's not for you to say."

"They're going to end up hating each other." The vehemence in his voice reinforced his distress. "I watched it happen to my parents. I can't stand to watch it happen to a man I think of as my brother."

She cupped his cheek, made him look at her. "No matter how much we love someone, we can't make their decisions for them. We wouldn't welcome them doing so for us and we owe them the same respect."

He sighed then pulled her into his lap, nuzzling the hair behind her ear. She wrapped her arms around him and hugged him tight. His arms enfolded her and they sat there for a while just enjoying the closeness of each other.

"She threw me over for my father."

Lindsay went still. "Who?"

"The woman I once got close to marrying."

"Oh, Zach." She tightened her grip on him and turning her head slightly, kissing him on the hard pec she rested against. "I'm so sorry."

"We met in college. My name didn't intimidate her, which was a real turn-on. It seemed all the girls I met were supplicants or too afraid to talk to me. Julia was a political science major. She said that was to appease her parents, that her real love was her minor, which were arts and humanities."

"She targeted you."

"Oh, yeah, she played me. Right from the beginning." He suddenly rose with her in his arms. "It's time to get out."

"I suppose we should." Her arms ringed his neck as he climbed out. She longed to hear more but had the sense if she pushed, he'd close down on her. So she kept it light-hearted. "I'm starting to prune."

He claimed her lips in a desperate kiss, holding her high against him as he devoured her mouth. His passion seduced her body just as his vulnerability touched her heart.

He carried her to the cabana where they'd left their towels. He released her legs and let her slide down his body. In her bare feet he towered over her, a dark shadow silhouetted by the nearly full moon. It took him a mere second to bridge the distance before his mouth was on hers again, hot and unsettling.

The right touch and she'd be lost to reason. From the reaction of his body to hers she knew he felt the same.

But he'd started his story and if she let this moment slip away, she may never hear the full tale.

She pulled back, leaning her brow on his damp chest while she caught her breath. "Tell me."

His hands tightened on her and then his chest lifted in a deep breath. He reached for her towel and wrapped it around her before grabbing his own.

She slid onto the double lounge and patted the cushion beside her. He joined her and pulled her into his arms so her back was to his front and the vista of Monte Calanetti spread out before them.

"She showed disinterest to catch my attention. And when I finally got her to go out with me, we just clicked so smoothly. We enjoyed all the same things. Had some of the same friends. She made me feel like she saw me, Zach Sullivan, as more than the son of William Sullivan. I reached the point where I was contemplating marriage. So I took her home to meet the parents. She was so excited. For the first time she asked me why I wasn't studying political science."

"With your family background, you'd think she'd ask that fairly early in the relationship."

"Yes, you'd think. I explained that I wanted nothing to do with politics. That technology was my passion. And I told her what she could expect with my parents. How they married to connect two politically powerful families and how they spent more time with others than with each other."

"And she went after your father."

"She barely spoke to me for the rest of the flight. I thought she was mulling it over, feared I'd put her off."

"You just gave her a new target." She held him tighter.

"She assumed because I grew up surrounded by politics

that I didn't need to study it. And when I let her know I had no interest in it, and revealed my father liked to play discreetly, she went for the big guns. I caught them kissing in his study."

"I'm so sorry. I know how debilitating it is to walk in on a scene like that. The shock, the embarrassment, the betrayal. But I can't imagine how much worse it must hurt for her to be with your father."

With a double betrayal of this magnitude in his past, she kind of got why he didn't like big weddings. And why he was concerned for his friend.

"I just wanted out of there. My dad stopped me and said she'd be the one leaving. She'd come on to him, surprised him with the kiss. He wasn't interested. After she stormed off, he told me he may not be the best husband, but he'd never put a woman before his son."

"Well, that was good, to know he didn't betray you. Still, it's not something you can unsee."

He rested his head against hers, letting her know he sympathized with her, too. "It meant a lot. It's the single incident in my life I can look back on and know he put me first."

Wow, how sad was that? And yet when she looked at her own life, she couldn't find one instance that stood out like that. The difference was that her mom may put herself first, but Lindsay knew her mother loved her. From what Zach described, his folks rarely displayed affection.

She rolled her head against his chest, letting him know she understood his pain.

"So you've never gotten close to marriage since?"

"No. I've never met a woman I could see myself with five years from now let alone fifty. I don't ever want to end up like my folks. I want someone who will knock me off my feet."

"Good for you. That's what you should want. Hear-

ing you say that about five years down the line, I realize
I didn't have that with Kevin, either. I could see myself
in a nice house with a couple of kids, but Kevin wasn't in
the picture."

"I can see you in my future."

Her heart raced at his words and she had to swallow
twice before she could answer. "Do you now?"

"Yes, all the way to tomorrow. I got a call from the
dealership. The Ferrari will be here by nine. I thought we
could drive to Sophia's."

She bit her lip, waffling a tad because she'd lost so
much time today it was hard to justify the drive when the
helicopter did the job so fast. Still she didn't want to make
him feel even guiltier about today's events.

And, truly, how often did she get the chance to drive
through the Halencia countryside in a Ferrari convertible
with a handsome billionaire by her side?

This was probably a once-in-a-lifetime adventure. So
why not stop fighting the inevitable and let the billionaire seduce her? She only had him for another couple of
weeks. Less, really. She didn't want to look back and regret not knowing him fully.

Because she was very much afraid she'd be looking
back a lot.

"Do I get to drive?"

"A little pixie like you? I don't think so." He laughed,
his body shaking with the sound. The good cheer was
wonderful to hear after his earlier despair.

"Come on. We both know it's not the size that matters, but what you do with it." His laughter shook her
some more. "I feel I earned the opportunity to drive it at
least once."

"We'll see."

"Oh, I'm driving." She snuggled into him. "I can tell
it's going to be a lucky day."

"Yeah? How?"

"Well, if you're going to get lucky tonight, it seems only fair I get lucky tomorrow."

He picked her up as if she was no bigger than the pixie he called her and set her in his lap. Using the edge of his hand he tipped her face up to his and kissed her softly.

"Am I getting lucky? What about your strict policies?"

She brushed his hair back, enjoying the feel of the silky strands running through her fingers. "I should stay strong, but you are just too tempting, Mr. Sullivan."

He leaned forward and nipped her bottom lip. "I like the sound of that, Ms. Reeves. Shall we start with a bath in the claw-foot tub?"

How did he know she'd been dying to soak in that tub? It was a modern version of the old classic and could easily hold the two of them. She'd just been waiting for him to be gone long enough to slip into the master bathroom.

Something was still off with him. Why else suggest walking back to the house and risk her coming to her senses? Seated as she was in his lap, there was no doubting his desire for her. Maybe his attempts at humor hadn't quite rid him of his funk in talking about his near miss with wedded bliss.

Unwilling to risk him coming to his senses, she leaned into him, looped her arms around his neck and pressed her lips to his. "Why don't we start here?"

He needed no other prompting. He rolled her so she lay under him. Her head was cradled in one big hand holding her in place for his kiss that belied the fierceness of his embrace by being tender. He cherished her with his mouth; seducing her with soft thrusts and gentle licks until she melted in his arms.

He pulled back, his face unreadable in the darkness of the cabana. A finger traced slowly down the line of her jaw.

"I don't want to hurt you," he said, his breath warm against her skin.

"Then don't," she responded and pulled him back to her.

There were no more words after that, her mind too absorbed with sensation to put coherent thoughts together. The balmy night and towels served to dry them for the most part but she found a few stray drops of water on his side and he shivered when she traced her fingers through the drops, trailing the wet across his smooth skin.

It thrilled her to know her touch affected him as strongly as his did her. He stirred her with his gentleness, but he ignited her when his mouth became more insistent, his touch more demanding. She arched into him, seeking all he had to give.

He grinned against her mouth, assuring her he'd take care of her. A moment later her bikini top slipped away and he lavished attention on the exposed flesh. Her nipple puckered from the rush of heat on damp skin. And the agile use of his tongue.

Wanting nothing between them, she wiggled out of the rest of her suit and pushed at his. Despite her efforts, the damp cloth clung to him.

"Off." She panted against his mouth.

He pushed it down and off without leaving her side. She admired his efficiency almost as much as she admired his form. He was so beautiful she would have liked to see him but he felt too good in her arms for her to regret anything.

Especially when his mouth and fingers did such wicked things to her.

She felt more alive, more energized, more female than any other time in her life.

Being outside made it a hedonistic experience. The night breeze caressed heated skin, while the scent of roses perfumed the air. The rush of emotion compelled her to reach for the moon that hung so heavy in the sky.

Her senses reeled from an overload of sensation. He made her want, made her sizzle, made her mind spin.

When he joined them with an urgency that revealed he was as engaged as she was, she was excited to know she moved him, too. It made her bolder, braver, more determined to drive him insane with pleasure. She loved when he hissed through his teeth, when he kissed her as if he'd never get enough.

When he lost control.

When the connection they shared took her to a whole new level.

Never had she felt so close to another person, in body, in spirit, in heart. He lifted her higher, higher until together they soared through the stars and she shattered in the glow of the moon.

And later, after they roused and he led her to the house for a warm soak in the claw-foot tub and then landed in the comfort of his bed for a repeat performance, she knew for her this was more than two bodies seeking each other in the night.

Somewhere along the way, she'd fallen in love with the best man.

Lindsay stared out the window of the passenger seat in the Ferrari, brooding to the point where the beautiful countryside flew by unnoticed.

She'd had such a lovely morning with Zach. Waking snuggled in his arms, she'd waited for the regret to hit. But no remorse surfaced. She loved Zach. Being in his arms is where she wanted to be.

That would change when she had to walk away. In the meantime she'd make the most of every moment with him.

Watching him put the new Ferrari through its paces on

the trip to Aunt Sophia's pleased her on a visceral level. Seeing his joy, absorbing his laughter, listening to him explain what made his new toy so special. His happiness made her happy, too.

The return trip was much more subdued, with Zach as quiet as she was.

Christina's aunt Sophia was a lovely woman, but a bit unorganized. Pia had called her, so she knew why they were there. She was so happy Christina wanted to wear the pin. Sophia had worn the brooch and she and her husband were still happily married after thirty-nine years.

Lindsay got her hopes up because Sophia seemed certain she had the brooch somewhere, but she'd already looked through her personal jewelry so she thought she must have stored it in the attic with other family heirlooms. Bad knees kept her from doing the search herself so she'd invited Lindsay and Zach to look all they'd like.

Luckily the attic was clean. And airy, once Zach opened the windows. But there was a lot to look through. She found a standing jewelry hutch and thought for sure the brooch would be there. Unfortunately not. Nor was it in any of the boxes or trunks they'd searched. In the end they'd left empty-handed.

"You okay?" Zach reached over and claimed her hand. "You did everything you could to find the brooch."

"I know." She summoned a wan smile, grateful for his support. "I just hate to disappoint the bride. Especially Christina. I've never had a bride disassociate herself so completely from the process so close to the wedding. It's almost as if she's afraid to invest too much of herself into the wedding."

"She's dealing with a lot."

"I get that. That is why I really wanted to find the brooch." With a sigh she turned back to the window. "It's the one thing she seemed to latch onto. It kills me not to be able to find it for her."

The car slowed and then he pulled to the side of the road. She looked at him. "What's wrong? Is it something to do with the car?"

"I needed to do this."

He cupped her face in his hands and kissed her softly. Then not so softly. Slightly breathless she blinked at him when he lifted his head.

"Much better." He slicked his thumb over her bottom lip.

He surprised her by getting out of the car and walking around the hood. He opened her door and helped her out. She looked around and saw nothing but green rolling hills for miles.

"What are we doing?"

"Well, I'm going to be riding. And you are going to be driving."

"Really?" Squealing in excitement she threw herself into his arms. "Thank you. Thank you. Thank you." She peppered his face with kisses between each word.

"Wait." He caught her around the waist when she would have run for the driver's seat. "You do know how to drive a stick, right?"

"I do, yes." This time she pulled his head down to kiss him with all the love in her heart. She knew he was doing this to distract her from her funk, which made the gesture all the more special because he'd categorically refused to let her drive earlier. "I'll take care with your new baby."

He groaned but released her.

She practically danced her way to the driver's seat. Of course she had to have the roof down. That took all of fourteen seconds. Too cool. He took her through where everything was and she pushed the ignition.

Grinning, she said, "Put your seat belt on, lover."

And she put the car in gear.

Grave misgivings hounded Zach as he stared down at the crystal bauble in his hand. Two hearts entwined side by side. Christina's lucky brooch. He'd given up on finding it, given up on sabotaging the wedding, but he'd opened a small tapestry box in one of the trunks in Sophia's attic and there it was. Tarnished, with a few crystals missing, but unmistakable nonetheless.

He'd had no plan when he'd taken it, but for one bright moment he saw a light at the end of the tunnel of Tony's train-wreck plan to marry a woman he didn't love. Without the brooch might Christina back out of the wedding?

With no more thought than that he'd pocketed the trinket.

Now as he clutched it, he realized what he'd done. Christina wasn't backing out. Tony wasn't listening to Zach's appeals to rethink the madness. And Lindsay would freak if she ever learned he'd taken it. On every level professional, friends, lovers, she'd see it as a betrayal.

How could she not when that's what it felt like to him?

He wished he'd never seen it. Never taken it. Never risked everything he'd come to care so much about. Hell, he'd invested so much time in this wedding, even he cared about it being a success.

If only Tony wasn't the victim in all this.

It killed Zach to stand aside while his best friend set himself up for such a big fail. But there was no going back now. It didn't matter that the brooch was not wearable. Didn't matter that he had regrets. The damage was done.

He thought back to the conversation they'd had in the car on the way back from Sophia's. With the brooch burning a hole in his pocket he'd voiced his concerns for Tony and Lindsay had warned him interference never paid off.

"Do you know how many weddings there are where someone doesn't think it's a good idea for some reason?" she'd asked him. "The timing's not right, someone's too young, someone's too old, their ages are too far apart. They don't know what they're doing. She's all wrong for him. He's too good for her. Every one. Show me a wedding and there will be a dissenter in the crowd somewhere."

"They couldn't all be wrong."

"Oh, yeah. Some of them were spot-on. But has it ever worked out well when they try to intervene? No. Because it's not their decision to make. The heart wants what the heart wants."

"What if it isn't love?" he'd demanded.

"Then the situation that brought them together wants what it wants. If the couple is consenting adults, then it's their decision to make."

He heard the message. Understood that a marriage was between the man and woman involved. Still, it was hard to swallow when he knew this was a wedding that was never meant to be.

Glancing around, he looked for a place to stash the piece. Spying a likely spot, he buried it deep. After the wedding, he'd find a way to return the brooch to the Rose family.

In the meantime it was time he got on board and supported his friend.

"Hey," Lindsay called out to Zach where he still sat sipping coffee on the terrace. "I'm doing laundry today. I'm going to grab your stuff."

She went into his walk-in closet and gathered up the items in the hamper. There wasn't that much and she could easily handle it with her things. Something thumped to the floor as Zach filled the doorway.

A crystal brooch, two hearts entwined side-by-side, lay on the brown-and-rust rug.

Heart racing, she blinked once then again, hoping—no, praying—the view would change. Of course it didn't. Christina's brooch lay on the floor at her feet.

It had been hidden in Zach's dirty laundry. Because it was his dirty secret.

Pain bigger than anything she'd ever suffered tore through her heart.

"Lindsay." He stepped into the room that had seemed so big a moment ago but was now tiny and airless.

"You found the brooch." As if it might bite, she backed away from it. A heavy ball of dread lodged in her gut.

"Let me explain." He reached for her.

She pulled away from him.

"What's to explain? You kept it from me. Hid it." Rather than look at him, she stared down at the crystal pin. The silver was tarnished, a few crystals were missing; a beautiful piece ravished by time. It would need to be repaired before it could be worn again.

She lifted anguished eyes to his. "You lied to me."

"I didn't lie," he denied. "I just didn't reveal I'd found it."

"How is that not lying when our whole purpose for being there was to find the brooch?"

"You have to understand, I just want the two of them to stop and think about what they're doing. A lucky pin is a joke." He bent and picked it up. "This is a bandage at the best and a crutch at the very least."

"I understand perfectly." Her stomach roiled as nausea hit. She circled to the left, wanting out of the closet without touching him. "You haven't been helping me at all. You've been using your position as best man to spy on the wedding preparations. Oh, oh." As realization dawned, she retreated from him. When her back hit the wall she sank and wrapped her arms around her knees.

"It was your fault. I thought you were confessing because you felt bad. But it was your fault. You knew exactly what you were doing when you hired Fabio—or had a good idea, anyway. It was all you."

He went down on his haunches in front of her. She shrank away from him.

"Lindsay, this wasn't about you. You were never meant to get hurt."

She closed her eyes to block him out. "Go away."

"You have to listen to me."

"I can't believe anything you say."

"Antonio is a good guy. Always thinking of others. He's kept up with his duties while working in America. He's invested in a lot of businesses here, supported charities. Now he's giving up his life to be king, devoting his life to his country. He deserves to be happy. He has the right to choose his own wife."

"It's his life, Zach. He made his decision. He trusted you." She swallowed around the lump in her throat. "I trusted you."

"You don't understand" He rolled forward onto his knees. And still he loomed over her. "There's more at play here."

"I don't want to understand. I just want you to go away."

I can't." He sounded as if he had a mouth full of glass shards. "Not until I fix this."

"You can't fix this." She shook her head sadly. These past few days with him had been so perfect; a paradise of working and living together. Finding time to escape for a drive or some loving.

But it had been a fool's paradise.

"There's no undoing what's been done."

"There has to be." He reached for her.

She flinched from him.

His hand curled into a fist and fell to his side. "After the deal with the palazzo grounds I stopped. I saw how upset you were and I couldn't be responsible for that. You were never meant to get hurt."

"Stop saying that. What did you expect to happen when a wedding I was planning fell apart at the seams?" How could he possibly believe she'd come out of the situation unscathed if the prince called off the wedding? She was right in the middle of it. Especially with all the little things that had gone wrong. Starting with him sitting on the wedding gown.

Oh, God.

Had he sat on the dress on purpose? Had he known even then who she was and planned to use her all along?

"No, of course not," he responded, revealing she'd spoken aloud. "I had this idea before I left home." He rubbed the back of his head in frustration. "I didn't know who you were when I boarded the plane. This wasn't about you. It was about saving Tony from a lifetime of misery. The wedding planner got paid either way. But I got the opportunity to save him."

Fury drove her to her feet. "You think I'm worried about getting paid? Damn you." She stormed from the closet, not stopping until she reached her room. Yanking her suitcase from where she'd stored it, she opened it on the bed and began dumping in clothes.

Of course he followed her. For such a smart man, he knew how to do stupid real well.

"Do you think I work for a paycheck? Is that all your work is to you? I bet not." She emptied the drawers into the case and went for her shoes. "I take pride in my work."

The shoes didn't fit. She forced herself to stop and fold. She would not come back here. She went into the bathroom and grabbed what toiletries she'd left down here. She clenched her teeth when she thought of the items now occupying space in the master bathroom. He could have them. No way was she going back in that room.

He still stood in the doorway when she returned to her room. His shoulders drooped and his features were haggard. He looked as though he'd lost something precious.

Good. He'd pulled her heart from her chest and stomped on it. Let him suffer.

"I take satisfaction in giving the bride and groom something special, a day they can look back on with pride and happiness."

She closed the suitcase, pushed on the lid a couple of times to mash it down and then started zipping.

"There's more involved than arranging the flowers and cuing the music." With her suitcase closed, she yanked it from the bed and pulled up the handle. Finally she lifted her chin and faced Zach. "But then, I know you don't put much value in what I do. I really should have listened when you said you hate big weddings."

"Lindsay, no—"

"What did you say?" She talked right over his protest. "Oh, yeah, the couple needs to distract the crowd because they're marrying for something other than love."

"Don't do this. Don't leave. I didn't mean you."

"Oh, and let's not forget, love is a myth best left to romance novels."

He groaned.

"No, it's good this happened. Foolish me. I believed I was falling in love. It's so good to know it's just a myth. In a couple of days I'm sure I'll be fine."

She passed him in the doorway, making certain not to touch him. "But you should know there's nothing fake about what I do. I put my heart and soul into my weddings. And the couple doesn't walk away empty-handed. I make memories, Zach. I intend to give Antonio and Christina a spectacular wedding to look back on."

She turned her back on him and walked out. "Stay out of my way."

CHAPTER ELEVEN

AFTER SEVERAL DAYS of brooding, of waffling between righteous indignation and hating himself for the pain he'd caused Lindsay, Zach finally came to the conclusion the first was really no justification for the second.

She still used the sunroom as her workshop, but mostly Serena worked there and when Lindsay did come by, she kept the doors locked; a clear signal for him to stay out.

As he had for the past two evenings, he sat in the shadows of the patio, waiting to catch her when she left for the day. Hoping today she'd talk to him. He hadn't seen her at all yesterday and his chest ached with missing her.

In such a short time she'd burrowed her way into his affections. Watching her work fascinated him; the way she gathered a few odd items together and made something beautiful. Her expression when she concentrated was so fierce it was almost a scowl. Many times he'd wanted to run his thumb over the bow between her brows to see if her creative thoughts might transmit to him and show him what had her so enthralled.

He missed her wit, her laughter, the way she gave him a bad time.

Steps sounded on the spiral staircase and he surged to his feet, meeting her as she reached the patio level. The sun was setting behind her, casting her in a golden glow. Strands of her hair shimmered as a light breeze tossed them playfully around. In juxtaposition her blue eyes were guarded and the skin was pulled taut across her cheeks.

She made to walk by him and he caught her elbow in a light hold.

"Won't you talk to me for a minute?"

She didn't look at him. But she didn't pull away, either.

"There's nothing more to say between us."

"There is." He ran his thumb over the delicate skin of her inner elbow. Touching her fed something that had been deprived the past few days. Still, he forced himself to release her. "I tried to explain, but I failed to apologize. I'm sorry, Lindsay. I didn't think hard enough about how this would affect you. I never meant to devalue what you do."

Her shoulders squared and she half turned toward him. "But you don't value it. You've seen the effort involved, you can respect that. But you don't see the value in a beautiful wedding because you see it as the prelude to a flawed marriage."

"In this case, yes."

She sighed. "Zach, I've heard you talk about your parents enough to know what growing up with them must have been like. And I know you love Antonio, that he's probably closer to you than anyone. Mix that with your dislike of big, fancy weddings, and I'm sure this has been hell for you."

"I meant well," he avowed, grateful she saw what motivated him. "I can't stand the thought of him making this mistake, of him being miserable for the rest of his life. But Tony isn't rational when it comes to Halencia."

"Why? Because he refuses to see things your way?" She shook her head, the disappointment in her eyes almost harder to take than the hurt it replaced. "I think that's a good thing. I think a king should be willing to sacrifice for his country. Considering what his parents have put this country through, I think that's exactly what Halencia needs right now. And I think as his friend and best man, you should start showing him some support."

Hearing it broken down like that made him pause and rethink. Hadn't he had the same thought just days ago?

She took the opportunity to walk away. "I understand

why you want to save Antonio. What I can't forgive is your willingness to sacrifice me to get it."

Unable to take anymore, Zack texted Tony.

Need to see you. I've messed up bad. You may want a new best man.

After sending the message, Tony wandered down to the pool to wait for the helicopter to arrive on the wide lawn they'd been using as a landing area. It would be at least an hour, but he had no desire to sit in the house so full of memories.

He stared at the pool and remembered the night he made love to Lindsay.

He couldn't regret it. Wouldn't.

Having her come alive in his arms was one of the high points in his life. He'd connected with her more closely than with any other woman he could recall. Her honest reactions and giving nature seduced him every bit as much as the silky feel of her skin and hair, the sweet taste of her mouth, the soft moans of her desire.

The few days he'd had her by his side had given him a brief glimpse into what the future could hold.

He wanted to scoff at the notion. To discount it as an indicator he'd been on one wild trip to Tuscany. But the truth was he could all too easily see her in his life. Not just here in Halencia but back in the States, as well.

And it scared the hell out of him.

The only thing that scared him more was the thought of losing her from his life altogether.

He knew the biggest betrayal for her was the intimacy they'd shared while she believed he'd been using her. But that's not what happened. He'd wanted Lindsay before he'd known she was the wedding planner. His attraction for her was completely disassociated from what she did.

Or so he'd thought.

Now he knew better. What she did was a part of who she was. She'd spoken of being disillusioned with her job. Her impassioned speech calling him to task for thinking a paycheck would suffice if the wedding fell apart proved she wasn't as lost as she'd feared. She'd been shaken because she let herself get caught up with Kevin and he'd used her.

It sickened Zach to realize he'd done the same thing.

Time to make it right.

The whoop, whoop, whoop of the helicopter sounded in the distance and grew louder. Finally. In another hour or so he'd see Tony, apologize for the mess he'd made of everything and put this whole fiasco behind him.

Being so close to Lindsay but parted from her drove him insane. He wanted to stay and fix it, but she needed to be here. He didn't. Hell, Tony probably wouldn't want him here when he learned what Zach had done.

He'd go back to the States and wait for her to come home. Then he'd find her and apologize again. No justifications, just a straight-up apology.

Ready to have this done, he strolled toward the helicopter. As he got closer he was surprised to see the pilot headed toward him. And then he knew.

"Tony." He broadened his stride and met his friend in a hug. "You came."

"Si, amico mio." Unselfconscious in showing emotion, Tony gave Zach a hard squeeze then stepped back to clap him on the arm. "Your text sounded serious."

"I've messed up."

"So you said. We must fix whatever you have done. I do not care to have anyone else for my best man."

"You haven't heard what I've done yet."

Tony had given up so much to support his country, would he be able to forgive Zach for messing in his affairs?

He couldn't lose both Lindsay and Antonio. Why hadn't he thought with his head instead of his heart?

"This sounds ominous." By mutual consent they headed toward the house. "You are my brother, Zach. You have seen how far I will go for my sibling. There is nothing you can do that will change my love for you. I need someone I can trust at my back during this wedding."

Zach walked at his friend's side. They were passing near the pool when Tony stopped. He looked longingly at the pool.

"Ah, the water looks good. I have not been swimming since I got to Halencia."

"You want to swim?" Zach grabbed his shirt at the back of the neck and pulled it off over his head. "It's as good a place to talk as any."

He stripped down and dove in. As soon as the water embraced him, he struck out, arm overhead, legs kicking, arm overhead, kick, again and again. He needed the physical exertion to empty his mind of everything but the tracking of laps and the knowledge Tony matched him pace for pace.

Tony tapped his shoulder when they reached fifty. "Let's hit the spa."

Zach slicked a hand over his face and hair and nodded.

In one big surge, he propelled himself up and out of the pool. He walked to the controls for the spa and flicked the switch to generate the jets. After grabbing a couple of towels from a storage ottoman and tossing them on the end of a lounger near the spa, he hit the mini fridge for a couple sodas and joined his friend, sighing as the hot water engulfed him.

"Grazie." Tony took a big swig and closed his blue eyes on a groan as he let his head fall back. "You don't know how good this feels. Hey, I know you're working with the

palace liaison on the bachelor party but can we do it here? Keep it tight and quiet."

"Sure. How about poker, cigars and a nice, aged whiskey?"

"Perfect." Tony laughed. "Now, tell me what's up."

Zach did, he laid it all out, not bothering to spare himself. "The good news is you'll still have a beautiful wedding, but I think I should go."

"It's not like you to run, Zach."

He barked a harsh laugh. "None of this is like me."

"True. You actually let her drive your new car?"

Zach eyed his friend still laying back and letting the jets pound him with bubbles. "Focus, dude. I almost wrecked your wedding."

"But you didn't." Tony straightened and spread his arms along the edge of the spa. He nailed Zach with an intent stare. "You messed up your life instead. You care about Ms. Reeves."

He got a little sick every time he thought about never seeing her again. But that wasn't something he was willing to share.

"She's a good person. And she's really worked hard to give you and Christina an event to be proud of. She found these cool candleholders that merge your two styles—"

"Stop." Tony held up a dripping hand. "I'm going to stop you right there. Dude, you're spouting wedding drivel. Obviously you're in love."

"Shut up." Zach cursed and threw his empty soda can at his friend's head. "You know I don't do love."

"I know you have a big heart or you wouldn't care so much about my future. You deserve to be happy, my friend, and I think the wedding planner makes you happy."

How easily Tony read him. Zach had been happier here in Halencia than as far back as he could remember.

But he'd ruined any chance of finishing the trip in the same vein.

"You deserve happiness, too. That's all I really wanted when I started this mess."

"I appreciate that you want me to be happy. But this is something I have to do. To be honest, the thought of a love match would terrify me. Watching the roller coaster that has been my parents' marriage cured me of that. I will be happy to have a peaceful arrangement with a woman I can admire and respect who will stand by my side and represent my country. Like your Lindsay, Christina is a good woman. We will find our way. You need to do the same."

His Lindsay. That sounded good.

"My being here hurts her. It's best if I leave and let her do her job."

"You mean it's easier. Well, forget it. You're my best man and I'm not letting you off the hook. Relationships take work, Zach."

That's what Lindsay said when she was talking about her mother's many marriages.

"If you care for this woman, and it appears you do, you need to fight for her. Apologize."

"I did. She didn't want to hear it."

Tony cocked a sardonic eyebrow. "Apologize again."

Zach nodded. "Right."

"Tell her you love her."

Love. Zach held his friend's gaze for a long moment, letting unfamiliar emotions—confusion, fear, sadness, exhilaration, joy, hope—rush through him. And finally he nodded. "Right."

A knock sounded at Lindsay's door. She ignored it. Now she was back at the hotel she was fair game for the press who thought nothing about knocking on her door at all hours. So pushy.

Another bang on the door.

She kept her attention on her schedule for the next week. Circled in red at the end of the week was *the* day. The wedding.

The rehearsal was in two days, four days in advance of the actual event because it was the only day everyone could get together. She'd have to see Zach, deal with him. As long as he didn't start apologizing again, she'd be fine.

She knew he'd meant well, that he loved Antonio like a brother. She even admired how far he was willing to go to ensure his friend's happiness.

But she couldn't tolerate the fact that she was acceptable collateral damage.

Why did men find her so dispensable?

She was fairly smart, had a good sense of humor. She worked hard; if anything, too hard. She was honest, kind, punctual. Okay, she wasn't model beautiful, but she wasn't hideous, either.

So what made her so unlovable?

More knocking. Ugh, these guys were relentless.

"Signorina? Signorina?" Mario called out. "Are you there? Mama says you should come."

Oh, gosh. She'd left the poor kid standing out there. Lindsay set her tablet aside and rushed to the door.

"Signorina." Mario greeted her anxiously. "Someone is here to see you. Mama says you must come."

Lindsay gritted her teeth. Zach. Why couldn't he leave her be? "Can you tell him I'm busy?"

His eyes grew big and he frantically shook his head. "No, *signorina*. You must come."

She'd never seen the boy so agitated. Fine, she'd just go tell Zach, once more, to leave her alone. Mario led her downstairs to a room she hadn't seen before. A man stood looking out on the rose garden.

"Zach you need to stop— Oh, sorry." She came to an

abrupt halt when the man turned. Not Zach. "Oh, goodness. Prince Antonio. Your Highness."

Should she curtsy? Why hadn't she practiced curtsying?

"Ms. Reeves, thank you for seeing me." He spoke in slightly accented English and had the bluest eyes she'd ever seen. They twinkled as he took her hand and bowed over it in a gesture only the European did well. "I hope you are not thinking of curtsying. It is entirely unnecessary."

His charm and humor put her instantly at ease. That ability, along with his dark, good looks and the sharp intelligence in those incredible eyes, would serve him well as King of Halencia. She wondered if they'd approached him about running for president.

"You're here to plead his case, aren't you?" Why else would the prince seek her out? He'd showed little to no interest in the wedding plans, even through his advocate.

Anger heated her blood. How dare Zach put her in this position? What could the prince think but that she allowed her personal business to interfere with his wedding preparations? Showing no interest and having none were two different things.

This whole situation just got worse and worse.

"I am." Prince Antonio indicated she should sit.

She perched on the edge of a beige sofa. The prince sat adjacent to her in a matching recliner.

"Your Highness, I can assure you the plans for the wedding are on schedule. And, of course, I will continue to work with Zach as your representative, but anything beyond working together is over. He should not have involved you."

"Please, call me Tony."

Yeah, that wasn't going to happen.

"You are obviously important to Zach and he is important to me, so we should be friendly, *si*?"

She meant to nod; a silent, polite gesture to indicate she heard him. But her head shook back and forth, the denial too instinctive.

"He does not know I am here."

That got her attention. "He didn't send you?"

"No. In fact he planned to leave Halencia, to concede the field to you, as it were. He wanted to make it easier on you."

"Oh." What did she make of that? He was supposed to be best man. Of course he'd have to tell the prince if he planned to leave. Had he already left? Was that why Antonio was here, to tell her she'd be working with a new best man?

Her heart clenched at the thought of never seeing Zach again. The sense of loss cut through the anger and hurt like a sword through butter.

"But he is my best friend. I do not want another for my best man."

"Oh." Huge relief lifted the word up. The feeling of being reprieved was totally inappropriate. He'd used and betrayed her. That hadn't changed. Just as her foolish love for him hadn't changed. It was those softer feelings that tried to sway her now.

Too bad she'd learned she couldn't trust those feelings.

"I have never seen Zach so enamored of a woman. Is it true he let you drive his car?"

She nodded. And she knew why. In piecing things together she figured that must be the trip where Zach had found the pin. She'd been brooding on the trip back and he'd felt guilty.

As he should.

The prince laughed, drawing her attention.

"He really does have it bad. I wish I could have been here to watch this courtship."

"There's been no courtship, Your Highness. Far from

it." She'd stayed strong for two weeks. Why, oh, why had she let his vulnerability get to her? Because she'd fallen for him. Her mom was fond of saying you couldn't control who you fell in love with. Lindsay always considered that a tad convenient.

Turned out it wasn't convenient at all.

"Antonio," he insisted. "I am hoping I can persuade you to cut him some slack. I am quite annoyed with him myself, but I understand what drove him. Zach is not used to having people in his life that matter to him. He is a numbers man. He would have calculated the risk factors and figured those associated with you were tolerable. If the wedding was called off, you would still get paid."

"So he said, but there's more than a paycheck involved here. There's my reputation, as well."

"Which would not suffer if I or Christina called off the wedding."

"It would if it was due to a jinxed wedding, which I can only speculate is what he hoped to achieve."

"Was it such a bad thing he did? Fighting for my happiness?"

"That's not fair." She chided him with her gaze but had to look away as tears welled. She had to clear her throat before speaking. "People don't use the people that matter to them."

Something close to sadness came and went in his blue eyes. "Yes, we do. We are just more up front about it. Zach told me you have the brooch."

It took a second for her brain to switch gears "Yes. It's in my room. It's damaged so I haven't mentioned we found it to Christina yet."

"This is good. If you please, I'd like to take it with me to see if I can get it repaired in time for the wedding."

"Of course. I'll go get it." She quickly made the trip

to her room and returned to hand him the antique piece. "It's really a lovely design."

"Yes, two hearts entwined side by side." Expression thoughtful, he ran his thumb over the crystals. "You can see why it represents true love and longevity."

"Indeed. I hope you are able to get it repaired in time. More, I hope it brings you and Christina much happiness."

"*Grazie*, Ms. Reeves. I can see why Zach has fallen for you. I think you will be good for him."

She sighed on a helpless shrug. "Your Highness."

"Antonio." He bent and kissed her cheek. "As you think about his sins, I wish for you to consider something, as well."

Cautious, she asked, "What's that?"

"Zach does not let anyone drive his cars."

She opened her mouth on a protest.

He stopped her with a raised hand. "Not even me."

She blinked at him as his words sank in, biting her tongue to hold back another ineffective "Oh."

He nodded. "Zach told you of Julia?"

She inclined her head in acknowledgment.

"Ah. Another sign of his affection for you. He does not talk about himself easily. He does not speak of Julia at all. He thought he should have known, that he should have seen through her avarice to her true motives. He's never been as open or as giving since. Until now."

Antonio stepped to the door. "Please do not tell Christina of the brooch. I do not want her to be disappointed if it is not ready in time." With a bow of his head, he took his leave.

Lindsay continued to look at where he'd been. She wrapped her arms around herself, needing to hold on to something. Because everything she believed had just been shaken up.

The Prince of Halencia had come to see her, to plead

Zach's case after he'd tried to sabotage Antonio's wedding. How mixed up was that? If Antonio could overlook Zach's craziness, could—should—Lindsay?

Hurt and anger gripped her in unrelenting talons, digging deep, tearing holes in her soul. She wanted to think this would let up after a couple of weeks of nursing the hurt as it had with Kevin, but this went deeper, stung harder.

What she felt for Kevin had been make-believe; more in her head than anything else. What she felt for Zach came from the heart. And it hadn't stopped just because he'd hurt her. The wrenching sickness in her gut when Antonio'd said Zach planned to leave proved that.

Seeking fresh air, she slipped out of the house and into the dark garden. Lights from the house showed her the way to a path that led to the back of the garden where a bench sat beside a tinkling fountain.

The earthy scent of imminent rain hung in the air. Lindsay looked up. No stars confirmed clouds were overhead.

Great. A storm. Just what she needed.

But it wasn't fear or an uneasiness that took control of her head. Memories of being stuck in Zach's car and staying with him at the farmhouse B and B in Caprese bombarded her.

He'd held her, a stranger, because she was afraid. He'd listened to her sad tale of being scared because her mother always cried during storms. The truth was her father left during a storm and deep down in her child's psyche, she'd feared her mother would leave, too, and Lindsay would be all alone.

Antonio had asked if Zach's fighting for his happiness was such a bad thing.

And the answer was no. She understood Zach's motivation. He'd grown up a victim of his parents' political alliance and the trip to see them en route to Halencia probably triggered the need to intervene on Antonio's behalf.

If this were just the summer fling she'd convinced herself she could handle, she'd forgive him and move on.

But she loved him.

She dipped her fingers in the fountain and swirled the water around. It was still warm from the heat of the day.

She missed the villa. Missed sharing coffee with Zach in the morning seated out on the terrace watching the city come alive down below. She missed his sharp mind and dry humor and his total ignorance of all things wedding-related.

But most of all she missed the way he held her, as if she were the most precious thing in his world.

And that's what she couldn't forgive.

He'd made her believe she mattered. And it had all been a lie.

She'd never been put first before.

Her dad had walked out before she even knew him. And her mother loved her. But Lindsay had always known her mother's wants and needs came first. Even when it was just Lindsay, work came first.

For a few magical days Zach had made her feel as if she was his everything. It showed in the way he'd touched her and by the heat in his eyes. It was in the deference and care he'd demonstrated, the affection and tenderness.

Maybe it was a facade he assumed and that's how he treated all the women in his life—the thought sliced through her brain like shards of broken glass—but it felt real to her. And she couldn't—wouldn't—accept less just to finish out a summer fling.

No more settling. She'd done that with Kevin and learned her lesson. She'd been willing to settle for a fling with Zach because she'd sensed how good it would be between them. And she'd been right. But she loved him, and a fling was no longer enough. She needed honesty, respect and a willingness to put your partner first.

How often had she watched her mother's relationships fall apart because a little work was involved? Her mom was so used to being the center of her world she didn't see that sometimes she needed to make her husband feel he was the center of her world.

Antonio inferred Zach cared for her. He made it sound as if Zach had planned to leave to make things easier for her. More likely he'd wanted out of this whole gig. But there was the bit about letting her drive his car when he never let anyone drive his cars, not even the man he thought of as his brother.

No. Just stop. She pushed the wistful thinking aside as she headed inside. His actions told the story. He didn't love her. He'd proved that when he'd put his friend before her.

Zach had said he liked storms, for him they washed things clean, made them shiny and new, allowing new growth. A good metaphor for him. He was the storm that allowed her to put the horror of Kevin's betrayal behind her. But would her heart survived the tsunami Zach had left in his wake?

CHAPTER TWELVE

Two days later Lindsay walked with Serena toward the Palazzo di Comparino chapel. The rehearsal started in twenty minutes. Nothing was going right today. She should be totally focused on damage control and all she could think about was the fact she'd be seeing Zach in a few minutes.

Her mind and heart played a mad game of table tennis over him. One moment she was strong and resolute in holding out for what she deserved. The next she was sure she deserved him, that his actions proved he cared deeply for the people in his life and she wanted to be one of those people.

"You just got an email from Christina confirming she will not make it to the rehearsal." Serena jogged to keep up.

Lindsay came to a full stop, causing Serena to backtrack. "What about Antonio?"

"He is still delayed at the palace, but he is trying to get here."

"Okay, we're talking a good two hours. Let me call Raffaele to see if he can move dinner up." Before the big blowup between them, she'd suggested to Zach that he host the rehearsal dinner at the villa. With her taking care of the details, he'd been happy to agree.

It was a no-brainer to put Mancini's in charge of the food. Still moving dinner up an hour would be a challenge. But so worth it if it allowed if at least one of the bridal couple to make it to the rehearsal.

"The prince's email said we should start without him."

"Wonderful. Zach will have to act as the groom and can you play the part of Christina?"

"Oh, Lindsay, I am sorry, but I cannot."

"Sure you can. I know these are high-profile people, but all you have to do is walk slowly down the aisle. No biggie."

"No, remember, Papa and I are meeting the glassblower to pick up the last delivery of candleholders. I have to leave in half an hour."

"Oh, yeah, that's tonight. Well, of course. Why should anything workout tonight?"

"Perhaps Papa can go on his own?" Serena made the offer hesitantly. Generous of her since Lindsay knew the two were looking forward to the road trip. A little father-daughter time before Serena went back to school.

"No, you go. I know this trip means a lot to you. I'll work something out."

"You could play the bride," Serena suggested.

"Uh, no. Thanks, but I have to keep things moving." So not a good idea. The very notion of walking down the aisle to Zach in groom mode messed with her head.

And her heart.

The elderly priest had other ideas. He looked like a monk of days gone by and he held her hand and patted the back ever so gently. He spoke softly, listened carefully, and totally took over the rehearsal. Everything must be just so.

He explained what was going to happen, who was going to go where, who stood, who sat, who would leave first and who would follow. He was quite thorough.

Because she found her gaze repeatedly finding Zach, who looked gorgeous in a white shirt and dark sports jacket, Lindsay ran her gaze over the participants. Everyone listened respectfully. Even Queen Valentina and the king, who sat holding hands. Apparently they were in an "on again" phase of their relationship.

The chapel looked lovely. A rainbow of colors fell through the stained-glass windows and standing candle-holders in white wrought-iron lined the walls from the back to the front and across the altar, illuminating the small interior. For the wedding they would be connected with garlands of sunflowers and roses.

And from what she observed, the palace photographer seemed to be doing a good job. He was the only extra person in the room. Serena had quietly made her departure during the priest's soliloquy.

"Come, come." The priest raised his cupped hands as if lifting a baby high. "Let us all take our places. You, young man—" he patted Zach on the shoulder "—will play the part of the groom. And you, *signorina*—" he looked at Lindsay "—will be our bride today."

No, no, no.

Pasting on a serene smile, she politely refused. "I'm sorry, Father, I really need to observe and take notes to ensure a smooth ceremony the day of the wedding."

"*Si, si.* You will observe as the bride. Come, stand here." He motioned to his right.

Zach stood tall and broad on the priest's left.

She swallowed hard and shook her head. She couldn't do it. She couldn't pretend to be Zach's bride when she longed for the truth of the position with all her broken heart.

"Perhaps Elena can play the bride?" she suggested. Hoped.

"Oh, no. Elena has her own role to play as the maid of honor. You are needed, *signorina*. Come."

There was no protesting after that. Plus, others would begin to make note if she made any more of a scene. Clenching her teeth together, she moved forward, holding her tablet in front of her like a shield, looking everywhere but at Zach.

She was fine while the priest directed the action from the altar, but when he stepped away to help people find their spots, Zach narrowed the distance between them by a step then two.

"Please don't start anything here," she implored.

"I'm not." He put his hands in his pockets and rocked on his heels. "How have you been?"

"We should listen to the Father."

"I've missed you."

"Zach, I can't do this here."

"You have to give me something, Lindsay. You asked me to stay away and I have."

She narrowed her eyes at him. "You've texted me several times every day." Crazy things, thoughtful things, odd facts about himself. She'd wanted to delete them without reading them, but she'd read every one, came to look forward to them, especially those that revealed something about him.

"I needed some link to you. I'm afraid I'm addicted."

"You're not going to charm me, Zach." She frantically searched out the priest. When was this show going to get on the road? When she looked back, Zach was closer still.

He bent over her. "You smell so good. Do you miss me at all?"

"Every minute of every day." Her hand went to her mouth. Oh, my dog. Did she just say that out loud?

"Lindsay—"

"The priest is calling me." Heart racing, she escaped to the back of the chapel where the wedding party congregated. The priest nodded when she appeared, as if he'd been waiting for her.

"*Si, si.* We will start with the procession. Just as I described. *Signorina*, you will be last with Signor Rose."

Lindsay took her place by the robust man who made no

effort to disguise his disapproval of Christina's absence. She wasn't Lindsay's favorite person at the moment, either.

Oh, gosh, instead of settling, her heart raced harder. Zach stood at the altar waiting for her to come to him. It felt too real. And, sweet merciful heavens, she wished it were real.

It mattered what he'd done. Yes, he'd meant well. And no, he hadn't known her when he initiated his plan. But it mattered.

The procession began to move. She closed her eyes and stepped forward. Her foot slipped on the uneven ground, so, okay, that wasn't going to work. She opened her eyes and concentrated on the smooth stones of the chapel floor.

He had apologized. And he'd honored her request to stay away. But he hadn't let her forget him, or the time they'd spent together.

Had that been him fighting for her? Or was that wishful thinking?

Suddenly, Mr. Rose stopped and Zach's strong, tanned hand came into view. She fought the urge to put her hands behind her back. All eyes were on her, on them, but this was for Antonio and Christina's wedding. Nobody cared about her or Zach; they didn't care that touching him would be a huge mistake.

She hated how her hand shook as she placed it in his.

He set her hand on his arm and led her to stand in front of the priest. And then he covered her hand with his warm hold and leaned close to whisper, "No need to be nervous. I'm right here by your side."

For some odd reason she actually found his promise reassuring. Facing the priest, not so much.

"Well done, well done." He motioned for the wedding party to be seated. "Lindsay, Zach, if you will face each other. Next I will begin the ceremony. I'll share a few words and then we'll go through the exit procession."

Lindsay turned to face Zach and he took both her hands in each of his. It was the most surreal moment of her life.

The priest began. "Today is a glorious day which the Lord hath made, as today both of you are blessed with God's greatest of all gifts, the gift of abiding love and devotion between a man and woman. All present here today, and those here in heart, wish both of you all the joy, happiness and success the world has to offer—"

"Stop. I can't do this." Lindsay tried to pull away. This hurt too much.

"Lindsay, it's okay." Zach's voice was calm and steady. His hold remained sure and strong as he moved to shield her from the audience. "Father, may we have a moment?"

"Of course, my son." The priest bowed and moved away.

"Breathe, Lindsay. It's going to be okay." Zach leaned over her. "I felt it, too. How right those words were between you and me."

Lindsay clutched at Zach's hands, clinging to him as emotions raged through her heart and head.

"I can't do this. I'm sorry." Aware her behavior embarrassed both her and him, she lifted bleak eyes to meet his gaze. What she saw made the breath catch in her throat.

His eyes were unshielded and in the dark, whiskey depths shone a love so big and so deep it seemed to go on forever. She felt surrounded in a cushion of caring, lifted on a throne of adoration.

"Zach," she breathed.

"I love you, Lindsay." The words echoed everything his eyes already revealed.

Hope slowly swelled through her as her love surged to the surface eager for all his gaze offered. Already weakened, her self-preservation instincts began to crumble as unleashed longing filled her heart.

"I hurt you and I'm more sorry than I can say that I let the fears of my childhood control my common sense when it came to Tony's wedding. You opened my eyes to what I was doing and he hammered it home. But even when I finally accepted the truth and apologized, something still nagged at me, a sense of wrongness that grew rather than diminished."

Behind him she was aware of movement and whispers, reminding her they were not alone. But all she heard, all she saw, was Zach and the raw pain filling eyes that had been overflowing with love just moments ago.

"And then the truth came to me. I couldn't get past how my actions hurt you. I wronged you, not just by disrespecting what you do and by making you work harder, but by putting Tony's needs before yours. That's when I knew the happiness I take in your company and the joy that consumes me when I touch you is actually love."

Now his hands were tight on hers. She ran her thumbs softly over the whites of his knuckles. Everything he'd said was just what she'd longed to hear. She let the last of her concerns melt away.

"Zach." She squeezed his hands. "I love you, too."

Relief flooded his features and he rested his forehead against hers. "Thank God. Because this is bigger and more terrifying than anything I've ever known."

A laugh trilled out of her. "Yes. I'm glad to know I'm not alone."

"You'll never be alone again." He raised his head and his love rained down on her. "Watching you walk down that aisle to me felt more right than anything else in my life. I love you, Lindsay Reeves. Will you marry me?"

"Yes." No hesitation, no need to think. Her misery had come from that same sense of rightness. She longed to spend the rest of her life with this man. "I would love to marry you."

"Right now?" His brown gaze danced with love and mischief.

She blinked at him. "What?"

"Will you marry me right now, in this beautiful chapel we refashioned together?"

Her mind slowly grasped what he wanted, and then her heart soared with excited anticipation. Still, she couldn't get married without her mother. "What about our friends and family?"

"We can have a lavish ceremony back in the States. As big as you want. But I don't want to wait to claim you as mine. So I made sure everyone who truly matters is here."

He stepped back to reveal the chapel filled with people. She saw Louisa sandwiched between Nico and Vincenzo. Raffaele and Daniella sat next to Eva and Mario. Alonso and Serena were here instead of on the road. And many more of the townspeople she'd met and worked with over the past month filled the pews, including the King and Queen of Halencia.

And standing with the grinning priest was Prince Antonio and...her mother.

"Mom?"

"I knew you'd want her here." Zach's hand rested warm and familiar in the small of her back.

"You must have been planning this for days."

"It's the only thing that's kept me sane." He lifted her chin, his mouth settling on hers in restrained urgency. When he raised his head, his eyes gleamed with the heat of desire, the steadfastness of love. "Shall we do this?"

She nodded slowly. "Yes."

Her answer ignited a flurry of activity. Antonio stepped forward while her mother grabbed her hand and hustled her back down the aisle and out the door. In an instant she was in her mom's arms being hugged hard.

"I'm so happy for you, baby. Zach is a force of nature.

If he loves you anywhere near as much as his actions indicate, you will have a long and joyous marriage." She sighed. "For all my marriages, I've never had anyone look at me with so much love."

Lindsay was too excited to have her mother here to care that her special day had circled around to focus on her mom's feelings.

"I'm so glad you're here. You look beautiful." Her mom wore a lovely, pale green silk suit that went well with her upswept brown hair and green eyes. "And you're wrong. Matt looks at you like that. You've just been too focused on yourself to notice."

"Lindsay!" her mother protested, but a speculative glint entered her eyes. "I'll let that slide. We need to get you ready."

"I think I'm as ready as we have time for." Lindsay glanced down at her flowing ivory dress that came to just below her knees in the front and to her ankles in the back and knew she'd been set up. Serena had insisted the dress was perfect for today; business moving into party mode. Of everything she owned this would have been her choice for an impromptu wedding gown.

"Oh, we have time for a few special touches." Darlene pulled Lindsay around the side of the chapel where a full-length, gold-framed mirror leaned against the side of the building, next to it was a garment rack with a flow of tulle over one end and a stack of shelves hanging from the other.

"Something old." From the shelves her mother lifted out a set of pearl-and-sapphire earrings.

"Grandma's earrings." Darlene had worn them for her first wedding and Lindsay recalled saying wistfully she'd wear them at her wedding someday. Her mother had remembered. Her hands shook a little as she put them on.

"Something new." A beaded belt and matching shoes adorned in pearls and crystals shimmered in the late-afternoon sun. While Lindsay traded her sandals for the high-heeled pumps, Darlene stepped behind her and clipped it into place at her waist. They both fit perfectly.

"Something borrowed." Mom smiled. "I saved this because you loved it so much." The tulle turned out to be a full-length veil scalloped on the edges in delicate pearl-infused embroidery. "Close your eyes and face the mirror."

Lindsay's heart expanded; she hadn't realized her mother had been paying such close attention to her reactions through the years. She closed her eyes against a well of tears while Darlene fussed with the veil and the lovely floral hair clip that went with it.

Next she felt a rouge brush dust over her cheeks and some gloss being dabbed on her lips. A tissue caught an escaping tear.

"You can open your eyes."

Lindsay did and was amazed to find a beautiful bride staring back at her. "Mom."

"You're stunning, baby."

Lindsay nodded. She felt stunning and ready to begin her life with Zach.

"Let's go. Your man is waiting."

Rounding the corner of the chapel, she spied the replica of the fountain from the plaza and thought of the wish she'd made with Zach. The wish for true love had been meant for Antonio and Christina. Lindsay supposed she'd been pushing it to make a wish for another couple, but she couldn't be disappointed that fate had chosen to grant true love to her and Zach.

This time when she walked down the aisle her mother escorted her and Lindsay's heart swelled with joy as her gaze locked with Zach's. He'd changed into the suit he'd been wearing when they'd met and she loved the symbolism of the gesture. He knew her so well.

There was no shaking as she placed her hand in his,

just a surety of purpose, a promise to always be there for him. The warmth and steadiness of his grip was the same as it had been earlier and she recognized he'd always be her rock. She suddenly realized something she'd missed when taking in the surprise he'd given her.

"What about your parents?" she whispered.

"They couldn't make it."

"I'm sorry." And angry. His parents didn't deserve him.

"Pixie—" he cupped her cheek "—you're all the family I need."

Her throat closed on a swell of emotion. She swallowed and pledged. "I love you."

"I can't wait for you to be my wife."

"Ahem." Antonio placed his hand on Zach's shoulder. "The priest is waiting."

"Right." Love and anticipation bright in his gaze, he gave the nod. "We're ready, Father."

"We are gathered together on this glorious day which the Lord hath made, to witness the joining of Zachary Sullivan and Lindsay Reeves, who have been blessed with God's greatest of all gifts, the gift of abiding love and devotion between a man and woman…"

* * * * *

ALL HE NEEDS

SHIRLEY HAILSTOCK

To my niece Tanesha for being there for me.

Chapter 1

Renee Hart stepped out of the conference room. She was going to burst. Without a word, she rushed past the secretaries and headed outside. The glass entry doors were the air pressure variety, yet she slammed them both open. Sunlight and humidity hit her like a hot oven. Renee welcomed it as she would a dive into a tropical pool. She needed a place to conceal the echo that was roaring inside her. She walked fast toward her car, but she knew she wasn't going to make it.

She got as far as the tree-lined divider that separated the upper parking lot from the lower one. Then she howled. She let the sound inside her go. All of it. Elation erupted like a volcano. Every emotion she'd ever had thundered and rolled with psychedelic pleasure.

She was happy, so happy. Tears broke from her eyes and ran over her cheeks.

Renee hadn't known when she'd accepted the bridal consultant position at Weddings by Diana that it would be the key to her heart's desire.

Two weeks ago she'd presented her idea to the two partners, and after jumping every time one of them opened her door, they'd finally given her the go-ahead today.

Standing under the trees, Renee smiled at the sky through the water in her eyes. The universe had finally favored her. She stood for several minutes, taking it all in. She didn't know how much time passed before she felt the press of heat and humidity on her skin again. Back on solid ground, she returned to the office.

Humming *one more wedding* as if the phrase were the lyrics to a popular song, she pulled up the file for the Griffin–Shephard nuptials on her computer. Twenty minutes later she was still staring at the screen with no idea what she should do next. Yet her mind was racing with things that needed to be done for her new venture.

A bridal magazine. Her own creation. Directed by her. With her ideas. There was so much to be done. Vendors, suppliers, layouts. Did she still have her contacts in the industry? She had to find a place to work, hire people…she needed to talk to Teddy about using her designs in the first issue. *The first issue*. She nearly screamed.

And a name.

What was she going to call the magazine? She had control, complete control—the partners had given it to her. Releasing a breath, Renee threaded her fingers through her hair, holding her long mane away from her face as her thoughts whirled. A boulder-weight of decisions crushed her shoulders. Where was she going to start?

And how long would it be before Carter found out?

Two weeks later, Renee's blood still sang with joy at the prospect of her new job. She was in New York, and she'd had several appointments to get the magazine's plan started. Initially, she'd been overwhelmed, but a little wine and a pen and paper calmed her down enough to begin cataloging the list of things she needed to accomplish. But before everything could begin rolling, she would have to be a consultant on one more wedding she'd already agreed to do. Then she could give her full attention to *Designed for Brides*, the name she'd chosen for the magazine.

The sun had set and she should be out with friends, painting the town as many shades of red as were in the rainbow. But she wasn't. She was walking toward Rockefeller Center, marveling at the heartbeat of the city and remembering the times she'd rushed past all the wide-eyed tourists and crowded commotion without a second thought.

Reaching Radio City, Renee turned toward Fifth Avenue. A couple holding hands raised them in an arch and she ducked through it. Renee looked after the lovers, remembering when that was her. She should have known better than to come to the city. It was too close to Carter. But New York was huge. Nightlife was abundant. There had to be a million places to go on any given night. The chances of her running into Carter Hampshire were minuscule. She was safe. And maybe he wasn't even in the city anymore. He'd told her he was leaving when he'd said he no longer wanted to see her. Maybe he was still away. Gone to parts unknown.

Renee had departed, too. She'd pulled up stakes and moved to Princeton, NJ, where, to her good fortune, she'd joined Diana Greer and Teddy Granville at Weddings by Diana.

But today she was back in the city she considered home. Out of the blue, her friend, Blair Massey, had called and invited her for dinner. How Blair had known Renee was in the city was a mystery she'd have to uncover later.

Renee had a wedding in Brooklyn tomorrow night. She was here to make sure all the final details were in order, but she couldn't help feeling nervous about reconnecting with people from her old life. That was how she thought of it—her old life. Back before she'd gone to Princeton, when she'd spent much of her time with people like Blair and Carter.

Her cell phone played the wedding march. She jerked around toward a shop window and stopped. Just being in New York put her on edge. She relaxed and put the device to her ear.

"Blair, I'm on my way," she said.

"Glad I caught you. I want to change where we meet," Blair said.

"Well, I'm good and hungry."

"I just discovered Villa Maria's is closed for renovations. Let's meet at Moonraker's on 48th Street."

"Fine," Renee said. "I can be there in fifteen minutes."

"See you then."

She felt a little better after hearing Blair's voice. The night had promise. Renee wouldn't think about Carter at all—he was out of her life. He'd been out of it for three years. There was no reason to think that on a Friday night, in a city this size, she'd run into the one man she never wanted to see again. He was probably in the Hamptons or out having fun with someone else.

Still, she couldn't help thinking about him. They'd worked together, then begun dating. She'd been well on her way to falling in love when—when he'd left her. It had been a clean break, nothing drawn out or lingering. No arguments, accusations or tears, yet three years later Renee felt as bereft as she had the day he'd walked out of her life.

She'd cycled through many possible reasons for their breakup: he wanted to marry someone else, his family disapproved of her, there was another woman, maybe he'd discovered he had a child. The truth was, she just didn't know. And without that closure, her wounded heart had no chance of healing.

Carter Hampshire sat forward in his chair and snapped the trade magazine as if he could shake the words off the page. Dropping it on the desk, he steepled his fingers as he looked down over the story. It was a small notice, but the name jumped off the page.

He hadn't heard about her in three years. Carter looked down again. Of all the print on that page, his eyes went straight to her name.

> Renee Hart, former director of the wedding magazine division at Hampshire Publications, is planning to start her own magazine for brides. The title for the new venture has not been determined at this writing, but Ms. Hart is actively making the rounds.

"Damn," Carter cursed. It couldn't be true. But in his heart, he knew it was something she was fully capable of doing. It wasn't inevitable, but it was logical for Renee. If she hadn't gone to work for one of his competitors, she'd be striking out on her own.

Carter walked to the windows on the 38th floor of the building that bore his family name. The night lights of New York emulated the postcards tourists bought every year.

"Renee Hart." He spoke her name aloud, checking the feel of it on his lips, the sound of it in the empty air. After three years, she still haunted him. A benevolent ghost, whose face and figure was as corporeal as smoke. But in his mind she was almost touchable.

And now she was returning to New York. It made sense that she would return to the city—New York was a publishing powerhouse.

Carter returned to his desk and picked up the office phone. He dialed a number and waited. Blair Massey answered on the first ring.

"Good, you're still there," he said without saying hello. It was seven o'clock, but Blair often worked late. He and Blair had known each other for years. She was a wizard at what she did, and she had mentored Renee. If anyone knew the whole story, it would be Blair.

"I was just on my way out."

"Meet me in the lobby." It was a suggestion, and Carter tried to keep the command tone out of his voice. He hung up.

Blair was waiting when he stepped out of the small paneled room. The fifty-year-old woman looked serious, although she was as impeccably dressed as any model on the fashion pages.

"Carter, I was trying to tell you I already have dinner plans," Blair said. She checked her watch. "And I'm already late."

He took her arm and moved her out of the parade of people. "Where are you eating?"

"At Moonraker's."

"Good, I'll walk with you."

He rushed her along, heading for the door and 48th Street. Blair stopped abruptly and moved to the side. "What's going on?"

"Renee Hart," he answered.

Blair's expression didn't alter more than a millimeter, but the slow breath she exhaled told him she knew.

"What about Renee?" Blair hedged.

"Is she going into competition with us?"

"Where'd you hear that?"

"It doesn't matter. Answer the question."

"She's starting a magazine. It's small stuff. We have no need for alarm."

"I'm not alarmed."

"Then why did you rush down from the 38th floor?"

"The news came as a surprise. How long have you known?"

"A couple of weeks," she said.

"Why didn't you tell me?"

She searched his face a long time. Carter held his expression still.

"It didn't seem that important. When the Weaver Group opened a magazine that competed with our how-to series on home improvement, you didn't consider it newsworthy. Why is Renee's small entry into the bridal market cause for concern? She hasn't even chosen the name of the publication yet. Unless your interest has nothing to do with the business…"

Blair was aware of Carter's past relationship with Renee. He'd never spoken a word to her about it, but Renee was her friend, and women talked.

She checked her watch. "I'm going to be late. Carter, if you're really interested, I'll find out what I can and call you after dinner."

"Find out?" he said. "Is Renee here? Are you having dinner with *her*?"

Blair looked at the sky, exasperated that she'd let him guess who she was meeting.

"I'm going," he said and took her arm. Carter should have thought better of it, but when had he ever been rational where Renee was concerned?

"Carter," Blair said. "She may not want to see you."

Carter stopped and thought about that a moment. "More than likely, she doesn't."

Renee loved to walk in Manhattan. The theater crowds were assembling for the eight o'clock performances. While the sun wouldn't set for another two hours, the streets looked like a parade was about to begin. Cabs blew horns, creating their own music, and Renee smiled as she took in the familiarity. She loved New York. She'd missed it. While Princeton had the university and its own personality, New York was incomparable.

Reaching the restaurant, Renee pulled the door open. She stopped the moment she stepped through it. Blair wasn't alone.

She was sitting with *Carter.*

Renee's throat went dry. Even with his back to her, Renee knew it was him. She wanted to turn and run. Every fiber in her body screamed at her to go, back out and walk away. No, *run* away. But her feet refused to follow instructions.

Then it was too late. Carter glanced into the mirrored surface in front of him and made eye contact. Spasms of memories raced into her. Time that had stood still for three years was unleashed. Memories of their entwined bodies on rumpled sheets broke, freely expanding into a new and confusing world.

Renee mentally shook herself. Carter was her past, her old life—not her present, and certainly not her future. She smiled widely and waved, and Carter turned around. The restaurant was dimly lit. She couldn't see the defined features of his expression, but she was sure he'd known she was coming. Blair must have told him, invited him to attend dinner with them.

Her feet suddenly got the message and she moved toward the table. Seeing Carter again had to happen sometime. She would have liked to have been more prepared for it, but tonight was as good a night as any.

He stood as she approached the table. Blair came around and hugged her.

"Carter, this is an unexpected surprise," Renee said. She put her hand out for him to shake, warding off any chance that he might try to hug or kiss her. She didn't want even the simplest embrace from him.

"How are you, Renee?" he asked.

His voice could be her undoing. It was as deep as she remembered it—in the dark of night, after they'd made love, she loved listening to him talk. She thought of the way the sound surrounded her, caressed her like a physical being that could capture and hold her. Renee felt the heat rise in her face and the burn of her ears. She forced the thoughts back.

"Let's sit down," Blair said.

Blair returned to the banquette seat. Renee took a step to follow her, but Carter pulled out the chair next to him. She looked at it for a second before sitting down. This close to him, she could feel the warmth of his hands near her shoulders.

"Blair tells me you've been working in New Jersey," Carter began as soon as the waiter took her drink order.

She glanced at Blair, a silent admonishment in her eyes. "Weddings by Diana," she told him. "It's a consulting firm. I thought I'd see what the other side of the table looked like."

"But now you're crossing back over," Blair spilled.

Renee wanted to throttle her. She quickly glanced at Carter. He was staring at her and didn't appear to have heard Blair's comment. Carter was a key partner in his family's magazine company, and Hampshire Publications had a division dedicated to the bridal industry. Renee had worked there. Along with bridal magazines, there were divisions covering every other aspects of publication. To Carter, her small entry into the market with Weddings by Diana must seem like a teardrop in the ocean.

"What do you do there?"

"I'm a wedding consultant, and now I'm working on a special project." She wanted to be as vague as possible. "How's Hampshire doing? Are you back there?"

He nodded. "I've been back a few months."

"I see," she said. But she didn't see. She hadn't seen it when he'd left, and she didn't understand it now. What was he doing here? Why had Blair brought him? He couldn't want to see her again, not after what he'd told her when he'd left. "How's the staff?" She needed something to say to get her mind off their relationship.

"There's been a lot of turnover," Blair answered. "At one point, I had to go back and fill in."

"But things have stabilized now," Carter added.

"Of course, if you want to return…" Blair sat forward and looked her straight in the eye. "I'm sure I could find a place for you."

The waiter arrived with their drinks, preventing her from replying.

"Are you open to that?" Carter asked when it was just the three of them.

"Open to what?" she hedged.

"Returning to Hampshire Publications."

Renee wondered if that was the real reason he was at this dinner. Had he come with Blair to ask her to return? And why? The two of them would not be picking up things where they had left off three years earlier. And after the way they'd parted, how could he expect that she would be open to working for him again?

"I'm satisfied where I am for the moment," she said. It was good practice to leave the door open to possibilities, so she did. But she had no intention of ever walking through that door, or even of ever seeing him again.

Their dinner arrived and Renee remembered little of the conversation after that. She was concentrating on the mechanics of eating. Cutting the steak, lifting it to her mouth, chewing and swallowing. Carter's presence unnerved her. Blair should have prepared her for his appearance. The conversation turned to their lives together, the life before. Carter spoke of the long nights in the office closing the magazine, the minor crises they'd averted just in time, the cold pizza they'd consumed when issues took three times as long to finish as expected.

Renee's mind tried to wander to other places—memories of putting the magazine to bed right before she and Carter went to bed—but she blocked those as much as she could. She smiled, laughed at the appropriate places and made a comment now and then to let them know she was listening.

By the time the waiter took dessert orders, Renee noticed she'd only pushed the food around on her plate. She refused dessert but accepted the coffee.

"Renee, how do you find working as a bridal consultant?" Blair turned the subject to the present.

Taking a sip of her coffee, she took a moment to answer. "The brides are a delight," she said honestly. "Their wedding day is the most important thing in their lives, and it was a joy making it happen."

"You didn't find the whole thing a little stressful?" Carter asked.

"No more than the stress of getting a monthly magazine out. For a wedding, I have an entire year to get all the details in place."

What was he trying to do? Renee wondered. Why was he deliberately baiting her? She wasn't the one who ran out on their relationship.

"What about yourself?" Blair commented. "Did working with all those real-life brides make you want to be one?"

Thankfully, Renee was not holding her cup. It was the last question she expected. She felt more than saw Carter turn to listen to her answer. Color flooded her face and burned up her neck to her ears.

"No," she said. It was a lie and she hoped neither Blair nor Carter could tell. "There are too many details that need attention for me to think of anything except the bride's plan. I never even thought of what I might want. Usually I'm just suggesting something to the bride or her mother."

"You must be the exception to the rule," Blair stated.

"What rule?"

"The one that says every woman plans her wedding the moment she enters puberty. I remember choosing my wedding gown while I was still in high school." She smiled as if the happy memory was only a day past. Blair had been married for seventeen years. Renee knew that Blair wanted that euphoric wedding feeling to last forever. That's why she'd gone to Hampshire Publications and had been there so long. When Renee had applied for the job in the bridal department, right out of college, it was Blair who'd given her the opportunity to prove herself. And it was Blair's enthusiasm that had rubbed off on Renee.

"One of the partners, Theresa Granville, designs gowns," Renee said.

"I've heard of her," Blair said. "She's making quite a name for herself."

Renee nodded. "She's had a couple of designs that stopped me in my tracks."

"So, you're interested in getting married." Carter stated it as if it was fact.

"A lot of people are." She skirted the question. "If they weren't, we'd all be out of a job."

He nodded, using that up-and-down movement of his head that was so slight that she wouldn't have seen it if she wasn't already familiar with it. It was Carter's way of conceding the point.

The waiter returned with a pot of coffee. She refused

a refill. It was time to put some distance between herself and Carter Hampshire.

"I'm afraid I'd going to have to eat and run," she began. "I have a wedding in the morning so I have to be up early checking the final details," Renee lied. Her wedding was actually in the evening, but she wanted some time to go over every detail. It was her last consulting job and she wanted it to turn out perfect.

Renee stood. Carter stood, too.

"Blair, thank you for dinner. We'll have to do this again sometime." She gave Blair a look that said, *alone*.

"Thank Carter. He's paying."

Renee looked at Carter, but said nothing.

"I'll see you to your hotel," Carter said.

"That won't be necessary. It's not far and Blair needs the escort much more than I do."

Blair stood up. "I have an escort," she said. At that moment, Campbell Massey came through the door as if on cue. Blair went into his arms and they kissed. Then he turned to Renee.

"Renee, it's great to see you." He swept her into his arms for a bear hug. He kissed her on the cheek and set her back with a happy smile. Renee liked Camp. She'd liked him from the moment they'd met almost ten years ago. "You are just as beautiful as ever."

"And you are just as much a flatterer as you've ever been."

"No flattery," he said. "Isn't she beautiful, Carter?"

Both Blair and Camp looked to Carter for an answer. Renee turned from Camp, her body suddenly going cold.

"She's quite ravishing," he stated, his voice low.

To her ears it sounded hungry, sexually hungry. Her knees threatened to turn to water.

"Well, we'd better be off," Blair said, taking Camp's arm. "Carter, you will see Renee back to her hotel?"

He nodded. The couple headed for the door, Carter and Renee trailed them. Out on the street, Renee turned to him. "I know you have a long way to go. You don't have to go with me. I'm not that far from here."

Carter looked over her head. "The Westley?" he said. It was an independent hotel. Renee liked patronizing small businesses. However, she hadn't realized she was so transparent to Carter.

Especially after three years.

But the truth was, he was wrong. She wasn't at the Westley, but there was no need to correct him.

Carter put his hand on her lower back to guide her toward the hotel. She stepped aside, forcing him to drop it. She walked quickly toward the hotel. It was merely three blocks from the restaurant. They covered the distance in silence. Outside the entrance Renee turned to Carter.

"Thank you. It was nice seeing you again." The words were false, but Renee wanted to get away from him as quickly as she could. She turned. Carter caught her arm and pulled her around.

"I want to talk to you."

"I have an early call. I really need to go," she said.

"I remember when we spent long nights together and still made deadline."

Her head whipped up and she stared at him. "We

were different people then," Renee said. She was in love then. He was not.

Carter pushed open the door to the hotel. He was right behind Renee. She had to move or feel his body form-fitted to hers. Avoiding the bar, she went to a collection of chairs near the back wall.

"What is it you want to talk about?" Renee asked.

He sat, leaned forward and rubbed his hands together as if it was cold. Then he looked her straight in the eye. "Are you sure you want to continue with weddings? You could just as easily return to Hampshire."

It wouldn't be easy and she knew it, even if he didn't. Renee took a moment, probing Carter's face for something to give her a clue to his motives. She found nothing. But she felt there was a meaning under his words. She couldn't pull it into focus, but Carter wanted something from her. She just didn't know what it was—yet.

"Renee?" he prompted.

"I've already given you my answer."

"But have you thought about what I'm offering?"

"No, Carter. Why don't you tell me? Just what is it you're offering that you think will entice me back to Hampshire Publications?"

Carter adjusted his position, clasping his hands between his knees. Renee's instinct was to move back, allowing herself more personal space. At the last moment, she decided to go on the offensive. She moved in closer as if they were conspirators about to exchange the plans for a secret weapon.

"First, you're in charge of everything." He spread his hands. "The entire bridal division is yours."

"And I would report directly to you? That is, I assume you're the head of editorial."

He nodded. Renee thought she saw the faintest look of smugness on his face.

"We've worked together before and that proved beneficial."

"That's not a positive," she told him and was rewarded by seeing his face fall. It was only for a moment, and only someone who knew his features intimately would have noticed it.

"Whatever you're being paid by that little business, I'll double."

Renee stood up. Carter got to his feet, too. She didn't like the way he'd insulted her business, as if only a huge company like his was worthwhile. Pointing out that his father had begun the huge empire would have been a waste of breath.

"Money," she said. "You think you can find my price, and I'll just return to Hampshire Publications." She shook her head, a satisfied smile edging the corners of her lips up. "I'm not for sale, Carter. And especially not to a Hampshire."

Chapter 2

Her last wedding. Renee watched as the new Mr.
and Mrs. took their places on the dais as the reception
began. Everything about the wedding had been technically correct.

Renee had had no complaints, hadn't had to talk
anyone down from a frantic rethinking of what marriage meant. She'd had no supplies arrive late, no mis-
haps with the bride's gown, no groom needing to be
reminded of when and where to stand and no issues
with any of the bridesmaids. The mothers of both the
bride and groom complimented Renee's efficiency. Everything was going like clockwork. For a wedding consultant, it was nirvana—the type of execution they lived
for. Perfect. The bride beamed and the groom's smile

was from ear to ear. It was exactly the swan song she wished for.

But all that efficiency did was leave her time to think about Carter. She'd tried for the last three years to put him out of her mind. She'd thought she'd done it. That was, until she'd seen him sitting at the dinner table last night. Her heart had thudded against her ribs so hard she'd thought he would be able to hear it.

It was frightening that he knew where she would choose to stay. The only reason she wasn't at the Westley was because Weddings by Diana had an unoccupied guesthouse available. They used it for brides who were from out of town and needed a place to dress before the ceremony. Occasionally, brides came into New York to check out accommodations. The guesthouse was part of some of the high-end packages.

Renee had allowed Carter to believe she was at the Westley. She'd even gotten on the elevator, but only ridden it to the mezzanine. After ten minutes she'd slipped out the back entrance and taken a taxi to the guesthouse.

A burst of laughter brought Renee back to the festivities. The bride and groom were laughing, yet the love in their eyes as they looked at each other was visible. Renee felt her own eyes mist over. For a moment, she saw herself as the bride and Carter as her groom. She blinked, shaking the image free. It was time to go.

Her last act was to let the bridal party know she was leaving and to make sure there was nothing left undone. Renee's smile was wide as she congratulated the couple, said her goodbyes and started the walk back to the car that would return her to the Brides by Diana guesthouse.

She hadn't thought she'd be as emotional as she'd been throughout the day. Maybe it was because she knew it was her last wedding. She'd even repeated the vows to herself as the minister spoke them. Or maybe it was her mixed feelings about the changes ahead. Although she was excited about the magazine, there was also a certain amount of fear in her mind.

She also thought of Carter and Blair, and their question about her feelings on weddings drifted into her mind. As she'd listened to the couple's vows, they seemed to have more weight than in the past. Did it have anything to do with Carter suddenly reappearing in her life?

There was a time when she'd entertained the thought of marriage. She'd fantasized about it, but that's as far as it had gotten. Even after moving to Princeton, seeing all the brides in their gowns made her imagine walking down the aisle with Carter.

It was safe, she told herself—she was leaving New York in a couple of days, regardless of what she'd said to Carter. She'd be back occasionally, and it was inevitable that they would meet at the same events. But Renee would be able to see him across a room and not have her heart jump.

Carter had changed. Gone was that boyish quality that used to vie for dominance on his face. His expression was more serious than before. His hair was shorter and the mustache that used to tickle her nose had been replaced with a clean-shaven look. He'd been on the basketball team in high school and college, and his body today still had the lean hardness of a twenty-year-old.

Renee wondered where he'd been for the last few years. He'd blown her off as if she were nothing to him. So why was it she still felt as if there was some unfinished business that needed closure? Carter had told her there was nothing between them. And there wasn't. They'd never gotten to the point where things change for better or worse. The place where you decide if you want to step over a line, or you realize the relationship has no place to go.

He hadn't waited for that moment. Carter knew earlier than the launch. And he'd spared her from any further involvement. At least, that's what she'd told herself. So what now? Why was her mind stuck on him and when she'd see him again? She thought their discussion last night would have discouraged him from trying to convince her to return to work at Hampshire.

Yet he'd called her cell phone during the ceremony and insisted on meeting with her at her hotel. No doubt he'd gotten the number from Blair. If she'd had time to banter with him, Renee would have refused the meeting. But in the back of her mind she knew she wanted to see him.

Back at the guesthouse, Renee changed from the suit she'd worn to the wedding. She wanted Carter to see her in control, happy with herself and commanding her own future. She put on a straight red dress and added a pearl necklace and matching teardrop earrings. She swung her hair up and to the side, anchoring it with a wavy pearl comb. Checking her image in the mirror, she left the town house in time to meet him in the hotel lobby.

Carter arrived through the revolving door just as

she stepped off the elevator and waited. It was all she could do to keep her breath from leaving her body. The contrast of his dark suit and white shirt emphasized his skin. She took in the broadness of the shoulders she used to lay her head on. If he'd gained an ounce in three years, she'd need a microscope to find it. He started toward her. Renee remembered his easy gait, the confidence that wrapped around him like a second skin.

What hadn't changed was his smile. White teeth gleamed at her, and try as she might, she had to return it. He stopped two feet away. Despite her five-foot-five-inch frame and the heels that raised her up four additional inches, she still had to look up at him to see his face.

"You look beautiful," he murmured. It was a whisper, so low she barely heard it.

Renee felt the rush of heat flush her cheeks.

"Thanks. You're quite the figure, too."

He moved a step closer to her. Renee instinctively knew he planned to embrace her. The thought made her both excited and scared.

Taking a step back, she said, "Don't."

Carter stopped. "I was only going to kiss your cheek. Isn't that what friends do? And we've known each other for years."

"No, we haven't." She shook her head. "We're strangers."

"Strangers?" Carter's brows rose.

"You've been gone for three years. For all I know, you could be married with three children. The same could be true of me. So we are strangers. You've

changed. I've changed. We're not the same people we
were three years ago. You wouldn't hug someone you'd
just met. So consider me that someone."

Carter took a step back. For a long moment he stared
at her as if assessing who this new woman was. Renee
withstood his scrutiny.

"I thought we'd go to Mile's End."

"My last wedding was today, and I'm leaving early.
Would you mind eating here?" She gestured toward
the restaurants that were at the back of the building on
the ground floor. "I've already made us a reservation."

Carter shrugged and smiled. Renee understood that
she'd thwarted his plans. She had plans of her own, and
traveling to a place they'd spent time together wasn't
on her agenda.

"I must admit, I was a little surprised to find you on
the other end of the phone asking me to meet you for
dinner," Renee said when they were seated.

He smiled. It didn't reach his eyes.

"I'm glad you came."

"Why is that? What do you want to talk about? I was
sure we'd settled everything last night."

He took a moment to gather his thoughts. Renee wondered if this meeting had something to do with them
as a couple. There was no *them*. There had never really
been a *them*. She'd thought there was, that there could
be, but obviously Carter had other plans.

"Your name has come up several times in the last
few days," Carter said.

She didn't react. She waited for him to go on. "Come
up where?"

"Along the avenues of publisher's row. There's a rumor going around that you're going into competition with me."

Renee leaned forward. "With *you*?"

"With my company."

"What kind of competition? There are several different kinds of businesses you're responsible for."

"Magazines," he said. "Specifically bridal magazines."

Renee smiled. She picked up her glass of wine and took a sip. Then she replaced it and sat back. "Not a rumor," she said.

"It's not a rumor?"

"Can't be a rumor if it's true." She waited a moment, then asked, "Weren't you listening last night when Blair mentioned my new job?"

His brows rose in surprise. "I didn't think she was serious."

Renee stared at him. "And the notice in the trades?"

She knew Carter read all the trade publications that detailed news about the various magazines Hampshire sold. He had a huge capacity for remembering and recalling what he read, and Renee knew he wouldn't miss the small paragraph bearing her name.

"You are serious?" he asked rhetorically.

"Don't look so surprised. I'm fully capable of running a magazine. You should know that. I ran Hampshire's division for three years."

"You're very capable."

"So, why are we here?" She spread her hands.

Again Carter waited a long moment before speaking. Renee wondered when he'd picked up that habit. He was usually decisive, in control, always knew what to say, how to act.

"I want you to come back to Hampshire Publications."

"You have got to be kidding," Renee said, her voice breathy and low. "We've already talked about this. I'm perfectly happy where I am. Why would I come back to Hampshire?"

"It's a profitable company, and it's a place where you fit in. You know some of the employees and they all respect you."

Renee looked at him. She knew Blair Massey. But with three years gone, she might not know most of the people anymore. Magazine publishing was a place that lent itself to turnover.

"Is Hampshire in trouble?" He'd said it was profitable, but that didn't mean the bridal division was afloat.

Carter shook his head. Renee looked for any sign of slowness, any inkling that he was hiding something. She found nothing to make her believe he wasn't telling her the whole truth.

"You're great at seeing what works and what doesn't in the magazine. Your ideas are always good and sales took an upward climb when you put your mark on the magazine. You could have the whole package with us. I can't imagine you would want to compete with us."

Hackles went up on the back of her neck. "I'm just a little business," Renee began. "In fact, at this point, I'm still scouting out the business. You're a conglomerate with magazines, textbooks, novels, comics and a score of peripherals. You can't be afraid of me."

"It's not fear. Hampshire wants you to be comfortable, and we don't want your reputation to suffer with a start-up."

"Well, that takes the cake. You believe that nothing outside of your control is worthy of doing?"

"I didn't say that."

"Didn't you?" She stopped and narrowed her eyes. "You said Hampshire wasn't in trouble. What about the bridal division? Has there been a dip in sales?"

Again Carter sat forward and looked at her. "I'll be frank with you. The division could do better. When you were directing it, it was at the top of the market. We've lost some market share—not enough to be concerned about. But we don't want to lose any more. Bringing you onboard would ensure that."

"Thanks for the vote of confidence, but—"

"Don't answer yet." He stopped her with one hand up. "Think about it overnight. Give yourself time to get used to the idea. We can meet tomorrow."

"I won't be here tomorrow," she lied.

"Renee, can't you give me a few minutes, lunch or dinner? Princeton can't have that great a need for you that you can't spare an old friend a few hours."

Renee felt guilty, although she had no reason to. She wasn't actually leaving until Sunday, and other than additional planning, she had a morning appointment tomorrow. After that, there was no one she could call, no arrangements she could make until Monday. But she didn't want Carter to think his presence influenced her in any way.

"All right, Carter," she said. "I'll meet you tomorrow. After lunch," she emphasized. He wasn't going to convince her to return to Hampshire Publications over a New York steak or a salad at lunch.

He smiled. She saw a little of the old Carter in that smile. A momentary flash of the man who wrestled the sheets with her burst into her mind. The same man who'd told her he was leaving and not interested in pursuing a relationship.

That was Carter Hampshire.

Carter paced the floor of his spacious apartment on Fifth Avenue overlooking Central Park. The view was spectacular, but Carter wasn't interested in it today. He punched the button on his cell phone disconnecting the call. Walking to the windows, he looked out on the traffic below. Was she down there? Renee Hart wasn't registered at the Westley Hotel. She hadn't been registered there and checked out. She'd *never* been there. Yet he'd taken her inside, seen her get on the elevator to go to her room. They'd had dinner in the restaurant last night, but she didn't have a room in that hotel. Why had she let him think she did?

Where was she?

They were supposed to meet today. Carter glanced at his watch. He wouldn't be able to meet her—he'd gotten word that his father was in the hospital and he needed to go to the Hamptons. His train left in an hour, but he hadn't been able to reach Renee. She hadn't answered her cell, and when he'd tried the hotel's number he'd been told there was no one named Renee Hart registered.

She had a wedding, he remembered. Maybe the wedding party hotel was where Renee was staying. Quickly, he went to his desk and dialed the number of the Waldorf Astoria. Renee was not registered there, either. He calmly thanked the person on the phone and disconnected.

"She lied to me," Carter said out loud. Getting up, he returned to the window. He needed to explain to her why he'd left three years ago. He'd wanted to do it last night, but the moment he'd seen her he'd known she wasn't ready to listen. So he'd tried to convince her to come back to Hampshire Publications. He wanted her there, and her job was open. When she'd been in charge, the magazine had led the industry. He knew she'd regain the share they'd lost, but she wasn't interested. Carter wanted to try and change her mind, see her again, but she'd evaded him. And now he had to go out to the Island.

He thought about how she'd looked. She was still the tall, thin woman he remembered, but there was more confidence in her appearance. And she was even more beautiful than she'd been three years ago. Her hair was black and glossy. When a curl had escaped, he'd almost reached across the table and threaded his fingers through it. Yet she'd told him he was a stranger. She couldn't know that she'd never be a stranger to him.

He was used to seeing models. Renee wasn't a model, yet her body mirrored that of the best he'd ever seen.

Her waist was thin and nipped in at just the right angle. Her hips curved to exactly match the contours of his hands. Carter's fingers trembled at the thought of touching her again.

A horn sounded below. He checked the time. He had to go now or he'd never make the train. Leaving Renee another text message, he left the apartment and headed for Penn Station wondering why she wouldn't take his calls and why she'd lied to him.

Renee sighed, one hand going to her breast as she studied the text message from Carter. He'd canceled their meeting. She wouldn't have to see him. Her shoulders dropped and she frowned. He hadn't said why.

Her morning meeting was over. It had been long and productive. To keep from being interrupted, she'd put her phone on silent. It had buzzed several times, but she'd ignored it. People who knew her knew she wasn't the type who instantly answered every call. With her brides, it was better to give them a little time before they reached her. By then, their crisis had been reduced to a minor problem or it had been resolved.

With nothing else to do, Renee returned to the Weddings by Diana guesthouse. The place was warm and inviting; however, it was not a place where anyone cooked. Renee had planned to have lunch before meeting Carter, and now she was hungry.

Opening the refrigerator she found only water and soft drinks. A few nonperishables were in the cabinets.

Carter had only said that something had come up. It must have been important, she thought, as she closed the refrigerator, or maybe he'd come to his senses and realized she couldn't be persuaded to return to Hampshire Publications.

She felt deflated. She'd worked herself up for another meeting with Carter, and he'd canceled it without a reason. This was just like three years ago when he'd left with no real reason. At least today he'd sent her a text. Squaring her shoulders, Renee made a decision.

She picked her phone up from the kitchen counter. Most of the people she knew in New York also knew Carter. She wouldn't call any of them. And Blair was out of the question. Then she had an idea. She sent a text message to her cousin Dana and invited her to dinner.

Often the two cousins shared a meal while they Skyped, but Renee wished she could see Dana face-to-face.

When? Dana's reply came almost immediately. Unlike Renee, Dana was always on her phone. If she hadn't answered immediately Renee would've wondered if something was wrong.

Six o'clock, Renee texted. It didn't take long for them to work out the details. Dana loved New York and said she'd come in from Connecticut and meet Renee at Grand Central Terminal.

She spent the afternoon catching up on email, then met Dana's train at the station. Taking a taxi, they got out of the tourist district and went to an Italian restaurant Renee was familiar with.

Dana smiled. "What's up?" She popped a fork full of lettuce into her mouth. They usually ordered salads and wine when they had these talks. But tonight Renee had ordered fettuccine Alfredo and a sangria.

"Not much," Renee said. "We haven't talked in a while. I thought it was time."

The two had grown up together and were closer than sisters. Renee had a twin brother, and she loved him, but there were things that only another woman would understand.

"So," Dana dragged the word out. A conspiratorial smile curled her lips. "Did you see Carter?"

Just like Dana to cut right to the heart. "You know, every time I come to New York you ask me that same question."

"And you evade it." Dana took another bite from her salad.

"I'm not here to see him."

"That wasn't my question," Dana said.

"He wasn't at the wedding."

"Again, not my question. Which means you saw him."

"Dinner, last night."

"Dinner! Do tell. Give me the details."

"No details. Well, one. He offered me a job."

"Back at Hampshire Publications?"

Renee heard the wonder in her cousin's voice. She took a moment to eat part of her fettuccine before nodding.

"What did you tell him?"

"That I was happy where I was."

"Are you?"

"Dana," Renee admonished.

Dana smiled slowly. "How does he look?"

"Good enough to eat."

"Well?" Dana prompted.

Renee said nothing.

Dana poked her bottom lip out like a child who wasn't getting her way.

"You can't want me to get involved with him again. After how he broke up with me. And what a basket case I was then."

Dana's face became very serious. Renee wondered if she was remembering her fiancé. He was a Marine who died in an explosion in the Middle East. Since then Dana had been alone, but she loved setting up her friends.

Dana leaned forward and said, "You wouldn't be getting involved *again*. Because you've never gotten over him."

"That's no reason to put myself in harm's way. I've survived the last three years. I can get through the rest."

"But what about when you move back to New York? You'll be in the same city and in the same profession. It's inevitable that you'll run into each other."

"So, we'll run into each other sometimes." Renee thought it couldn't be any worse than the meeting last night. Then she'd been ambushed. Next time she'd be prepared for his possible appearance, even expecting it.

"You can handle that?"

"Sure I can." Renee's voice was strong, but she wasn't that sure of herself. She'd been tested last night, and she'd survived. It had to get easier as time went by.

But even though it had been three years, her heart had jumped into her throat when she'd seen him.

She would have to weather whatever came.

"I'll be fine," Renee told Dana. "Besides, in the next few months, I'll be too busy to think of anyone. Getting a new venture off the ground is a day-and-night proposition." Renee hadn't mentioned it to Diana and Teddy, but she wanted to launch in six months.

Dana gave her a long look, then dropped her eyes. "What's happening with the new magazine?"

Her cousin had been the first person Renee had called when the project had been approved.

"Oh, good progress. And I found a place to live."

"Where?"

"It's a house. Not an apartment. And it's in the museum district."

"How'd you do that?" Dana's brows rose.

"Remember my Aunt Olivia?" Renee asked.

"Vaguely."

"She lives in the museum district."

"You're going to live with her?" Dana frowned.

Renee didn't answer immediately. She knew Dana was trying to determine Aunt Olivia's age. She was a spry eighty-three-year-old.

"You were never a favorite of hers, if I'm remembering correctly," Dana added.

Renee smiled. "She mellowed after I started working at Hampshire. I used to visit her often."

"And now you're moving in with her?" Dana's voice showed incredulity.

"Not exactly," Renee responded.

"Okay, stop dancing around and explain it to me."

"I called her a few weeks ago and she invited me to lunch. During the afternoon she told me she was leaving the city. She'd put the house up for sale but had no offers."

"Where's she going?"

"She's got a brother in North Carolina. She's going there to be near him."

"Doesn't she have children? I mean eighty-three is a hard age to pick up and move."

Renee shook her head. "She had a son. He was killed in Vietnam."

"So she's selling you the house?"

She's letting me rent it with an option to buy."

"That was lucky."

Renee nodded. "There are some legal papers I have to sign tomorrow."

Renee's cell phone rang and the photo of the caller appeared. Renee stared at it.

"Aren't you going to answer it?"

Renee said nothing. The ringing continued, causing a high-pitched whine in her ears. A sound she hadn't heard in years. It couldn't be coming from the phone, but pinging back and forth inside her brain.

"Renee, are you all right?" Dana asked. "Who's on the phone?"

Renee lifted the small device and held it up. Dana drew in a mouthful of air.

Carter's photo stared back at her.

Renee hit Reject to stop the ringing. It rang three

more times before she and Dana left the restaurant and
returned to the town house.

As they stepped in the door, the ringing began again.

"You're going to have to answer it sometime. Obviously, the man is persistent," Dana said. "And it could
be something important."

A hundred thoughts flashed through Renee's mind,
but she couldn't pin any of them down. Why was he
calling still? Why hadn't she deleted his photo from
her cell phone? She hadn't seen it in three years, hadn't
thought of it. It just stayed there, like some specter waiting for the perfect time to strike.

Renee pulled her phone out of her purse. She didn't
hear Dana leave the room, but as she inspected the
phone, Renee noticed she was alone. The phone continued its insistent ring. Renee continued to stare at it.
Her finger hovered above the reject button. Then she
quickly pushed Accept. She wouldn't let him intimidate her any longer.

"Carter," she said, using her happiest smile, one she
did not feel.

"You deliberately deceived me about where you were
staying," he began without a hello.

"I did," she admitted. She heard him swallow. He
obviously wasn't expecting her to admit the truth.

"Why?"

"It's a privacy thing. I didn't want to be disturbed."

"I disturb you?"

She saw the shadow of a smile on his lips.

"Not in the way you're thinking," Renee told him.
"And you canceled our meeting today. So we're even."

"I had to cancel the meeting. My father is in the hospital. I had to come out to the Hamptons."

"Oh," she said. "I'm sorry. Is he going to be all right?"

"They're still doing some tests, but you know my dad. He's a powerhouse. And he's not as bad as my mother made me believe."

Renee knew Joseph and Emily Hampshire—Joseph had run the magazine empire for years. He was a fair man and loved by his employees. She liked him a lot. His wife, Emily, was a fashion designer, and she could be excitable. Having a sick husband qualified as a good reason.

"Please let him know he's in my thoughts," Renee said.

"He'll like that. He always liked you," Carter said. "When I get back, I want to reschedule our meeting."

"Carter, we had a chance three years ago. You chose to end it. I've moved on with my life, and I suggest you do the same."

"I didn't call you to rekindle a love affair."

Renee took a deep breath. She felt a knife slip into her heart. They hadn't had an affair, and the love had only been on her side. "Then why are you calling?"

"We talked about a position at Hampshire last night. You were supposed to give me an answer tonight."

"I respectfully decline," she said.

"Respectfully?" he questioned. "Are we going to be that formal?"

"It's considered good manners to be formal with people you've just met. Remember, we are strangers."

"Oh, right. We're strangers. So, if we are strangers,

then why don't we act like we just met and we can discuss my offer like adults?"

"We've already discussed it, and I'm happy with my current position."

"I hear you have a house."

Renee gulped. How could he know that? She hadn't even told Blair.

"I guess that means you're moving back to the city permanently."

Did she hear hope in his voice? Did she want to hear it? Renee mentally shook herself. Carter didn't want her, only her expertise in the bridal industry.

"I'll be working and living here. But, like I said, I'm keeping the position I have. And how did you know?"

"So, you're not leaving town as you said."

"No," she answered. And you didn't tell me how you knew."

"My mother told me."

"Your mother?" Renee frowned.

He nodded. "My mother designs for Lealia Sauvageau. She and her husband own the house next to the one you bought."

"I recognize Lealia Sauvageau's name," Renee said. "What does she got to do with this?"

"She'd ordered a gown from my mother and would no longer need it since she and her husband have sold their house and are moving. In the course of conversation, Lealia told my mom that the house next to them was being rented by a bridal magazine owner."

"And you naturally thought I was the only owner of a bridal magazine in town?"

"Naturally," he replied. "Especially since you're the only one coming from Princeton."

Renee closed her eyes.

"Small world," she said flatly.

"Isn't it? Lealia thought she was helping my mom by giving her a lead for another place to showcase her designs."

"I see."

"Anyway, now that you're going to be here, we can have that dinner tomorrow night. It'll be a small celebration, marking your return to New York."

"Carter, I'm very busy and we've already met for lunch once. We don't need to prolong this…" She didn't know what to call it. It wasn't friendship.

"You're not afraid of being across a table from me, are you?" he interrupted.

She laughed. "You're not going to play the fear card. You know I have no fear where you're concerned. But I decide who I want to eat with and that has nothing to do with you laying down a challenge."

"So the answer is…"

Renee weighed the invitation for a long time. She saw Dana in the doorway gesturing for her to accept. Dana could only hear one side of the conversation, but she could tell Carter had asked to see Renee. Renee knew it was best to stay away from him, but if she was going to live in New York and inevitably run into him, she would have to become comfortable in his presence.

"Fine," she said. "Dinner tomorrow."

"You're not going to stand me up, are you?"

"I keep my word," she said.

"Where are you staying?" he asked.

Renee was not about to give him the address. She knew he often showed up early for a date, and then they wouldn't make it out.

"You discovered I'm renting a house, yet you don't know where I'm staying." She paused, then said, "I'll meet you at the Rainbow Room at seven."

She heard his sigh through the phone. "Rainbow Room it is."

"Tomorrow, then."

"Good night, Renee."

She clicked the end button without saying anything. The tone of his voice with those three words had taken away her power of speech. Did he know he was doing that? Was it on purpose, designed to throw her off guard? She'd heard those words in the dark, after a fervent night of lovemaking. They'd wrapped around her, folded her in a blanket of warmth, the way his arms had. She'd voluntarily gone there, taken his hand and run with him into an unknown place that held the promise of forever.

Renee had never wanted to leave it. She'd wanted to see the next bend, open the next door and find what surprises awaited her. She'd wanted to jump from cloud to cloud and go with the man of her dreams.

In his arms, she had been blinded. She'd forgotten that dreams have the permanence of smoke. And it had blown up in her face. The relationship had hardly begun before the burning between them had been doused, leaving only smoke and cinders. It had taken her a while to get herself under control, to not open her eyes in the morning and find herself thinking of him. But she was at that point now. And there was no way she was allowing him back into her heart.

Chapter 3

Renee took a deep breath and stepped off the elevator on the 65th floor of Rockefeller Center. She wore a formfitting red dress with shoes that sparkled. It had taken her a while to decide what to wear. This wasn't a date, she kept telling herself. But who goes to the Rainbow Room just to eat? Then she decided to throw caution to the wind and dress as well as she could. She'd show Carter what he was missing and then not let him touch it.

Carter was standing by the door when she arrived. He smiled, looking her over.

"I should have worn sunglasses," he said, his smile wide. "You're dazzling."

Renee couldn't help returning it. "Thank you."

He didn't wink at her, but the slight change in his

eyes told her he approved. The thought warmed her in places she wished it didn't. He reached to give her a hug, and Renee steeled herself. She stopped him before he could pull her into his arms.

"Still strangers?" he asked.

"Good evening, Carter." Renee ignored his question. He was dressed in a black suit with a gleaming white shirt and shoes that had a mirror shine. The man could be a GQ model instead of a publishing magnate.

"Your table is ready," the maître d' said.

Renee followed the black-coated man to a table for two next to the large windows that looked out on the city. The night was clear, giving them a panoramic view of the Empire State Building and Washington Square Park.

For a while, Renee buried her face in her menu. She knew what she wanted, but spent time looking over the selections as if she were deciding. She was avoiding looking at Carter, and now that they were here, she wondered what they had to talk about. It couldn't be their past.

"Are you hiding?" Carter asked.

She closed the menu and laid it on the side of the table. "I was checking over the new entrées. It's been a while since I was here."

For a moment he only stared at her. Renee stifled a smile. She'd accomplished her goal. Carter gazed at her with appreciation, and she could see a glimmer of attraction in his eyes.

A waiter brought them a bottle of champagne and went through the ritual of opening and pouring the wine into flutes. Taking their order, he quietly disappeared. Carter raised his glass and Renee clinked hers with it, the bell sound of the crystal rang clear.

"Congratulations," he said.

"On what?" Renee asked.

"Your move."

"I haven't moved yet."

"Tell me about the new house. Where is it?"

"It's up in the museum district." She avoided giving him a specific address. It wasn't like he'd show up on her doorstep, but if she was going to keep her heart intact, she wanted him to know as little about her as possible.

"Will you be launching your magazine from there?"

Their food arrived, and she took a moment to take a bite and swallow before answering. "Now that I've secured living space, I'm looking for offices for the magazine."

"So you'll be back for a site search."

Renee felt the color creep under her skin. She'd walked into that. "I will."

"When?"

"I have no current plans."

"Will you let me know when you return?" he asked straight out.

"No," she said without hesitation.

"Why not?"

"I'm not here to see you. When I come, my time will be limited. As you've said, launching a new magazine takes a lot of work."

"So you're not dating." He stated it as a fact.

The switch in subject gave her whiplash. "My love life is not your concern," she told him. "And yours is no concern of mine, but why is it you're here with me instead of being out with some other woman? As I remember, you never had a problem getting dates. I don't imagine that has changed."

"I'm between women at the moment."

Renee took a bite of her food, but she regretted it the moment she put it in her mouth. She was sure she couldn't swallow it. Yet the fact that he was unattached caused a small flutter in her stomach.

"What about you? Married? Divorced? Is there someone back in New Jersey waiting for you?" Carter asked.

"Not married, not divorced. If you're asking if I'm dating, yes," she lied.

There was no one special back in Princeton. There were men she knew, and if she needed a date, she'd have no trouble getting one. But there was no one she'd run to with good or bad news.

"Anyone special?" Carter persisted.

"You're getting really personal," Renee said.

He sat back as if he was backing off. "I apologize. It's just been a long time since we've seen each other. I was only trying to catch up."

"I see." Renee said it slowly. She put her fork down and folded her arms along the edge of the table. "I have a question I've been dying to ask for three years," she said.

Carter didn't hesitate, but Renee could see the change in him. He must have known what was coming. "Go ahead," he said.

"What happened three years ago? I felt like we were going along smoothly, then the floor fell away and there was nothing holding me up."

"It was timing, Renee. It just didn't work."

"Well, answer this, then. What's changed in the past three years that you want to be in my company now?"

The air around their table grew instantly heavy and despite the conversation of the other diners, the room felt utterly quiet.

"Nothing's changed," Carter said. And he meant it. He still felt the same way about Renee as he had when he left to go to Afghanistan.

Carter had known this question would come sometime. When he'd left there had been no guarantee that he would return, and he'd wanted to save Renee from what could happen. Three years ago it had seemed like the right thing to do. But tonight, as he looked at her beautiful face and the way her body moved in that red dress, he wasn't so sure.

He had to tell her, but not right now.

"Do you mind if we postpone that question until the end of the night? I will explain, but I don't want to start the evening with that."

Renee nodded. Carter could tell this was not the response she was expecting. But he needed more time to decide how to tell her.

"What's it like working as a consultant?" he asked, hoping to lighten the mood.

Renee leaned back and seemed to relax. The tension bunching the muscles in the back of his neck relaxed.

"It's the other side of the table," she said. "Working directly with the people who buy the gowns we put in the magazines gave me a totally new perspective on what they want and how to please them."

"Do you like that side of the business?"

She nodded. "Like any job, it has its good and bad moments. For the most part, they were good," she said. "I love the gowns, and I love seeing the glow on the brides' faces when they see themselves for the first time in white lace or satin. Often the emotions surprise them so suddenly that tears spill down their faces. That's something we can't duplicate in the pages of a bridal magazine."

"Is that what you want to do?" Carter asked. "Return to the magazine world so you can infuse emotion into the pages?"

Renee seemed to take a moment to ponder that. "Yes," she said, speaking in a whisper. Her face showed she'd hadn't thought of it until that moment. "I like production and development. I like layout and finding new ways of presenting the designs. Otherwise, I wouldn't be about to launch a magazine."

"But now you know what you want to do to make this one different from the crowd of bridal issues already on the newsstands."

"I suppose I shouldn't have admitted that to you. After all, we are going to be in competition with each other."

"I promise to keep your secret." He leaned forward as if they were conspirators. "And that's only one idea.

As much as I'd like to know more, I can't get in your head and see what else is in there."

Renee swallowed. He could tell she knew there was a double meaning in his words. Carter had fallen for her the moment Blair introduced them. He hadn't understood the attraction. It was much too fast, and he'd never had any feelings as immediate as those before.

Resisting them seemed the natural thing to do. But he'd found himself taking more interest in the bridal division. His eyes were always on her when they were in a room together. He loved talking to her, sharing opinions. But then he'd had to leave, and making her play the waiting game would have been unfair.

A burst of song came from another room. Both of them glanced toward the door.

"It's a wedding," Renee said.

"Ever crash one?" Carter asked.

"I never needed to."

She smiled and Carter felt the warmth of it. This was the first time she'd really smiled at him. The others had been imitations, put on at the right time, but not genuine. This one was, and he wished he could capture and hold it.

"Wanna crash this one?"

"You're not serious?" she whispered as if the entire wedding party could hear her.

"Come on." Carter stood, holding his hand out.

"We haven't finished eating," she told him.

"The food will wait."

Renee put her hand in his. He wanted to hold her, and slow dancing at a wedding would give him an excuse.

"We'll be right back," he told the waiter as they headed for the reception.

"Hi, Renee, I didn't know you were going to be here."

"Hello," she said to Roni, a wedding consultant from one of the New York companies. "We're only here for a dance." Renee looked at Carter. "Roni, this is Carter Hampshire. Carter meet Veronica Edmonson. She's a wedding consultant for a company here. We met a couple of years ago."

They shook hands and exchanged pleasantries.

"We won't be long," Renee said.

Carter turned Renee into his arms. They began slowly moving to the music. "Do you know everyone in the business?" he asked.

"Not everyone, but it helps to know people. You never know when you'll need a favor."

Her lips were close to his ear as she said that. A tremor went through him, and his arm around her waist tightened, pulling her intimately close to him. Taking a slow breath, he inhaled her scent, felt the softness of her body and forgot everything except how good it was to hold her again.

They stayed for three more dances. The last one was slow and Carter hummed the song in Renee's ear. She couldn't help closing her eyes and giving herself up to the moment. At the end of the dance, Carter kept his arm around her back as they returned to their dinner table. Renee missed dancing with him. She missed everything about Carter, although she wouldn't admit it to anyone. She wanted to relax in his arms, melt into him and let the music take them away, but that was dangerous. And she was unsure of Carter's goals. He obviously had a reason for insisting that she spend time with him. On the surface it was to get her back at Hampshire Publications, but while he had his arms wrapped around her, she wasn't sure.

"That was fun," Carter said, holding her chair as she sat.

Renee noticed his voice was deeper.

"We should do it more often," he continued.

The promise of a future together was in his words. She suppressed the excitement that rippled in her heart, but she didn't miss his tone. It was that midnight-in-the-dark sexy voice that once wrapped her in its sound. Only now they weren't alone in the dark together, because Carter had dumped her. Without a reason. He'd only said it wasn't working for him and he was moving on. So why was he here now? Why had he insisted that she have dinner with him? Was he trying to wear her down, hope they could pick up where they had left off three years ago?

She guessed he'd had plenty of women who had filled her position for longer than she had had it. She frowned, wondering what he could want. It had to be something. Renee wondered if it was the business. Did he not want her to succeed at her magazine? Could he be that petty? Quickly she dashed that idea. Carter was honorable. At least, in everything except his relationship with her.

They spent a couple more hours over dinner, talking and laughing, although she was careful of what she said. She didn't want to reveal anything that could come back to haunt her. And she continued trying to discover his motives for wanting to be in her company. There had to be something going on.

Finally it was time to leave. Renee preceded him from the dining room into the hall. She wasn't looking forward to sharing the intimacy of a taxi, but she knew Carter wouldn't let her go home alone. As they stood waiting for an elevator, a happy couple joined them. The man swung the obviously inebriated woman around in a dance move as they laughed. Renee thought she'd seen them on the dance floor. However, as spacious as the hall was, the couple bumped into Renee and Carter.

"Excuse me," the woman said, backing away and continuing to giggle.

Renee barely acknowledged her. Her attention was on Carter. He'd grabbed her around the waist to steady her and she was now in his arms. Heat flashed through her. She trembled against him but pushed herself away as the doors of two elevators opened simultaneously. Rushing into the small sanctuary, she took a deep breath and Carter followed her in.

"Should I apologize?" Carter asked as they began the descent to street level.

Renee didn't pretend to misunderstand him. She shook her head.

Carter stood next to her and took her hand. Electricity skidded up her arm, but she didn't let go.

The taxi ride to the East Side was short and they spent it in silence. At the guesthouse, Renee opened the car door.

"You don't have to get out," she said. "It'll be hard getting another taxi in this area."

She slid out. Carter didn't take her advice. He got out, too, but he asked the driver to wait.

At the town house's door, he surveyed the facade and asked, "Is this yours?"

"No," she said without further explanation.

"Who lives here?"

"No one."

"No one?" His brows rose.

"I'm using it temporarily."

"Until when?" Carter persisted.

"Until I go back to Princeton."

He stared at her, waiting.

"Carter, I enjoyed dinner. Thank you for asking me." She sounded like some high school student from a B movie.

"I did, too."

Renee made the mistake of looking up at him. She wanted to know if he was being sincere. His eyes connected with hers in the low light of the outside bulb. She couldn't look away. She couldn't stop herself from watching his head come down toward her and his lips settle on hers. She pulled away almost immediately.

"What's wrong?"

"We are. We've done this before, and we know it doesn't work."

"We don't know that."

"Should I refresh your memory?" Renee asked. "I can recite the words for you. You told me point blank and to my face. 'I don't love you.' Then you disappeared, and I didn't hear from you again."

Putting her hand on the doorknob, she stared at him. The indication was that he should leave. Carter stood his ground, and a staring war ensued between them.

Renee didn't move when Carter finally took a step. She was ready to push the door open and go inside. Before she could twist the knob, his hands imprisoned her and his mouth seared hers. She couldn't do anything captured between his body and the wall, both as solid and unforgiving as granite.

She tried to resist his mouth, but her resolve wasn't strong enough. She melted into him, joining him in the kiss and letting go of all thought. Her eyes fluttered close and she clung to him, lifting herself higher on her toes.

He lifted his mouth, yet their lips still touched. She could taste him as he stared into her eyes. Then he removed the millimeter of space and kissed her again. This time his mouth was questioning, asking if it was all right to go on. His lips brushed hers, sweeping back and forth with a touch so light it was disconcerting. Renee turned as his arms gathered her closer, spanning her waist and sides. Without thinking, she went up on her toes, pressing her mouth closer to his. Her arms circled his neck and he crushed her against him for the second time. It had been too long since she'd felt like this. No one had held her or kissed her or made her feel as loved as Carter Hampshire.

She knew this was wrong. She shouldn't do this. She and Carter had no future. There was a time when they could have had a relationship, but when they'd reached that fork in the road, they'd stumbled. Still she couldn't deny herself the pleasure of being in his arms. Carter swept his tongue into her mouth. Shockwaves of emotion ran the full length of her body. She felt her leg rising, brushing against his pants leg.

Then, like a splash of ice water, she remembered where she was and what she was doing. She pulled her mouth away from him and stepped out of his arms.

Carter looked down at her. The dim light from the street lamp was bright enough to show the desire in his eyes. Renee was sure her mouth was swollen from the aftermath of his invasion, a wanted invasion.

"Carter," she whispered. She could manage no other words.

"Good night, Renee." He stepped down to the street and got back in the taxi.

Renee opened her clutch, and if her keys hadn't been immediately visible she was unsure if she would have been able to find them. Or slip them into the lock and open the door.

She stepped inside and turned to look at Carter. Neither waved or said a word. She closed and locked the door and heard the taxi drive away. Looking out the side window, she watched as the cab bore Carter Hampshire out of her life for the second time.

Carter's family had a house in the Hamptons and a summer home in North Carolina, but he lived in a two-level apartment on Fifth Avenue, where one room was dedicated to music and entertainment. Pulling his tie aside, he unbuttoned his collar and took the stairs two at a time to get to the music room.

A wall unit held his CDs and an enviable collection of LPs and vinyl records. There were times when only the original medium would do. He hunted through the LPs. Renee was on his mind. She could no longer say they were strangers. After that kiss on her doorstep, there was no doubt in his mind that they were more than familiar with each other.

Fire and Desire, a Rick James favorite, was what he was looking for. Finding the album that contained the track, he placed it on the turntable and listened as the sound of love filled the cavernous room. Lowering the lights, he looked out on the city toward East 65th Street where he'd left Renee.

He wondered what she was doing. Had she changed from the red dress she wore into something sheer enough to see through? He imagined her lying on the bed, her skin tone contrasting with the white sheets. The thought aroused him.

The song ended, and Carter used his remote control to start it again. He listened to it play seven times before finally turning the machine off and heading for his bedroom.

Carter replayed their kiss over and over in his mind. It was the last thing he thought of before sleep claimed him. But his sleep was fitful. Dreams of Renee filled the night. She wasn't pliable in his arms, but pulling away, eluding him and running whenever he tried to catch her.

Waking with a headache, he swung his legs to the floor and hung his head. Light filtered through the sheer curtains and hurt his eyes. Going to the bathroom, he found some headache medicine and downed two white pills. Thirty minutes later, he was dressed for work. His headache had only abated slightly.

The coffee timer pinged as he walked into the kitchen. He poured a cup and picked up his cell phone. It might be early, but he remembered that Renee was an early riser. He dialed her number. The phone went straight to voice mail, but the recording told him she was not accepting calls at this time.

"Damn," he cursed. If he couldn't wake up with her by his side, he at least wanted to talk to her on the phone.

Taking a sip of his coffee, he wondered if she was already on the train back to Princeton. She hadn't said when she'd return, and she had told him she would not contact him when she did. But that should all have changed last night outside her front door.

He hadn't answered her question, Renee thought as the train rolled toward Princeton. He'd never told her the reason he'd left, like he'd promised he would.

Then there was the kiss at her door. That had rendered her unable to think clearly. All she'd wanted after that was to get on one side of the door and leave him on the other. This weekend had been a test, and according to her own standards, she'd failed.

There was no available taxi at the Princeton train station when Renee arrived. By the time she walked the short distance to Nassau Street, she had a plan. She wouldn't see Carter again. Getting the magazine up and running would consume her for several months. Any invitations that included him, she'd refuse. Any calls from him, she'd ignore.

Renee sighed as she entered her home. It felt good to be back, welcoming, even though no one was there. She'd be moving out soon, but not selling. She'd decided to rent the house. Princeton was a college town and there were always people looking for residences. Mentally, Renee kept planning, forcing her mind to remain on tasks instead of thinking about the weekend and Carter.

She'd barely gotten unpacked before the phone at her computer rang. The signal told her it was a Skype call. Renee knew it was Dana calling to find out how the weekend had gone.

"Hi, Dana," she said cheerily.

"How was it?" Dana replied.

"Dinner was fine. The food at—"

"I'm not interested in the food," Dana interrupted. "How did it go with you and Carter?"

"As it always did," she replied.

Dana smiled. "Really?"

"It's not what you think. We had a normal dinner and spoke like friends."

"Friends!" Dana's face fell. "I thought you two might mend some fences."

"Why? Why would you think that?"

"Renee, this is me. Dana. I know you're still in love with him. You've been that way since time began."

"That's not true," she began. "We weren't together long enough for that."

Dana, raising her finger, stopped Renee from continuing. "It only takes a moment," Dana said. "Some relationships can take years to develop and others can happen in the blink of an eye."

Or a glance, Renee thought. "Well, it usually takes two people to make a relationship."

"Do you think he wants one?"

Renee frowned. "I'm not sure. He wants something. I could feel it each time we've met, but he hasn't really said what it is. For sure he'd like me to return to Hampshire Publications, but I'm committed here and I have no intention of returning there."

"Well, be careful. I don't want you to be hurt again."

Renee smiled.

"So, when are you moving?"

Renee sat up in her chair and relaxed her shoulders. The change in subject removed a weight from them.

"Next month, after Aunt Olivia moves out. I have to have her house cleaned and painted, get a manager for this house and hire a moving company, plus pack while planning the magazine."

"A plateful, I see."

"Isn't it always like that?"

Both she and Dana thrived on keeping busy and getting things done. As teenagers, Dana had visited Renee wherever her father was stationed.

"When you do move, I'll come to the new house and help you unpack."

"Thanks, I'd love the company."

Renee's cell phone rang and she glanced toward it, but it was too far away for her to see the caller ID.

"I guess people know you're home," Dana said. "I have to go anyway. Talk to you again soon."

Dana disconnected the call. The cell continued to ring. Renee expected it to be Carter. She took a deep breath and stood up. If it was him, she'd ignore the call.

Lifting the phone, she turned it over.

Teddy's face appeared in the small window.

Chapter 4

Three weeks later, Renee was back in New York. She'd heard nothing from Carter in all that time, and she was beginning to think things were settled between them. Yet the memory of her performance in his arms outside of the guesthouse wasn't as easy to put behind her.

"I have a wonderful place for you to see," her real estate agent, Eloisa, told her. "It's within your budget, centrally located and immediately available."

Renee had been searching for office space for a week with little result. There was plenty of property available, but everything had at least one problem that made it unsuitable. When she saw a place that would work, the contract had clauses that were deal breakers.

She met Eloisa down the block from the next space they were viewing, and they walked toward the building together. But she resisted when Eloisa pulled open the glass door and waited for her to enter a building Renee was so familiar with she could navigate it blindfolded.

"Is something wrong?" Eloisa asked.

Renee moved to the side, stepping out of the flowing sea of humanity moving around her. "This is the Hampshire Building," she said. Her voice was quiet, the kind of quiet that showed desperation. Renee wasn't angry. Eloisa hadn't known. It was almost like her words were an explanation to herself, to calm her down.

"They have wonderful offices and the space is available."

"But Hampshire Publications has a bridal division and my magazine caters to that market. We'll be in competition with each other."

The likelihood of running into Carter in an elevator or on the street increased tenfold if she even considered this space.

"I checked the contracts and there is no exclusion related to other magazine publishers."

"But it's unethical," Renee said.

Eloisa inclined her head in a gesture of surrender. "I can find you other spaces to consider," she said, "but they'll likely have a higher rent."

"Let's look at them," Renee said. Even though she was tired of looking, tired of negotiating and tired of discovering unsuitable locations, she would continue the search.

Two weeks passed, and finally Eloisa confronted her. "We've been everywhere. I'm at a loss to find you anything unless you increase your price point or your location."

Renee wished she could, but she had a budget and she had to stay within it. The Weddings by Diana partners had already been more than generous with her start-up cost estimates.

"How about we revisit the Hampshire Building?" Eloisa suggested with a happy note to her voice. "The least you could do is look at the space."

Renee nodded, but her heart sank.

Twenty minutes later they were in the office space, and Renee knew it was perfect for her needs. Very little renovation would be necessary. Some of the items she'd budgeted for were already present.

"What do you think?" Eloisa asked after a long while.

"It's perfect," Renee said without enthusiasm.

"Great." Eloisa didn't inject any excitement into the word. "Does that mean you'll take it?"

Renee looked at her. She nodded, unable to speak. All she could think of was that Carter Hampshire was only twenty floors above her. Thankfully, she'd noticed that the set of elevators that serviced her floor was different than the ones that went to his. They weren't even in the same hallway. She wouldn't run into him if she was lucky.

But where Carter was concerned, luck had never been on her side.

Numbers don't lie, Carter thought. It was a mantra his father had taught him when he was showing him the business. And Carter didn't like the numbers he was seeing. He was going to have to do something about it soon.

He heard a tap on his door. "Come in," he called.

Blair opened the door and smiled as she walked into his office.

"What's new?" she asked. "You usually like to come down and walk through the office."

Carter did. Instead of asking his division heads to come to his office, he'd go to their offices. That way, he could smile at the staff and get to know them. Again, this was something his father had taught him and Carter continued to do it. It was also how he had first met Renee.

Suddenly, she walked into his mind and filled it with her presence. He imagined her standing in the middle of the conference room. She was talking and the glass wall allowed him to fully stare at her.

"Carter," Blair called him, doing the same thing now that she'd done years ago.

"I've been looking at the reports on the bridal division," he said.

"We've had a setback, but we discussed that. We'll bounce back."

Carter stood up and walked around the office. "Do you think so?"

"What?" she asked. "Do you think Renee can have that much impact on the market with a small magazine?"

"It's not Renee. Her magazine hasn't launched yet, despite all the buzz in the air. But we've been losing market share for some time now. If we don't get sales up, I'm going to have some very bad reporting to do."

"It's the market," Blair stated. "The number of weddings is down, so we won't have the same number of brides looking for magazines."

"The number of weddings is actually up," Carter corrected her. "I thought that might be the reason, but after getting the statistical reports, I found the opposite to be true."

"Well, we'll just have to come up with a campaign to put us back on track."

Carter didn't smile. "That will be a start," he said. "But we'll have to keep it up issue after issue. Confidentially, we've now begun losing money on this division. If we don't turn it around, we'll have to put it up for sale or close it."

"You're not serious," Blair said. The surprise was genuine on her face.

"I've been covering for the sales for a while. I can't keep operating the division without it holding its own."

Blair looked directly at him, although she remained in her seat. "I guess we'll have to come up with something so irresistible to the bridal market that they have to buy it. But don't worry. I have an idea or two up my sleeve."

Moving day was never easy. Renee knew that from the many times she'd moved with her family. Her father was in the military, and every couple of years they'd pull up stakes and relocate, most times to another country. The army had packed and shipped their things, but her mother insisted on unpacking and putting everything away, along with the help of her twins, Renee and her brother, Roger. During summers, Dana would come and stay with her until school started. They'd had some of the best times of their lives those summers.

Renee's new house was filled with boxes, and she could barely walk around. But instead of completing her home move, she was focusing on setting up her new office space. Everything and everyone was there at the same time: electricians, the phone company, furniture deliveries. So much for an orderly move. The place was chaos central. The only person who wasn't there was Carter, and she had to be thankful for that. He was twenty floors above her and she hoped she could avoid him for the rest of her life.

The sun had set ages ago, and finally the place had some semblance of order. She didn't worry about organizing her office as long as the heavy pieces, like her desk and cabinets, were in place. The other areas of the office space had desks and equipment. She was also in the process of hiring people to fill those spaces.

There was a small kitchen along the opposite wall from her office. Renee headed there to make herself a cup of coffee. Even though the sun had gone down, she had hours to go before heading to her new home, where an equally chaotic bedroom awaited her. She wasn't planning to open anything there tonight.

"Do you mind if I have one of those?"

Renee jumped at the sound. Twirling around she saw a thin woman with long red hair standing in the doorway. Renee had seen her most of the day, directing and helping with the placement of furniture.

"I'm sorry. I thought everyone from the moving company had gone."

Renee poured a second cup of coffee and handed it to her. "Milk is in the fridge and sugar on the counter."

The woman smiled and added milk and one sugar to her cup. She turned back to Renee.

"You don't have to stay after you finish your coffee," Renee told her. "I can handle things from here."

"I'm not with the moving company," the woman said. She smiled as if she had a secret. "I'm Wanda Guilliard, your three o'clock."

"My interview! I totally forgot." Renee stood up straight. "I am so sorry." She looked at her watch. It was nearly seven o'clock. "Why didn't you stop me?"

"You were so busy and you looked like you really needed help." Wanda looked through the kitchen door at the chaos that was still in the outer rooms. "When I arrived, a man thrust a box at me and said to put it over there." She indicated one of the offices.

"But you worked all afternoon. I saw you and I thought you were with the movers. I did wonder why you were wearing a skirt, but only in passing."

"I was dressed for an interview. But I had walking shoes in my tote bag, so I changed into them." She put a foot out and Renee looked at the tennis shoes.

She laughed. Wanda joined her. "I can't thank you enough. If you work as well with the computer as you did with the move, the job is yours."

"I am qualified," she said.

Renee gestured for her to sit down. They both moved to one of the two round tables.

"I have a degree from Columbia. I studied design and business, and I can show you my portfolio of other publications I've designed. I can break down and troubleshoot the insides of a computer and I'm fluent enough in Microsoft Office to teach."

"How are you at digital publishing?"

"I know it cold."

"You're very confident," Renee said. Despite her selling herself so hard, Renee liked her. Even if Wanda could only do half of what she professed, she would fit in. Renee had managed before and she knew that if someone didn't work out, she would terminate them.

"I don't mean to be overbearing. I can do what I say and probably more. It just depends on what you need."

"I need someone who can run the digital design side of the business. We will produce a full print issue each month, and I need someone to lay out the pages so they can be sent to a printer for the final product."

"I'm sure that won't be a problem," Wanda said.

"Have you ever worked for a magazine before?"

Wanda shook her head. "I'm currently employed at Parks, Kagen and Cooper, a law firm in Jersey City."

"What do you do there?"

"I run their website. And before you ask, I'm looking for something more challenging."

"I'm sure we can fill that bill," Renee commented. "How many people will be in the production and design department here?"

"Right now, there's only you."

"Does that mean I have the job?" Wanda bit her bottom lip.

Renee smiled. "If the salary meets your requirements." Renee told her what she'd budgeted.

"We're good," Wanda said. "When do I start?"

"You tell me. We have to do a background check. And I suppose you need to notify the law firm of your decision."

"Two weeks will work for me," Wanda told her.

"By then I'll have this mess in order." Renee smiled again. She liked Wanda. Apparently, she was a pitch-in-when-and-where-needed type of person. And Renee needed someone like her.

"If you don't mind, I'd like to help with the computer setup and arrangement," Wanda said. "I want to make sure all the programs I need are properly installed and ready for use."

Designed for Brides officially had its first employee. Wanda wasn't afraid to get her hands dirty, and she didn't ask for much direction. She was exactly the kind of person Renee had hoped to find.

One down, seven to go, Renee thought when Wanda waved good-night. Renee went around turning out the lights and locking up the place. She'd be in the next day to continue putting things in order. One office at a time, she told herself.

She left the building by a rear exit and walked around to the front heading for the subway.

"Renee." Carter's voice stopped her. She'd reached the curb and was waiting for the light to change.

A shudder went through her at both the sight of him

and the way he said her name. She glanced over her shoulder, hoping there was someone or something there that would give her an excuse to get away from him quickly. Nothing materialized. Her day had been long, and she wanted nothing more than to grab something to eat and take a long bath before going to bed.

"Late day?" he asked.

She nodded.

"Just going to pick up something and go home," she answered.

"I was about to get something to eat. Why don't you join me?"

"I'm a little tired. I think I'll just go home."

"Renee, you have to eat. And it's only a quick bite together, not a full dinner. Although we could go to dinner if you wish…"

"I'm just going to pick something up, but thank you. Good night." She darted across the street and buried herself in the crowd.

In front of her was her favorite deli, but she walked by it. There was another one on the next corner and she'd rather not have Carter following her inside a place so close to the office. There was a traffic jam of people already standing in line to order something to eat before heading home, and Renee joined the crowd. She could cook her own dinner, but she was too tired. Her back and neck hurt and doing nothing when she got home was her goal.

Placing her order, Renee stepped back. She bumped into someone and instinctively turned to apologize.

"I'm sorry," she said. Then she saw who it was.

"Carter, what are you doing here? I thought you'd spend your dinner hour in a fancy restaurant with the opposite sex."

"And look at you, the bridal wizard, fulfilling every woman's dream of grabbing a sandwich and a drink and taking it back to your lonely kitchen."

"You don't know that," Renee said.

"Don't I?"

The clerk called her order. It was obviously a sandwich for one. Renee took it, paid and left, hoping to get away from Carter before his order was ready.

He caught up with her before she could find a cab. Without asking, he took her arm, hailed a passing taxi and pushed her inside.

"Where are we going?" she asked.

"Your place," he said.

She leaned back, her eyebrows raised.

"Would you rather go to my place?" He leaned forward and put his hand on the latch of the connecting window.

"No!" she stated too quickly and too loudly.

Renee gave her address and Carter slid the window back in place.

He relaxed, leaning back in the seat and sighing.

"Bad day?" Renee asked.

"A little more than usual."

"Wanna talk about it?" Renee regretted her words as soon as she said them.

Carter looked at her. Both of them remembered when they'd worked together. When he'd had a bad day or she'd had one, they would always vent about it together.

That was how it had begun. Those talks at the end of the day. Soon they'd added food delivery, then picking up something and eating together, until finally dinner and making love had followed. She wasn't going down that road again. They no longer worked together, and they were no longer lovers. They weren't even friends anymore. They were rivals.

"I'll work it out," he said.

Renee wondered if he hadn't answered because it had to do with the bridal division. Her heart constricted a moment. She missed their long after-work conversations. She couldn't stop the regret that spilled out of its hiding place.

They might be colleagues, but friends they weren't. And lovers they would never be again.

Carter's week had been one crisis after another, mainly in the bridal division where two graphic artists had resigned. He barely had time for anything but the office and thoughts of Renee, whom he hadn't seen since that night in the deli.

Heading into the Hampshire Building, he wondered where Renee's offices were. They had to be close by or he wouldn't have run into her.

Carter stepped into the office elevator. For a moment his finger hovered over the buttons before he punched thirty-eight.

He'd been trying to reach her for the past two weeks. But each time he dialed her number, it went to voice mail. Obviously, she did not want to talk to him. Carter understood when no meant no. And Renee was telling him no. He'd thought that after the frank conversation about the layouts that the two of them were heading toward a new road. But something was still going on to cause her to refuse his calls.

Exiting the elevator, he spoke to pockets of people as he made his way through the hall toward his office. Two secretaries carrying cups of coffee passed him. He looked into the room where the coffee machine sat and decided to stop and get a cup.

"Good morning, Carter," Marjorie said. Marjorie worked as an assistant to the company's legal director.

"Good morning."

She poured a cup of coffee, then headed in the direction of her office.

Just before Carter reached the door to his own office in the corner he heard a name that stopped him.

"Renee Hart. I was so surprised to see her. It's been years."

Carter turned back, coffee in one hand, his briefcase in the other.

"What's she doing here? I thought she moved to New Jersey." The other woman asked.

"I don't know, but she looks like wherever she's been, it agrees with her."

"She was always beautiful. I wish I had her complexion, so smooth and clear."

They started to walk away, when Carter called out. He didn't intend to, but he heard his voice. "Sandra?"

She turned toward him as the other woman walked away.

"You saw Renee? When?"

"This morning. A few minutes ago, actually. It was

strange. I got on the wrong elevator, the one that only goes to the twenty-fourth floor, and she was there. I was talking and turned into the first bank instead of the second.

"I didn't realize I'd gotten in the wrong elevator until we'd passed the sixth floor where I could switch from one bank to the other. So I rode up with her."

"Where did she get off?"

"On eighteen," she said with a sly smile.

"Thanks."

Sandra gave him a look that said she wanted to ask a question, but thought better of it. She turned and walked away. Carter went into his office and pushed the door closed.

Here? What was she doing here? Who was she visiting on the eighteenth floor? Carter put his coffee and briefcase down and opened his computer. As soon as it booted, he pulled up a list of tenants. Filtering them by floor, he checked the names of businesses and there it was. The name jumped out as if it was a viper. *Designed for Brides*. It was the only business on eighteen. She'd taken the entire floor. As the building's owner, Carter had access to other information about the tenants. Opening the file for *Designed for Brides*, he saw the space was leased to Weddings by Diana with a contract that had been signed by Renee Hart.

Renee was opening her magazine in his building. In the same place where he had his own bridal magazine's offices. Had she thought he wouldn't find out?

Carter closed the file, clicking the mouse button harder than necessary.

He wouldn't go down there. She had a right to lease the space. Her magazine was just a start-up, and there was no need to worry that it would cut into the profits of his company. Carter opened the sales figures for the previous day. Usually he started with the men's magazines, body building and car repair, but today he went straight to the bridal sales. Releasing a sigh, he checked the numbers. Sales were exactly as expected. Quickly he did a comparison of sales for the same week last month and last year. They were slightly down, but that was understandable. None of it had anything to do with her.

She hadn't launched yet, a voice inside his head gave him the logic. Sitting back in his chair, Carter stared at the screen and wondered when she planned to launch. There was nothing to worry about. Renee had been away three years, and she hadn't even been working in the industry. Three years was a lifetime in the magazine business. It didn't matter how well she'd done three years ago. It was all about who advertised in the magazine and what was happening in the bridal industry.

"Carter." His secretary poked her head in the door. "You're going to be late for the staff meeting."

Carter glanced at the clock on his desk. Grabbing his leather notebook, he stood up and headed for the conference room.

The rest of the day slogged by. He couldn't remember how many times he checked the clock. Renee was on his mind, and he wanted to go to the eighteenth floor and see if she was there. He wanted an explanation as to why she wouldn't take his calls.

But he vowed not to do it. After all, he understood *no* when he heard it.

The office quieted down after five. Carter had done little other than wear the carpet out between his desk and the panoramic windows. He told himself he needed to catch up on the trade journals he hadn't read, but he couldn't focus. When he did finally open one, he was looking for information on Renee's new venture. Other than that small announcement in the issue he'd read a month ago, there was nothing.

"I thought I'd find you here."

Carter looked up. Blair stood in his doorway.

"You know, it's not a crime to go home before the late news is on." She walked to the front of his desk and took a seat in one of the guest chairs. "Or go down to the eighteenth floor."

"You know?" His brows rose.

"It's the talk of the building. People who used to work with her have been disappearing all day."

"Was one of them you?"

She shook her head. "I ran into her on the street the other day. I didn't know she had space in this building. We're having a drink Friday after work." Blair raised her hand, warding him off. "And this time you are *not* invited."

"I ran into her, too. Why would she take space in this building?"

"That's easy. We're located in the middle of all the

services a magazine needs. We had available space. And there's not a rule against another publisher moving in."

Carter stared at her.

"I checked," Blair said.

"But why here?"

Blair smiled. She relaxed in the chair, crossing her legs and putting her elbow on her knee, while her hand supported her chin. "You think she came to be near you?"

"I don't. I think she doesn't want to see or hear from me."

Blair frowned.

"I've called her several times in the past few weeks. Her phone goes straight to voice mail and the recording says the number is not accepting messages And if she wanted to see me, all she'd have to do is go down to the sixth floor, cross over to the other elevator bank and come up."

"And she hasn't?"

He shook his head.

Blair stood and walked across to the windows. She cut quite a figure, having been a model in the past. Her hair was totally white, cut short and styled to emphasize her best features. For a woman over fifty, she had few lines on her face, even though her smile was infectious. She walked to the door of his office and turned back to look at him.

"There is one thing you probably forgot, Carter."

"What's that?"

"The elevator goes up *and* down."

* * *

Renee stretched her back. Slipping her feet out of her shoes, she stood and reached for the ceiling, extending one arm higher than the other, then reversing the exercise, air climbing to relieve stress. She'd been putting in fifteen-hour days for the last three weeks. Tomorrow would be another one.

Mentally she went over the last three weeks' accomplishments. She'd contracted with two sales forces, one to handle advertising and one to work with the various designers. Both started this week. Wanda, although talkative, had organized the computer network and tested all the machines. She was already laying out details for their debut issue.

Renee had hired a production team and a marketing director, and they were now nearly fully staffed. She turned and looked at the electronic production board that was mounted on the wall of her office. If all went well, they would launch in the spring. She smiled. Her back hurt, but she was satisfied. Night had already fallen. She shut down her computer and the board went dark.

Slowly she walked through the office turning off any unnecessary lights. By the time she'd collected her shoes and purse, only the light in reception remained illuminated. She switched it off. Gasping, her heart jumped into her throat as she saw Carter on the other side of the double glass doors. Renee's heartbeat jumped several hurdles. Her hand went to her heart and she let out a long breath.

Carter's features were distorted by the etching of the

Designed for Brides logo on the door. The computer automatically locked the doors at six o'clock, but since Renee had stepped in view of the motion detector, a click unlocked them to let her out.

Grasping the curved handles, Carter pulled both doors open and stepped inside. Renee retreated a step.

"Welcome to New York," he said sarcastically. "I am truly surprised to find you here."

She didn't know what to say. She should have known that, with Sandra seeing her in the elevator and the number of people who had come to say hello, word would get back to Carter. But Renee thought she'd evaded him for one more day.

"Why are you here?" Carter asked, his tone almost demanding.

"The space was available and had everything I needed. And the building staff has been wonderful in helping me set things up."

"Stop talking about the staff. Why didn't you answer my phone calls?"

"Carter, let's not go through this again. If my being here is going to disturb you, I can find another location."

"You could have told me," he said. "Not only are you going into competition with one of my magazines, but you're going to do it in the same building."

"I'm not the only other publisher in this building. I'm also not the only one who publishes a magazine that competes with one of Hampshire Publications'. So you're not here to talk about my use of space. Why are you really here?"

He didn't immediately answer. "I want us to go back three years and start over."

"You know that's not possible."

"You're being literal," he told her.

"I am," she agreed. "The last three years happened. We can't pretend they didn't."

"Could we sit down?" Carter asked.

Renee looked around. Behind her was a loveseat with a coffee table in front of it. On either side of the table, facing the two seater, were individual chairs. She took a seat in one of the singles. Carter sat on the sofa close to her chair.

"If I apologize for leaving you, could we at least be friends?"

"I never said I wasn't your friend."

"You said we were strangers."

"And that's true," she said.

"Not anymore," he said. "Not after that night on your doorstep."

Renee's face flooded with heat. She was glad the lights were off. The soft glow from the hall didn't reach her features.

Renee looked at her still-bare feet. "I'd rather not talk about that night."

"Why not? Because it proved that you're not as immune to me as you wish?"

Renee took a deep breath. "You're right, Carter. I'm not immune to you. But I will not open my heart to a man who crushed it three years ago and has the gall to ask me to be his friend."

"If you won't be my friend, be my love."

Renee choked. She dropped her purse and the shoes she'd been holding. "You can't be serious," she said.

"I'm dead serious."

"Why?" Renee deliberately made her voice soft. "You're a good-looking man. There are at least ten women on the same floor as you who'd give their eye-teeth to hang on your arm. Why do you want me there?"

"Because you aren't one of the ten women on my floor."

"How do I know you're not asking this to find out what I'm doing to get this magazine off the ground?"

"You mean, to sabotage your efforts?" He didn't wait for an answer. "That's beneath you."

"You offered me a job at Hampshire Publications. Since I turned it down, this could just be another method of you getting what you want."

"It isn't," he said.

She wanted to believe him. Every fiber of her body wanted her to stand up and rush into his arms. But things had changed. Their lives were different.

"Where did you go, Carter?" Renee asked.

"War," he said.

Renee wasn't sure she'd heard him. It was a single word and her mind tried to think of something that she might have misheard, but nothing replaced the single word.

"War?" she asked.

"Afghanistan."

"You went to Afghanistan?" She leaned in a bit, then stopped.

"Two years."

Renee had no air. "Why didn't you tell me?"

"I couldn't. If I had told you, you might have waited for me until I got back, *if* I got back. It was my second tour. I'd seen guys get messed up over there. I didn't know what would happen to me. And I didn't know if things would change between us while I was gone."

Renee thought about Dana losing her fiancé. How would Renee have felt if Carter had been killed? She shuddered at the thought.

"Are you all right?"

"I'm fine," he said. "I came home without a scratch."

"What about the mental part?"

"I've been back a year. I take part in counseling returning soldiers. I think I'm all right, but sometimes the effects take time to set in. I can't guarantee that I'll always be fine, but for right now, I've been cleared of all medical issues."

"Carter, I am so sorry. I didn't know."

"Few people did. They thought I was working somewhere else. Some thought I'd had a disagreement with my father. Others thought it was you."

"Why keep it a secret?"

Carter stood up. He walked about the small space as if he were an animal and needed more than the cage he'd been assigned. He turned, stopping under the light near the door. "I didn't expect to return," he said. "I thought I was going to die."

Renee gasped as a mental picture flashed through her mind.

Moving more quickly than Renee thought he could, Carter was next to her, taking her hand. "We hadn't been together long. I thought if I asked you to wait, even if I told you where I was going, and then I died, it would make your life worse."

She snatched her hand free and stood, stepping away from him. "So you did this for me? You made a unilateral decision for *me*? You didn't give me the opportunity to think, to choose, for myself?"

"I can tell you don't agree with my decision, but it was for the best. What would you have done had I told you?"

"I'd…" She stopped. "I suppose we'll never know the answer to that question."

Was there a word that meant being both right and wrong at the same time? Carter asked himself as he opened the door to his apartment. It had been a mistake not to tell Renee where he was going. But Carter had known their relationship was new and soaring. He'd felt more for her after a single date than he'd ever felt for any other woman. And he'd known she was falling hard for him. But he had to go—he'd already been called. If anything had happened to him, he didn't want her feeling guilty or lost. It was better that they'd ended their relationship before it moved any further. Whether she believed him or not, he did it for her.

His phone rang. Carter pulled it out of his pocket, hoping he'd see Renee's photo. He hadn't changed it when he'd left for Afghanistan. He'd kept it with him and looked at her picture often during his two-year absence.

Carter blinked at the display. He blinked again. Renee's photo smiled back at him. It was the one she'd used on the website when she'd worked at Hampshire. It was the only one he had. The ringtone whirred again. He pushed the button for the speaker.

"Hullo." He cleared his throat, finding his voice was deeper than usual.

"Carter?"

"I'm here," he answered.

She took so long to say anything that Carter checked the display to see if she had ended the call.

"Renee, are you still there?" He heard her breathing. She was obviously struggling with something. "Where are you?"

"Across the street."

Carter walked to the window and looked down. He saw her standing in the light of a street lamp. She looked up at him. Carter dashed from the apartment and ran down the five flights of steps. He couldn't wait for an elevator. He crossed Fifth Avenue to the tree-lined median where she stood, still holding her phone to her ear.

He gazed down at her, unsure of what to say or do.

"I thought I should say something," she said.

Carter moved to stand next to her. Traffic sped by on the major road.

"Come with me." He took her arm and looked both ways. When the traffic opened, he pulled her across the street and shuttled her into his building. He didn't stop until they were inside his apartment and he'd closed the door. Carter didn't know how she knew where he lived. The few times they'd spent the night together it had been at her place.

Getting two glasses of wine, he gave her one and they took seats. She chose a chair instead of sitting next to him on the sofa.

Renee sipped the white wine. "I came to apologize."

"I'm the one who owes you an apology," he said.

"I started walking. I walked for a long time. And I thought for a long time. I thought about your question. What would I have done, had I known. I'm not sure, but I know I would have worried that you wouldn't…"

She struggled for words. Carter didn't move.

"Then I found myself across the street. I wish you'd told me before you left," she said. "But the fact that you didn't is no reason for me to hold a grudge against you, especially since we're bound to run into each other from time to time."

Carter didn't allow her to get any further. Lightning propelled him across the room, and he hauled her into his arms and seared his mouth to hers.

His arms encased her, gathered her to him as his kiss deepened. Renee didn't resist. She didn't want to and knew that it was impossible. Her arms went around Carter and she melted into him.

She'd missed being kissed, held and loved. She missed the smell of him, the way his fingers threaded through her hair. The way his arms felt as they held her. Their heads bobbed from side to side as wet kisses covered her face before he returned to her mouth.

Carter brought out feelings that no one else could. She was aware of everything about him—she knew the weight of his arms, the strength of his embrace, the smell of his cologne and the unique scent that was his alone.

Carter's tongue invaded space she gladly yielded. It was like the last three years hadn't existed. And today she wanted him to go on kissing her until time stopped. It seemed she might get her wish. Carter's mouth changed, becoming gentler, more loving, so much so that the emotion flooding her system overloaded.

Carter raised his head, sliding his mouth from hers and cradling her like a baby against him. Renee's heart pounded and her breath came in short gasps. She could feel the pulse in Carter's neck. She knew she still affected him the way he affected her. Moments later he pushed her back and looked down at her. Renee's eyes opened slowly and she looked into his. They were dark and deep with desire.

Behind him Renee notice a lamp, and the light somehow recharged her brain.

"This doesn't change anything," she said, getting to her feet. "I wanted to apologize, but I didn't come here for...this."

"Why did you come?"

"I explained that."

He nodded. Renee inched closer to the door. "I'll go now."

"Renee?"

She stopped. She looked directly at him, not wanting Carter to think that he intimidated her.

"You can't win," he said.

"Maybe not, but it will be a worthy fight."

* * *

You can't win. Renee sat up in bed. Carter's words
came back to her. Why did these revelations always
come at night, disturbing her sleep? Pulling her knees
to her chest, she clamped her arms around them and
rocked back and forth. She hadn't been able to sleep.
It was the smile—no, the smirk—on Carter's face as
she'd left his apartment that kept her awake. What had
Carter meant? Was she interpreting his parting words
differently than he'd intended? She'd assumed he was
talking about the business at first. That she couldn't
win in the bridal market against a conglomerate that
controlled the industry.

But the words came on the end of a passionate kiss.
And the smirk, that I-know-something-you-don't look,
was keeping her awake. While she'd spent hours, days,
months planning for every eventuality in the business,
she hadn't planned for a you-can't-win smirk from her
prime competitor.

Pushing the cover aside, she swung her feet onto the
floor and stood up. There was little chance of any more
sleep tonight, so she might as well get up and unpack
some of the boxes littering every surface of her house
from the door to the back wall.

The unpacking worked until sunrise. By then she
was ready to go back to bed. Unfortunately, it was time
to shower and head for the office, an office where she
could, at any time, find her nemesis standing on the
other side of a glass door.

Renee knew taking this space wasn't the best idea.
However, if she wanted a prestigious address and a

place of business that was central and met all her requirements and budget, the Hampshire Building was it. It only had one drawback, which was Carter.

Work was the panacea. After several hours at the office, she no longer felt tired and she no longer thought of Carter more than three or four times a minute.

She called Wanda into her office, and the two of them spent the rest of the day developing something unique that could help when they launched the magazine. Eventually the day ended, and she headed home. In the lobby, Carter emerged from his elevator bank just as her elevator door opened. He fell into step with her near the front entrance, and the two of them passed through the building's exit at the same time. Neither spoke a word to the other, yet the look that passed between them spoke volumes.

Once she was in the crowd on the sidewalk, she decided to change her routine. She quickly lost sight of him and went to a deli in the opposite direction of the one she usually frequented. Carter must have had the same idea—she saw him the moment she walked through the door.

"In our attempt not to run into each other, we keep running into each other," he said.

"I'm beginning to think you're stalking me." She didn't really believe that, but she did wonder if he was baiting her, forcing her to remember and relive the scene that had taken place in his apartment.

Renee ordered her food. She hoped Carter would leave, but he remained and they left together, almost as if they'd planned to meet there.

"How are things going?" he asked. She knew his question was just to fill the silence. They weren't the small-talk types.

"If you mean how my magazine is coming along, it's right on schedule."

When they got to the subway station they had to part ways, and Renee turned to say goodnight.

"I suppose running into you is something I can't control," she said.

"And I'm not stalking you," he said.

"You said I couldn't win. Did you mean that you don't think I can make my magazine a success?"

Carter stepped closer to her. Leaning down, he kissed her cheek and whispered in her ear.

"Winning has nothing to do with any magazine."

As Renee turned and bounded down the subway stairs, heat radiated through her. Why did he have the ability to render her speechless? With anyone else she was articulate, intelligent and logical, but the moment Carter entered the room she became awkward and unable to formulate complete sentences.

"Maybe it wasn't about winning," she said aloud. Checking around her, no one seemed to notice that she was talking to herself.

She would win. She was unsure of what the rules were, but she would devise her own. She knew a lot about Carter, and anticipating his playbook wouldn't be that hard. The problem was that he knew hers, too.

By the time Renee got home, she was too tired to prepare a meal. But having meals at home would keep

her from bumping into Carter at local delis again and
again. She sighed.

So winning wasn't about the magazine. It was about
them. Yet there was nothing between them. If she didn't
participate in his games, there could be no outcome.
And she could resist that. She'd concentrate on the magazine. She'd show him. And in the place it would hurt
the most—business.

She and Wanda were planning a revolutionary
change to the way brides viewed their gowns. No one
had anything like it. It might take some time for her to
win the game he was playing, but this one would set
him back a step or two.

Carter hated dinner parties, especially those given
by his parents. While his father had retired from Hampshire Publications when Carter returned from Afghanistan, he still liked to keep track of the movers and
shakers in the magazine business. His mother just liked
entertaining. She had her own set of industry people
who came to their house in the Hamptons two to three
times a year. Her expertise was in the fashion business,
which complemented the magazines.

Usually his mother was either trying to push someone into the spotlight or she was parading possible
future daughters-in-law for his benefit. But it never
worked. Carter was perfectly capable of finding his
own bride, if and when he wanted one.

"Mother." Carter grasped her shoulders and kissed
her on the cheek. She went into his arms and hugged
him. She was short, only three inches over five feet.

There was a time when she'd had hair long enough to reach her waist. He used to brush it before his younger sister took over the task and Carter grew old enough to want to play baseball instead of do girly things. Now her hair was salt and pepper, and had been cut into a chic style that tapered at her neck.

"No date?" she asked instead of saying hello.

"What, and have you making wedding plans before I even get a drink?"

"I wouldn't do that," she said. "I'd wait until after you got a drink." Both of them laughed.

"I see you have quite a turnout from the city," Carter commented. "Which one have you singled out for me?" He looked over the crowd of dressed-to-the-nines females. Most people he either knew by name or recognized.

"Darling, I thought you might come with Renee Hart. I hear she's back in the trade."

"Who's back in the trade?" His father joined them. Dressed in his white tie and tuxedo, few people would know Joseph had been in the hospital recently. Thankfully, his diagnosis hadn't been very serious. However, he did need to take things easy.

"Renee Hart," his mother said.

"I liked her." His father didn't hesitate. "I could live with her."

"It wouldn't be you who would live with her," Carter told his dad. His father was the one person who knew how he felt about Renee.

"I've heard she's back," Carter said, hedging.

"Between the two of you, I'm surprised she isn't

here." The look that passed between his parents told him they knew something. "She isn't here, right?"

"Right," his mother answered.

Carter let a breath out.

"But…she's expected," his father finished.

"I can't believe you two. I'm thirty-two, not thirteen."

"We didn't invite her just for you," his mother said. "She's an up-and-coming force in the industry. When she worked for you, she was invited. It would be a slight not to invite her now that she's back in the industry."

There were other competitive publishers in the room, and while Renee had not launched her magazine yet, she was still causing a buzz in the backrooms and board-rooms along publisher's row.

"Let's get a drink," Carter said. *I think I'm going to need one.*

The three of them headed toward one of the bars, but his dad was stopped halfway by a guest and his mother paused to greet one of her fashion models, Melanie Esterbrook. Carter continued walking. He didn't want to get caught up with his mother introducing someone beautiful, thin and unmarried. Carter already knew Melanie, but that wouldn't keep his mother from re-introducing them and beginning her sales pitch on the woman's attributes. Not that he wouldn't hear it later in private, but it was much easier to fend off if Melanie wasn't standing in front of him.

The bartender was as much a regular at these parties as his parents. He knew exactly what Carter preferred and reached for a glass when he saw him coming.

The bartender smiled, poured a finger of scotch in a glass, added water and handed it to Carter.

Moving away from the bar, Carter circled the room, talking to the guests, but always aware of the door and that Renee had yet to appear.

"How's it going?" someone from behind him asked.

Carter turned to see another one of his mother's models. She must've been new since Carter didn't recognize her. But then, the faces of models sometimes merged together. He'd been around beautiful women all his life and he supposed he'd built an internal immunity to them and the admiration they expected.

"JoAnna Snow," she said, and offered her hand. She wore a one-shoulder chiffon gown that showed off her creamy skin. She'd pulled her hair to the side, and she looked like she was ready for a photo shoot.

"Carter Hampshire," he said, taking her hand.

"I know." Her voice had just the right amount of sultriness to it.

He knew what was coming, but he smiled and decided to try and sidetrack her request to be on the cover of one of his magazines. "Snow? Is that a real last name or a model identity?"

"It's real. And I'm not a model."

Carter's brows rose. "Most of the people here are either in the fashion business or publishing. Where do you fit?"

"Fit?" She said it as if it was a dirty word. "I hope I'm not being put into a box."

"I apologize. My word choice was poor. It's that my parents usually invite people within the same industry to their parties."

"Apology accepted," she said with a winning smile. "I'm with The Women's Project. We're a nonprofit group that helps women restart their lives."

Carter nodded. It was a noble career.

"Your mother has been very influential in getting donors for us."

Carter glanced across the room at his mother. "She's like that."

JoAnna nodded.

"Did she by any chance tell you that Hampshire Publications would donate to your cause?"

"She did." JoAnna smiled.

"Did she also give you the amount of our donation?"

JoAnna shook her head. Her curls bounced. Carter thought of how Renee's hair bounced when she walked.

"Why don't you call me on Monday, and we'll work something out?" He could see his mother smiling from across the room. She probably knew exactly what had just transpired between them. "In the meantime, would you like to dance?"

That would satisfy his mother, seeing the two of them together. They stepped to the dance floor and circled it a couple of times before Carter saw Renee enter the room. A man came up behind Renee and placed his hands on her arms. The gesture was intimate. Losing his focus, he stepped on JoAnna's foot.

Carter hadn't realized he'd stopped moving and now just stood staring at Renee.

What a reception, Renee thought. She looked around the huge house—it was brightly lit and filled with people. Renee had been surprised the Hampshires still included her among their guests. But when the invitation had arrived, she couldn't refuse it. And she couldn't go alone. She needed to convince Carter that there was nothing and there would be nothing between them. But there was no one she could ask to escort her who wouldn't read more into it than was there. So she called the only person she knew would fill the bill: her twin brother, Roger.

Renee knew where the bar was, and taking Roger's hand, she headed that way. The bartender recognized her.

"Sweet white wine?" he asked.

Renee smiled. "You remembered."

He nodded, but the smile on his face said more. Roger's presence probably stopped him from the flirting that she knew would have come. From the other room, the band started to play "Night and Day." Carter stood in the doorway, his arms wrapped around a tall woman with dark hair.

Had Carter asked the band to play that song? She wasn't sure how to read his expression. Roger took her elbow and she snapped out of her trance. They walked toward a group of people Renee knew, although she was unsure if she'd be capable of coherent speech.

"Night and Day" had played over and over on the first night they'd spent in bed. Renee had it on a CD and somehow she'd hit the repeat button. Images of them in bed accosted her. She slipped her arm through Roger's and held on tightly.

"You all right?" he whispered.

Releasing her viselike hold on him, she looked up and nodded. For that night, Renee wasn't going to tell anyone Roger was her brother. She'd only introduced him as a biomedical investor, which was technically the truth. Roger did invest in biomedical research. He was the researcher and had his own business that was supported by venture capitalists. Biomedical research was about as far from publishing and fashion as you could get, but he enjoyed explaining it to whomever asked for more information.

"Maybe I'll get some donations from this," he told Renee as they walked into the ballroom and began greeting people. Most of the conversation centered around Roger, since he was the only one there not part of the trade.

Renee's mind was on Carter and the woman he was dancing with. Renee didn't recognize her, but why would she? She was Carter's date. Renee was silently thankful her brother had agreed to escort her.

As they circled the ballroom, Carter suddenly appeared in front of them. Renee was forced to introduce him. The urge to blurt out the truth was on the tip of her tongue, but Roger interrupted her and offered his hand.

"Nice to meet you," Carter said. "I hope you're enjoying yourself."

"So far it's been good," Roger stated.

Carter checked over his shoulder. "Mind if I ask Renee to dance?"

Roger shook his head and Carter took her hand, giving her no chance to refuse.

"Who is he?" Carter asked, shuttling her around the room.

"My date," she answered. "Someone you don't know."

"Where did you meet him?"

"I think that would fall under the heading of none of your business," Renee said. She had a smile on her face. No one looking at them could have gauged the tension that wrapped around them like shrink-wrap. "Who was the long-haired woman who captured your fancy?"

Renee saw him frown a moment as if he didn't remember the woman. "That was one of my mother's charity directors."

"And you're the charity?" Renee asked, regretting her words the moment they came out. "I'm sorry. I didn't mean to say that."

She stopped dancing, and Carter bumped into her. "I am not the charity, but I will be donating to her cause."

Realizing they were standing in the middle of the dance floor, Renee stepped back. Another couple bumped into them. The music ended and she excused herself. She wove through the crowd looking for her brother. He was nowhere in sight. Forcing herself to walk slowly, she went to the bar and ordered another glass of wine. She moved through the crowd and ended up in a quiet room where many of the current Hampshire magazines were lying on the tables. Renee was naturally drawn to the bridal ones, of which there were three issues.

"Fantastic, aren't they?" a man said near her.

Renee looked at him. She recognized the photographer, but she couldn't remember his name. He'd joined the company just as she was leaving.

"The cover is mine, but the layout inside is a work of art. Are you one of the models?"

Renee shook her head as she opened the magazine and found something she had done in the past.

"I tell you, the last three issues of *Hampshire Bridal* have really rocked," the photographer said.

Renee looked closely and saw that all three issues had used her interior layouts. The gowns inside were new, but everything else had simply been slipped into an existing template she had originally created. She tried to act as if it didn't matter to her, but in fact it did. She was surprised that Carter was allowing this to happen.

"They're not really that new," she said.

"I know. I mean, nothing is really 'new.'" He used both hands to symbolize quote marks. "But the way these have been laid out, the entire flow is stunning."

Renee took her wine glass and excused herself. She passed Carter's father on her way out, and he stopped her.

"Renee, how nice to see you."

He caught her in a bear hug. Joseph Carter had always been friendly. His smile was wide and genuine. Renee liked him.

"I heard you were back at the magazine," he said. "I know it'll be back on top with you in charge."

For a moment, Renee was unsure what magazine he was talking about. "You mean *Hampshire Bridal*? No, I'm not back there."

Joseph Hampshire looked confused. "Then where are you?"

"I'm starting my own magazine."

"You are?"

She nodded.

"Don't you want to head up our division?"

Thankfully, she was saved from answering. Joseph was abruptly pulled away into another conversation.

She stared after him. She'd met Joe Hampshire a few times, mainly at parties and trade events. He was a joker, but always happy. Renee assumed it was his marriage that made him seem as if he walked on clouds. She smiled, hoping one day she'd have someone that made her that happy.

Turning around, she found Roger talking to Carter and her heart stopped. Before she got close to them, they shook hands and Carter left.

"What was that about?" she asked as she joined Roger.

"He was just asking some questions about investing."

"Really?"

"He could have been testing me to see if I knew my stuff, or he could be genuine."

"What did you think?"

"Genuine," Roger said.

Renee felt good about that. She wouldn't want to find out that Carter had been interrogating her brother. But why should she care? Carter was nothing to her. So why had seeing the tall woman in his arms bothered her? The thought came unexpectedly. And why had she felt like Cinderella dancing in his arms?

"Are you ready to go?"

Roger's head turned too quickly. "I'm enjoying this."

"As you are enjoying following that woman in the green dress around."

"You noticed that?"

"Roger, I'm your twin. I just know."

"Well, don't get lost." She leaned close to him and whispered in his ear. "And don't blow my cover."

After-parties were usually laugh-fests. That's what they had been when Carter was in college. He thought of all the nights he and his friends had stumbled out of bed and relived the antics of the night before. After his parents' party, he and his dad had talked most of the night, but no part of their conversation had been humorous.

His mind, as his conversation had been, were about Renee. Carter wondered what she'd done for the rest of the weekend. And he couldn't forget the man she'd been with. Carter had gone to the party stag. Yet she'd come with a date. It was foolish of him to think that there was no man in her life. Renee was a beautiful woman and he hadn't seen her in three years. It was natural that she'd moved on. Hadn't that been exactly what he wanted her to do? What he'd told her to do when he left?

So why did he feel like there was a hole in his heart? Even when he was away, the one thing he thought leaving her behind would do, hadn't happened. He didn't realize how much he would miss her, how much of her he'd taken with him when he went to Afghanistan. The universe was funny. While Carter thought he was saving both of them, the universe didn't allow it. He'd taken all his feelings and more with him when he'd boarded that plane.

While he was away, he wondered where she was and what she was doing. He wanted to know whom she was with and did she still use the same shampoo. He wanted to know if her hands were still as soft as they were when he held them and if the smile she'd always given him was now being given to someone else.

Carter had his answer. He saw it Friday night in the way she danced with the man whose arm she held. He saw it in the easy manner that the two of them communicated. They almost looked like two halves of the same whole. Had they ever looked like that when they were a couple? Had their communications been that easy?

"You're awfully quiet," Carter's father said. Sitting in the passenger seat, Carter looked out on the scenery between his parents' home and the train station.

"It's getting close to Monday. I was thinking about the office."

His father's laugh was one that said he didn't believe his son for a moment. "Carter, I remember the first time you lost your heart to a girl. You were thirteen. At thirty it's no different. Why don't you tell her how you feel?"

"She's not ready to listen yet. Maybe she will be soon, but right now she still sees me as the man who left her behind. I'm taking it slow. I don't want to push her."

Joe Hampshire parked the car and they got out. Carter reached in the back and pulled his overnight bag out.

"Good advice," Joe said. "Just remember, there are

other men out there who might also have an eye for Renee."

Carter nodded. The image of Renee hanging on the arm of the man she was with at the party had him suddenly ready for battle. "I'll remember."

"I hope so," Carter's father said. "Because I believe your first test is about to happen."

"What?"

His father hitched his chin toward something behind him. Carter turned and looked. Tension tightened his body at what his father meant. Renee stood next to a stairway with the same man she'd been with at the party. She laughed at something he said. Then he hugged her and kissed her cheek. Turning, she bounded up the steps, almost as if she had added buoyancy to her step.

Carter thought she had gone back to New York Friday night. Yet here she was, still on the Island and still with the same man she'd been with at the party. Carter opened his free hand that he'd balled into a fist before loosening his grip on the overnight bag. He hadn't realized he was holding it so tight.

His father's laugh broke into his thoughts. "Have a good trip back. It's bound to be interesting. I'd sure like to be a fly on the wall during your trip."

"I won't even be in the same car with her," Carter said. "She won't know I'm even on the train."

"Yeah, I believe you," his father said, shaking Carter's hand and pulling him into a man-hug. Carter could hear his dad's strong laugh as he backed away and returned to the car.

Turning around to the stairway, Carter scanned the

area, looking at as much of the platform that was visible. Renee was no longer in sight. Carter couldn't decide whether or not that was a good thing. For his peace of mind, it was better that he kept some distance between them.

But could he?

Did he want to?

Carter heard the train coming and headed for the platform. When he came out to see his parents and took the train, he usually sat near the end of the train. There were less people there and he could get some work done. Stepping through the door in his usual place, he put his bag in the overhead rack and took his usual seat. He wasn't going to go car by car and find where Renee was sitting.

Ten minutes later the train pulled out of the station. Carter's laptop lay unopened on his knees. Staring out of the window, he watched the platform end and rooftops begin to slide by. The train picked up speed while he thought of Renee sitting ahead of him a few train cars away. Another ten more minutes passed and he opened the laptop and looked at the blank screen. However, he hadn't done much more.

Making a snap decision, he closed the laptop and stood up. Grabbing his bag from the overhead rack, he walked determinately to the car door. Pulling it open, he ignored the Do Not Cross Between Cars While Train is in Motion sign and stepped across the gap. She wasn't in the next car. Carter kept moving. As he opened the doors, all heads were facing front. He would have to identify Renee from the back.

Five cars up, he saw her. The morning sun beamed through her dark brown hair adding halos of red highlights. He could have picked her out no matter which direction she faced. The seat next to her was empty. He walked directly to it, tossed his bag on the rack next to hers and dropped into the seat.

She glanced at him, then did a double take. The book on her lap fell to the floor. Both of them reached for it. Their hands met and Renee quickly pulled hers free.

"Carter!" she said.

"Have a nice weekend?" he asked.

For a long moment, Renee said nothing. She was obviously too surprised at seeing him to speak.

"With all the seats on this train, why do you want this one?"

"Time goes by faster when you're with a friend," he answered, and offered her the book.

"Friend? We're not friends."

"Of course we are. You don't want to toss people out like Kleenex. You'll find yourself alone in the world."

"Maybe I'd prefer that."

"Believe me, you wouldn't. So, did you have a nice weekend? I thought you went back to the city Friday night, but I see you had company."

"Do you really want to say that and leave yourself open for the obvious reply?"

"That you didn't go back Friday?" he asked.

"That there are a lot of things you don't know about me?"

"We can fix that," he said.

"We can't," Renee contradicted. "But for the record,

I had a wonderful weekend. Your parents were gracious to invite me. They've always been very nice to me, especially when your father still ran the business."

Carter felt the obvious barb she'd thrown. "He speaks well of you. In fact, he wondered if you were back at Hampshire Publications."

"Does he still come into the office once in a while?" Renee asked.

"He says he doesn't want to step on my toes. And that he enjoys sitting by the ocean and letting other people do the work."

"I doubt that. He was always so active."

"He still is. He got a job at the local newspaper, one of the free ones, and writes a weekly column on business. And he's taken up tennis and golf."

"Exercise is probably good for him."

Carter nodded. "His doctor suggested he get into a routine."

"What about you? Are you still swimming?"

"I got some laps in while I was there. I go to the fitness club several times a week and swim." Carter had been on the swim team in college and he still enjoyed the pool.

"What about you, after the party? Did you get in any exercise?" He hated the way that sounded.

Renee smiled. "I did," she said. "In fact, I got a lot in."

"With…" He stopped the question. "What did you do?"

"We ran along the beach"

"We?" he interrupted.

"Roger and I, the man who came to the party with me."

Carter nodded. "Does he live on the Island?"

"He has a house there. It was very relaxing to spend the weekend by the sea. I hope to do it more often."

"Did Roger invite you back?" Carter hated the way he talked about the man she'd been seeing. He wanted to know about him, but then he didn't.

"Roger is a biomedical researcher. I'm considering investing in his business."

"That could be very risky. You could lose your entire investment."

"I know, but Roger would take care of me," Renee said. She tossed her head and pushed her hair away from her face. It was curly and Carter wanted to run his hands through it. He knew it was thick and silky and he could get just as much tangled in it as he could in her. He wondered what she meant by Roger would take care of her. Was he doing that now? Did she need someone to take care of her? Why hadn't she turned to him?

Carter knew why. He knew that he'd left her almost standing at the altar. They weren't engaged. They hadn't gotten that far, at least not with spoken words, but they knew they'd crossed the line. And that was when Carter had decided to end things. He was leaving and he didn't want any entanglements behind. He never expected to feel so strongly for Renee, especially when he knew he would be gone in weeks.

But the fire between them flared, then raged out of control. Telling her he didn't want to see her anymore was the hardest thing he'd ever had to say. Now seeing her, being within reach of her and not being able to say what he wanted, to touch her, hold her, make love to her was tearing him apart.

The train reached Penn Station in New York faster than he thought possible. Passengers got to their feet, preparing to disembark. How could he keep Renee from leaving? He didn't want to part from her. He wanted to stay near her, even if he couldn't touch or hold her. He still wanted her around.

"Do you have a car waiting?" Carter asked.

"I'm taking a taxi," she said. "I only have a small bag. Everything else I left at Roger's."

The mention of the man's name pierced him as surely as a switchblade knife would have. What kind of relationship did she have with him? Carter swallowed his retort on what he thought of Roger.

They exited the train together. Throngs of people spilled out of the train and headed in all directions. Some scrambled to make connections. Others headed for the New York Subway System. Some rushed outside to catch an available taxi. Carter focused on keeping up with Renee.

"Here, let me take that for you." Carter took her backpack before she could refuse. She couldn't ditch him if he had her makeup and jewelry. He was sure that's what she carried. He wasn't sure that green gown she'd worn was inside, but whatever was there was valuable to her and she'd want it back.

Renee looked at him suspiciously, but allowed him to keep the bag.

"How do you find being back in a place where people are always moving? Tourists never stop coming, no matter the weather and there are crowds everywhere. I guess it's a lot different from the streets of Princeton, NJ."

"Every city is different," Renee said. "I like New York with all the things you mentioned. I also have a house in Princeton that I kept. So if the crowds, tourists and anyone else…" she glanced at him when she said that "…gets in my way, I have a sanctuary."

"Do you think you need a sanctuary?"

"You never know. After all, this is a very big city. I might need some place to relax."

They reached the escalator leading up to Seventh Avenue. A car was waiting by the curb. Carter went straight for it. He opened the door and stood back for her to get in. Renee looked at the taxi stand and the long line of people waiting.

"I'll take you wherever you need to go," Carter said.

"It's out of your way. I'll take my backpack and be gone."

She reached for it. Her hand touched the strap and Carter turned to face her. Someone bumped into them, pushing them closer together.

"You're not so scared of being alone with me that you can't accept the offer of a ride, are you?"

"Of course I'm not afraid of you. I wonder that you want to be in the area with me."

She stepped around him and slid into the back seat. Carter knew she had no idea how much he wanted to be in the same place with her.

* * *

Renee gave him her address and the driver pulled away from the curb. As much as she chided Carter, she was nervous of him. Her body was hot and she could feel a stream of sweat rolling between her breasts. The car was air conditioned, but it couldn't keep up with her personal furnace. The drive was amazingly short.

The driver opened the door and Renee slid out without answering his question. Carter came out behind her.

"I'm all right, Carter. There's no need for you to come. The door is barely ten feet away and it's broad daylight."

"It would insult my mother's teachings if I didn't see you safely inside."

Renee looked up at him. He was clearly the most handsome man she'd ever seen. "Does that mean you need to check every room inside to make sure no terrorists or ninjas have eluded my alarm system in the last three days?"

"Only if you think it's necessary."

Chapter 5

Wanda and Pete arrived in the bridal department at the same time the next morning.

Renee looked at Pete with concern. "You look like you didn't sleep at all last night," she said.

"I didn't," he said.

"Why not?" Wanda ask. "We don't launch for a while. If you can't sleep now, by the time we get there, you'll be a nervous wreck."

"I'm already a wreck. Did you pick up a magazine on your way in today?" Pete asked Renee.

She shook her head. She usually did. She knew exactly when the new magazines hit the newsstands. And she was often there to get a first copy. Today, she'd been a little preoccupied. It wasn't that she didn't sleep well.

She'd hadn't been thinking about the magazine. Carter was on her mind.

Pete lifted a copy of the current issue of *Hampshire Bridal* he was holding and slid it across the desk. Renee picked it up.

"Beautiful isn't it?"

She gasped at the cover. Coming forward in her chair, she pulled the magazine closer. Opening it, she leafed through the pages. Color drained from her face.

"I know," Wanda said. "It's gorgeous. I had the same reaction."

Renee's reaction was different. She recognized a lot about it. It was different in some places, but for the most part, Renee was familiar with the layout. Why was it here? There were only so many ways to put people on a page, and Hampshire did own this layout. There was no reason they couldn't use it. Renee was just surprised to see it.

By the time she left work that night, she was still thinking about *Hampshire Bridal*. Going to a news-stand, she panned the array of copies like the one she was taking home with her. Laying it on the coffee table in her living room, she found it staring at her each time she passed. She had to find the truth. When she'd moved to Princeton, she'd put a lot of her things in storage. She had yet to get them out and unpack them. She couldn't get a physical copy or a previous magazine, but she might be able to find the CD where she'd saved the files.

It took her two hours to find it in one of the boxes that was still unpacked and sitting in her would-be home office as soon as she had time to organize it. The files were over three years old and the program that had created them had been updated several times since. She hoped it would open.

Renee put the CD in the disc drive and waited. Finally it opened and she watched the screen. Looking back and forth between the computer and the book on her desk, she saw the similarity. More than similarity. If there was such a thing as plagiarizing a previous issue, Hampshire had done it. And done it with a past layout that she had designed.

Sighing, Renee knew there was nothing she could say or do about it. She'd been employed at Hampshire when she created it. And it belonged to them to do with what they wished. But why were they recycling a previous spread? And why were they making it so obvious that they had done little to disguise it.

The next time she saw Blair, she would ask. Then Renee thought better of it. It was none of her business. If Hampshire wanted to use a previous design and layout, they had every right. And he might think she was trying to take credit for it. It was better to leave it alone. She had *Designed for Brides* to worry about and there was enough going on there to keep her busy until the launch. She didn't need to get sidetracked by a misinterpretation with Hampshire.

After a moment, a smile stole across Renee's face. They were afraid, she thought. She could hear her own voice as a whisper in her mind. They were afraid of her. The smile widened. Renee lifted the glossy book and looked at it. She could tell their fear had translated into imitation. They couldn't stop her, couldn't even discover what she was doing to launch her project, so they were going to match her using her own designs. Suddenly, Renee's energy level soared as if she'd had a drug infusion.

Fear was a powerful motivator. Renee saw it in the pages of *Hampshire Bridal*. And Hampshire had reason to fear. They just didn't know how much.

But they would find out and soon.

Not having to go into the office, even for a single day, made Renee feel less claustrophobic. A shipment of dresses for a scheduled photo shoot was expected, and since the office was being painted and set up, there was no place to store them. Renee had moved into her own space, so she'd had them sent to the guesthouse. Dana had come to the city for the weekend to visit, and Renee enlisted her to help with opening boxes and hanging gowns.

"Oh, this is gorgeous," Dana said as she pulled a gown from a box.

She'd said the same thing for each box she opened and each gown she hung. Renee laughed. Dana's comment took her back to her consulting days. They weren't that far behind her, yet hearing a bride find the perfect dress for her special day still gave her goose bumps.

"Renee, you have got to let me try some of these on."

"I take it you're not superstitious," Renee said sarcastically.

"Not in the least." Dana held up a dress covered in Battenburg lace. The sigh she gave was audible and appreciative. "Teddy should do this all the time."

"It is taking more and more of her time. I wouldn't be surprised if sooner or later, she and Diana hire someone else to do the consulting while Teddy concentrates full-time on design."

"And with the magazine you're doing showcasing these dresses, she'll be busier than ever."

"That's the plan," Renee said and smiled.

They had ten boxes to unpack. Seven contained gowns and the other three held accessories.

"When is the shoot?" Dana asked. "I want to be here for that."

"It's on Monday. Can you stay over? I could use the help."

Dana looked at her as if she'd been granted access to Fort Knox.

"I can stay," she said quickly. "That is, unless you have plans." Her brows went up. "Like, is that hunk Carter coming over?"

"Dana," Renee warned. She kept her head down, looking at the task she was performing. "I've told you more than once that Carter and I are history. We never really had a history, so even that may be a misnomer."

"You have and I've heard you, but I'm not convinced that all is done."

"All is done. You sound like someone out of the eighteenth century.

"It must be the gown." Dana held up a retro dress made of delicate lace and covered in pearls. "I think I'll die if you don't let me try this on."

The gown was definitely a magazine cover. She wondered which model was destined to wear it for the shoot on Monday. But for the moment, her cousin would be the first.

"Do you think it will fit?" Renee asked.

"I don't know. It doesn't have a size." Dana looked for a tag. "And models are usually super thin."

"Let's try it."

Moments later, Renee was holding the dress and slipping it over Dana's head. Delicately, she helped Dana pull the gown down and Renee meticulously buttoned her into it.

"Oh," Dana said, looking down at herself.

"You are going to be a beautiful bride," Renee told her cousin. Renee pulled a full-length mirror designated for the shoot in front of Dana. "Look," she said.

Dana's hand went to her breasts. "Is that me?"

"See what a great gown can do for a bride?"

Dana twisted from side to side, looking at herself.

"Let me get the veil and gloves."

"And my phone so I can take a picture," Dana called. "It's in my purse."

The gown could have been made for Dana. The train was long and Renee pulled it out, unfolding the lace and spreading it behind her cousin almost to the length of the room. Renee found a veil and stood on the sofa to set it on her cousin's head.

"Oh," she sighed when she jumped down and looked at Dana. "Oh, my," she whispered, awed by the way her cousin looked. "It's you."

Standing back, Renee snapped a photo on her phone.

"Take one on my phone," Dana said. "I want to show it to my mom."

Renee laughed and took several pictures. "Be careful with that. You know what will happen. You'll have to explain to your mom why you were trying on wedding gowns."

"It's only *one* gown."

"She'll overlook that point," Renee laughed, thinking of her aunt. "She'll want to know who the guy is, why she hasn't met him and whether there's a date yet."

Renee continued to click the shutter. Dana turned about as if she was truly modeling the gown.

"All right. Give me a happy pose. One that you'd find on the cover of a romance novel."

Dana laughed. She pulled the veil off and held it in her hand while it dragged on the floor. Then she threw her head back and arched her back.

"Perfect." Renee was having fun. "Send these to me, especially that last one."

Dana took the phone and pressed several buttons.

"They're in your email. Now you."

"I could never look like you in that dress."

"Not this one. I saw you looking long and hard at one of Teddy's originals. Come on, I tried one on. You can do the same."

"All right," Renee said. She helped Dana take the dress off, then went to the collection they'd hung on the makeshift rack. Sorting through them, she found the one she loved. The strapless bodice was covered in Swarovski crystals shaped like flowers. Between them other crystals dripped like falling teardrops. The bottom of the gown was two layers of white satin over a huge underskirt. The bodice was covered in lace appliqués that picked up the crystals. The train wasn't as long as the one Dana had worn, but it spread out in a perfect semicircle.

Dana found fingerless gloves that reached Renee's elbows and again sported the dripping crystals. While Renee pulled them on, Dana placed the matching veil over Renee's hair.

"Wow," she said stepping back. "You should be one of the models. You look…" Dana stopped.

"Dana, are you crying?"

"Of course I'm not crying…" Her voice broke. "Where's my phone?" Covering her tears, Dana found the cell phone and took several photos. "Turn around," she said. "I want some with the train twisted."

Doing as Dana said, Renee turned a step. Dana pushed the mirror around and Renee got a glimpse of herself. She gasped at the reflection. For a moment she couldn't speak.

"Stand over here," Dana instructed.

Renee moved. The dress and all its slips were heavy. Renee went up two steps and turned back.

"Right there," Dana raised a hand and Renee stopped. "Don't fix anything. It's perfect."

The camera clicked as Dana took one shot after another. "Take some with my phone," Renee said.

"I want a romance cover pose, too," Dana said.

"Fine, but I need a romance cover hero."

"I suppose you'll have to pretend Carter is holding you."

Renee stood up straight and stared directly at Dana. "You think Carter is cover model material?"

She nodded. "Go ahead, lie to me. Tell me you don't think Carter Hampshire could compete with any of those shirtless, airbrushed men on the books you read."

"All right, I concede. He'd a good-looking man."

"He's a great-looking man. I'm sure women are falling all over themselves to get to him."

"Do you mind if we don't talk about Carter?"

Dana hunched her shoulders and snapped another photo.

"Enough," Renee said. "If we're going to make that play tonight, we need to finish this."

Renee came down the steps and turned so Dana could unzip the gown.

"Just a minute. I want to send some of these to myself. I can't be the only one my mother sees in a wedding gown. Where are your contacts? Never mind—I see them."

Setting the phone on the coffee table, she unzipped the gown and held it as Renee stepped out of it.

Renee took the dress and delicately replaced it on the padded hanger. Then she slipped it back into its plastic bag and went to the dress rack. Why did Dana have to bring up Carter? Now all Renee could think about was him holding her in that romance cover pose. As soon as Dana had said it, Renee had gone all warm inside, as if she could feel his strong hands holding her. Suddenly she wished they were holding her.

The pool water was refreshing. Carter swam his thirtieth lap, then pulled himself out of the water and grabbed a plush towel. Drying himself, he breathed hard as he flopped down on a nearby chaise lounge on the fitness center's roof swimming deck. He could feel the sun through the overhead glass panels. It was warm and Carter relaxed for several minutes. A single note that pinged on his cell phone told him he had a new message. Usually he turned the sound off on weekends and late at night. Since he was expecting a call from his sister and she was partial to texting, he'd left it on. The ping, however, wasn't a text. It was an email.

And it was from Renee.

He sat up straight, staring at the phone. Seeing her name and her photo was so unexpected Carter nearly dropped the phone. Leaning forward, his legs balanced on both sides of the chair, he opened the message. There were no comments, only several attached image files. Why would Renee send him picture files? And why was there no message accompanying them?

Carter checked the address. It was hers and there were no other addresses in the email indicating that it could be spam mail or a virus. Curiosity got the best of him and he clicked on the first file. It took a moment, but a photo of Renee appeared wearing a wedding gown. All the air seemed to leave his lungs when he saw her. She was as beautiful as any of the models he'd seen in the magazines.

What did this mean, he asked himself.

He opened the second file. Again, it was Renee. She wore the same dress, but her position and pose were different. Carter had the same reaction. Not only did his breath stop, his heart hammered. What was going on? Renee had rebuffed him at every turn, then out of the blue she sends him wedding photos as if she was part of the upcoming spread in a Hampshire bridal magazine.

There had to be a reason. Renee was a straight forward person. She'd told him in no uncertain terms that she wanted nothing to do with him. So what the heck was this?

Carter opened the third file. Renee's eyes were dreamy. She had the look a photographer would give anything to capture—the look of love. Staring directly at him, love poured from Renee's eyes, showing whoever she was looking at or thinking about that she loved him. Carter was sure it was a *him*. Should he read anything into these photos? He was too confused. Why had she sent them? And without a message. What was she trying to tell him?

He had to know.

His calls to Renee had been unanswered and unreturned. However, Blair told him she had a photo shoot Monday morning. *Well models weren't the only thing she was going to see that day*, he thought.

Chapter 6

Monday came way too soon. Renee and Dana had re-lived the old days, when they were carefree and only interested in talking their dads into buying them new dresses for the school dance. They'd spent a night at a play, then followed it up with drinks at a local bar, which turned into a dance marathon. Recuperation on Sunday would have been ideal, except that Renee had to make sure all the details were set and ready for the shoot early Monday morning.

And it wouldn't be just morning. They had to be ready before sunrise, while the mist was still in the air. They were beginning in a park north of the city. But the photographers had other places they wanted to photograph the models, including a ruined mansion. Thankfully, all the models were there on time. Renee had sent cars to pick them up to make sure. It was going to be a long day.

"All right people, let's do this," the photographer shouted. The first group of models came out of the temporary dressing room, each holding her dress and train to keep them clean.

Dana sidled up to Renee. "Excited?" Renee asked. "Have you ever been to a shoot before?"

Dana shook he head. "This is fascinating. I wish I could model that gown I fell in love with."

"You've got the pictures," Renee told her.

Dana pulled her phone out as a model emerged wearing the dress. Both women looked at the phone and then at the model in front of them.

"That is one gorgeous dress," Dana said. "And she's wearing it to death."

"She doesn't look any better in it than you did," Renee chided with a smile.

"She's had a hairstylist and a makeup artist work on her, plus she's tall as the Empire State Building."

"But how did you feel in the dress?"

"Like it was *my* day."

"Wait, here comes your dress. Let me pull up the photo." The two of them watched as image after image of Renee flashed by. Dana frowned and started the sequence over.

"What's wrong?" Renee asked.

"Some of them are missing." She went through her photos again. Renee peered from next to her.

"Where's the romance one?" Renee asked.

"You sent it to yourself. It should be in your email."

"Right," Dana said and pulled up her email. Renee saw her name in the unopened messages. Dana opened the file and clicked on the photos. The two of them looked as Dana smiled for the camera and her cousin. "Wait, these are the ones of me. I opened the wrong file."

She went back to the inbox. There was no other message from Renee.

"They're on my phone." Renee pulled her phone from the pocket of her jeans and opened her email. "Here they are." Again the two of them looked at the photos and at the model wearing the gown.

"Wait a minute," Dana said. "Why don't I have those on my phone, too?"

"Check your sent folder," Dana said. "Maybe the files are still in your outbox waiting to process."

Renee opened her sent folder and froze. There was the email Dana had sent from Renee's phone. But it wasn't addressed to Dana. It was addressed to Carter.

"Oh, no!" Renee wailed. Everyone in the yard turned to look at her.

"What's wrong?" Dana asked.

Renee could barely speak. "You didn't send those pictures to yourself."

"I did," Dana defended. "You were standing there when I sent the message.

"Look." Renee held up her phone and pointed to the message in her sent folder.

Dana gasped. "I couldn't have done that."

Renee understood what had happened. Carter was in her address book and Dana had had a hard time finding the contact list. When she'd pressed the small key for her contact information, she'd probably hit Carter's instead.

"I'm so sorry, Renee. I never intended to send those photos to him."

Renee didn't say anything. She nodded to her cousin. As much as Dana teased her, she would never have sent those photos without Renee's knowledge.

"What are we going to do now?" Dana asked.

"It's my problem," Renee said.

"I can explain it to him," Dana said. "It was my mistake. I can fix it."

"You can't," Renee said quietly. She took Dana's arm and squeezed it, letting her know she understood it was an error. Renee should have removed his number from her contact list years ago. But she hadn't.

Suddenly, Dana grabbed Renee's arm and squeezed it so tight it hurt. Renee cried out in pain and Dana loosened her grip, but did not release her. "Don't look around," she whispered.

"Why?"

"He's over there. Behind you."

Fear raced through Renee, cold and heavy. "Who?"

"Carter Hampshire."

Renee was tired. Strain from finding Carter staring at her and her need to direct the shoot warred in her mind and body. Life had been a whirlwind for the past three weeks and it culminated with her needing to explain the misdirected photos.

"Let me go tell him what happened," Dana said for the second time.

Renee shook her head. "I'll do it."

Giving Dana a quick smile, she turned and went toward Carter. His face held the slight reflection of a smirk. She wondered if he knew how uncomfortable she felt.

"Great photo," he said the moment she was within earshot.

"I can explain that."

"Don't. I'd rather imagine it. I wish I could have been there," he teased.

"Carter, I need you to delete those pictures."

He crossed his arms and planted his feet. "Now why would I do that?"

Renee knew only the truth would do. "The gown I wore is the centerpiece of our first issue. I need to make sure it's not unveiled until the launch."

Carter looked at the sky as if he was thinking.

"I know you won't use the dress to embarrass me." She appealed to his sense of honor.

He slipped his phone from his pocket and punched in his security code.

Renee held her breath, hoping his intent was to comply with her wishes.

"Is this the one?" He turned the phone so she could see the display.

Renee nodded, although she was sure Carter knew that was the one. Dana had only sent one message to his address.

Going back to the message, he clicked the file to select it. His finger hovered over the delete key. Before pressing it he looked at her.

"What do I get for doing this?"

Renee stepped back as if the question pushed her. "You want to negotiate for the photos?"

"Seems like a good time to me." His smile was white and irritating.

Vowing to remain calm, she asked, "What do you want?"

He stepped closer to her and leaned in. Renee felt the heat of his skin.

"I get the photo back after the launch."

Relief spread through her. Renee's mind had gone in an entirely different direction.

"Is that all?" she asked.

"All for now."

Carter smiled at the mocked-up layout on his desk. "Blair, these are fantastic. Did you hire someone I don't know to design these?"

Blair was shaking her head. Her smile was huge. Carter supposed he'd been harsh with her when he'd rejected the campaign she'd brought to him previously. She had to be relieved that he now liked what she'd presented.

"It was hard to take, but you know when we have to come up with something fantastic, we stand up to the challenge."

"And that you did," Carter said. "You should have been doing these all along. I think they can compete with anything out there. Not only compete, but surpass."

"Thanks," Blair said. "I have more on the drawing board if you'd like to see them now."

"These six are fine. You have my approval," Carter said. "Go with them. We'll have to check out some of the designer collections and get the results of the photo shoots. But I have to say, I am impressed."

Blair gathered the layouts. "We've been working hard in the department."

"Well, please thank everyone for the work. Usually these designs take months. You've done them in just a few weeks."

"And I'm exhausted," she said. "It was a gargantuan effort. Thankfully, we don't have to continue at that level. We've got six months of layouts ready to go under our belts. Now we can breathe a while."

Carter nodded. He felt so much better. For some reason he knew *Hampshire Bridal* would compete with whatever Renee was doing. When her first issue launched later this year, he wanted to have something that was comparable, if not better. Blair had come through, but then she knew this business backward and forward. After all, she'd hired Renee and tutored her. Then Renee's talent had taken flight, and the magazine sales had begun surpassing all projections. It hadn't been the same since she'd left, since he'd forced her to resign.

He was happy that she was using her talent again. It was impossible for him to want her to fail.

It was impossible for him not to want her.

"You seem to have found your energy barometer," Wanda said when Renee arrived at the office the next day.

She smiled but offered no answer. She knew it was

the plan she had in motion that had caused the change in her.

"Sit down," Renee said. "I want to explain an idea I have. I hope with your design wizardry you can make it a reality."

By the time Renee stepped into the elevator that night, she was walking on air. If the two of them pulled her idea together, the industry would be set on its ear and she'd sell a ton of magazines.

Checking the hallways for any sign of Carter, she began walking toward the exit. Sighing as the fresh air hit her, she felt as if she'd escaped him one more day. Yet she felt a twinge of loss. She didn't want to run into Carter, but when she didn't she felt as something was missing.

Renee turned left out of the building. She lived toward the right, but that's how Carter would head. Ten steps later, she noticed a commotion at the curb. Two men were talking in a panic in front of an open car.

One of them was Carter.

What was happening? Without thinking Renee rushed to him.

"Carter, what's wrong?"

"I have to go." He pulled the car door open. "My dad had a heart attack."

His voice was slightly emotional. Renee put her hand on his arm.

"They don't think he's going to make it."

Renee sucked in a breath. "He's on the island, right?" The Hampshires had moved to the Hamptons when Carter's father retired.

Carter nodded.

"You're not driving?" she questioned.

"No other way to get there. The next train doesn't leave for two hours."

Renee bit her bottom lip. Then, making a snap decision, she took his keys and slid into the driver's seat.

"I'm driving," she said. "Get in."

Carter waited a long second, staring into her eyes. Emotions she was unaware of crowded into her.

"He'll be all right," she said, her voice only a whisper of sound.

Carter shut the door and moved to the passenger seat. Renee pulled into the traffic flow as soon as he'd clicked the seat belt.

Carter was quiet for the ride through the city. Once they got through the Midtown Tunnel, his shoulders relaxed a little.

"The doctor called," he said without her asking. "He said the heart attack was serious and that I should come."

Renee let him talk. Putting her hand on his leg was all the comfort she could give. Carter covered her hand with his, and Renee bit her bottom lip.

They drove straight to the Hampton Regional Medical Center. Carter was out of the car the moment she cut the engine. He didn't wait for her as he headed for the entrance, but Renee was only a step behind him. They found his mother in the hall on the third floor, and Carter went into her arms.

"How is he?" Carter asked.

"He's sleeping." She glanced at a door. Carter followed her glance.

"I'm going in." He took his mother's arms from around him and stepped back. He kissed her on the temple and went through the door.

Renee went to Mrs. Hampshire. The woman looked up at her in confusion, then recognition. "Renee?" she said.

Renee nodded.

"You work for Carter?"

"I used to," she corrected.

Renee draped her arm around the woman. She seemed small and lost. Renee led her to a small room with seats where they sat down. Renee had met Emily Hampshire several times and liked her. She always dressed like a fashion model and wore only her own designs. Today, though, she just looked like a distraught wife unsure of his husband's condition.

"Carter's been in there a long time," she said.

"It's only been a few minutes. He'll be out soon."

She patted Renee's hand. The action was nervous and self-conscious.

"Can I do anything for you?" Renee asked. Emily Hampshire looked like she needed sleep. "I have a car. I can take you home to rest for an hour or so."

"No!" She drew away. "I can't leave."

Renee pulled her back and let her lean against her. "We'll wait."

Carter came in a few minutes later, and Emily popped up like a champagne cork. Her steps took her back to Carter.

"The doctor came in while I was there," he explained. "He's in serious condition. There's no guarantee. The next twenty-four hours will tell."

"Twenty-four hours, then what?"

Carter sighed. Renee knew the answer and knew he didn't want to say the words out loud.

"He'll be fine," Renee said, coming up behind her. "The best thing you can do is go home and rest."

"No," Emily said again.

"You want him to see you at your best. You can rest, eat and come back."

Renee glanced at Carter. He nodded. "I'll stay here," he told his mother. "I'll call if there's any change."

Reluctantly, she nodded. Carter walked them to the door. He hugged his mother, then squeezed Renee's hand.

She looked up at Carter, and they locked eyes.

Carter needed her.

Chapter 7

The Hampshire home was a sprawling three-story mansion accented with fish-scale shingles. At the end of the house was a double-story attached gazebo. The back faced the sea, and Renee smelled the water. It was beautiful and breathtaking. During the party, she hadn't been able to see the water, but she knew what the view looked like from other parties she'd attended.

A maid opened the door as soon as Renee stopped the car. Together they took Mrs. Hampshire inside.

"She needs to rest and eat," Renee said.

The maid directed her to the master bedroom and left them to get her a tray.

The inside of the house was just as beautiful as the outside—open, bright and happy looking. Renee had been there before, but never above the ground floor. Together she and Mrs. Hampshire went up a staircase that any five-star hotel would be proud to display. Carter's mother didn't argue about resting, and she was nearly asleep when the maid came in.

After eating half a sandwich and drinking some tea, she refused everything else and fell asleep. Renee took the tray and quietly stole out of the room. As she descended the stairs, she heard a car door slam. Checking the window, she saw a yellow cab and the top of a man's head. A moment later, the front door opened and in walked a man resembling Carter. He was an inch or two shorter, but they had the same dark eyes and smooth skin. Dropping an overnight bag by the door, he looked up at Renee.

"Who are you?" he asked.

"I'm Renee Hart. You must be one of Carter's brothers." She knew he had three brothers and a sister.

"Sean," he said. "Where's my mother?"

Coming to stand in front of him, she said, "She's sleeping. I got her to eat a little. Carter's at the hospital."

"How is he?"

She knew he referred to his father and not Carter.

"The doctor said it's too early to tell. They're hoping to know more by this time tomorrow."

"I'll run up and see my mom, then get my car and go there."

"Try not to wake her. She's really tired," Renee said.

"Are you a nurse?" he asked.

"No, I'm just a friend." Although right now the lines of what she was seemed to be blurring.

Renee was in the living room looking through the windows at the darkness when Sean came back down.

"I'm on my way out," he said.

She turned. "I'll stay with her until she wakes. Carter promised to call if there was any change."

He started toward the back of the house.

"Sean?"

He stopped.

"Take this." Renee handed him a small insulated pouch. "It's got juice in it for Carter. He's not a big coffee drinker." She didn't add that coffee made him restless. He was probably restless enough.

"You must know him well."

"We used to work together," she offered. "When everyone was drinking coffee, he'd have a bottle of juice."

Sean took the bag from her. "You're Renee, right?"

She nodded, wondering if he'd forgotten her name or if he was remembering it.

"Thanks," he said. But it was his smile, so like Carter's that made her feel that he knew more than he was letting on.

Carter didn't call. Mrs. Hampshire was still asleep when Renee looked in on her two hours later. Renee didn't know her well enough to know if she should wake her or let her rest. She opted to let the woman rest. Neither of her sons had returned to the house, and they would have come or called if there was any news.

At sunrise, a group of people came through the door. Their noise woke Renee, who'd fallen asleep on the sofa. She pushed her hair out of her face.

"How is he?" she asked, pushing her bare feet to the floor.

Carter came to her. "He's out of danger."

Renee stood up and Carter pulled her into his arms. She closed her eyes and held on, relieved about his father, but also loving the feel of being held by him. Loving it too much. She needed to push him back, but found it was too hard.

"Do you think we could get introduced to this woman in your arms?"

The voice came from the only other female in the room. Carter stepped back and turned, his arm remaining possessively around her waist. He introduced her to his other brothers, Sloan and Shane, and his sister Julia. Renee smiled and shook hands with them all.

"It's good news about your father," she said.

"What news?"

All eyes went to the staircase. Mrs. Hampshire was halfway down. Her children moved to her, and only Carter stayed behind.

Renee turned to him. "I have to go back now."

"Don't go."

She so wanted to fall into the darkness of his eyes, but she knew better. "I have things to do. Your father is out of danger. You have your mom and your family for support. I need to go back to work."

Carter sighed, but didn't try to stop her. "I'll drive you to the train station."

Renee nodded and said goodbye to the group. His mother came over and thanked her with a hug.

At the station, Carter got out of the car and waited

on the platform with her. It was crowded with the morning's rush hour commuters.

"You don't need to wait. You've been up all night, and you need to get some rest."

"The train will be here soon. And I wanted to thank you for all you did."

"No need." She looked down at the platform.

"You dropped everything you planned for the evening, drove me out here, listened to me in the car, cared for my mother and remembered that I needed juice."

Renee laughed at the last.

Carter smiled.

"Only a friend would do that," he said. "We can't be strangers any longer."

The wind blew against her, but the heat invading her body was no match for it. Looking over her shoulder, she saw the train's engine light in the distance.

"That's my train," she said unnecessarily, but feeling like she needed to say something to keep her emotions in check.

"I'll see you when I get back," he said.

Renee nodded. Carter pulled her into his arms and kissed her. His mouth was hard on hers and Renee's was just as hard on his. Strong arms circled her body, pulling her close, until the train whistled.

"I have to go," she said, her voice hoarse and her emotions raw. Pulling away, she moved onto the train, turning back to look at Carter. The crowd forced her further away from where he stood. She wanted him, needed him. When he'd come through the door at his house, he'd come straight to her and taken her into his arms as if it was the most natural thing to do. As if it was what he should do.

For the merest moment, Renee felt as if she belonged there. As if she was part of that family and they were part of hers.

The next day, Renee woke refreshed and ready to go back to her work plans, which were becoming more concrete by the day.

As long as she lived, she would consider hiring Wanda one of her smartest moves ever. The woman was incredible. The two of them had worked tirelessly for weeks coming up with the computerized program that was the first part of the plan Renee had in mind. Neither had told anyone what they were doing. They were almost ready for the launch party, and Renee planned to invite Diana and Teddy up for the unveiling. They were using one of Teddy's creations, which Renee would model while Wanda would handle the graphics.

The final result came at midnight two weeks after Carter returned to the office. Renee hadn't seen him. But the tension of potentially running into him had a greater force than it had in the past. Renee knew it had to do with the kiss on the platform. With all his kisses.

"It was an absolutely stupendous idea," Wanda said as they looked at the spinning gown.

Her comment pulled Renee's attention back to the present.

"I wish I'd thought of it."

Renee discovered Wanda liked to speak in superlatives. Everything was over the top.

Renee's idea was to use a new technology that would create a hologram of a wedding gown. They had needed a hologram expert, and so Wanda had called in Pete Cooper, who she knew did this kind of work. He was fabulous. Renee had hired him as a consultant, but eventually changed his position to full time employee.

They were about to finalize the last test to make sure the system worked.

"You were so right to patent this," Pete told her as he fiddled with the device on his arm.

"Just wait until the competition finds out what we have. We won't be able to keep these magazines on the newsstands," Wanda said, her fingers flashing over the computer keys like lightning striking.

"I hope Ms. Teddy is ready for the onslaught of brides," Pete said.

"I've already given her a heads-up. They're planning to be ready."

Renee was holding ground-breaking technology. It would bring business in, and not just for the magazine. Teddy had a store in Princeton, but there was no New York facility, not to mention all the places across the United States where the magazine would be available. She needed to call Teddy and set up a meeting. This was a new business and they needed to plan for the operation.

"How close are we to being ready?" Renee asked.

"Just inches," Pete said.

"Call me when we're ready for the test."

"I'd say you should go refresh your makeup. We're

that close." Wanda took a moment to glance at her and smile.

Moments later Renee stood in the middle of the floor. Wanda stood on one side of the room, Peter on the other.

"Ready," he asked.

"As ready as ever," she said. Lifting her arm, she pressed the button on the strap Wanda had hooked on her. A mockup of the magazine was propped against the desk, with one of Teddy's gown designs facing her. She pressed the button.

"Ahhh," Wanda said, clapping her hands like a three-year-old on Christmas morning.

"It works," Peter shouted.

Renee glanced at the projection. She turned fully around. What she saw was herself, wearing the gown that was in the book. *She* was the hologram. The gown glittered as if it was real.

Pressing the button again, the office went back to normal. For a long second, the three of them looked at each other. Then they rushed together and shouted in a group hug.

"You try it," Renee said to Wanda.

Wanda smiled and stood up. She walked to the place Renee had stood and pressed the button of a second prototype. It worked like magic.

"Look at me," Wanda crooned. "I love this." She twisted around, checking the dress from all angles.

"Especially the shoes," Pete chimed in.

Renee looked at the red sneakers on Wanda's feet. She usually wore high heels, but after seven this evening, she'd changed into more comfortable footwear.

"What about you, Pete? Try it," Wanda encouraged, already removing her device.

"Those are women's gowns."

"Yep, and you're a man." She made fists and raised her arms, imitating a macho bodybuilder. Pete was far from a bodybuilder, but he was lean and tall and the women in her office checked him out every time he passed.

"We could just as easily create a tuxedo for the men," Wanda stated.

"We should have done that," Pete said, his voice indicating he'd love to work on another project.

"One magazine at a time," Renee cautioned.

"Come on, Pete. Show us your feminine side." Wanda clamped the projection device on his arm and stood back.

With a heavy sigh Pete stepped into place and pushed the tiny pink button. The two women broke into gales of laughter.

"We'll have to redo your hair." Wanda could hardly get the words out.

Pete hit the button again, killing the image of himself. "I've seen my feminine side, and it sucks," he said.

They laughed again. A moment later, Renee heard the main entry buzzer sound.

"Expecting someone?" she asked. Blank stares looked back at her.

The three of them headed for reception.

"Carter," Renee said.

"What's he doing here?" Pete whispered. Both Wanda and Pete knew Carter owned Hampshire Publications, but they didn't know anything about her relationship with him.

"It's all right," Renee said. "I'll take care of this."

The door clicked. She pushed it open and stepped outside. It locked behind her.

"I came up to say hello, but I heard a shout. Is everything all right?"

"Everything is fine."

"It's pretty late," he said.

She looked at her watch, only there was no watch there. The device was still in place.

"What's that?"

"Just something I was working on." She put her hand down, slipping it behind her back. "You're here very late."

"I had to catch up on the work I missed when my dad was sick."

"How is your dad?"

"Almost back to his normal self." He smiled. "That means he's being a pain to everyone around him."

"What about your mom? Is she all right?"

"She asked about you."

Renee looked up at him.

"She wanted to thank you for all your help."

Renee smiled. "I didn't do much."

"And she said she'd like you to come to dinner when everyone is better."

"That would be nice," Renee said. She didn't want to commit to anything.

"Are you finished here for the night?" he asked. "I'd like to take you to get something to eat."

Renee hesitated.

"I owe you. You were there when I needed you. Be gracious enough to accept."

Renee glanced behind her.

"Don't mind us," Wanda shouted through the glass door. "Pete and I have plans."

Renee knew Pete and Wanda had no relationship that didn't involve a computer.

"It's a little late for a meal. I think I'll just go home. We have a ton of work to get done in the next few weeks."

"Then I'll see you home," Carter said.

Renee couldn't think of any reason to refuse, especially since she could see Wanda gesturing for her to accept.

"Let me get my things."

When they were on the street, Carter took her hand and threaded it through his arm. Renee felt his strength. She didn't try to pull free, but knew if she wanted to, Carter wouldn't allow it. Taking a cue from him, she leaned her head against him.

They walked several blocks, sauntered through Grand Central Terminal and got a taxi at the 42nd Street entrance. Renee gave her address and the taxi pulled into the evening traffic.

Renee settled herself against Carter in the back seat.

"Tired?" he asked.

"It was a long day," she yawned. "But a productive one."

"What were you working on so late? You haven't

launched, so it couldn't be the deadline for getting everything to press."

"Just a few projects. But we'll be ready soon." *And then all will be revealed.*

The taxi stopped in front of her house and they both got out. Carter saw her to the door and said goodnight, but he didn't leave. Renee looked up at him, and he quickly pulled her to him and clamped his mouth to hers.

It was the kind of kiss that said they couldn't deny each other. They couldn't go on as they had in the past. The world for them had changed, and they must change with it. It was a new beginning kiss, an I-know-we've-been-apart-but-we're-back-now kiss. Renee raised her arms and circled his neck, giving up any thought. She wanted Carter.

The waiting taxi beeped his horn reminding them that he was there. Carter lifted his mouth and sighed into her hair. He pushed her back and looked into her eyes.

"One day I'm going to kiss you inside a place where there are no steps, no train platforms and no waiting taxi."

A free weekend. Renee couldn't think of the last time she'd had one of those. As a consultant, her weekends were booked with weddings. Since returning to New York, she'd put in weekend hours too numerous to count at *Designed for Brides*. And as soon as they launched the magazine, she'd have precious little time, so she decided to take a day off from the office.

Finally, all the boxes sitting on the floors of the various rooms in her house had been unpacked and their contents stored. Renee sat on the floor of her home office surrounded by bridal magazines. She wanted to re-familiarize herself with the competition. For the most part, the magazines were the same. There were full-page photos of bridal gowns, ads for tuxedo rentals, accessories for the bride and her bridesmaids.

Designed for Brides needed something more. Something unique that would set it apart from the many bridal magazines on bookstore shelves and newsstands. Renee leafed through the pages. While the gowns were gorgeous, nothing really spoke to her. After going through the issues for several hours and reading everything in them, an idea struck her. But she needed help.

She needed Wanda and Pete.

Renee had an idea, but her skills were only rudimentary for executing it. Maybe Pete could do it. If not, they might have contacts. Renee liked the talkative woman and the quiet spoken man.

Picking up a magazine, she looked down at the cover. It was from Carter's company. Renee analyzed the elements. She pulled eight other magazines and spread them out in front of her. They could be mirrors of each other. All had a bride on the cover, usually the one that some designer had paid to have there.

For *Designed for Brides*, she would have control over what went on the cover. They were going to go with one of Teddy's creations for the first issue. Brides expected to see a dress on the cover—it was a mental trigger as to what was inside, what they could expect. Renee wouldn't tamper with that, but she wanted to present it differently. Taking another look at the covers, she perused them one by one, giving each one enough time to determine if there was anything that stood out to her. If she was a bride and looking for a magazine, she'd choose the one with the dress that most appealed to her. The dress on *The New Bride,* distributed by News Publications, Inc. was the one she'd choose.

She spent another twenty minutes looking at *The New Bride,* then decided she'd need more time to come up with a presentation.

Renee got up just as her doorbell rang. She turned toward the door, staring at it as if she could see through the heavy wood. She wasn't expecting anyone. She looked through the peephole and found Carter standing there. What could he want?

She opened the door. "Carter, I wasn't expecting you."

She held the door close to her arm, not opening it fully.

"Is it all right if I come in?"

Renee reluctantly opened the door and stepped back. Carter entered and she closed it.

"Would you like something to drink?

"I'll have what you're having."

She'd opened a bottle of wine, and a single glass sat on the coffee table. She got him a glass then resumed her seat.

"Buzz is all over the building that something secret is going on."

"Did you come to see what it was?" she asked.

"Just looking for ideas," he said.

Renee gathered the array of magazines and put them in a pile. "That's exactly what I was doing. I'm trying to find something that will appeal to brides and not be the same designs they've seen before."

"I believe I've heard you say that before."

"Carter, is there something you wanted? You've never been one to steal ideas, so I don't think you're here to see what I'm doing. And since we're rivals, you can't be here to help."

"I thought you might want to go out for a cup of coffee or a glass of wine." He saluted her with the wineglass.

"Well, you don't drink coffee, and we already have the wine."

"Then how about we just walk. You've been locked in here all day. A little exercise might do you good."

He couldn't know she'd been in all day, but Renee didn't argue the point.

She couldn't dispute that she needed exercise. She was a jogger, and in Princeton she'd had a daily routine of running through town before she began her day. After moving to New York, most of her energy had gone into working, first *on* the office, then *at* the office. Even her nights were filled with analyzing her competition.

"Come on." Carter offered her his hand.

Renee stared at it. Yet her heartbeat went up a notch and she found her hand moving into his. Grabbing her keys and purse from the hook by the door, she followed him out into the late afternoon.

The park wasn't that far away and they walked toward it. Carter kept hold of her hand, and Renee felt hers grow clammy.

Three years, Renee thought. She remembered the office party where they'd first gotten together. He worked on thirty-eight, and she was two floors below that, but he often came to discuss things with Blair. When the McGuinn deal had been signed, sealed and delivered, the champagne had been brought out and a celebration had begun.

Carter had congratulated her and everyone had toasted to the huge contract. When the cases in the office were all empty, they continued at a local bar, where more wine was drunk and the loud music made others get up to dance. Carter didn't ask her to dance, but she happened to bump into him. They'd laughed and talked and finally danced. As the night wore on and people began to leave for trains and buses, she found herself next to him.

His car service arrived and he offered to take her home. That had been the turning point. From the moment Renee made the decision to allow him to drive her home, her life would never be the same. She couldn't go back and change history, even if she wanted to. And she wasn't sure she did.

She'd been as happy as any of the brides displayed on the covers of their magazine. She'd thought the relationship would follow the normal cycle. But that wasn't what happened.

Renee looked at the ground and shrugged the memory off. She'd walk and not think about what was happening. Nothing was happening. Their relationship was in the past and it had no future. She was on one side of the magazine playing field and he was on the other. There was no crossing the barrier.

Renee couldn't say she hadn't thought of resuming a relationship with Carter. It had been on her mind since her heart lurched in the restaurant that night she'd met Blair for dinner.

She'd told herself they were competitors, but that wasn't the complete truth. She was just plain scared of having her heart broken again. What if the chase was all that interested Carter? What if something or someone else came along and he decided to leave without discussing it with her? Could she go through the heartache again?

That wasn't how a relationship worked. Renee hadn't been seriously involved with anyone since Carter. She'd had dates. She'd gone out with people she liked, but none of them touched her heart the way Carter had.

"Are we just going to walk or are you going to tell me why you felt the need to come to see me today?" Renee finally asked when they reached the park. Carter made her nervous, especially when he showed up without notice. His unexpected arrival at her doorstep was no different.

"I wanted to see you?"

Her heart lurched again.

"I went to your office, but all I could get out of your receptionist was that you'd taken the day off.

"I needed some down time," she said, looking away from him.

"But you spent the day working from home."

She didn't say anything, she couldn't deny it. The array of magazines he'd seen on her floor told him she had been working, but it wasn't the tiring kind of work that took all her energy when she was in the office. Maybe because she knew Carter wasn't an elevator ride away from her.

"What did you do today?" she asked.

"I thought of you."

Renee stopped as if a barrier had been placed in front of her and looked at him. Her throat went dry. She couldn't speak.

"We've got to talk about us sooner or later." Carter's stare was direct and unwavering. "Don't say there is no us. We both know that's not true."

"Carter, I can't go through that again."

"I won't ask you to."

"Don't you think it would be better if we—"

"No," he didn't let her finish. "Our emotions won't allow it. It doesn't matter how far or fast we run, we're supposed to be together."

Renee remembered them continually running into each other when she was trying to avoid him. It was like some type of force that kept putting them in the same place and time.

"And you didn't know that three years ago?" she asked.

Renee watched as Carter winced.

"I did, but it was out of my control."

"But you feel that you have control now? That nothing else will come up and force you to leave again."

He nodded. "I can't speak for the future. No one

can. But I know that I will never make the same decision as I did before. I know I want you in my life. And you know it too. No matter how much you try to deny it. All I need to do is touch you and…"

He didn't need to finish the sentence. Renee's body reacted to his words.

"I can't do this now, Carter."

"Can't do what?"

"I can't concentrate on you and me. And I'm not saying that there is or will be a you and me. I have a lot riding on this magazine. I'm being tested with this project. Not so much by Diana and Teddy, but by myself. There's a whole industry out there and not all of them are rooting for me. I have confidence that I know what I'm doing. But I can't afford any missteps or any distractions. Can you understand that?"

"I understand," he said, although Renee wasn't sure he did. She could hear the disappointment in his voice.

"Does this mean you'll give it some thought once everything is done?"

"I will, Carter," she said. "When this magazine is put to bed, I'll think about it."

The truth was Renee hadn't been able to think of anything other than her and Carter. He'd given her some room. She didn't run into him every night or find him waiting in the reception area of her office. However today she expected to see him.

Renee was at the Magazine Expo trade show, admiring the Hampshire Publications booth. It covered the space of ten booths. The staff was mainly marketing and sales people. Renee didn't know many of them, but there were a few left over from her days.

She noticed the bridal section was bright and had a large part of the real estate, but not the greatest amount. That went to magazines on fitness and sports. Renee spent several hours walking through the show and looking at what publishers chose to display. Market share was obvious to anyone who knew how to see it.

She headed to News Publications, Inc. Their space wasn't as large as Hampshire's, but it was close, and they also had a bridal section.

"Surveying the competition?"

Renee turned to find Blair next to her.

"I am," she answered honestly. "I've already been to Hampshire. Frankly, I thought the section for brides would be larger."

"We have an adequate showing."

"It's impressive," Renee said. They did have an impressive showing, but in the back of her mind, she felt Blair was unhappy. She was smiling, but there was a sadness in it. Renee had seen that before.

"I have to get back over there. If you have a moment, have lunch with me."

"I can't. I already have plans."

Renee was seeing one of the wedding gown designers over lunch, and she would be discussing using some of his designs in her magazine. Justin Millard was relatively new to the business and she felt she had a good chance of picking him up before the world of fashion understood that he was destined to be a force in the business.

Renee said goodbye to Blair and left the expo for her appointment. She and Justin were getting together off-site—Renee didn't want any prying eyes to notice who she was meeting. Teddy had brought him to Renee's attention. Both had looked at some of his designs and felt they would augment her magazine. Justin came prepared for a presentation, even though they were in a restaurant. Renee looked through his work, forgetting her meal. She liked what she saw, and when she emerged an hour later, they had an agreement. One of Teddy's designs would be on the front cover, but Justin would get the center of the magazine. He went away smiling and agreed to come to the offices in a couple of days so they could finalize everything.

Renee went back to the convention center after lunch. The crowds were now massive, and she ended up only a row from the Hampshire display when she came face-to-face with Carter.

"Well, hello."

Renee nodded. Seeing him was like getting a narcotic elixir pumped into her blood. "I saw Blair. Things appear to be going well." She glanced toward the booth, but the crowds prevented her from seeing straight through.

Carter looked in the same direction. "I guess you'll be here next year with your own displays."

"Probably not as large as the one Hampshire is taking up, but I put in a request." The trade show was a major event for sales and marketing. Booking space a year in advance was common.

"You were always thinking about the business."

Carter smiled at her and suddenly she wasn't thinking of business at all. She had a mental picture of the two of them rolling around on the bed. Business had been the last thing on her mind then.

"It gives me something to do between breakfast and dinner." She almost said between breakfast and bedtime, but caught herself. She didn't want any references to bed.

"What do you do after dinner?"

Color rushed up her face into her hair. Renee had walked into that one. "I sometimes go out with friends."

"Anyone I know?"

"I doubt it," she teased."

Renee didn't ask if there was anyone in his past. She knew there had to be, but she didn't care to have it confirmed. It had been three years, and there could have been many women between then and now. Knowing Carter had shared his days and nights with someone else tortured her. Renee pushed aside any thoughts of Carter and another woman. She focused on the magazines in front of her, but saw only a blur of color.

"Renee." She heard her name called and turned to see a friend rushing toward her. "I've been looking for you. That guy you wanted to meet is in the booth now. Come with me."

Renee looked at Carter. "Jean, this is Carter Hampshire of Hampshire Publications," she said. "Jean Raymond. She's the—"

"Art director at Wineman and Sons," Carter finished for her.

Jean offered her hand and the two shook.

"Your reputation precedes you," Carter said.

"As does yours," Jean replied.

"Carter, I'll see you later," Renee said. She was glad to have a reason to leave the aura that seemed to surround him. Renee felt as if she couldn't pull air into her body whenever he was near.

"I need to get back, too. Nice meeting you, Jean." He left them.

"What a hunk," Jean said. "Who knew he was so good looking? Much better than any photo I've ever seen of him."

"Where's the booth?" Renee asked.

She glanced toward Carter's retreating back before the crowd swallowed him up.

Chapter 8

It had been a mistake to let her go, Carter thought making his way back to the Hampshire booth. Not only was she beautiful, but she was intelligent and had a sense for the market. He had no doubt that the magazine she was developing would be a success. He'd seen what she had done with his own bridal magazine. And she had Theresa Granville designs. They were new to the market, a fresh look, and from the reports he'd seen women were falling over themselves to get one of her originals.

That alone would make the magazine sell. But he felt Renee had another surprise up her sleeve. She was an innovator. He wasn't totally unaware of her methods as a wedding consultant. She'd done some pretty fantastic weddings. Even though he was two floors above the bridal division at Hampshire, Blair often came up to give him a rundown of Renee's work. She was good at what she did.

He wouldn't do anything to discourage or sabotage her efforts, but he wished she was on his side instead of part of the competition.

He wasn't sure what would happen between them after she launched, but he was determined to make sure any conflict between them was settled.

Launch day for *Designed for Brides* was only a breath away, but before that the marketing department had set up a prelaunch party to get the buzz about the magazine started.

Every detail of the demonstration was ready, and it was time to share it with the world. Renee inhaled deeply, glancing at her staff. Wanda, Pete, and her marketing director, Stacy Costain, each gave her a smile and a double thumbs-up.

"We're ready," Stacy whispered encouragingly.

Renee walked to the head of the room. An array of bloggers, journalists, trade publication executives and influential news people stopped their conversations.

"By now you're all wondering why you were required to sign a confidentiality agreement before entering."

There was a smattering of laughter and a few groans that followed.

"The windows have been blocked, the waitstaff has left the room and there is security outside the doors."

A murmur went through the crowd.

"Don't worry," Renee stated. "We haven't locked you

in. However, it's extremely important that we keep what you're about to see confidential until our magazine, *Designed for Brides*, launches." She paused. "We're giving you a sneak peek at our creation so you can have your blogs, columns and interviews ready to go in three days when the magazine hits the newsstands."

Renee surveyed the gathering. They looked inquisitive, skeptical and confused.

"You should all have received your wristband. We're called it a DR Device. DR stands for Dress Rehearsal, and it allows every bride to instantly see what she looks like in a designer gown."

Looking at the doorway, Renee saw the staff was ready. Again they gave her smiles and nods.

"Ladies," she said, extending a hand to them. Her staff funneled into the room carrying the first edition of *Designed for Brides*. It had a slick cover sporting the latest gown by Teddy. They placed copies of the magazine in prearranged locations, then moved to stand behind Renee.

"Wanda," Renee called.

Wanda walked to the center of the room amid applause. Smiling, she turned around in a full circle as if she was a runway model.

"Wanda has agreed to demonstrate. Please notice her attire *and* her shoes." Dressed in multicolored leggings with a long red T-shirt and her signature stiletto heels, she looked nothing like a bride.

"Show them," Renee said.

Pushing the pink button of her DR, Wanda's projection flashed across the open space, showing her dressed in the gown from the magazine's cover.

A collective *ahh* came from the crowd. Renee watched as eyes opened wider and mouths dropped. Three seconds of silence held the room in awe before questions flew from frenzied reporters.

"How did you do that?" someone called.

"Does mine work?" came another.

Others shouted louder, each trying to be heard and to get an answer. Questions came fast and from every direction. Renee fired replies as fast as she could.

The chaos died down and Wanda pressed her device button, returning her image to her personal attire. The room quieted and Wanda joined the small group behind Renee.

"Your devices are operational," Renee told the assembly. "Feel free to try them."

"It's working," Pete stated as the room filled with projections of one of the four gowns that beamed from the open books.

"We're going to stomp the competition," Stacy said. "I can hardly wait to see it."

"I want to see the look on Mr. Carter Hampshire's face when he hears about this," Pete said.

Renee turned to look at him.

"And when he sees it," Wanda said, then she noticed Renee's stare. "I mean, he's handsome as the devil, but he's got nothing like this."

"No," Renee agreed. "He's got nothing like this."

* * *

"What's going on down there?" Carter asked the moment Blair came into his office.

"I haven't been able to find out anything. The glass doors are blacked out and anyone who's come out of there refuses to speak about what they learned. The only thing that appears strange is they're all wearing a bracelet."

"A bracelet?" Carter's brows rose.

"The same bracelet. It has a little pink jeweled button on it. When I asked what that was for, the only thing I got was that it was a gift for attending."

Carter paced the room. Renee was up to something. It had to be big if she'd gotten the bloggers and media people to remain closed-mouthed about what was going on.

"I heard they had to sign a nondisclosure agreement. So they can't talk about what happened."

"Nothing here has ever been that secret." Carter spoke more to himself than to Blair.

"I know. There were even hired guards. I tried to get in, but my name wasn't on the list and they barred me totally. I tried every approach, even called Renee's cell. I got a message saying the line wasn't accepting calls or voice mail."

"She launches in three days," Carter said. "Someone has to know what happened."

"True," Blair said. "I know it's intriguing, but it doesn't really affect us."

Carter glared at Blair. "Our sales are declining. This is

a new venture by someone who used to run our bridal division. She's planning something that directly affects us."

Blair walked to where Carter stood. Putting her hand on his arm, she turned him to face her and looked directly into his eyes. Carter didn't want her to see anything there for fear of what he might reveal, but he didn't look away.

"What's this really about?" she asked. "In three days we'll know everything. We've never been this concerned about a start-up before. Is it the magazine that's bothering you, or is it Renee?"

Carter kept his eyes from wavering. Several answers flashed through his jumbled mind, but in the end he opted for the truth.

"A little of both."

Blair waited a moment before dropping her head and her hand. "Did you answer her invitation yet?"

Carter cleared his throat. It was suddenly clogged.

"It doesn't matter," Blair said. "Like I said, we'll know everything in a couple of days."

Blair left him staring through the window. He looked down wishing he could see into Renee's offices. But more than that, he wanted to see into her mind. What was going on there? He hadn't seen her in a week. And when he left the office each night, he'd pass a delivery guy bringing in food for the whole staff on the 18th floor.

The truth was, Carter wanted to see Renee. He wanted to be close to her, to spend time together, eat together, and make love early and often. He wanted to know if she was thinking of him. Did their conversation in the park have an affect on her? He realized it was a gradual process with Renee. Their history put an obstacle in his way and negotiating it was a delicate operation. He was making progress, but it was slow.

Renee no longer flinched at his touch or pushed him away when he got close enough to take her arm. She accepted his kisses and he knew his touch penetrated her defenses. But he wanted more, and he was sure she did, too. Even if she refused to admit it. Yet their history had burned her deeply. Somehow they needed to reach a point where she would allow herself to trust that their relationship had enough strength and promise to survive a future together.

The entire staff from Weddings by Diana arrived for launch day. The magazines hit the stands at four o'clock in the morning, and Renee hadn't been able to sleep the previous night. Her stomach was tied in knots when she stepped into the office. The day looked ordinary. They wouldn't know anything about the sales until later in the morning.

Would her plans work? As she'd hoped, buzz about the magazine had been building in the streets of the bridal district. Phone calls and email had clogged their lines and inboxes, but her staff had remained tight-lipped. The bloggers' help was greater than she'd anticipated—they were already alluding to a coming tide of change, without saying what it was. But they invited their readers to return on launch day for the anticipated reveal. Preorders of the magazine tripled as Renee had expected. And she'd been approached by the morning shows to appear because of her *revolutionary game changer*, their words. She'd agreed, and now she found herself in the studios of one of the major morning talk shows. Teddy and Diana were with her for moral support, but Wanda opted to watch from her apartment. And Pete said he wouldn't miss a single moment of the unveiling.

Renee's knees knocked as she was led from the greenroom to the on-air studio. She was microphoned and seated. Teddy gave her a smile and a thumbs-up signal as the lights came on and the anchor took her chair. Pete smiled, something he didn't do often. Renee relaxed as the interview began.

It was customary to invite your competition to the launch party. It was also usual for them to refuse. But Carter and his bridal division staff accepted. Rumors abounded about something radical, brand new, never before seen that was coming from Renee's new venture. Unfortunately, he hadn't been able to discover what it was. He'd gone to her offices, and while she no longer barred him from her presence, she was extremely uncommunicative about what her plans at *Designed for Brides* involved.

The party would begin at eight in the evening, and it was only seven in the morning now. Carter knew she was on a talk show today; she'd mentioned it herself during one of his drop-in visits. He'd picked up one of her magazines from the newsstand in the lobby on his way to his office.

There didn't seem to be anything different except

a few thick pages. Soon he and the rest of the industry would find out what all the hoopla, not to mention
secrecy, was about. In the back of his mind, he clos-
eted the hope that she'd live up to the implied promise.
Anything less would devastate her and kill her business, not to mention the impact it could have on their
relationship. Carter switched on the live streaming of
her interview on his computer.

He'd missed her introduction and the quick banter
thanking Renee for appearing. The commentator went
right to the meat of the interview.

"Ms. Hart, from what we've seen, you're about to
revolutionize the magazine industry."

Renee's face filled the screen. She could be a model
herself. She looked gorgeous in a high-necked lace dress
that could have been a wedding gown. The unexpected-
ness of it hit him like hot water. He thought about the
photo Dana had mistakenly sent him. Renee would be
a gorgeous bride, and he wanted her to be his.

The launch of a magazine wasn't usually newsworthy. Crossing his arms, he paid silent homage to Renee
for the marketing efforts she was orchestrating. Yet he
was still a little apprehensive that she could pull this off.

"We have a new invention that will allow every bride
to model the designer wedding gowns in our issues,"
she said.

Carter frowned. This was the rumor he'd heard.

"There's nothing strange about that. Brides often try
on as many as twenty dresses before they find the one
they wish to buy," the commentator said.

Renee smiled. Carter could tell by the way his heartbeat accelerated that there was more to come, and she knew it.

Then he noticed the bracelet on her arm, a black velvet strap holding a rectangular box the size of an elegant watch. In the center there was a stone that looked like a pink tourmaline or pink topaz. It was faceted and shaped like a heart. Blair had mentioned this gift item when Renee held her secret meeting.

"That's the average," Renee was saying. "But many don't get to try on the designer dresses they find in magazines."

Then the commentator asked the question that was on Carter's mind.

"How is your magazine going to make that happen?"

"May I demonstrate?" she asked.

The commentator nodded. Carter moved closer to the screen.

Renee stood up and took a step forward. Whatever she faced, the camera didn't show. While she positioned herself, the commentator continued.

"This is the new magazine, *Designed for Brides*." The anchor held the glossy cover up to the camera. Carter noticed the design, the placement of text on the cover, the font used as a branding element. It was well designed. He wouldn't expect any less of a product that had Renee's name attached to it. And it was the same magazine that lay in the center of his desk.

The camera panned back so both Renee and a portion of the studio floor were visible. Nothing appeared in front of her. Raising her arm, she pushed the pink heart on the bracelet and a life-size version of herself seemed to step off the page and become a 3-D projection on the floor in front of her. She appeared to be fully dressed in the gown shown on the cover. There was an audible gasp from the crew in the newsroom.

Carter, in his office, gasped, too.

The anchor never lost a beat or showed surprise in his voice. "As you can see, Ms. Hart has a method that will basically take your breath away. It's something every bride can do in her own home. Tell us what you've done," the anchor prompted.

Carter's phone rang. Not taking his eyes off the screen, he picked it up and pushed the accept button.

"Are you seeing this?" Blair's voice boomed through the phone.

"I'm not sure I am."

"How did she do that? Do you realize this magazine will cause a rush for the newsstands?"

"Calm down, Blair."

"We don't have anything like this. You don't even have a director for the bridal division. I've been keeping up with it. But this…"

She trailed off, allowing him to hear what Renee was saying. "We have a patent pending on this technology, so I can't reveal how it's done."

"Damn," he cursed to himself. They'd locked up the process.

Carter was torn. In front of him was the woman he loved, and she'd outdid him. Beaten him at a game he should know. He'd been in this business for decades. She had only taken it up a few years ago.

Carter didn't want Blair to know how he felt. Renee's creation wouldn't just change things, it would turn their world upside down. She now had a huge advantage over every other magazine on the market, and not just bridal magazines. Her innovation had the potential to change how people read, how they worked, how they shopped. Even if the magazine failed, the royalties she could charge for this technology could eliminate their competition.

Where had this idea come from? And why hadn't anyone on his staff thought of it? Why wasn't *she* on his staff? Because three years ago he'd told her they had no future.

He wondered how many other competitors were suddenly planning to attend that launch party.

The phones were already ringing on every desk when Renee walked into the office. The receptionist was trying to take messages. She thrust a handful of papers at Renee. "Your voice mail is full," she said. "And I can't answer them as fast as they're coming in."

Renee went to her office. She was still dressed and made up for the cameras.

"They're sold out," Wanda, followed by Stacy, joined Renee as she reached her desk. The smile on her face was ear to ear. "I went by three places a few minutes ago. Every magazine seller said the people descended on them in droves to get copies. One said he never saw a launch issue sell out so fast."

Renee's phone rang. She looked down at the display. It was from News Publications, Inc. Renee knew no one there, but she was sure they wanted her to answer the same questions she'd answered on the morning show.

"Do we have any more copies?" she asked.

"Sales reps have been calling for the last hour asking for more," Stacy answered. "Marketing had the second printing released. Orders will be filled within the hour."

"Good."

The day went by that way. The phone rang every few seconds. Everyone in the office was on phone duty. By noon, things calmed down as the second delivery was being made.

"Whew," Wanda came in. "I never thought I'd hate answering a telephone, but today I could do without this invention."

Renee looked up from her desk. "You'll have time to relax. And the party is tonight."

"I hope I'll have enough energy for it."

The phone on Renee's desk rang again. She smiled and automatically picked it up.

"How's your day going?" Carter asked.

His was not the voice she expected to hear. "It's going fast," she answered, giving nothing away. She had the feeling Carter knew exactly how her day had begun and how it was at this very moment. "Why do you ask?"

"It's your launch day and I see your issue is making history. That is if television can be believed."

Ahh, Renee thought. "You saw the morning news."

"Me and several million media professionals, I'm sure."

Renee smiled. Just hearing his voice made her heart beat fast.

"Those who didn't see it are probably burning up the internet getting a look at the phenomenon. And the lucky ones who already got a copy of the magazine aren't doing any work today. They're too busy looking at themselves wearing a Theresa Granville gown."

Renee laughed.

"Don't laugh. Not only is every woman in my entire company doing nothing today, but you should be indicted for shutting down the workforce of the entire United States."

"We shipped some overseas too," she said, proudly.

"Congratulations!" Carter said, no detectable sarcasm in his voice. "You've pulled off the coup of the fashion century."

"Thank you."

"What time should I pick you up for the party tonight?"

Renee hesitated. Her heart jumped to see him, but caution was still necessary. "Carter, that's probably not a good idea. You're the competition."

"With the excitement going on over the magazine, I doubt anyone will notice who you walk in with."

"You are wrong. I have guests from my parent company to entertain. I'll see you at the party, and I'll make my own way there."

"As you wish," he said.

Renee could hear his smile through the receiver. She also heard a whoop of laughter in the background.

"I'd better go before Hampshire Publications has to

declare today a holiday for every female employee, as well as some of the men, who are ogling them in wedding gowns."

"Is one of them you?" She couldn't resist asking.

"I only ogle you," Carter said. "In case you don't know, you look beautiful in a wedding gown."

Renee was riding on adrenaline alone. She'd been rushing around all day. The only downtime she'd had was the few minutes she'd used to talk to Carter. His comments had made her face hot and her cheeks bloom with its own internal makeup. Then the frenzy had begun again with more newsstands and stores clamoring for the magazine. All copies except the ones needed for the party had been sent out.

It was going to be tight, Renee thought as she got home with barely enough time to dress before the limousine picked her up. She put the finishing touches on her outfit then stepped into the limo, which drove her to the Waldorf Astoria for the party. A separate limousine picked up Diana and Teddy, and brought them, along with their husbands, to the event. And it was an event worthy of a Hollywood premiere. The weather was beautiful, warm with just the hint of a breeze. The car pulled up to the curb, and the door opened. Renee took the driver's hand and stepped out.

Inside, Renee was one of the first to arrive. Wanda and Pete were already there. The event planners were checking all the details. Fifteen minutes later, the first guest walked in—Carter.

As hostess, Renee was at the door. He leaned down

and kissed her cheek. "You look good enough to eat," he whispered. She turned her head and smiled. His mouth was very close to hers, and she wished she could kiss him. She wore a strapless gown of deep purple, and the full skirt was made of huge roses that ended in a small train. Dotted here and there throughout the roses were sparkling crystals that caught the light.

Behind Carter, Renee heard a noise. His arrival started the parade of guests. Renee shook hands and greeted people she knew: suppliers, vendors, bridal shop owners and competitors' company executives. Some were strangers, but she knew they were there to find out what she, Wanda, Stacy and Pete had done to create the sensation that was storming the day. As soon as the morning show had aired, the phone calls had come in from people who wanted to come and had missed the date to RSVP.

They all had an excuse, but neither Renee nor the agency handling the party details was surprised. They'd planned for them at Stacy's insistence.

Dana came in at the end of the first wave. "I'm so glad to see you," Renee said as they hugged.

"I see Carter is already here."

Renee nodded but didn't say anything.

"Are you two on better terms now?" Dana asked.

"We're civil toward each other." Renee felt bad lying to her cousin. The two had always shared everything, but how she truly felt about Carter was a secret she was keeping to herself.

Dana moved around as other guests arrived. "I'll talk to you later," she whispered and headed toward Carter.

Renee followed her progression, wondering what the two of them would talk about, since she was the only subject they had in common.

Diana and Teddy arrived, taking her attention away.

"I wasn't expecting this," Teddy said, surveying the room. "This is truly overwhelming,"

"And it's affecting the office back in Princeton," Diana added.

"Did something happen?" Renee was concerned.

"We knew it would be a sensation, but we underestimated the sales it would pull into the shop," Teddy said.

Pete and Wanda came up to them smiling. When the guys left to get drinks, Teddy explained, "We hired a temp to maintain the office while we came up for the party, but it didn't work out."

"What happened?"

"She couldn't handle the orders or the number of people in the Princeton store."

"Did she leave?" Renee asked.

Teddy shook her head. "It's our fault. You'd warned us that the magazine launch would create huge demand for the gowns, but we didn't expect the number of orders to overwhelm us this much. If it hadn't been for one of our new designers cutting a vacation short and taking over the order processing, we'd be in over our heads."

"Everything is under control," Diana said. "So we can relax and enjoy the party. But tomorrow we'll head back to help with the overload."

"I'm sorry," Renee said.

"Don't be." Diana waved her concern away. "This is the best thing that could have happened to the business. Don't think about it again. Enjoy this night—it only happens once."

They smiled and accepted the wine their husbands brought. After a sip, they went off to look at the huge posters around the room of wedding gowns.

Waiters moved through the crowd with drinks and trays of food. By eight-thirty, the incoming flux of people had slowed, and Renee left the door. Carter appeared next to her with a wineglass.

"Drink this," he said. "It's sparkling water."

How had he known she was parched? The drink tasted of lemon and bathed her throat. Renee intended to rejoin Diana and Teddy and introduce them to some of the people who'd worked hard to get the magazine launched. However, the moment she looked up from her drink, she was surrounded by magazine executives.

She knew what they wanted. To find out how she'd pulled off the holograms. And those who wanted a quick five minutes alone with her also wanted to steal her away from *Designed for Brides* and have her come and work for them.

With a smile of appreciation, Renee turned them all down. But she walked away on air.

"You look like someone who's won the lottery." Carter came up beside her as she completed her conversation with the vice president of News Publications, Inc. and moved away.

"Close," she said. Renee saw another executive heading her way. When the man saw Carter, he veered off and stopped at one of the bars. Turning to Carter, she smiled, thanking him for something he was unaware he'd done. But Renee knew she couldn't allow Carter to stay with her for long. He wasn't her protector, and he'd already made the same bid for her services as the other executives were.

"How's it going?" he asked.

"As expected," she said, trying to be noncommittal in the conversation.

"They're all vying for you to join them, or at least have a meeting on the technology."

"Exactly," Renee said. "And like I did with you, I turned them all down." She took a moment to poke him with a purple fingernail.

"I wasn't totally turned down," he said, drawing that sexy note into his voice.

Renee's thoughts went straight to the night in his apartment. Mentally shaking herself, she dispersed the images. Across the room, the event planner waved her over; it was time for introductions and her speech. Excusing herself, Renee headed for the stage.

The band played a few bars of a song, then abruptly ended it, causing the crowd to quiet down and turn to face the bandstand. Models in wedding gowns formed a line and moved onto the stage set up for them. Posters of the inaugural issue's cover descended from the ceiling as if they were lights. They'd been especially made and sealed so they wouldn't flap in the air. Twirling on pearl ropes, they were illuminated by spotlights. On the floor, the brides stepped forward and created a circle. The music began as they faced the audience with linked arms. The wedding gowns projected in front of them.

As the circle revolved, each woman's image changed to a different gown.

The audience burst into applause. The brides stopped turning and returned to their places along the edge of the floor. The projections disappeared one by one and a spotlight appeared on Renee.

She gave her short speech, thanking her team and introducing them and the owners of Weddings by Diana. Then she invited everyone to enjoy themselves for the rest of the evening.

As the music began, Carter captured her before she left the floor and pulled her into his arms for a dance. Renee said nothing. She didn't resist but went easily into his embrace. She wanted to rest her head on his shoulder and allow the music to carry her away, but she was mindful of where she was and that many of the people in the room were keeping careful tabs on her. Renee didn't want to appear to favor any of the companies that were courting her.

Yet Carter's arms were strong, and she liked the way they secured her to him, the way he whirled her through the steps. They'd danced this way before. Renee remembered that office party years ago. When she'd also found herself wrapped around Carter, and she'd wanted to stay there, live there, spend an eternity there. Tonight was no different. She could easily get lost with him, especially with the music surrounding them like invisible love strands. She heard the lyrics of a love song and knew the singer was directing them to her and Carter.

Renee allowed the night to take her away. She'd

pulled off a coup in the industry, and tonight was her night.

"Renee, where are you?"

Carter whispered in her ear, but she barely heard him. Her heart was hammering and heat cocooned her in a bundle of electrical nerves.

"Renee." Carter spoke her name again.

Somewhere in her mind, she realized the music had ended. She stopped and looked up at him. Whatever was in her eyes changed what was in his. Desire was raw and obvious in their gazes.

"We'd better get something to drink," Carter said.

His voice snapped her back to reality. She looked away from him, checking to see if anyone was staring at them. Only Dana seemed to find them of interest. Carter's arm, still wrapped around her waist, led her to the bar. He ordered her more sparkling water.

"If you have anything alcoholic," he said. "You'll probably forget where you are."

Renee shook herself, remembering where she was. She had to remember that all eyes were on every move she made.

Taking his own drink, a glass of wine, he walked her away from the bar and back toward a table. Wanda and Pete were on the floor, each dancing with someone Renee didn't recognize.

"Who was that?" Teddy asked coming over when Carter excused himself.

Renee checked over her shoulder, watching Carter's straight back. "That's Carter Hampshire...the same one who runs Hampshire Publications."

Teddy glanced over Renee's shoulder. "Good-looking man," she said.

Renee nodded.

"You two seen to know each other well."

Renee felt the color rise in her face, but Teddy knew her story. Renee had been very open after she took the job as a consultant. Over the three years she'd worked at Weddings by Diana, she'd told Teddy the entire story of her reasons for leaving Hampshire.

"Are you two getting back together?"

Renee was shaking her head before Teddy finished speaking. "We're history."

Yet she'd promised Carter she'd think about a relationship with him after the magazine launched.

It was officially public now. She'd just told Teddy they were history.

But were they?

Chapter 9

Renee knew exactly how Eliza Doolittle felt after her ball. It wasn't the dancing all night that had her floating—she was high on the whole event. They had done it. With Wanda, Stacy and Pete's help, the publishing industry would never be the same.

The crowds were winding down in the ballroom, and Dana found Renee near the bathroom. "We're going to have to talk," she said.

"About something important?"

Dana smiled broadly. "About all this." She looked around, encompassing the entire room, which had thinned out a lot. Renee had a collection of business cards in her beaded bag and invitations to have lunch from at least a dozen people.

"Call me tomorrow afternoon," Renee added.

Dana hugged her, draped a silk shawl over her shoulders and started for the door.

Renee, too, was ready to leave. After saying goodbye to several more people and promising to keep in touch, Renee found herself facing Carter.

"You must be tired," he said. "Sit down."

Dead on her feet, she didn't argue. Carter knew her moods. She took a seat at an empty table. The magazine lay at her place, front side up.

Pulling a chair around, Carter sat. He reached down and took her feet in his hands. Removing her sequin-encrusted heels, he lifted her legs to his knees and began methodically massaging her insteps. Renee's eyes closed at the pleasure his strong fingers evoked. She leaned back in the chair. The sensation felt so good—too good, she thought. While she wanted it to continue, she knew better. Pulling away, she placed her feet down and slipped her shoes back on, despite the fact that her feet hurt.

"It's time for me to go," she said.

"Can I drive you somewhere?"

"I have a car service," she told him.

"Cancel it. Let the guy go home to his family. I'll drive you."

She hesitated.

"It's a drive, not a commitment," Carter said.

Renee knew his views on commitment. She also knew tonight wasn't a night that she should get into a dark car with him and rest her head on his shoulder. And she was too tired to talk about them as a couple.

"He's waiting," she said. "I'd better go."

Carter didn't move to stop her when she started walking. Renee refused to turn and look over her shoulder, but she knew he was watching her.

Half an hour later, the limousine pulled up in front of her house and the driver helped her out. Thanking him, she went up the few steps to her door. She unlocked it and waved the driver away. Stepping inside, she heard a car door close and looked toward the sound. Carter smiled as he crossed the street and came up the steps.

"What are you doing here?" she asked.

"I came for my good-night kiss."

Renee was stunned. Pulling her inside, he closed the door behind them. She took a step back, but he caught her around the waist, tightening his embrace. She offered no resistance as his long arms gathered her close. Renee smelled Carter's cologne—she remembered it from a past life. Three years of feelings rushed into memory at what they had once shared.

For a moment, Renee thought of pushing him back, but she wanted to be in his arms. For just a few seconds of pleasure, she told herself, she'd remain where she was. She relaxed, allowing her body to accept all the pleasure signals she was getting. Carter's kiss was soft on her mouth. His hands crushed the purple satin as she pushed herself closer to him. Her arms snaked around his neck and she let the full force of sensation drive her up the sensual ladder to a higher rung of pleasure. Carter's hands banded her body. They were warm as they slid up her spine to rest on the bare skin of the low-cut gown.

Delirium was setting in. Renee raised a leg up Carter's

and settled between his legs. She felt his erection and the heat that told her he was aroused. The thought triggered her own arousal. She knew this was the point to push back; if she went further, there would be no return. She'd told herself this was it. Either stop or be prepared to follow this to the end.

Carter lifted his mouth from hers. His eyes held desire, but he was restraining himself.

"That was some kiss," she said.

"For me, too," he returned.

"Would you like something to drink?" she asked. The heat they'd produced with only a kiss had burned the air dry.

He shook his head.

For an eternity, they stared into each other's eyes. Neither spoke, neither moved. Then, as if there was music somewhere in the background, they began to slow dance across the foyer and into the main room. Carter held her tight, but not so she couldn't escape if she wanted to get away.

She didn't.

They were alone. No one here to see them and no one expected. Renee stopped moving. She looked up, and her eyes rested on Carter's mouth. His lower lip quivered slightly. She wouldn't have noticed if she weren't a kiss away from him. Raising her hand, she touched his mouth. He kissed her fingertips gently. Fire plowed through her skin, working in circles and folds through her fingerprints and burning through to her flesh.

Moving her hand, she pushed herself up and put her mouth on his. This time the kiss wasn't soft or chaste.

It was raw, wet and hungry. His mouth assaulted hers. Their heads bobbed from side to side as sensation ran through them like lightning bolts looking for a grounding wire. Renee forgot the years of separation, forgot that she and Carter had new lives and careers. All she knew was that she wanted him, and he wanted her.

Her dress crisscrossed at the back, threaded by a white ribbon that tied at her lower back. Carter found the bow and pulled. The dress loosened and fell. Renee caught it between them. Cool air rushed against her back but was quickly replaced by the heat of his hand. When he smoothed his strong hands over her bottom, Renee instinctively seized as new arrows of electrical current shocked her. She knew his hands, knew the feel of them, the size that was perfectly fitted to the exact curvature of her body.

She ran her hands over his arms and around his back. His mouth continued to work magic on hers. His head pushed her back, bending her over as the two seemed to merge into one. Renee didn't know how her dress slipped from her shoulders. Only when Carter's hands found her bare breasts and patted his thumbs over them, causing her to utter a cry of pleasure, did she realize the dress hung near her arms.

His mouth followed his hands, and she arched toward him as the erotic stroke of his tongue introduced her to a world of sensual pleasure. Slipping her arms from the dress, it fell like a pile of purple roses around her feet. Carter lifted her out and carried her toward the stairs. Renee laid her head between his shoulder and neck, and teased his ear with her tongue as he staggered like a drunk man up the stairs.

There was a soft light coming from her bedroom and Carter headed that way. Inside he took her to the bed and slowly let her slide down his body until her feet reached the floor. He looked down at her. Renee felt as if she was the most loveable person in the world. With only his eyes, he could tell her everything she needed to know.

When he kissed her again, his mouth was back to the tender, thoroughly satisfying kiss that, despite its gentleness, wrung everything from her. It forced her to want him, to use her hands and the soft movement of her hips to tell him she was ready for him. She wanted his body merged with hers, wanted to feel their joining and wanted to enjoy the pleasure of making love.

Renee pulled Carter's bow tie loose, unbuttoned his shirt and pressed her wet tongue to his slightly moist skin. Tasting the salt of his body, she felt his hands squeeze her bottom as he pulled her tighter against his erection. Holding on to her sanity, she pushed his jacket over his arms. One at a time, he slipped his arms free. The jacket fell to the floor, but Renee was oblivious to it. Her eyes were trained on the uncovered skin of his chest. For a long moment she only looked at him. His darkened skin was smooth and contoured, as if some hand had personally outlined him, not in plaster or bronze, but in flesh and bone. Renee's throat went dry.

Yet her need multiplied. She pressed herself to him, running her hands over his shoulders and arms, feeling sparkles of electricity. Hooking her arms around his neck, she kissed him. She was only a head shorter than his six-foot frame, yet she went up on her toes. She loved the taste of him.

His breathing was hot against her mouth and her heart thumped so hard, she thought it would burst through her chest. She couldn't take this torture much longer. She needed him now. Wanted him more than she'd ever wanted anyone.

She wanted to know that the beauty they had created three years ago had only been on hold, had not died away. She brought her hands to his belt and released the buckle. In seconds they were both naked. Carter lifted her and placed her gently on the bed. He stretched out next to her, kissing her so lightly it was like being caressed, yet he was driving her wild. His mouth traveled over her contours, kissing her eyes, her mouth, her shoulders. Taking his time, he moved from one area to another. Large hands massaged her back and came around to skim over nipples that stood erect at his touch.

Carter rolled over her, cupping her face and looking down at her. Her hair had come loose from its moorings, and he threaded his fingers through it as his mouth descended to take hers. Inside her hunger and need combined to a pleasure–pain paradox. Carter reached over the edge of the bed and found his pants. In seconds, he had a condom out of its package and had placed it over himself.

Renee didn't wait for him. She pulled him down on top of her and opened her legs for his entry. When it came, her eyes fluttered. The rhythm was slow to begin, but soon changed to a frenzied pace that she didn't think she could maintain. Yet the deep pleasure drove her further and further along the ride with Carter.

Guttural sounds mingled in the air. Renee was unsure if they came from her throat or Carter's. She didn't try to distinguish one from the other. He was here. With her. She'd forgotten how good they were together, how his body completed hers, how they moved in unison and gave all. She held nothing back. Whatever she felt, she let Carter have. He filled her time and again, their bodies meeting, retreating, meeting again. Each drive had her eyes closing and her body taking in the passion that only the two of them could create.

Carter rolled her over the big bed, carrying her over and under him. Renee was immersed in the pleasure he granted her. Biting her lip, she took the pleasure his body offered her. Yet neither Renee nor Carter would give in. She reached for more and more until the scream she'd pinned inside her wouldn't remain quiet. It was about to release.

She moved, rolled, reversed positions with Carter until she was over him, her body pumping his. His hands smoothed over her belly and squeezed her breasts. The action released something wild that lay dormant inside her. Like a suddenly awakened tiger, she ravished him. Hunger for him drove her to oblivion.

Somehow they rose to a higher level than ever before. For a space of a lifetime she held the pleasure. Then she collapsed onto his sweat-slick body. Renee could say nothing. Carter's arms embraced her. Large hands roved over her back and the curve of her bottom. Their breath was ragged and loud, but the air was filled with the aftermath of lovemaking.

Carter brushed her hair aside and kissed her forehead. Renee had never felt more cherished.

Sanity returned with the sunlight that streamed through the windows. Renee smelled coffee and bacon. Opening her eyes, she pushed herself up on her elbows and looked at the empty place where Carter should be sleeping. He was gone.

"A man who cooks," she said out loud as she smiled.

Dressing quickly, she rushed down the steps and burst into the kitchen.

"You're cooking," she said needlessly.

Carter wore one of her aprons and boxer shorts. Nothing else. The sight had her body going into overdrive.

"I'm starving," he said.

He turned to face her, and Renee felt all the heat of last night's bedroom gymnastics return to claim her. Carter placed breakfast on the table. The two of them ate in silence, yet their eyes spoke, their hands talked and the smiles they offered each other told a story that only they would understand.

Over coffee and juice, the English language returned to their minds. "Shouldn't you already be at work?" Renee asked.

"I called in and told them I'd be late."

"How late?" Renee smiled tantalizingly.

"How late do you want me to be?" Getting up from the table, he came to her and pulled her out of her seat.

He kissed her, long and hard. Renee tasted the juice he'd drunk. Her knees went weak, and she wondered if he'd always have that effect on her.

She lay against him when he lifted his mouth. His heartbeat was steady in her ear. She liked being where he was, felt as if this was where she belonged. But they were competitors. They were going to have to discuss their relationship soon. But not now, she told herself. Now, she just wanted to stand here in her kitchen, with the morning sun streaming in, and be wrapped in Carter Hampshire's arms.

Grand Central Terminal was packed with weekend travelers. Renee searched the cavernous structure for Dana. They'd agreed to meet by the double staircase in front of the three tall arched windows facing the main concourse. The sun shone brightly through them, and Renee squinted as she searched the room.

She spotted Dana walking across the marble floor, holding two cups of coffee.

"Do you have time?" Renee asked, accepting one of the cups.

"My train leaves in forty minutes."

They climbed the stairs and found a seat away from the moving mass of people.

"What did you think of the party?" Renee asked.

"It was wonderful!" Dana's eyes opened wide. "You and whoever created those graphics are geniuses. I imagine sales are through the stratosphere."

"They're greater than projected. And, by the way, who did you leave with? I couldn't see his face."

Dana looked down, a shy smile on her face. "He is an advertising director at Juvenock Magazines. He saw me to my hotel, chastely kissed me on the cheek and promised to call." She took a drink from her cup. "This morning, when I checked out, there was a card waiting saying he enjoyed last night and would call later today."

Renee smiled. "Maybe I should go back to being a wedding consultant for one more wedding."

Dana sat up straight. "Not so fast. We live in different states. You know that rarely works out in the long run." She smiled brightly again. "But for the time being, it might be fun."

Renee knew Dana's situation and how cautious she was with men. The loss of her fiancé had changed her. It had taken her a long time to get over that, and even longer to begin dating again. Renee was glad to think that her cousin was healing.

"What about you? Are you and Carter...*friendlier*?"

A frisson of emotion ran through Renee. Just hearing Carter's name raised her temperature and pumped her heartbeat.

"We're friendlier," she admitted.

"Did he ever explain why he left three years ago?"

Renee understood that was a question that Dana broached with caution. Renee took a sip of her coffee and looked Dana in the eye. She explained what Carter had told her.

"He was in Afghanistan?"

Renee nodded. "Our relationship hadn't developed very far and he didn't want to have someone worrying about him at home."

Dana sat quietly for a very long time. Renee wondered what she was thinking. Did this remind her of her lost fiancé?

"I know you might think that doesn't sound like a good reason, but it was."

"How can you say that?" Renee asked.

"Renee, he was protecting you."

"How do you figure that?"

"Answer a question. Were you in love with him when he left?"

Renee waited a moment, then nodded.

"Did he know that?'

"Not in words. I'd never said it."

"But we all know when a relationship crosses the line and changes, matures, turns more serious."

Renee couldn't deny that. She nodded quickly even though Dana had not asked a question.

"He was saving you from pain in case something happened to him."

Renee weighed her words.

"But why didn't he tell me?"

"Because it wouldn't have spared you. If you'd known, you'd have waited, written, called. You'd have done all the things I did." She stopped.

Both women stared at each other.

"Then when you couldn't reach him by phone or mail, when you got no responses to anything, you'd have fallen off the deep end, like I did."

Renee gripped her cup with both hands. "I fell off of it anyway."

"You did, but there's a difference."

"What's that?" Renee asked.

"You have another chance. He's back, safe…" Dana didn't go on. Her voice cracked.

Renee reached over and squeezed her hand.

It was time for Dana's train, and the two walked to the platform together and hugged goodbye.

"Renee, think about giving him another chance."

"I'll think about it," she said. "Carter asked me to think about it too."

Dana smiled, hugged her again and got on the train. She waved from one of the windows, but her words hung in the air as the huge silver cars rolled out of the station.

The office was less frantic then it had been the day before. Renee and Carter hadn't arrived together. He'd had to go to his apartment and change clothes, and she'd had to meet Dana, but not before they had spent a long time in her shower and then again in bed before parting. Renee could still feel the evidence of their night together. Throughout the morning, she kept smiling as she remembered the two of them making love and holding each other. She wished it had never ended.

Dana's words rang in her ears. *Give him another chance.* What was last night, if not a chance?

The phones were ringing, and the office was full of flowers, bottles of champagne, some of the world's best chocolate and notes of thanks from several of the past evening's guests. Renee continued to get job offers and questions about sharing their technology from some of the publishing professionals.

News reporters wanted interviews, but Renee wanted to escape. For a short moment, she considered going up to the 38th floor and hiding out in Carter's office. But Carter was one of them—the competition that was desperate for her technology. He didn't feel like one of them when she remembered his hands on her body, but her brain knew going upstairs would be a monumental mistake.

Diana and Teddy's arrival was a godsend. Her secretary would hold all her calls, giving her some needed downtime. Now that the first issue was history, they had work to do to get the second one to press and get a head start on the next six. She'd finally feel comfortable when they were months ahead of the curve.

"Did you enjoy yourself last night?" Renee asked the two partners.

"I had more fun that I thought possible," Teddy said. "I loved the show. Those covers coming from the ceiling and the gowns in the circle…wonderful idea."

"You can thank Wanda and Stacy for that," Renee said. "We had an event planner, but Stacy came up with the idea."

"Which one is Stacy?"

Renee glanced through the door. Stacy was standing near her secretary. "She's the blonde right there." Both women followed Renee's nod. "She's the one who worked with me on numbers for the expected orders of gowns. We sent you the projections."

"And she was so right," Teddy commented. "From what I heard, the phone orders continue to be brisk.

And we had to expand the bandwidth on our website to keep up with the traffic."

"Other than that, tell us about the man you spent a lot of time with last night," Diana asked.

"Man?" Renee asked. "What man?" Her body grew warm. She knew exactly what man they were talking about.

"The man who danced with you several times. The one who couldn't keep his eyes off you even when you weren't dancing."

"His name is Carter Hampshire. And he's the competition," Renee said. She glanced at Teddy who already knew who Carter was. Obviously, Teddy had not shared the information with Diana. Renee thanked her silently for keeping her confidence. "He owns this building, or his family does."

"And he couldn't keep his eyes off you," Teddy teased.

"I'm sure you're wrong."

"I wonder," Teddy said.

Renee left it at that. But Dana's words echoed back. *Give him another chance.*

Life fell into routine after a couple of weeks. Renee was busy working on the next several issues. Advertisers were knocking down the door, even though their prices were through the roof and they had a waiting list. Bridal designers vied for callbacks so they could secure a spot in an upcoming issue. Every one of them wanted their dress to be featured as one of the four spots that used the hologram. She referred their calls to the sales reps, but found she was constantly required to sign off on some deal.

After each exhausting day, she and Carter would continue their lovemaking at either her house or his apartment. So far neither of them had broached the subject of their relationship and the fact that they were competitors. Renee knew it would have to come sooner or later, but she'd rather it be later. Her feelings for Carter were securely in place, and she didn't want to give up her secret meetings with him.

Was it the fact that their relationship was a secret that made lovemaking so exciting? Renee didn't know and didn't care. All she knew was that she was in love with Carter Hampshire and together they created fireworks. She now understood the yearning of brides for their partners, the love that wove its way around and inside them, creating that invisible bond that seared them together. She knew the obsessive need to give, to please, to crave understanding.

Now, Renee stretched in Carter's big bed. Her hand touched his arm and he immediately took it, pulling it to his mouth and kissing her fingers. The familiar reaction to his touch sparked through her. She smiled, loving the way he made her feel. She looked up as his hand brushed her hair back, and he rolled toward her and kissed her hairline.

Renee couldn't remember ever being this happy. Her heart virtually sang every night when she knew she'd meet him. They'd cook together, have dinner, discuss everything from world politics to the price of an internet connection. Never did they talk about the magazine business. Then they'd retire to his bedroom or hers and make love throughout the night.

"What are you thinking about?" Carter asked.

"Marbles," she said.

"Marbles?" Carter laughed. Renee felt his body shake against her. "What about marbles?"

"I don't know. I don't seem to have any."

"Where did you lose them?"

They both laughed at the old joke. Renee knew where she'd lost hers. Well, they weren't lost—she'd given them away. Given them to the man holding her. Yet she hadn't told him. Not yet. But she would.

Reaching up, she kissed him, brought her lips to his and tasted the essence of Carter. His hand slipped over her bare belly and around her body. When he pulled her into alignment with him, she felt the entire length of his long, strong body. Their legs entwined and they looked into each other's eyes. It was that look that started the burning. Carter's gaze marked her as surely as if he'd touched her, and Renee felt the heat rising.

Carter fell back against the bedding. Her body fit into his as his erection hardened and pressed into her. Renee initiated a kiss. She felt the restrained lion in him that controlled strength he held tightly until she was ready, until it was impossible not to release the tension within them.

Climbing on top of him, she stretched down his body. Moving slowly against him, she felt the ecstasy of love beginning. Carter's hands thrust into her hair and clamped over the back of her head. He held her that way for an eternity, his mouth taking hers and working its magic, the tension within her coiling and tightening. Finally, pushing her aside, he found a condom and she took it from him. Watching Carter's joy, she slipped it over him. His eyes rolled back as pleasure took control of his features and Renee slipped her hands up and down over him. His hands grabbed hers and he stopped her with a groan.

He pulled her down, reversing positions. He gazed into her eyes until she felt something snap within him. In seconds he was inside her. Passion flooded them. Fire flared into a roar and the rhythm between them moved with a fury strong enough to topple the Earth.

Renee heard herself moan at the pleasure that coursed through her. Her arms hugged him and her body matched the speed of his. Her throat was parched as she breathed through her mouth. She kissed his shoulders, his chest, as her body writhed beneath his. She grasped his shoulders, holding on as Carter pushed her legs up and took them higher on the ecstasy scale. As control was lost between them, she felt a hard wave rising. It was higher than any that had come before. Clamping her mouth closed, she waited, held back, tried to stop it from cresting too quickly.

It was impossible. The wave broke through. She felt more than heard her scream, and Carter's groan was audible in her ears. Together they climaxed and collapsed onto the bed. Renee let her breath out. Carter, lying on her, his chest taking long drags of air, as if it was a liquid he could drink.

"Wow," was all Renee could say. Even the other times they'd made love hadn't compared with this. He slid sideways and caressed her against him. Carter kissed her neck, holding her and taking long breaths. Renee didn't think he could speak—she knew she couldn't.

The way Carter made her feel was life-changing. She knew it was for him, too. Could it always be this way? Would she be able to keep this bright star of love alive in the future? She didn't know if she could, but she was sure going to try.

Something woke Renee. Turning to reach for Carter, her hand felt the coolness of the sheets where he should be lying. Her eyes flew open. Where was Carter? Glancing at the clock, she saw it was just after four o'clock in the morning, too early for breakfast. She didn't smell the coffee or the bacon that he loved to eat in the morning. Where was he?

Slipping out of bed, she grabbed one of his shirts and pulled it over her naked body. There were no other lights on in the hall. Quietly she went toward the living room. No light filtered in from the outside, but there was a light coming from his office.

Was he working?

She smiled. The man was diligent. Renee went toward the light and pushed the door open. Carter swung around in his chair. Renee looked over his shoulder, immediately recognizing her own work. *Her* layout. Her designs for upcoming issues of *Designed for Brides*.

"What is this?" she asked, her eyes fixed on the screen.

"Renee, it's not what you think."

"Those are my designs, and you have them. You stole

them," she accused. "That's why you've been so good to me. You wanted them all along."

"Renee, let me explain."

"What could you say?" she shouted. "That you've been trying to get my designs? First you ask me to take a job with you. When that fails, you decide to steal what you can."

"That's not how it was."

Renee stormed back to the bedroom. Putting her clothes on over the shirt, she gathered what things were readily within reach and bolted for the door.

"Renee, we have to talk."

"We've done all the talking we need to. Get out of my sight. I never want to see you again."

Renee rushed through the door and grabbed the first taxi that came by. She held on to her tears until the driver dropped her off at her home. Inside she backed up against the door, but her knees were too weak to keep her upright. She slid to the floor and let the sobs burst.

Chapter 10

Blair Massey sauntered into Carter's office and slipped into a chair. "What's up?" she asked.

Carter stood behind his desk. He'd paced the entire room waiting for her to arrive. He couldn't believe what he'd seen. There had to be a logical explanation, something reasonable, something understandable.

"Have you checked our sales and projections in your division?"

She nodded. "Since Renee's launch we've been seriously down in sales, but I expect them to pick up once the wedding season is in full swing."

"This layout you sent me yesterday," Carter said, restraining his voice to something approachable. "It's wonderful, better than anything I've seen in years."

"Thank you. We strive for the best." Blair recited the bridal division motto.

"Who in the department thought of this? I want to be sure to give credit where credit is due."

"That's just like you, wanting to give praise. The entire department worked on it, but the initial idea came from me. I'll pass your thanks on to the rest of the group."

Carter rounded his desk and sat down. He looked into the smiling face of a woman he never thought he'd have to say these words to. Blair stared back at him. After a while, she realized the serious expression on his face meant something.

"What's wrong, Carter?"

"I've seen this design someplace else."

Blair sat up in the chair. "Someone's stolen our idea?"

He didn't move, didn't nod or shake his head. "No one stole our design."

"Where did you see it?"

"On Renee Hart's desk at *Designed for Brides*."

"How did you happen to see that?" Blair was uncomfortable. Carter knew her well and he knew how she sat, what her mannerisms were when she was nervous. She pursed her lips and licked at her lipstick.

"Why did you steal it, Blair? We don't need to do that."

She got up and stood behind the chair she'd been sitting in. "Why do you think I stole it?"

"You just admitted it was your idea."

"I did but...when we were working, the design just

grew. No one stole it. We came up with it independently."

"Blair." Carter's voice held a warning. "You stole the design."

"Well, what did you think I would do? We needed something big to compete with her magazine. I tried to get something. The department worked night and day trying to come up with something that would make the industry look at us. Nothing compared. Then I saw the designs in her office when we had a lunch date. She got called away for several minutes. I had a jump drive with me. I always carry one—it's a habit. I can't tell you what came over me, but I put the drive in and copied it."

Carter stared at Blair as if he'd never seen her before. She'd been employed by Hampshire for over twenty years. He'd trusted her.

"Blair, you're fired."

The words stunned her. Her face paled to the point that Carter thought she'd pass out from lack of blood flow.

"Fired?"

"I have no choice. Do you know the number of laws you've broken? Do you realize your actions could ruin not only the bridal magazine division, but the entire business?"

"No one knows. Our magazine will get to the stands before hers. It'll look like they stole ours. It'll put them out of business."

"Blair, how can you even think that's something this company would have any part of?"

"It's done all the time. This is business."

"That is not the kind of business I run. And until a few days ago, not the kind you did either."

She looked at the floor, then up at him.

"You have to go, Blair."

There was nothing else to say. Blair opened her mouth to speak, then closed it. She'd done the unforgivable. And Carter was going to have to do some serious damage control, both for the company and for his relationship with Renee.

Carter lifted the phone and called security.

"Security will be here in a few minutes to escort you from the building."

Word of Blair's firing raced through the office like a forest fire. It reached Renee just before lunch. Blair had worked at Hampshire Publications for more years than some of the people there had been on the planet. And now she was gone. Renee wondered why, but she couldn't call Carter and ask. She wanted nothing to do with him.

Was he blaming Blair for stealing her design? Was he using her as the scapegoat for his theft?

Renee's phone rang.

"Hello," she said.

"Ms. Blair Massey is here to see you."

Renee swallowed. Blair? Here?

"Shall I send her back?"

"Of course," Renee said.

What could Blair want? Maybe she was here to ask for a job. Renee stood and waited to see her come around the corner. She'd aged years in just a few hours.

"Blair," she called. "Come on in."

Renee closed the door and offered Blair a seat. She sat in front of the desk. Renee took the second guest chair next to her.

"You've heard," Blair began.

"I think by now the news has reached the Jersey Shore." Renee tried to lighten the mood that had descended on the room. She hadn't expected to see Blair. In fact, by now she would have expected Blair to be halfway home. "I'm surprised you're still in the building."

"I'm sure you are," Blair said. "That gauntlet I just passed through looked like they had their claws out." She glanced at the door.

"They're curious, that's all."

Renee looked through the glass wall. The entire office was pretending to work, but they were really trying to discover what was going on.

"How can I help you?" Renee asked.

"I believe I'm here to help you."

Renee stared straight at her, but kept her face unemotional. The comment was a lead-in to a job interview.

"All right, how can you help me?"

Blair smiled as if she knew something Renee didn't. "You're all wondering why Carter fired me?"

Renee leaned forward in her chair and stared directly at the woman. "Yes, we are. You're a staple at Hampshire Publications. You're at the top of your field, and you've run more of those magazines than anyone else. I don't understand Carter."

"It wasn't Carter," Blair said.

Renee frowned. "What wasn't Carter?"

"Carter fired me, but you're the reason I got fired."

"Me!" Renee was stunned. "How could I have anything to do with it?"

Blair hunched and dropped her shoulders. "You're good. You're brilliant. Your marketing plans are beyond great. And they sell. That thing you did with the launch magazine was historic. And not just for magazines. I've heard the reports of how other industries want to adapt it to their particular products. I could never come up with anything even remotely resembling it."

Renee felt as if she should say thank you, but it also seemed inappropriate. So she said nothing.

"Let me get to the point. You know I'm a good person. But…" Blair paused. "Everyone, good or bad, has a breaking point. Carter fired me because I stole them."

"You stole…you…not Carter," Renee stammered. "What plans?" Renee's heart began to beat faster.

"The ones for the next year, I copied them and used them as my own."

Renee again leaned forward. Her hands went to the computer keys on her desk.

"Don't bother," Blair stopped her. "They're there, exactly as you expect them to be. I used a jump drive to copy them the day we went out for lunch."

"How… I…" Renee stopped. She was at a loss for words.

Blair stood up as if the interview was over and she was ready to go.

"About the plans…" Renee began.

"Don't worry. I never got to use any of them. Apparently, Carter found out where I got the ideas. I have no idea how he knew."

Renee felt heat paint her skin.

Blair went to the door. With her hand on the knob, she turned back. Renee had the feeling she was a character in a play on Broadway. She was an understudy who didn't know her lines.

"I may not know how he got them, but I'm sure you have some idea." With that, Blair opened the door.

"Blair, one more thing," Renee said.

The woman she'd called her friend for nearly a decade turned back, her brows raised.

"Why are you telling me this? Why admit it?"

"I'm sure in the long run Carter would tell you anyway, but I admire you. I don't know what slant someone else would put on the story, but I wanted you to hear the truth. From me."

"Thank you for that."

Renee felt numb. She hadn't expected the day to go this way. She'd lost a friend and a lover. How could she have been so wrong? He'd told her he'd never do anything to encroach on her business. Yet she hadn't even given him the benefit of the doubt. She'd immediately assumed he was there to steal. That he'd been using her all this time, just to get her designs.

But it wasn't just the designs. She hadn't trusted him. Or even given him the opportunity to explain. She couldn't blame him if he never spoke to her again.

Renee flopped against the back of her chair. She took in a long breath, feeling as if she hadn't had air since Blair had walked into her office.

Closing her eyes, Carter came to mind. She'd accused him of theft. He was innocent...but he must have recognized the plans. Why hadn't he told her? Maybe he thought she stole them from Blair, and not the other way around? But how had he found out the truth?

And what was she going to do now that she'd destroyed his trust?

The 38th floor felt very far away. Renee's elevator trip up to the offices of Hampshire Publications was like ascending to a high office to be called on the carpet. Carter may well throw her out, and he'd have every right to do so. She'd broken his trust. She didn't know if that could be mended. She hoped so.

The elevator doors opened onto a highly polished hallway.

"Ms. Hart," the receptionist stood up and came around her desk. "It's so good to see you." She hugged Renee.

"I'm here to see Carter," she explained. "If you don't mind, I know the way."

For a moment the receptionist looked confused, then she smiled and pressed a button to let her through security. Renee held her head high as she walked through the door and passed several offices. Some of the people she knew gawked at her. Renee nodded to them, but didn't slow her pace. She was on a mission. Silence followed her movements. People thought she was there for a fight and that an explosion was imminent.

She saw Carter's secretary. "Is he in?" she asked, passing the woman without altering her stride.

The secretary stood up, but had no time to say anything before Renee opened the door and went inside. She closed it, hearing a click of finality. Carter turned around in his chair. The expression on his face told her she was the last person he expected to see. Her heart thundered. He could order her out. She expected him to do so.

"We need to talk," she said. "No, I need to talk."

Carter stood, but said nothing. Moving across the room Renee stood in front of his desk. She didn't sit. What she had to say needed to be said standing up.

"I apologize," she began. "Blair came to see me."

He frowned. "She did?"

"She told me the truth about the designs. That *she'd* stolen them. You didn't. It was all her."

Renee waited for Carter to give her an indication that she should go on, that there was some kind of forgiveness. She found none.

"I'm sure you don't want to see me again, but I wanted to tell you how sorry I am for mistrusting you."

"Apology accepted," Carter said.

Renee waited a moment. Neither of them seemed to have anything more to say. Renee glanced at him, expecting it would be the last time she saw him alone. She turned to leave.

"Renee." She stopped at the sound of his voice.

"You said we needed to talk. I have something to say."

She turned around.

"Please sit down."

Renee took a seat. If he wanted to level accusations at her, she deserved them.

"I'm sorry Blair did what she did," he said. "But it forced me to make a decision. I'm going to need your help to accomplish it."

Renee frowned, then blinked several times. She had no idea what Carter was getting at. "It's about the magazines, both yours and mine."

Renee nodded, but was still confused.

"I think they should merge or—"

She jumped up as if propelled. A business deal. He was offering her a business deal? "You're suggesting I merge *Designed for Brides* with *Hampshire Bridal*?"

Carter raised his hands, palms out. "That's not what I mean."

She put her hands on her hips and stared at him. "Then what do you mean?"

"I lied to you about the bridal division at Hampshire," he said.

"How?"

"It's not doing as well as I told you it was. But that magazine is your baby. You love it and the love you feel for it is evident in the product you produce yourself. Since you left three years ago, things haven't been the same."

"And your solution is…?"

"I sell Hampshire's bridal division—to you."

The silence was deafening. "Are you kidding?"

"Not in the least." Carter's face was serious.

"I sell the bridal division to you. You can either

merge it with *Designed for Brides* or add it as a second magazine. The choice is yours."

"I don't understand. You're giving up the business?"

"There is one condition. Well, two conditions."

She knew there had to be a catch.

"You keep the staff. Their benefits remain intact. They're good people, and they'll put out an excellent magazine."

"I don't understand." Renee's head was spinning. They hadn't had a competitive fight, and they must still be profitable enough to make the business valuable to the larger company.

"I'll be honest with you. The magazine hasn't been pulling its weight for several years. It's reached its cycle with us. You can bring it back to life, give it another name, another look, make it successful."

"Carter, you have more experience than I do with magazines. You know how to reinvent a magazine."

"That takes a lot of work, and we don't have the manpower or creativity to do it. I have confidence that you can turn it around in a short period of time. It's why I wanted you to return to Hampshire. Since that is not possible, the decision was to close the division or sell."

He walked around the desk and came to stand in front of her. "Do we have a deal?"

"I can't make a deal like this without first discussing it with my partners."

"I understand. Then do we have a tentative understanding of a deal at least?"

"You said there were two conditions. What's the second?"

"My mother gets one of her designs featured at least once a year for the next three years."

Renee smiled, then laughed. "I think that can be arranged if we go through with this. But I'll have to see the books, and I'll need everything disclosed."

"Absolutely, I'm sure your accountants and mine will be able to work together."

"In that case, we have an understanding."

Carter thrust out his hand. Renee stared at it. She couldn't remember them ever shaking hands. And at this moment, she was afraid to put her palm against his. Slowly, she raised her hand and he took it, encasing it in his. Then he released it and returned to his desk.

"I'll have our lawyers draw up some proposals to get the ball rolling."

Renee nodded and turned to leave. She stiffened her back and walked to the door. He'd brushed her apology away as if it had meant nothing. The business deal had been more important than her telling him she was sorry.

The weight of the world got heavier and heavier as she stepped into the elevator and held on as it descended thirty-eight floors. The sun was bright as Renee walked out into the warm afternoon. She took a deep breath and dropped her shoulders.

She'd survived losing Carter once before. She could do it again. But this time she wouldn't be leaving New York or changing her profession—there was no running away. She was in love with him, but she'd killed that love with her mistrust.

Renee walked away from the building. She'd walk a while, then head for home. A long plaza led to the street. As she reached the three steps that led down to the public sidewalk, she stopped.

This was not the way it was going to end, Renee thought. Not this time. Quickly she whipped around and crashed into Carter.

"You don't think I'm letting you get away a second time, do you?" Carter asked.

"Are you...what are you saying?"

"I'm in love with you. I've been in love with you since you first came to work here. I couldn't risk telling you three years ago, but I love you, and I'm not letting business get in the way of our happiness."

"Carter..." Renee said, but had no idea what she wanted to say. "What just happened in your office?"

"I offered you a business deal and you accepted it—tentatively."

"And now you're telling me you love me," she stated.

He nodded. "I first had to clear away any obstacle between us. And the magazine was one of them. I want your love more than I want that business. Is that okay?"

"I'm sure I can handle that."

He smiled. "Is that all you can handle?" He raised his eyebrows. "Can you handle me being in love with you?"

"How do I know you won't decide to leave me again the way you did three years ago?"

"I explained where I went—"

Renee put her hand up to his mouth, silencing him. "I know," she said. "I know you can't promise that."

"But I will," he stated. "If you'll forgive me, I'll never leave you again."

"I forgave you long ago, Carter."

"But you never said anything."

"I did, just not in words. I know your decision was to protect me in case something happened to you. It was a noble gesture."

"But I understand now how unfair it was," Carter said. "I should have told you the whole truth. But I knew there was no guarantee that I'd return. If anything happened to me, I wanted you to be free."

"I would have chosen you. Even though we'd only been together for a short time, I was certain of my love. And, yes," she said, "knowing you love me means I can handle anything. Can you handle it, too? The fact that I'm in love with you?" The words came easily to her lips. "I love you," she repeated.

Carter pulled her into his arms and standing on Madison Avenue, oblivious to the crowds passing by, he kissed her. Kissed her hard and long. Kissed her with all the passion of a man in love.

Renee returned it. She had nothing to hold back. Her arms climbed around his neck and she let her heart open up. Love poured out in torrents. And she was happier than she'd ever been.

Epilogue

June—Twelve Months Later

The gown was a Theresa Granville. And it was real. Not a hologram. Not a projection. Not controlled by a bejeweled arm band. Renee stared at herself in the triple mirror. Dana stood behind her, a hand to her heart, her mouth open in a silent "O". Her eyes were misty, quickly filling with tears.

"Don't start crying," Renee admonished her voice full of emotion. She knew if Dana cried, her own tears wouldn't be far behind.

Dana grabbed a tissue from the box on a table in the church basement and dabbed at her eyes, careful not to damage her makeup.

"I'm not crying," she said, her voice breaking. "It's just that you look…you look…" Her hands flailed.

"You've seen me in a wedding gown before," Renee told her, remembering their dress up session.

"It wasn't real then. This time you're getting married." Again her voice broke on the last word.

Renee turned to her cousin and hugged her. After a moment, Dana pushed back, sobering.

"It's about time we started this show," Dana said, sniffing and covering her feelings.

Dana's words brought a storm of activity. The door opened and a parade of people came through it. Her mother led the group with Carter's mother right behind. Both stopped. Their hands then came up to their breasts and their mouths opened in awe. A fresh wave of emotions raced through Renee.

"You're beautiful," her mother said, her voice no louder than a prayer.

Renee swallowed, unable to reply.

Moments later the room was in utter chaos. Renee knew this was normal for the bridal party just before the ceremony would begin. The bridesmaids were all making last-minute preparations for their walk down the aisle. The chatter raised the noise level to a volume so high she wanted to cover her ears.

She'd witnessed and participated in a score of weddings. But some how everything seemed different, more pronounced, yet surreal. She couldn't explain the sensations that flooded through her, one after the other, as she stared in the mirror at herself.

She reached out at nothing in particular, but her

mother grasped her hand and held it. She understood, Renee thought. Without words, her mother had come to her rescue.

Turning she hugged her mom.

"He loves you," she whispered.

"I love him, too," Renee said through the lump in her throat and the love that swelled in her heart.

"I know." Tears glistened in her mother's eyes. She blinked them away. "I could tell the first time I saw you two look at each other."

Teddy came in then. She had insisted on being the wedding consultant for *one of their own* as she'd put it.

"Time to begin," she called over the crowd. The room immediately went dead silent. With quiet authority, Teddy lined the bridesmaids up and sent them to their assigned places.

While Renee and Weddings by Diana's bridal consultants had been called upon to create some very elaborate weddings, Renee's was going to be small and simple—well, almost simple. The entire nuptials had been planned around the number two.

Both mothers stood at the sanctuary entrance. Her mom gave her a final smile and turned to the doors. The music began and the promenade started with the two women being escorted to their seats. Renee swallowed as she waited out of sight of the guests. Her two sisters were her bridesmaids. Dana and Diana served as maids of honor.

When they were all inside and the doors had been closed, Renee imagined the groomsmen rolling out the carpet. She knew her two flower girls were excitedly

peppering it with rose petals before joining the group
that included two ring bearers, at the front of the church.

Teddy called Renee forward. Both her father and
brother were giving her away. With an arm through each
man's elbow, and her bouquet held with both hands, the
wedding march began. She could hear the assembly
stand. The doors opened and Renee heard an audible
gasp from the congregation.

However, the only man she saw was Carter. He
waited for her, appearing unnerved with a smile. It was
an *only you* smile and as Renee took the first step toward her new life, she knew she'd remember that smile
into her old age.

* * * * *

THE FIREFIGHTER'S FAMILY SECRET

SHIRLEY JUMP

To all the unsung heroes in my life, who put out
a helping hand to others when they need it most.
You make the world a better place.

Chapter One

The last thing Colton Barlow expected while visiting Stone Gap, North Carolina, was for opportunity to come knocking.

He wasn't a man given to living by the seat of his pants, and, in fact, most everyone who knew him would say Colton was deliberate. A planner. A man who set a course and mapped his route carefully. It was how he had always approached a fire on the job—assess the situation, know the risks and variables and plot the battle with care. Rushing into a blaze with no forethought was what got people killed.

And Colton Barlow had already made that mistake.

He'd spent the past six months trying to settle back into his job. Most days he did okay. Some days he was lucky if he could shrug an arm into the heavy turnout coat. But he told himself he was fine, just fine, and everything was on track.

Until the information that upended his life, told him everything he thought he knew about himself was wrong and led him to a small Southern town and three half brothers he hadn't even realized existed until a month ago. For almost thirty years he'd been Colton Williams—his mother's last name—and now it turned out he was a Barlow. That last name still felt like a new pair of shoes—a little uncomfortable, a little odd. Maybe if he kept thinking of himself as Colton Barlow, the name would grow on him.

His family had, so far. He'd finally met the other Barlow brothers—Jack, Mac and Luke—at Jack's wedding last week, and in the process, he stumbled upon a job opening on the Stone Gap Fire Department.

A job he hadn't even been looking for. But once the idea took root in his head of a change, a new start, Colton thought it wouldn't hurt to at least check it out. Maybe at a new department, people wouldn't look at him with eyes filled with a mixture of pity and mistrust. Maybe he could finally leave the shadows behind him and begin again. He'd lost his love for firefighting after the accident, and wondered sometimes if he'd ever get it back. Then he'd talked to Harry and the first glimmers of excitement about his job returned.

That's what had him turning around almost the minute he got home to Atlanta. He'd returned to Stone Gap, both to have a little time to get to know his brothers and father, and to meet with the fire chief for a formal sit-down. Except Fire Chief Harry Washington wasn't a formal sit-down kind of guy, more a walk-and-talk, see-how-it-goes man. Which was why Colton was strolling through downtown Stone Gap, while Harry gave him a guided tour of the town.

"Best apple pie in the county is served right there," Harry said, pointing at a little restaurant on the corner. A bright red-and-white awning above the Good Eatin' Café pronounced the same thing in a dark blue curly script. Harry, a short and slightly pudgy man with a white buzz cut, looked as if he might indulge in the pie on occasion. He had a wide smile, a twinkle in his eyes and a friendly manner, which most everybody in Stone Gap seemed to respond to, given how many people had shouted a hello on their walk so far. "And if you ask Viv real nice, she'll give you an extra scoop of ice cream on top."

So far, Harry had talked about the best place to buy a pair of work boots, how to unclog a drain, the top menu items at Mabel's diner and a whole host of other topics that didn't have a damned thing to do with firefighting. Colton kept expecting some kind of questions about his skill set, but in the half hour since Colton had met Harry at the station and they'd started walking, nothing related to his occupation had come up in conversation. Maybe Harry was a circuitous guy, Colton thought. One who needed to be brought back around to the real reason he was here. "Sir, if you want my résumé—"

Harry put up a hand. "Let me stop you there, son. I don't hire people based on a piece of paper. You and I both know how quickly paper disappears when you set it ablaze. I make my decisions based on the person, not their fancy-dancy credentials."

"But surely you want to know if I have experience—"

Harry squinted in the sun. "Do you like fishing, Colton?"

The non sequitur made Colton stumble over a crack in the sidewalk. He pushed his sunglasses back up his nose and fell back into place beside Harry. "Uh, yes, sir."

Harry nodded. "Good. Go home, grab a pole and meet me down at Ray Prescott's place 'round three this afternoon. We'll do the whole formal interview thing then."

"While we're fishing?"

Harry grinned. "It's called multitasking, son. Now, if you ask my wife, she'll tell you I can't talk and breathe at the same time, and while that may be true, I sure as hell can talk and fish at the same time." He gave Colton a little salute then strode off down the sidewalk toward the brick fire station.

Colton stared after him for a long time, then decided that if he wanted a job in Stone Gap—and he still wasn't sure he did—then he should get a fishing pole. Not that Colton had gone fishing much. A few times with his uncle Tank, but that was about it. He'd been too busy trying to be the man of the family, a job thrust on him from the minute he could walk. Even now, even all these miles away from his mother and sister, he felt that mantle of responsibility. Of course, Katie was all grown up now, and their mother…well, she was what she liked to call "a work in progress."

Which meant Colton shouldn't feel bad about doing something for himself for once. Like going fishing.

Especially considering how much his life had changed in such a short period of time. A month ago he'd been working for the Atlanta FD, spending his free time working on his mother's run-down car and urging his sister to take some time off, live a little, someplace other than the accounting firm where she spent a minimum of eighty hours a week. In return, Katie had needled him about being the quintessential bachelor, with an apartment as empty as a store going out of business. Sure, he had the occasional fling, but he wasn't interested in serious relationships, and he made sure the women he dated knew it. He'd thought his life was more or less complete.

Then he found out that Uncle Tank—his real name was David, but no one ever called the barrel-chested, hearty man by anything other than Tank—whom Colton had always thought was just a family friend, was actually his real uncle, and that his biological father—a man his mother had never spoken about— lived in Stone Gap, along with the three sons he had raised. Robert Barlow had ignored Colton's existence for thirty years, a fact that still stung, even though Colton told himself he was far too old to care whether he'd had a dad to teach him how to complete a layup or tell him how to win a girl's heart.

But he did care. And working through the roller coaster of emotions that meeting his siblings and father had awakened was part of what had kept Colton here in Stone Gap. A saner man might have just turned his back on all of this and left town forever, but Colton had this need to know where he came from. His mother had called it his curiosity gene, the same need that had driven Colton to dismantle the dishwasher when he was eleven, and ask a thousand questions in every class he ever took.

Now he had a thousand and ten questions for Bobby Barlow, but Colton had hesitated to ask them. Had delayed seeing his father again, because Colton wasn't so sure he wanted to hear the answers.

Nor was he so sure his father would want a relationship with him. Colton wasn't the success that Mac was, the war hero Jack was or the second generation partner that Luke was. Sure, Colton was a firefighter, but he was barely hanging on to the job he had in Atlanta after the disaster that claimed two of his coworkers six months ago. A disaster that Colton could have avoided, if only he had tried harder.

The memory of that night had a way of stealing Colton's breath when he least expected it. He'd catch a whiff of smoke or hear a crash, and he'd be there again, screaming into his mask for Willis and Foster. He'd see the burst of flame, hear the crack of the overhead beam, feel the heat crushing his gear. And see the yawning cavern that opened up like a hungry beast and swallowed the best men—and the best friends—Colton had ever known.

He pinched the bridge of his nose and willed the memory back into the shadows. It took a while, four deep breaths to be exact, but then he opened his eyes and reminded himself he was in Stone Gap, North Carolina, on a vacation of sorts. And about to go fishing.

Get it together, Barlow.

He jogged across Main Street, avoiding the lone car going south. He shook his head in amazement. Stone Gap wasn't a hundredth as busy as Atlanta had been. That alone might be a nice change if he got offered a job at the department here.

If he even wanted to stay. Living in Stone Gap, becoming part of the fabric of the community, would mean being around his father on a regular basis. Dealing with all those questions that kept needling at his thoughts, the ones he wasn't ready to face.

At the same time, it would mean having three brothers, three men who were the kind Colton had as friends back home. Three men he already genuinely liked. A lot.

He spied a familiar pair of legs sticking out from under the body of a Ford pickup truck at Gator's Garage, the Barlow family business. Colton hesitated for a moment—this whole thing with his brothers was still so new, he wasn't sure how to handle things like running into Luke downtown—then decided the only thing to do was to just go over there and say hello.

Colton ambled into the garage. He'd always liked garages, the smell of motor oil, the myriad tools, the puzzles of the cars that needed fixing. Gator's used to be run by his father, until Bobby had knee-replacement surgery and needed to slow down. Now Luke was in charge, while Bobby worked part-time.

Colton took in the pegboards filled with tools, the

tall red chests stuffed with parts, and imagined his father here, teaching Luke how to change the oil in a Chevy or rotate the tires on a Ford. The thought made Colton a little envious. Maybe getting to know Luke, Jack and Mac better would help ease some of those feelings. Colton looked down at the work boots below him. "Hey, Luke."

Luke pushed out from under the car and grinned up at Colton. He had the same dark brown wavy hair and blue eyes as the rest of the Barlows, Colton included. Looking at his brothers was eerily like looking in the mirror. "Hey, Colt. Good to see you! Guess we didn't scare you off, after all."

"I'm not so easy to get rid of." He chuckled. "Plus, I had an interview with Harry, the fire chief, so I figured I'd come back here and see it through." Colton shrugged. "Not thinking it's going to lead to anything, but it's a shot. Might as well check it out."

Luke nodded at that, then got to his feet, grabbed a rag and cleaned off his hands. "Glad to hear you're staying a bit. You can help me torture Mac now that Jack is off on his honeymoon. But I have to warn you, Jack and I have a good routine going that keeps Mac at the center of a lot of merciless teasing. You gotta be on your toes to hang with us."

Colton laughed. He liked the relationship the brothers had. Jack, a former soldier, was a good guy, solid and clearly head over heels for his new wife, Meri. Luke was the prankster of the family, though his heart was with his new fiancée, Peyton Reynolds, and their daughter Maddy, while Mac was the overachieving tycoon who had made millions in buying and selling companies, but had recently met and fallen in love with local girl Savannah Hillstrand.

"Sounds like a plan." Colton shook his head. "I still have to get used to having all this family. It's been just me, my sister and my mom for so long, and now all of a sudden, it's like I'm tripping over Barlows."

Luke chuckled. "We're pretty much everywhere. Just ask the neighbors, who blamed every broken window and torn-up lawn on one of us."

"Rightly so?"

"You know it." Luke grinned. "But I'll never admit to the crimes of my youth, at least not in front of my impressionable daughter, who I'm trying to steer away from my mistakes." He made a circle in the air. "So between you and me, I was a Goody Two-shoes."

That made Colton laugh. "And people are going to believe me when I say that?"

"Hell, no. But that's okay. I just blame all my misdeeds on Mac. I love seeing his face get that scrunched-up look." Luke tossed the rag on the counter then grabbed the clipboard that held the day's jobs. "Listen, I'd love to sit around and shoot the breeze, but I have a bunch of work on tap for today. Ever since I took over for Dad, this place has been hopping. What say we grab breakfast tomorrow morning, you, me and Mac?"

"Sounds good." Colton feigned coolness, but he was secretly pretty pleased the other Barlow boys had welcomed him so easily. He didn't expect the road ahead would always be smooth, but he was glad they'd started off so well. His brothers had brought him into the fold as easily as inserting a card into the deck. Maybe if he started with the brotherly relationship, he'd be able to ease into the one with his father. "Hey, where's the best place to get a fishing pole around here?"

Luke grinned. "Let me guess. Did Harry invite you? That man would be a professional fisherman if he could get paid for it. Go on over to Ernie's across the street. They have pretty much everything."

"Thanks." It didn't seem like enough to say to Luke, because it didn't capture all that Colton really wanted to say, but he was a guy, and *thanks* was pretty much the extent of what he was capable of. "See you."

Luke nodded. "See you tomorrow."

Tomorrow. Breakfast with his *brothers.* The word still sounded weird in his head, even weirder when he spoke it aloud. All the things he had lacked all his life, right here in this tiny little town. Yeah, maybe staying a while was a good idea.

He ducked into Ernie's Hardware & Sundries, which sported a hand-drawn sign advertising a special on night crawlers. Colton waited a second for his eyes to adjust to the dim interior, the rows of shelves and the bins of garden tools.

"Good morning. Can I help you?"

He turned toward the lilting sound of a woman's voice. That was what hit Colton first—her voice, which, even in those few syllables, seemed to have a sweet, happy tone to it, as if his coming into the store was the best thing that had happened to her all day.

Then he saw her, and decided maybe seeing her was

the best thing that happened to *him* all day—because the woman behind the counter was stunning.

His grandmother would have called her *willowy.* She was tall and thin, with long, straight, light blond hair that was so pale it seemed ethereal. Her dark green eyes were wide and deep, and matched by a welcoming smile that made him feel warm inside. She wore a white button-down shirt with big silver buttons with the sleeves rolled up, tucked into a pair of dark jeans that hugged her curves.

"Uh…yeah, good morning," Colton said, wondering when he'd become a guy who stammered. "I'm looking for fishing rods?"

"Right this way." She crooked her finger, beckoning to him, and made her way down one of the aisles. He would have followed her to Timbuktu with just that one gesture. Not to mention the view he had from behind.

She stopped in the middle of the aisle and waved toward a display of tackle and fishing poles. "I don't know what you're looking for, but if you were to ask my dad, he'll tell you the best one is this graphite bait caster right here. Lot of folks go for this spinning combo—" she pointed to another, fancier pole "—but my dad always says that the right pole sits in your hand like it was made for your palm. Not too heavy, not too light, and when you go to pull up on the hook, the pole does the work."

It was all pretty much Greek to him. "Okay, let me see one of the graphic things."

"Graphite." She grinned at his mistake then handed him the pole. "It also matters where you're fishing and what you're fishing for."

"Well, I don't really know the second answer. I'm meeting Harry Washington over at Ray Prescott's place. It's a job interview. Sort of."

She laughed. "I know Harry. He's not much on formalities. Ray's place is right on the water, so chances are you're doing a little surf fishing. That's a different animal from fishing in the lake. You might want to try this pole instead." She pulled yet another from the seemingly endless rack. "It's got a heavier reel. That will help you if you're going for some striped bass or red drum. And the gear is heavy enough, in case you accidentally hook a shark."

He took the new pole she handed him and hefted it in his palm. It seemed strong, solid. "Sounds like you know what you're talking about."

She turned and gave him a grin. "Well, when you're daddy's girl, and the only kid at that, you play soccer and catch fish and learn how to shoot a rifle. At the same time you're learning how to curl your eyelashes and pick out lipstick and wear high heels."

He chuckled then put out his hand. "I think with a line like that, we should be formally introduced. I'm Colton. Colton…Barlow." The name sounded strange still, but it was beginning to grow on him.

Confusion muddied her eyes. "One of *the* Barlows? With Jack, Luke and Mac?"

Small-town living, Colton thought and grinned. "Sort of. I'm their half brother. From Atlanta. Firefighter, novice fisherman and decent first baseman."

He didn't know what made him give her that mini-résumé, but then she laughed, and it made his day.

"Pleased to meet you, Colton Barlow from Atlanta. I'm Rachel Morris, daughter of the famous Ernie. Expert fisherwoman and not-bad shortstop."

"Maybe you could teach me a thing or two about catching the right one."

Her smile reached into her eyes, lighting up her entire face. A flirty, teasing look in those green depths toyed with the edges of her lips. "Is that what you're here for? Because we don't sell matches made in heaven. Just fishing poles and garden rakes."

"I'm just talking trout and bass." He picked up another pole from the ones she'd pointed out to him, hefted it for weight, put it back and reselected the one she'd given him. From feel at least, it seemed like Rachel's choice was the best. "Definitely not long-term commitments."

"Just what this town needs. Another confirmed bachelor." But she laughed when she said it, took the fishing pole from him and walked back to the register. She punched in a few keys then recited the price and thanked him when he handed over a credit card.

While she was finishing the transaction, Colton racked his brain for something else to say. Something to prolong the moment before he had to leave. He liked Rachel. Found her intriguing. And it had been a long, long time since he'd met a woman who interested him like that. "So, have you lived here all your life?"

Yeah, way to go on the lame question. Clearly, he was out of practice.

"Pretty much. I was born and bred here." She printed out the credit card receipt and handed the white slip of paper to him, along with a pen. "Are you thinking about moving here? If you get the job with the fire department?"

"Maybe."

"Still testing us out, huh?" She grinned. "Well, I can tell you this much about Stone Gap. It defines small town. If you sneeze over your Wheaties at breakfast, half the town is lined up for a flu shot by lunchtime. Most everyone here grew up in each other's pockets, as my dad likes to say. Which means everyone knows pretty much everything about everyone else."

"Sounds…suffocating."

"It can be." She shrugged. "But in a small town, someone's always there if you need help. If you're down, there's a neighbor or a friend to pull you back up. Stone Gap has its faults, like any place, but at its core, it's a great town to live in. And you can't beat the weather or the fact that we're right on the water."

He chuckled. "Are you with the welcoming committee?"

She blushed, a soft pink that stole across her cheeks. "No, I just…finally learned to appreciate this place."

"I've never lived in a place that I loved like that. Atlanta's fine, but it's a big city. You can get…lost there pretty easily." His voice trailed off, and he shook his head.

"Lost in more ways than one?" she said softly.

Colton cleared his throat. He wasn't about to unload his life history in a hardware store with a woman he barely knew. Even if every time she smiled, she made him want to linger for hours on end. "Well, thanks for the tips about Stone Gap. I'll keep them in mind."

"Sure. Anytime. And if you want the twenty-five-cent tour, you know where I am."

"Twenty-five cents? That's it?"

She blushed again. "It's a small town."

That made him laugh. "Harry already told me where the best apple pie is."

"Then you're down to the twenty-cent tour. Unless you have already discovered the best place for making out." The blush intensified. "I meant, for the teenagers."

"Of course." Making out? That made him think about climbing in the backseat of his car with Rachel and seeing where it might lead. Not a good train of thought to follow, but that didn't stop him from a quick mental image. "Us old people are too mature for that."

"Definitely."

Yet everything in the undercurrent of their conversation said differently. He might be out of practice in the dating arena, but he sensed some definite attraction in the air. He had the strangest urge to lean across the counter and kiss her right now.

"Uh, I should sign this." He bent his head and scrawled his name across the receipt then handed it back to her.

"Thanks," she said. She lifted the fishing pole and gave it to him. "Need anything else?"

Your phone number, his brain whispered. Because he definitely wanted to get to know Rachel Morris, fisherwoman and shortstop, much better. But he was leaving in a few days, so asking her out wouldn't make any sense.

But as he headed out of the store, Colton had to wonder if maybe forgoing her number was the thing that didn't make any sense, because she lingered in his mind long after he cast the first line into the water.

Chapter Two

Rachel dusted shelves that didn't need dusting and tidied displays that were already tidy. It was a Tuesday, one of the least busy days in her dad's shop. Her only customer had been the tall, good-looking firefighter in a faded blue T-shirt and stonewashed jeans that hugged his legs and told her Colton Barlow was a man who worked out. A lot. Good Lord, his biceps alone were enough to make her mind start fantasizing. Hot and yummy, and a definite change from the older, potbellied retirees who usually came into the store.

Men who looked like Colton Barlow, and had a killer smile like his, didn't come to Stone Gap very often. He'd stayed long enough that she almost thought he was going to ask her out. But in the end, he just paid for his purchase and headed out the door. Clearly, she'd read him wrong. Of course, she hadn't helped things by being such a dork and blushing every five seconds, or making that stupid comment about the best place to make out. It was as if she was back in high school again and crushing on the cute boy in English class.

She shouldn't have been disappointed—after all, she was the one who had sworn off men until she had more than five minutes of free time a day—but she was. It would have been nice, really nice, if he'd noticed more than just the type of rod and reel she was selling him.

At six she locked up, got in her car and drove across town to the three-bedroom bungalow where she'd grown up. The flower beds were overrun with weeds, the trees in desperate need of trimming and the white picket fence out front had faded to a dingy gray. It was as if time had stopped in that house, and now everything else was slowly giving up the fight.

Rachel sighed, parked her car in the drive then headed inside. Just like the outside, the interior of the house was dark and dingy, coated with a fine layer of dust and despair.

Before her mother's death, her father had been at his store day in and day out, clocking in when the shop first opened and staying as long as anyone needed to buy something from him. Her mother had manned the ship at the house, keeping up with the plants and dishes and creating a home with everything she did.

But then cirrhosis had taken Rachel's mother last year, leaving all of them with a hole too wide to fill. It had hit Ernie especially hard. He'd made himself a hermit in the house, losing interest in the store, in fishing, in his life. For that entire year, Rachel had run the shop single-handedly, putting her own life on hold, leaving her father to grieve while she ordered supplies and paid bills and swept the floors.

For ten months he hadn't asked her a single question about how the store was doing. But she'd come by every day nonetheless and given him a recap. Then one day he'd called her in the middle of the day, asked her how it was going. It wasn't much, but her father's spark of interest had given Rachel hope that maybe, just maybe, she could get back to her own venture someday soon. Assuming she still had one, given the dent one year of not working had made in her bridal business. Just when Happily Ever After Weddings was getting off the ground, Rachel had to put it all to the side. She'd lost several bookings, and had probably given up all the ground she had worked so hard to gain the year before. But her father had needed her, and that was all that mattered.

Someday he'd be back in charge, and she'd go back to her life. Someday.

She found her father sitting at the kitchen table, a crossword puzzle in front of him. He had filled in only a handful of clues since she'd left him this morning in the same place, with the same folded section of newspaper in his hands. The breakfast dishes still sat in the sink, and there was nothing in the stove for dinner. Rachel worried that if she ever stopped coming by, her father would stop eating altogether. It was as if losing his wife had made him lose his motivation to move forward. Move anywhere, period.

"Good evening, Dad." She pressed a kiss to his unshaven cheek. She missed the scent of his cologne, the smoothness of his skin after he shaved. "What's for dinner?"

"I…uh…haven't thought about it." He blinked, his eyes bleary and red, probably from getting a few fitful hours of sleep in the recliner in front of the TV. His white hair stuck up on his head, and his T-shirt looked as though it hadn't been washed in a month. "The day goes by so fast sometimes. I didn't even realize it was that time already."

"Why don't I just throw some chicken on the grill?" Rachel pulled open the fridge and pulled out a package of meat, acting like everything was okay. That it didn't make her heart hurt to see her once robust and busy father sitting here like a lump of clay. "You still have those potatoes?"

"Potatoes?"

"I bought them at the store yesterday. Remember?"

"Oh, yeah. I forgot about them. Well, I haven't eaten any potatoes, so they're probably in the bin in the pantry. You know, where Mom always kept them? Never store them with the onions, she'd said, but I can't remember why." He shook his head then turned back to the crossword. "What's a five-letter word for *in fashion*?"

"Umm…" She thought about it while she sprinkled some seasoning on the chicken, then dug in the bin in the pantry, unearthed a few potatoes, washed them and pricked their skins. "Try *vogue*."

"Works for me." He penciled it in. "Been working on this crossword all day. It's a tough one."

It was what he said every day. She wasn't quite sure how her father spent the hours between breakfast—when she got here at eight and put his coffee on and fixed him some eggs—and six fifteen, when she got back from the store. She didn't want to think of him sitting at this kitchen table, staring out the window, mourning. But truth be told, that was what she knew her father probably did every day.

"Have you called Daryl? He was in the other day. Said he wanted to get you up to the lake, see what's biting." Her father's best friend had been in almost every day over the last month, checking to see if Ernie might have come in for the day. Daryl had tried calling and coming by the house, but if Ernie didn't want to deal with someone, he just ignored them. Rachel hoped that if she kept on mentioning Daryl and her father's favorite pastime, it might get him out the door.

Her father waved that off. Again. "Maybe when the weather is better."

Rachel glanced out the window at clear skies, a sunlit day. "Today was a great day for fishing, Dad."

That made her think of the firefighter again. Colton Barlow. Novice fisherman. Decent first baseman. And very hot guy in general. She wondered how his fishing trip had gone, and whether he'd be back to the store. Whether he'd ask her for coffee—

Then she glanced at her father and realized she probably didn't have time to date. Heck, she barely had time to take care of herself. There were dishes to do, laundry to process, some weeding to tackle, then she had to go home and take care of her own chores, sleep, get up, work the store and come back to her father's house again. Rinse and repeat, day after day, until her father got back into his life. "Dad, I'm going to get this on the grill, then I'll come back in and do the dishes."

"You don't have to. They can keep." He never even looked up from the crossword. "I'll do them later."

She sighed. It was what he always said, whenever she offered to clean for him, but he never swept or washed or did anything about the mess inside the house or the weeds out front. And all the other thousand little things that had gone undone for months.

She put the chicken on the grill then came back inside. She fished out the register report from her pocket and smoothed the paper on the table in front of her father. "Here's today's tally. Things were a little slow." She didn't mention that her only customer had been the firefighter.

The store had barely been surviving in the last few months, but she never told her father that. If she did, his disappointment—in the store, in her—would likely make him retreat even further. So she tried to keep things upbeat, positive. There were days when even that was a challenge.

Her father gave the paper a glance. "Business will pick up."

He'd been saying that for months. But business had dropped to a dangerous low, and right now it was costing more to keep the lights on than she was taking in during the day. She was doing her best, but the people of Stone Gap loved her dad, came to him for his expertise, the way he made everyone feel welcome. She was trying, but she wasn't Ernie. "I think everyone misses you down at the shop."

"I'll be by." His focus was back on the crossword. "Someday."

Rachel slipped into the seat opposite her father and put a hand over her dad's. "Someday…like tomorrow? Come on, Dad. It'll be good for you to—"

He shoved the chair back so fast, it squealed against the tile floor. "I'm fine right here. So let it go."

Then he stomped out of the room, down the hall and into his bedroom. The door shut with a slam, and Rachel was left alone, with the same mess she'd been trying to clean up for the past year.

She fixed the chicken, did the dishes and processed a load of laundry. Then she left her dad a covered plate and a note that said she loved him before she headed out the door. Rachel sat in her car for a long time, debating whether to go home and do the same at her house, then work on the books and orders for the store.

Or maybe, for once, do something for herself.

That made her think of Colton again. He was here on vacation, she presumed. Did that mean he was out tonight? Sitting on a bar stool somewhere, or still fishing? Or was he the type to fill his evenings with a long run or a good novel?

When was the last time she had done any of the above? Had enough time to buy a book, never mind read one? Take a long, lazy walk on a warm summer evening? Sleep in on a Sunday and dawdle over the paper with a cup of coffee and a cinnamon roll?

As she neared the street toward the cozy apartment she lived in, she saw the sign for the Sea Shanty. She debated at the stop sign then finally turned left, away from home and toward the restaurant. She rolled down the windows, let in the ocean breeze and tasted the short burst of freedom in the air.

The Sea Shanty wasn't much, as restaurants went, but the food was good, and they'd recently started featuring live bands almost every night of the week. Rachel picked up her phone, pressed a button and waited for the other end to answer. "You up for a glass of wine and way too many calories?"

"Hell, yes." Melissa, Rachel's best friend since grade school, let out a throaty laugh. "Tell me where and when, and I'll get Jason to watch these kids so I can escape the shackles of motherhood for a few minutes."

"The Sea Shanty. As soon as possible."

"Hold on a sec." Melissa covered the phone then yelled to Jason, "I'm going out so you've got the rugrats for dinner." Then she was back. "Give me ten minutes."

"I can't wait." Rachel pulled into the lot, parked her car and tucked her keys in her purse. How long had it been since she'd had dinner and drinks with friends? Clearly, way too long if she couldn't remember. She had to find a better way to balance her life. Otherwise, she had a feeling she'd wake up a year from now and realize she was still in the exact same place as before. She wanted to date again, go out more often, get her business running. Coming here tonight instead of going home was a good first step, but Rachel had a feeling she was going to need a miracle if she wanted to carve more than an impromptu dinner out of an already tightly structured twenty-four hours.

Yeah, definitely a miracle. She still had a pile of paperwork to do at home, the end of the quarter financials to finalize and a restock order to process. She didn't have time for a long dinner—maybe a quick bite and the rest to go. Melissa would understand, Rachel hoped. Maybe in a few more months…

But even Rachel didn't hold out hope for that. Her father was all she had left, and there was no way she was going to abandon him. If it took one year or ten, she would be there, taking care of him and doing what she should have done—

Before her mother died.

The guilt rolled through Rachel like a wave. Those two years after her mother got sick, Rachel had been so invested—too invested—in her own life. Her father hadn't even told her about her mother's illness early on, and she'd missed all the subtle clues that something was awry. Rachel had been pouring herself into her new business, into getting it off the ground, and by the time she realized her mother was sick—

It was too late.

Her father had been the one who had dealt with the doctor's appointments, the long, sleepless nights, the funeral plans at the end. Her mother had told her, just before the end, that she had begged Ernie not to tell Rachel about the cirrhosis, because she wanted her daughter to be happy, unburdened by an illness that took full-time caregiving. Her father had agreed, and the two of them had done their best to shield their daughter from the situation until the weakness and changes in her mother's face spoke the truth.

That was why Rachel had dropped everything to be there for her father now. She may have let him down before, but she wasn't going to do it again, regardless of how long it took.

The Sea Shanty was half filled with diners, and several people sat at the outdoor bar. Rachel opted for an outdoor table, since the weather was warm, the breeze light, the ocean waves lapping at the shore like a quiet song in the background. The band was tuning up, a three-piece group she'd heard before and liked. They did a lot of covers of popular songs, but had a strong female singer who could belt out a ballad, too.

Rachel was just opening her menu when she caught a glimpse of Colton Barlow, just settling down at the end of the bar. He ordered a beer then picked up a menu.

Damn, he was a good-looking man. He'd changed since this morning, into a fresh pair of jeans and a pale blue polo shirt that stretched across the muscles in his back. His dark hair was damp, which had her picturing him in the shower. Naked. Soapy.

Crap, crap. He'd turned and caught her looking. She jerked the menu up to her face and prayed Melissa arrived, like right now. Instead, Colton slipped off the bar stool, crossed the wooden deck toward her and, in less time than it took to flip a burger, derailed all of Rachel's careful plans.

The pretty clerk from the hardware store blushed when Colton approached. He liked that. She'd come across as so self-assured in the shop, and yet when he caught her eye now, a shy smile flitted across her face, and she dropped her attention to her menu. Avoiding him? Or embarrassed that he had caught her staring?

"You seem to be everywhere I am," he said. Not exactly a winner as far as opening lines went, but in his defense, he was a little rusty. It had been at least three months since he'd been on a date, almost a year since he'd been in anything remotely approaching a relationship.

"It's a small town. It's bound to happen." She put her menu to the side and crossed her hands on her table. All business now, the last traces of her blush gone. "So how was the fishing?"

"Great. The rod you sold me worked out well. Caught two striped bass, but no sharks."

"Just as well," she said, and a smile flitted across her face. "If you got bit while you were staying here, it might put a dent in our tourism industry."

He arched a brow. "Stone Gap has a tourism industry?"

"Well, only if you count the Fullertons, who come down every winter to vacation with the Whitmans." Then she glanced at him again, and her cheeks grew pink. "Well, them…and you, of course."

"Of course." He looked down and noticed another place setting and a second menu at the seat across from her. For a date? Colton had no right to care whether Rachel was dating anyone or not, but a part of him did. He knew he should just let the conversation drop, let her go. He was leaving town in a few days, after all, and anything he started with this beautiful woman he would never be able to finish. Except he couldn't seem to get his feet to move. "I wanted to thank you for the fishing advice you gave me."

She waved that off and gave him a smile. A genuine one that brightened her eyes, her whole face. Something deep inside Colton warmed. "It was nothing. The advice comes free with the purchase of the rod and reel."

Maybe so, and maybe she wasn't interested in him, but in that moment Colton decided he wasn't going to walk away with regret a second time. So maybe he was only going to be in town for a short while. And maybe she was waiting on a man. But he loved the way she smiled and especially loved the way she blushed, and he didn't want to return to his seat without knowing when he was going to see her again. "Let me take you to lunch tomorrow."

"Oh, I can't." She shook her head. "I'm working and it's…difficult for me to get away."

"Then dinner."

"I have… I, uh, don't think I can. I'm sorry." Another head shake, this one a little slower and sadder.

"Are you just playing hard to get?" He grinned. "Or are you really this busy?"

"No, really, I am this busy. My life is…complicated right now."

"Join the club. Mine is a bit of a mess." He glanced again at the second place setting and decided maybe she simply wasn't interested in him. "I'm sorry. I should let you get back to your date."

"Good Lord, don't do that. This poor girl hasn't had sex in months."

Rachel turned red as a beet. Colton spun around to find a short brunette with a big smile and an even bigger purse pulling out the second chair. She thrust a hand toward him. "I'm Melissa, her married best friend. Who is desperately trying to get Rachel back into the dating scene again before she shrivels up and dies like a prune. And you are…single and employed?"

He laughed. "Yes to the first, and sort of to the second. Colton Barlow. I'm a firefighter in Atlanta."

Melissa grinned up at Colton, then shot another grin at Rachel. "He's cute, did you notice?"

Rachel looked as though she wanted to run from the restaurant. So Colton pulled up another chair, spun it backward and straddled the seat. Which only made Rachel blush harder and piqued Colton's interest more. "Maybe," he said. "Seems like a nice enough town. With a lot of nice people."

Melissa nodded. "Very nice. Rachel here is—"

"Trying to order dinner," Rachel cut in. "Did you look at the menu yet, Melissa?"

Melissa waved a hand in dismissal. "I know the menu here. It never changes. Whereas the population of Stone Gap, well, looks like that is changing. And

weren't you just saying the other day that there were
no good men to date in this town?"

Rachel choked on her water. Colton choked back a
laugh then cleared his throat.

"Then maybe you should take me up on my lunch
invitation," Colton said to Rachel. "So you can eliminate one more single man from the list."

"He asked you to lunch?" Melissa said. She leaned
across the table. "And you said no? Why on earth did
you say no?"

"I'm busy and—" Rachel threw up her hands. "I am
not having this discussion. I'm ordering some food."
She signaled to the waitress. A young blonde came
bouncing over to the table, readying a pad of paper.

"What can I get you?" the girl said. She chewed a
stick of gum while she talked, which added a snap to
each syllable.

"I'd like the fish tacos," Rachel said. "And a glass
of chardonnay. Melissa?"

But Melissa wasn't paying attention. She was staring at Colton as if he was the last man on earth and she
was going to wrap him up and deliver him to Rachel
for Christmas. "Did you say Barlow? As in related to
Mac, Jack and Luke?"

He nodded. "They're my half brothers."

"Well, then, that's a whole other vote in your favor.
Everybody loves the Barlows." Melissa leaned in toward Colton and lowered her voice. "Rachel is a bit…
stubborn, and she is busier than anyone I've ever met,

but believe me, she is worth whatever hell she puts you through to date her."

"Melissa!"

"What? I'm just making a case for you." Melissa grinned. She turned to the waitress, who was standing there, tapping her pen on her pad. "Bring me the seafood salad. Those darn kids have left me on a perpetual diet. And for the gentleman—"

"Who isn't staying," Rachel cut in.

"See what I said? Stubborn." Melissa grinned at Colton. "But don't let that… Oh, look. It's Bobby and Della."

Colton turned and saw his father, standing by the hostess station with another couple, and Della, his wife—and the mother of the other Barlow boys. At the same time, Bobby noticed Colton, and he stiffened. He whispered something to Della, and she turned toward Colton. She worked up a smile and gave Colton a little wave.

Colton stared toward Bobby, but a pained look filled his father's face. The other couple, unaware of the tension filling the restaurant, started chatting with Bobby. He gave Colton a half nod then turned his attention back to the people he was with. A second later the hostess gathered up a pile of menus and started waving toward a table on the far end of the room.

A deep ache started in Colton's chest. The father he'd always wanted, the father he had finally found, and despite the auspicious beginning they'd had at Jack's wedding, Colton could tell Bobby still looked uncomfortable with the idea of welcoming his illegitimate son into the family fold.

It was a small town, after all, and that meant they would inevitably run into each other. Colton told himself he hadn't expected a warm, familial welcome, but—

He had. He'd hoped for some Hollywood reunion, with his father trotting him around town with pride, telling everyone that Colton was his son.

A son who let two of his best friends die in a fire? Did you really think he'd want to spread that *news?*

Colton shook off the thoughts. If he let the guilt in, he knew it would take over every thought, and he'd be stuck in that limbo he'd barely climbed out of. He needed to move forward, make a new start. Not dwell on the past and choices he couldn't undo.

"I'll let you ladies enjoy your dinner," Colton said, then got to his feet. He crossed over to Bobby and Della as they made their way through the room, thinking maybe he had misread the look on Bobby's face. But no, the closer Colton drew, the more Bobby's face pinched, and the deeper the dread sank in Colton's gut.

"Hi, Colton," Della said. She was a warm and welcoming woman with dark copper hair and a wide smile. Colton had liked her on the spot. If there was one word he associated with Della Barlow, it was grace. Despite finding out her husband had had an affair, and that the relationship had produced a child, Della had treated him as one of the family. For that, Colton was grateful.

"Yeah, uh, hi," Bobby said. The five of them had

stopped in the center of the restaurant, twenty feet from the empty table. "Nice to see you again, Colton."

A tall, thin man with glasses as round as salad bowls looked over at Colton with a mixture of familiarity and confusion. "Come on and join us, son." The man squinted. "Wait. Are you Mac?"

"No. I'm Colton."

"Colton?" The man looked at Bobby. "Who's Colton? One of the cousins?"

"Yeah, uh, look, why don't you go grab the table, Jerry? Della and I will be right there."

"Sure, sure." Jerry and his wife took a seat at the table and accepted menus from the hostess. They sent over one more confused glance in Bobby's direction.

"How…how are you?" Bobby said.

"Good. Pretty much the same as yesterday."

"That's good." Bobby shifted his weight. "Uh, you're staying in town?"

"For a few days, yeah."

He waited for his father to invite him over, to ask him to join them for dinner. Instead, Bobby glanced over at his friends then back at his son. "Uh, Colton, we need to…" Bobby waved toward the table across the room with that pinched look in his face again.

One of the cousins, that's what his father had agreed Colton was. If anything told Colton where he ranked in his father's life, that did it. Why was he still here? Why was he still hoping for a miracle that wasn't going to come?

"Well, good to see you. Enjoy your dinner." Colton turned away then fished a twenty-dollar bill out of his pocket, tossed it on the bar and walked out of the Sea Shanty. He'd been a fool for coming to this town and thinking he could manufacture a father-son relationship out of thin air. And an even bigger fool for thinking if he stayed any longer he might find all the things he'd been looking for.

Rachel watched Colton exit the restaurant and told herself she was relieved. She didn't have time, after all, for a relationship. And especially not one with a man who wasn't going to be here for more than a few days.

"That was one delicious hunk of man," Melissa said. "Tell me again how you met him?"

"He came into my father's store. Bought a fishing pole." She shrugged.

"Well, I think that's an auspicious start already."

Rachel laughed. "Auspicious start? I wasn't aware anything was started."

"Then you didn't see the look the two of you exchanged." Melissa arched a brow. "Definitely something started. And he's interested in fishing—"

"He bought one pole. A couple of things for tackle. Said he hadn't fished in a long time."

"Close enough to interested." Melissa leaned forward. "Did you give him all the ins and outs of pole handling?"

Rachel laughed. "Did you really just say that? 'The ins and outs of *pole handling*'?"

Melissa grinned. "What? I'm stuck at home with kids all day. When I do get out, it's like I got a free pass from the warden. I get in all kinds of trouble."

Rachel laughed. "Is that what we're doing tonight? Getting into all kinds of trouble?"

"Well, my trouble can only last till nine o'clock. Then this pumpkin has to haul her butt home because the baby will be up at the crack of too early." Melissa let out a long sigh. "Anyway, enough about my pre-ball Cinderella life. How are you doing?"

"I'm good."

Melissa arched a brow. "This is me you're talking to, remember? You've had a lot on your shoulders lately, and I worry about you putting everyone else first and yourself at the bottom of a very long list."

"Spoken like an expert." Rachel grinned.

"True." Melissa laughed. Her friend was always running her kids here there and everywhere, rarely finding enough time to go shopping or get her hair done. "I'm just as bad. The way I see it, all us kettles and pots need to stick together, since we're all in the same boat."

That made Rachel burst out laughing. "That is the worst mash-up of trite phrases I've ever heard."

"Hey, everyone has to have a special skill." Their food arrived, and while they ate, they exchanged small talk about Melissa's kids, several friends they had in common and the hardware store.

A little while later, Melissa glanced at her watch and let out a sigh. "Sadly, it's time for this pumpkin to hit the road. Maybe we can grab coffee later in the week? Two of the kids are in a summer camp, which means

I actually have freedom. Or at least as much freedom as a mom with a baby strapped to her hip can get."

"You love those kids and you know it."

A sweet smile stole across Melissa's face. It was the smile of someone in a secret club, one where only those who had children knew the password and the handshake. For a second envy rolled through Rachel. How she wanted the same for herself, for her own life. Considering she wasn't even dating, never mind married, that kind of thing was going to have to wait. Besides, she had enough on her plate, as Melissa had said, with her father and trying to run his business, while also stealing a minute here and there to keep her own afloat.

They paid the bill and walked outside together. The fireman was nowhere to be seen, and Rachel told herself she wasn't disappointed. But she was.

Melissa gave her a tight hug. "Promise me you'll take time for yourself this week," she said.

"I don't have—"

"You do," Melissa said. "If I have five minutes for a little girl time and an extra-long shower, then you can find a couple hours to go out to dinner with a hot fireman."

"How do you know I want to go out to dinner with Colton?"

"I may be a tired, worn-out mommy and a wife who hasn't had a conversation with my husband in months that hasn't been interrupted by someone puking or yelling, but even I can still recognize interest when I see it." Melissa gave her a hug. "Life is a train, Rachel. You gotta reach out and grab on for the ride before you miss it entirely."

Chapter Three

Scrambled eggs.

Who would have thought all three of the Barlow boys sitting in a booth at the Good Eatin' Café would have the exact same taste in breakfast? Two eggs, scrambled, wheat toast, bacon, extra crispy. Luke, Mac and Colton had recited their orders then laughed when they parroted each other. Even Viv, the owner of the diner, couldn't resist a chuckle. "Do you boys know that is the exact same breakfast your father orders when he's here on Sunday mornin'? Y'all are a bunch of peas in a pod."

Luke chuckled as Viv walked away. "Guess we have a lot in common," he said to Colton. "Let me guess. Your favorite pizza is—" he put a finger to his lips and feigned thought "—pepperoni."

Mac gave Luke a gentle slug. "Everyone loves pepperoni."

"Well, everyone in *our* family does." Luke arched a brow in Colton's direction. Outside, rain began to fall in a curtain. In seconds the sunny day turned gray, and the pavement was speckled with fast-forming puddles. "Am I right?"

Colton grinned. "Yup. Though the real question, and the one that determines if we're brothers is…" He glanced at Luke and Mac. "Red Sox or Yankees?"

"Oooh, them's fightin' words," Luke said. "Everybody with a brain knows the Yankees are the only team worth cheering for."

Mac scoffed. "And that's why I'm the smart one. The Red Sox are the best ball team. Hands down."

Luke and Mac turned to Colton. "Fess up. Which one do you root for?"

Colton started to answer when the door to the diner opened and Rachel walked in. She was wearing a pale yellow sundress and her hair was tied back in a ponytail. She shook off the rain, brushing the drops off her bare arms. Even damp from getting caught in the storm, she looked…fun. Like something he'd been looking for and didn't know he wanted to find until he saw it. "I'll be back in a second."

He heard his brothers' laughter as he left the table and went over to Rachel. She was just slipping onto one of the counter stools when he reached her and dropped into the empty seat beside her. "Good morning."

She turned to him with a slight lilt of surprise in her brows and a smile toying with the edge of her lips. "Good morning. You seem to be everywhere I go lately."

He put up his hands. "I swear, I'm not stalking you."

She laughed. He liked her laugh. It was light, airy, sweet. "It's okay. Sometimes living here feels like living in a circle. I run into the same people, at the same time, in the same places."

"That's the complete opposite of Atlanta. Outside of work, I rarely run into people I know. It's kind of like being invisible."

"And do you like that?"

"I don't know. I haven't lived anywhere else before. So I guess I don't know what I really want or like in a place to live. I do know that it's nice to be in a place where life is a little slower. I feel like I can..." He shook his head. "God, I'm going to sound all sentimental if I say this."

"Say what?"

She seemed so interested that he figured even if he did sound like a total dork, it would be okay. "Here, I feel like I can stop and smell the roses." He chuckled. "Seriously, I'm not normally this sappy. Must be the rain."

"Or maybe Stone Gap is rubbing off on you. Before you know it, you'll be taking the chief's job offer and buying a house."

"How do you know Harry offered me a job?"

"It's a small town, Colton, remember?" She grinned. He liked her smile. Liked it a lot. A part of him ached to reach out and trace the sweet curve of her lips.

"Word spreads, especially when there's a hot eligible firefighter in town."

He grinned. "You think I'm hot and eligible?"

A faint blush filled her cheeks. "Well, people think you are. That's what I hear."

He wanted to know if she was one of those people. If she wanted to kiss him even half as bad as he wanted to kiss her. He wanted to see her again, wanted to spend a long, lazy afternoon with her. He fished in his pocket and pulled out a coin. "Here," he said, taking her hand and dropping it into her palm.

She gave him a grin. "What's this for?"

"Prepayment for the twenty-five-cent tour of Stone Gap."

Rachel laughed and started to hand back the coin. "That was just a joke. And I really am swamped right now. I don't think I even have time for the nickel tour."

He closed his hand over hers. "Keep it. And if a hole opens up in your schedule, I'd love to see Stone Gap from your perspective."

Electricity arced in the space between them. It was only a quarter, and a simple touch of hands, but Colton could swear he felt the same current from her. Rachel's eyes widened, and she glanced down at their joined hands, then pulled hers away. She didn't try to give back the quarter again, and he took that as a good sign.

"So, you're, ah, here with Luke and Mac? Is Jack still on his honeymoon?" she said as the waitress deposited a cup of coffee before her. Changing the subject, but still talking to him. Another good sign.

"Yes and yes. The three of us were grabbing breakfast." He glanced over his shoulder at his brothers. Luke arched a brow and shot him a grin. Mac was busy on his phone, probably working.

If Colton lived here, he'd probably see the three other Barlow boys a lot more often. That would be nice. Real nice.

As for his father...that was a work in progress. Somehow, Colton had had this crazy idea that everything would be good just because their first meeting went well. But his father hadn't been as warm and welcoming as his brothers had been, and Colton wasn't quite sure if he should continue to reach out or just let it go. Either way, it hurt, even if he was too damned old to care whether his daddy loved him.

Living here would mean seeing Bobby around town, too. That might not be such a benefit, given the rocky road they were on right now.

"As much as I complain about living in a circle and running into people I know everywhere I go, life here...grows on you," Rachel said, her voice soft and sweet. "It sounds like something from a Hallmark card, but living in a small town is like having a houseful of your favorite family and friends. They'll get on your nerves from time to time, but you're also so glad to see all those friendly faces whenever life gets tough." She ran a finger along the rim of her coffee cup, her eyes downcast, her voice even softer now. "When my mom died, it was the people of this town who helped me keep the shop running, and they've been the biggest supporters I could ask for. People keep trying to help my dad, too, but he's...stubborn."

Colton chuckled. "I think we all know someone like that. My mom is a stubborn woman, too. She…does things the way she wants to do them when she wants to do them." That was probably the nicest way he could say that his mother had been mostly consumed with her own life, leaving him and Katie to fend for themselves more often than not.

"You said you're their half brother. So you're not… Della's son?"

Even though Colton was old enough that he shouldn't care what people thought about how he was conceived, that didn't stop a little hesitation in his answer. He wondered if maybe Bobby was dealing with similar reactions to Colton's arrival. "No, I'm not. My father met my mother when he was working in Atlanta."

No need to divulge the family history that he had been the product of a brief affair. The Barlows were well loved in this town, and his conception had been more than thirty years ago. Ancient history that didn't need to be dragged forward. Colton was a man who much preferred to live in the present.

"How long have you known the rest of the Barlows?" Rachel asked.

"I just met them a couple weeks ago. I didn't know about any of them until now." He glanced over at Luke and Mac, who were grinning at him like a couple of fools. Clearly, there was going to be merciless teasing when he returned to the table. Which he should have done a long time ago, but he really liked talking to Rachel. Watching her smile, the way that gesture lit her eyes and brightened her face.

"Wow. That's a lot to digest in such a short time frame. No wonder you seemed a little...discombobulated when you came in the shop."

He chuckled. "Yeah, it's been a lot. But my brothers are great and that makes it easier."

"Well, you're in a good family. Mac, Luke and Jack are great guys."

It heartened him that his brothers were well liked. He wondered if maybe—by extension—Rachel would paint him with the same brush. "Does that approval umbrella extend over me, too?" Colton asked. "And encourage you to say yes when I remind you that I asked you out?"

She took a sip from the white mug, avoiding his gaze. "I thought I said no to a date."

"You were...vague. So let me try this again." He spun the stool until he was facing her head-on and looking into those deep green eyes. He knew he probably wasn't staying in this town for long. Knew he was crazy to date a woman he barely knew, a woman he wouldn't see again if he went back to Atlanta. But he wanted more of those smiles that seemed to light her from somewhere deep inside. "Would you like to go to dinner with me tonight, Rachel?"

She opened her mouth, closed it. "Tonight? As in this evening?"

He smirked. "That's usually the time people have dinner."

"It's just that I usually bring dinner to my dad's house and eat with him."

"Oh, okay. I understand." Disappointment weighed

in his gut. That no was a lot more definite. He laid a hand on the counter, inches away from hers, got to his feet. "Well, I'll let you enjoy your breakfast."

Just as he turned away, she covered his hand with her own. "But maybe I can meet you a little later. Like...seven?"

It was like he was fifteen again and the pretty girl in algebra had sent him a note across the aisle. He tried not to look like too much of an overeager dork. "Seven would be great. Let me pick you up. Make it an official date and everything."

"An official date?" She shook her head and let out a little laugh. "I haven't been on one of those in so long, I don't think I remember what to do."

"Just smile, Rachel," he said, reaching up and tracing an easy line along the curve of her smile. Wanting to do so much more than that. "The rest will fall right into place."

Just smile.

That was pretty much all she did the rest of the day. She smiled as she went over the bills. Smiled as she restocked the shelves. Smiled at Harvey when he came in with the daily bait delivery and smiled as she stacked containers of worms and crickets in the small refrigerator by the door.

The bell over the shop door rang a little after two, and Ginny Wilkins strode into the shop. Rachel had known Ginny pretty much all her life. The younger girl had been a cheerleader in high school and one of the most popular debutantes in all of Stone Gap. She came from a family that could trace its roots almost all the way to the Mayflower and had a six-acre property just on the edge of town, presided over by a two-story white antebellum mansion that had withstood hurricanes and the Civil War, and would probably outlast them all.

Ginny was also a girl known for extravagance in everything she did, which included the bright pink tea-length dress she was wearing, paired with an even brighter pink purse and flats. Her platinum-blond hair was done in bouncy curls that danced along her shoulders. "Rachel, I am so glad you are here!" Ginny said. "I need your help."

Rachel slid around the counter, a little perplexed as to why Ginny, the girliest girl she'd ever known, would be in a hardware shop. Maybe buying a gift for her father or boyfriend? "Sure. What do you need? We have a sale on—"

"I'm getting married!" The words exploded out of Ginny, complete with a little squeal and a wild flourish of a giant pear-shaped diamond on her left hand. "And I need you to plan it for me. I haven't the foggiest idea where to start or what to do."

"Ginny, I'm not doing that right now. I'm working here, at my dad's shop. I—"

"But you have to! You're the only one I trust. I mean, you did such a fabulous job with Arnelle Beauchamp's wedding and, oh, my, the venue you set up for Lucy Coleridge's wedding—amazing. I know you can do something even better for me. And that will make those two gooses green with envy over how amazing my wedding was." Ginny grinned. "You know there's nothing I like better than going further over the top than anyone else."

That was true. If there was one woman in Stone Gap to add more ruffles, more pink, more flowers, it was Ginny. She'd never been the kind to sit sedately in a corner. Everything she did, she did loud. Planning her wedding would be fun, Rachel thought. The kind of no-holds-barred event that would not only be an adventure, but also get people talking about Rachel's business.

The exact kind of jump-start she needed to get her company running again. If Ginny's wedding was a year or so away, there would be plenty of time for Rachel to both run the shop and get the event planned. And by then, surely her dad would be back at work every day.

Yes, she could make it work. Just thinking about getting back to the wedding-planning world that she loved caused a little tickle of excitement in Rachel's stomach. It was an incredible opportunity.

"I know the ideal location, Ginny. Perfect for the kind of wedding you want to have. There's this new hotel two towns away that's really something to talk about. It's pink and white and giant," Rachel said. She could already see it decorated in Ginny's signature color, imagine the band on the stage, the guests dining on something extravagant. It would be amazing, as Ginny had said.

"Pink? My favorite color!" Ginny exclaimed. The woman used more exclamation points in her daily speech than an Oscar winner. "All my bridesmaids are going to wear flamingo pink, and I'm going to have bright pink roses in my bouquet and a trail of them down the back of my dress, and it will look like I'm walking out of a garden. It's going to be all pink, all the time!"

Rachel bit back a grin at Ginny's ideas. That would be a wedding to remember for sure. "This hotel also has the most amazing outdoor patio, overlooking the water. You could have a gazebo on the patio and get married right there, with the boats in the background."

"Do you think we could get all the boats to have pink sails?" Ginny asked.

"I'm not sure," Rachel hedged. She could just see herself making that kind of request in the harbormaster's office. "That's a pretty tall order. But I'm sure we could hang pink organza from the gazebo and along the aisle."

Ginny clapped her hands. "Oh, my, that sounds too perfect for words! And do you think you can get it all done in three months?"

"Three…months?" A stone sank in Rachel's gut. "As in ninety days?"

"I know it's fast, but when you fall in love, you just don't want to wait. And I love my Bernard so very much." A smile stole across Ginny's face, the kind that only a woman truly in love wore, as if she had a secret no one else in the world possessed. It almost made Rachel jealous.

"There's no way I can get a wedding pulled together in three months," Rachel said, and tried not to let her own disappointment show through. This would have been the opportunity she'd needed, the big break that would breathe new life into her gasping business. "I'm still running this store full time. And the amount of work involved in such a short time frame…" She let out a long breath. "I'm sorry, Ginny."

"But you *have* to do it, Rachel. You are seriously the only one in the world I trust to handle my wedding. Can you please, pretty, pretty please, just think about it? Just for a day or two." Ginny cocked a hip to the side and wagged a pink-tipped nail in Rachel's direction. "You know, my wedding should make all the papers, and if my daddy has anything to say about it, it'll end up on the local news, too. That should be great for your business! A bonanza, for sure!"

It would be fantastic for her business. But Rachel couldn't see a way to make it work. There simply weren't enough hours in the day to do both. She couldn't let her father down, couldn't abandon his store. But instead of telling Ginny that straight out, Rachel found herself saying, "Yeah, sure, I'll think about it."

Ginny squealed, then drew Rachel into a tight hug. "Awesomesauce. I'll call you in a couple days or you call me. I'm so excited!"

After waving as Ginny pulled away from the curb in her pink Mercedes, Rachel let her smile falter as she slowly walked back into the empty shop. There were no customers, and the full shelves and almost empty cash register seemed to mock her. She was spending her days here, trying to keep her father's dream alive, while her own died a slow death.

On the back wall hung a series of plaques and a small shelf of trophies. Best Fisherman, Biggest Catch, Good Neighbor Award. All the things that made up her dad and his life here in Stone Gap. It was like walking through her memories, remembering the fishing trips to the lake, perched in the back of the boat when he reeled in the biggest bass anyone had ever seen, sitting on a hard metal folding chair in the lobby of the town hall while the mayor of Stone Gap handed her father a plaque and a citation for his help the day after a hurricane whipped through Stone Gap and leveled half the town.

That was the kind of guy her dad was. Hard-working, competitive, considerate to his neighbors, to everyone who knew him. She couldn't abandon him.

Couldn't put his dreams on the shelf while she went after her own. Even if a part of her heart broke as she thought about letting her dream flutter away in a cloud of pink.

Chapter Four

Colton had never been the kind of guy that anyone would describe as romantic. He didn't remember Valentine's Day, rarely thought to bring flowers and stumbled over his words whenever he tried to say something poetic.

Yet here he stood in the Garden of Eden flower shop in downtown Stone Gap a little after six in the evening, debating between roses and lilies. They all looked the same to him, a jumble of pinks and yellows and reds, and he realized he didn't know enough about Rachel to tell which she liked best.

God, this was a stupid idea. He could buy the wrong kind of flowers, or buy too many and make her wonder about his intentions. Maybe he should have picked up one of those solitary roses in the bucket on the counter at the gas station. Or nothing at all. Colton started to turn and leave when a familiar figure walked into the shop.

His younger brother Luke. A very, very welcome sight.

"If you ask me, roses are overrated. Women like something creative," Luke said. He slipped into place beside Colton, the two of them squaring off against the colorful refrigerator case like two gunfighters. "Something that tells them you thought it through, or at least made a stab at thinking."

"Does staring at all these options for twenty minutes, too damned confused to pick anything out, count?"

Luke chuckled. "Nope. Sorry." He gestured toward the refrigerated case stuffed with fresh flowers. In the background, a saleslady in a green apron hovered, ready to jump in at any time. She'd already offered her help three times, but Colton had thought he could do this on his own.

Ha-ha. Yeah, he pretty much sucked at this romance thing.

"So," Luke said, "I take it the agonizing over flowers is part of your campaign to impress the beautiful and intriguing Rachel Morris?"

Even though his brothers had teased him when he'd returned to their table in the diner that morning, he hadn't told them he had asked Rachel out. He'd just changed the subject when the food arrived, and the two of them had let it drop. Colton thought maybe his conversation with Rachel—and his interest in her—

had dropped below Luke and Mac's radar. Yeah, not so much. "How did you know that?"

"For one, you ditched us to talk to her—"

"Sorry." Luke was right. The time he had with his brothers was limited, and he should have stayed at the table instead of getting distracted so easily.

"No need to apologize. Pretty women always take precedence. Though you should expect some serious teasing in the days ahead." Luke grinned. "All part of the initiation."

"There's an initiation?"

"Of course. You didn't expect us to just let you become a Barlow without one, did you?"

Colton chuckled. "Guess not." Then he glanced over at his brother, half his flesh and blood. When it came to his brothers, Colton already felt like he was part of the family. With his father…not so much. "Though I don't think it's quite that simple."

"You talking about Dad?" Luke let out a sigh. "I don't think it's anything personal. I think he's just struggling with the whole thing. You being here, what that means in…"

"In what?" Colton prompted.

"In a town this size. People talk, you know, and most people talk more than they should. About crap they know nothing about."

That was what Colton had been afraid of. That even at his age, being an illegitimate son was mostly an embarrassment. What had he been thinking, just showing up here last week? At Jack's wedding, at that?

His uncle Tank had warned him that Bobby might

be…difficult. *It's going to take some getting used to*, Tank had said. *My brother isn't one to embrace change. He's a stick who is very happy staying in the mud.*

Maybe this was how his relationship with Bobby would be going forward. Was that enough for Colton? If it never progressed beyond small talk and awkward pauses?

"Maybe it would be best if I went back to Atlanta," he said.

Luke scoffed. "Best for who? Not for me and Mac. Not for you. And not for Dad. I love my—our—dad, don't get me wrong, but he's being an ass." He put up a hand before Colton could argue. "Now, back to the top priority. The pretty woman. You need swoon-worthy flowers, and I need flowers that say, *forgive me for being a Neanderthal*."

Colton smirked. "They sell those here?"

Luke laughed. "They better. Or I'm in trouble again tonight."

"What'd you do?"

"I had a fight with Peyton." Luke threw up his hands. "I know, I know. But in my defense, it was a busy day and I was a little tired. And missed lunch."

Colton chuckled. Even he knew an empty stomach wasn't grounds for an argument with your fiancée. Luke was smart to be buying flowers.

"I don't even know what to tell you."

"Just help me pick out some flowers that say, *I'm sorry I was an idiot*." A sheepish grin filled Luke's face. "I love Peyton too much to argue with her for more than five seconds. All I want to do is see her smile again."

At the mention of the word, a slow smile curved across Luke's face. Colton envied that look. That pure…joy on his brother's face when he talked about the woman he loved. Colton had never felt that way about anyone before. Had come close a few times, but never opened his whole heart like his brothers had with the women they clearly adored.

"Now, for you," Luke said, "I recommend the almost-deluxe bouquet. You get a little of this, a little of that, not so many you're walking in there with a garden in your hands, but enough to say, *Hey, I like you.* An almost-deluxe bouquet is not so fancy that it screams *trying too hard* and not so casual that it says *yanked off the highway median at the last second*." Luke put up his hands. "Been there, done that. The results were… unsatisfactory."

Colton laughed. "I'll keep that in mind."

In the end, he settled on a midsize bouquet with white and yellow daisies, a few pink lilies and a bunch of dark purple flowers he didn't recognize. The saleslady wrapped it in thick paper, giving him all kinds of instructions about water and trimming the stems and something about a packet of floral pre-servative that she tucked between the stems. He just nodded and said yes to everything. Luke did the same, and a few minutes later the two of them were standing on the sidewalk.

"Good Lord. We look like Cupid's minions," Luke said.

Colton chuckled. "Might have to turn in our man cards."

"It's all worth it, big brother, when she smiles that sweet smile of hers and says your name." Luke clapped him on the shoulder. "Now I better get out of here before we both need some Kleenex."

Colton watched his brother walk away, Luke's steps light and his smile wise. Colton never had been a romantic guy, but maybe it was time to change his ways—if doing so meant having the kind of happiness that hung around Luke like a ray of sunshine.

"You're fidgety this evening," her father said. He set his crossword puzzle to the side and laced his fingers together. "What's going on?"

"I…ah, just had too much coffee today." If she told her father she had a date, there'd be all kinds of questions. She wasn't sure this thing with Colton would go anywhere past an appetizer, so better not to say anything at all. It was just a dinner, nothing more.

Her father peered at her over the bridge of his reading glasses. "And that's why you're wearing a new dress? And fancy shoes?"

"How did you—"

He leaned across the table then reached around her neck and pulled up a tag. "You forgot something."

That was what she got for being in a rush today and buying the dress in the few minutes she had between leaving the shop and going to her dad's. It was a wonder she'd made it out of the store at all, given how nervous and rushed she'd been. Rachel scrambled to her feet and fished the scissors out of the junk drawer. She reached over her shoulder but couldn't quite grasp the small tag. Her father got to his feet, crossed to her, lifted the tag then took the scissors from her hands. "Let me do that for you," he said. "You've done more than enough for me."

"Thanks, Dad."

He pressed the small price tag into her palm. "You're welcome." Then his pale blue eyes met hers and his gaze softened. "I'm sorry."

"Sorry? For what?"

"For taking up every minute of your life with my... inertia." He waved at the cluttered kitchen table, the dirty dishes in the sink, the pile of clean laundry waiting to be put away. "You deserve your own life. I'm glad you're going out tonight. You don't need to spend every night here, taking care of a tired old man."

She cupped his cheek, settling her palm against the rough stubble of his unshaven beard. "For the record, you are neither tired nor old. And I enjoy spending time with you."

His smile turned bittersweet and his eyes shone with unshed tears. "Get out of here. Go on your date. I'll be fine."

"But what about dinner and—"

"I know how to make a peanut butter sandwich. I'll be fine."

She thought of all the meals her father had skipped. All the times he'd fallen asleep in this very kitchen chair, forgotten to take his daily heart medication... there were a thousand things he hadn't done, a million ways he hadn't been fine. "I should stay..."

"You should go." He waved her toward the door. "I mean it."

She started to argue again, but saw the determination in her father's eyes. Maybe he was feeling better, and maybe he was going to start being more independent. Doubts clouded her thoughts, but in the end, she relented. "Okay, but if you need anything—"

"I know how to dial a phone." Her father smiled. It was a dimmer-watt smile than the one she knew and loved, but nevertheless, it was a start. "Have a good time, sweetheart."

She nearly turned back toward her dad's house three times on her way to her apartment. Picked up her phone twice at a stop sign to call and check on him. She pulled under the carport, parked then stared at the phone in her hand and debated. He had said he would be okay. If she hovered too much, he'd never move forward. But if she didn't hover enough…

Surely her dad would be okay for a few hours. Besides, this date could be over before dessert. She might not like that hot single firefighter with the crooked smile.

Uh-huh. That was a likely scenario.

If she didn't finish getting ready, he'd find her outside her apartment half assembled. Not that she probably wouldn't look like that, anyway. Rachel was the complete opposite of a girlie-girl. She was happier in jeans than heels, and more comfortable in a faded T-shirt than a fancy dress.

She turned off the car then headed inside. She had

ten minutes until Colton arrived. Just enough time to check her makeup and hair for the thirtieth time.

Just as she was about to dial her father's number, Rachel's cell rang. Melissa's smiling face popped up on the caller ID. "Before you ask," Rachel said when she answered the call, a knowing laugh in her voice, "yes, I did go with the black heels."

"Those strappy ones with the silver buckle?"

"The very ones." Melissa had been the first one Rachel had called after she'd agreed to the date with Colton. Her friend had cast the deciding vote among the three dresses Rachel had found in a little shop downtown between work and her dad's. She'd been the one to talk Rachel into a pair of shoes she never expected to wear again, though she had to admit they looked really cute. "My feet have totally forgotten what it feels like to wear heels, and I think they're going to stage a coup very soon."

Melissa laughed. "If you're lucky, the heels won't be on for long."

"It's just dinner," Rachel said, reminding herself as much as Melissa.

"Who says you can't have an appetizer first? Or dessert after?" Melissa let out a throaty laugh. "Preferably both, if you get lucky."

The thought of ending up in bed with Colton sent electricity through her veins. A man like that, with a rock-hard body and a ready smile, was the kind who would leave her breathless at the end of the night. And it had been so long—way too long—since she'd been with anyone that just the mere thought of curling around him in her queen-size bed was almost too much. "I hardly know the man."

"Trust me, that's a good thing. Once you know them well, they start leaving their socks on the floor and belching at the dinner table. Better to go with a stranger who at least has a semblance of manners. And mystery."

"You love Jason." Rachel had always envied Melissa and Jason's marriage. They still shared secret smiles and private jokes, and nearly every opportunity they got they were either holding hands or leaving a little touch on the other's shoulder. It was a nice relationship, the kind Rachel dreamed of having for herself someday. When she had more than a couple hours on a weekday evening to devote to dating.

"I do love my husband. I just don't love all his manness." Melissa laughed. "Who am I kidding? Of course I do. But sometimes I wish he would go back to being the guy I dated. The one who tried so hard to impress me with his chivalry that he broke a toe opening the door to The Chalet restaurant too fast."

Rachel laughed. "I remember that. And then he spent the rest of the night trying to pretend it didn't hurt."

"Until I insisted on taking him to the emergency room, and spending our first date between a guy who had been stabbed in the thigh and a woman with the flu. Hold on a sec." Melissa's voice moved farther from the phone. "Jason, Jr., you cannot feed your little sister your peas. And no, you can't give them to the dog, either." She came back to the phone with a sigh. "Want some kids? Free of charge."

"Not tonight, but I promise to babysit Friday night so you and Jason can get a night out. Maybe *you'll* get lucky," Rachel said.

"Right now my version of getting lucky is him remembering to see if I'm in the car before he pulls away," Melissa laughed. "Anyway, have a great time tonight with that hunk of burning love. And don't disappoint me by being home before midnight."

Rachel said goodbye then peeked in the mirror yet again. She debated the dress and shoes for the thirtieth time—too much? Too fancy? Too sexy?—then decided if she changed, Melissa would never let her hear the end of it. Then the doorbell rang, which meant she was out of time to stall.

She let out a deep breath then pulled open the door. "Hi."

Colton smiled. It was the kind of smile that washed over her and sent a little thrill through her veins. "Hi yourself. You look…amazing."

Just to see that look in his eyes made the purchase a total win. Her gaze took in the rest of him, the clean-shaven chin, the pale blue button-down shirt open at his neck, the dress pants that outlined a very trim, very nice, body. The conversation with Melissa—and Rachel's fantasy about ending up in her bed with Colton—rushed back to her mind, complete with images of unbuttoning his shirt, and tugging those pants down his legs. Good Lord. She was going to have to start fanning herself any second. "Thank you. I'm not normally dressed up like this," she said, waving a hand over the outfit. "I feel like a fish in an evening gown."

He chuckled. "I'd say more like a mermaid. You are beautiful, no matter what you wear."

She blushed, a burst of crimson that filled her cheeks and trailed down the V-neck of her dress. He decided he should make her blush more often. "Thank you again. You look great, too."

"Oh, these are for you." He thrust a bouquet of flowers at her.

White and yellow daisies, pink stargazer lilies, long stalks of purple lavender peppered with stems of baby's breath, all wrapped in a thick paper cone. It was a sweet bouquet, one that went beyond the cliché of roses. She wondered what sort of meaning he attached to their date as she caught the heady scent of the lilies.

He seemed nervous, which made her smile. Maybe she wasn't the only one who hadn't been on a date in a while. She brought the flowers to her nose and inhaled. "They're gorgeous. Thank you."

"You're welcome." He gestured toward his car. "Should we go?"

"Let me put these in water first." She glanced back at him. "Do you want to come in for a minute?"

As soon as he entered her apartment, the space felt too small, too confined. He was six feet two inches of brawny man, with his smile and his big blue eyes that reminded her of the ocean on a sunny day. Nerves fluttered in her gut, which was crazy. She never got nervous, never got flustered around guys. Or at least she never had—

Until she'd met Colton Barlow.

Now the man had her thoughts running in twelve different directions, half of which led straight to her bedroom. The nine hundred square feet she lived in made that bed seem awfully close. Too close. Too tempting.

She reached for a vase above the fridge, and her silly nervous hands nearly dropped it. Colton was there, right behind her, his body so close to hers, all she'd have to do was inhale and she'd be pressed against him.

"Let me get that," he said, his voice deep beside her ear.

"Thanks." She knew she should step away, but she stayed where she was, in the few inches of space between Colton's chest and her refrigerator. He grasped the vase and brought it down to her in one slow, liquid movement. She took it with one hand then turned to look up at him.

Her heart beat. Her breath flowed in, out. And her gaze locked on his, on the ocean depths that seemed to darken as one second passed, then another, another. "Thank...thank you."

"My pleasure."

The word *pleasure* sent heat spiraling through her. How far away was her bedroom? Twenty feet? Thirty?

God, what was wrong with her? She couldn't haul the man off to her room before they even had a date. She started to step to the side, but Colton moved at the same time, and they collided, chest to chest. Heat erupted inside her, a deep, yawning want that nearly took her breath away. She looked up at him, the vase forgotten, the flowers a distant memory.

And held her breath.

Slowly, oh, so slowly, Colton brought his face down to hers. His eyes never wavered from her gaze, and she thought a girl could get lost in that sea. His fingers danced along her cheek, trailed down to her jaw, skipped over her lips. She opened her mouth—to protest, to agree, she wasn't sure—and then his lips were on hers, and she was lost.

His kiss started slow, sweet and easy, like sliding into a warm pool on a cool day. He shifted against her, and she reached up, gliding her hands along the cotton of his shirt, inching over the ridged muscles of his back.

He deepened the kiss, the two of them moving in concert now, her mouth opening to his, his tongue darting in. She let out a little mew and arched into him, wanting, needing, seeking more.

His fingers tangled in her hair, and she swore he whispered her name against her lips before his tongue swept in and urged hers to dance. He was hard against her, and she pressed into him, wanting more, wanting... *everything*. He felt so good, so right.

He brought his hand down to her cheek again, a tender, sweet touch, then he shifted back, away from her. The kiss ended, but he hovered there, just inches from her face. "This is going to go...somewhere it shouldn't, very fast. We should go to dinner before..."

Before they ended up in her bedroom. A part of her wanted to say, *But I want it to go there. I want it to go twenty feet down the hall, to that queen-size mattress and those crisp white sheets.*

Then her sanity returned, and she nodded. "You're right. Let's go." She started to reach for her purse on the counter.

He touched her hand, drew her back. "The flowers?"

"Flowers?" she repeated, confused.

A grin quirked up one side of his face. "Remember? The vase that started all this?"

Her face heated. "Oh, yes. I just…forgot."

Got totally distracted by he-of-the-blue-eyes-and-incredible-kissing-ability, was more like it. She spun away, grabbed the vase and busied herself with filling it then trimming the stems and dropping the bouquet into the glass container. She set it on the window ledge over her sink then left the light on above them. Not that the flowers would know or care, but when she came home tonight, it would be nice to see the flowers there.

Nice because they would remind her of the way this night had started. And if that was any indication of what lay ahead, she was already happy she'd agreed to go out with Colton Barlow.

Chapter Five

His dinner at the Sea Shanty could have been cardboard, for all Colton noticed.

All of his attention was focused on the intriguing, beautiful woman across from him. A woman he had kissed—and who had made something as simple as that seem like the most incredible experience he'd had in a long, long time.

In her elegant black dress and heels, she was as feminine as a debutante, but then she got talking about baseball, and she could have been one of the guys. Except he never looked at the chest of one of the guys and fantasized about trailing kisses down the valley between their breasts.

"When Henderson stole third in that Yankees game back in '85, he was incredible to watch, though I didn't see it live, just on a replay of old games I watched with my dad. Every Saturday we watched those classic games, and Henderson was his favorite player," she said. "No one mastered the art of the stolen base like Henderson did."

"He had, what, eighty steals that season?" Colton said. "He was like David Copperfield out there."

She took a sip of her wine. "In '83, he stole one hundred bases in one season. No one's done that, before or since. Amazing stuff."

Colton buttered a slice of ciabatta and set it on the edge of his plate. "I don't think I've ever met a woman who knows as much about baseball as you do."

She shrugged. "Only child syndrome. My dad wasn't into playing with dolls, so we bonded over baseball. He taught me how to play, and we watched tons of games together. One year we even took a trip to Louisville to visit the slugger museum. I still have the bat he bought me and had engraved with my name." A sad smile stole over her face. "I miss those days with my dad. Ever since my mom died, he hasn't wanted to go to a game, or sit through one on TV. Never mind do anything else he used to do. It's like he just stopped living."

"That's got to be hard for you."

She shrugged again, but he could see the stress in her face, the burden on her shoulders. "He's my dad. I'm going to support him however I can."

"But you have a right to a life, too."

She waved that off. "It can wait. He needs me now."

Yet another reason to like Rachel. She was the kind of woman who did the right thing, who stuck by her family when they needed her. He'd known far too many women—which probably went back to his bad choosing skills—who were more interested in the label on their back than the people in their life. Rachel's lack of self-centeredness certainly made her stand out.

Colton thought about his sister and his mother. For nearly all his life, he had been the one taking care of them. Making sure his little sister got up for school and took a lunch with her. Making sure the house doors were locked tight for the night after his mother got home from work. Making sure there was gas in the car, the trash put out on the curb, a little more money in the bank. Katie was an adult now, living on her own and highly successful at the accounting firm where she worked, while his mother was still flitting from job to job, living arrangement to living arrangement. He'd only been gone for a few days, but he still worried about them.

"I understand putting family first," he said. "I guess I always felt it was my responsibility to take care of my mom and sister. I was the only man in the house, know what I mean?"

"Even when you were little? Because you didn't have your dad then?"

Colton wondered how his life would have been different if his father had been involved from the start. Uncle Tank had been great, a regular presence at the house, but it hadn't been the same as having a full-time dad. His brothers had turned into great men, as far as Colton could tell, which meant their father must have had a good influence.

"It just seemed like the right thing to do. To take care of them, to protect them," Colton said. "I don't know, maybe it's an instinct for men."

"Not all men." She shook her head, and a smile filled her face. "You're pretty incredible, you know that? Helping to take care of your mother and sister, then becoming a firefighter, where you rescue people from burning buildings for a living? You're like a hero."

He cut his gaze away. The cozy restaurant suddenly seemed ten times smaller. In his head he could hear Willis and Foster, hear their shouts grow in pitch and volume as concern turned to worry, turned to panic. And Colton, trying so hard to get past the wall of burning timbers, trying to climb in there and grab a hand, a foot, anything. But then the ceiling came down in a shower of sparks and wood, and then the screams stopped—

"Colton?"

Rachel's soft voice drew him back. He shifted in his seat and picked up the bread, swirling it in the sauce. "Sorry. My mind...wandered."

"Okay." She fiddled with her wineglass, and he could tell she knew he was keeping something from her.

But how could he tell her that he had watched two of his friends die? That the man she thought was a hero was still paying the price for what had happened, was still carrying the weight of his own guilt?

What he needed to do was change the subject, swing them back around to the fun conversation they'd been having earlier tonight. Because as much as he told himself he shouldn't get any more involved with a woman he was probably never going to see again, Colton craved more of her smile, more of her voice, more of everything. More of her.

Tomorrow would take care of itself. For now he had tonight, and an intriguing, beautiful woman sitting across from him.

"You know, you still owe me the twenty-five-cent tour of Stone Gap," he said as the waitress took their empty plates away. "And I think we should start at the Good Eatin' Café, because I hear they have the best apple pie in the county, and all the Sea Shanty is offering tonight is cheesecake. I don't know about you, but I'm a pie guy."

She laughed. "They do, indeed. And the best pecan pie in the world. I'd eat it every day, if I could."

That had him suddenly craving pie in the worst way. "Then let's get out of here and go get some pie."

She nodded. "I think that sounds like a great idea. Though I have to warn you, after that, there's not a lot to see."

His gaze raked over the woman before him, with her dancing green eyes and warm, welcoming smile. "I think there's a lot worth seeing in this town."

Rachel was trying really hard not to like Colton Barlow.

She had her life all mapped out, her days planned to the last minute, and falling for a guy like Colton made her want to ditch those plans. Even tonight she was ignoring the books for the store, and the orders she should be placing, to run around town in his rental car with the windows down and the breeze in her hair.

But it felt so good to be doing something so...relaxing. No bills to worry about paying, no sales to worry about increasing, nothing but just being in the car with a sexy man who was interested in her. She'd worry about tomorrow later. For now there was only Colton.

They stopped in at the Good Eatin' Café first, where Viv rushed right over and seated them in a booth. "Oh, I'm so glad to see you, Rachel, and out with a handsome gentleman, too."

Rachel flushed and decided the best course of action was to ignore Viv's comment. "What kind of pies do you have tonight?"

"Apple, pecan and a strawberry rhubarb."

Rachel glanced at Colton. He nodded. "How about a slice of each?" she said.

"Coming right up. Extra whipped cream?" Viv asked.

"Definitely," Colton said.

When Viv was gone, Rachel crossed her hands on the table and smiled at Colton. "We had the same exact thought."

"We both know a good pie, or rather pies, when we hear it." He grinned.

Viv brought the pies a second later, along with two cups of decaf and a pair of forks. "Enjoy, kids."

"Thank you, Viv." Rachel picked up her fork, then cut off a piece of the pecan. "Here, taste this first, because it's a pie to measure all others against, believe me."

"If I was a gentleman, I'd insist you take the first bite, but…" He leaned forward and took the bite.

Rachel could hardly concentrate. There was a dollop of whipped cream on Colton's lip, and she was dying to lean across the table and kiss it off. "You…you have a little…" She rose in her seat, closed the distance between them and instead of kissing it or licking it, she swiped the whipped cream off his lip with her finger.

Before she could sit down again, he grabbed her hand and gently licked the little bit of whipped cream off her finger. Her hormones sent up a loud cheer, and her gut tightened. "Thank you," Colton said.

"You're…welcome." She could barely eat her slice of pie, because every time she glanced at the dessert, she thought about the whipped cream on Colton's lip, and the sexy way he'd…

Stop, Rachel. Just don't go there.

Too soon—or maybe not soon enough—they had finished the pie and were heading back out to his car.

She was going to concentrate on showing him around Stone Gap. Not the thought of climbing in her backseat with a canister of whipped cream—

No. That wasn't a productive thought. At all.

"Now this isn't going to be your ordinary tour," she said. "We're going to start with the haunted house. And if you're still hungry later on, we can move on to some cookies from Betty's Bakery and then possibly some beach time. There's nothing like walking on the beach when it's dark and all you have for light is the moon."

"So, what's the theme of the twenty-five-cent tour?"

"All you can see for twenty-five cents worth of gas."

"That's not going to get us far."

"It's a small town." She grinned and pointed to the street ahead of them. "Take a left here then your first right."

He did as she instructed, and a moment later they pulled in front of a dilapidated mansion. Once, it had been amazing—Rachel had seen photos of it in a book in the library—but those days were long past. The front of the house stood tall and erect, as if it was putting on a brave front against the powers of the ocean winds at the back. The white paint had grayed and peeled, the expansive wraparound porch leaned into the back of the house, collapsed onto itself. Most of the windows were broken, the shutters hanging askew, and the landscaping was so overgrown it almost blocked the first floor from view. "Rumor has it that Gareth Richardson killed his family in this house," Rachel said, "and he still walks the floors at night, moaning his regrets."

"Should we go inside?" Colton asked. "Go pay Gareth a visit?"

She laughed. "I don't think it's safe, but…"

Colton was already out of the car and coming around to her side. He opened her door and put out a hand. "You're with me, remember? I'll keep you safe."

She slid her hand into his warm, firm grip. She wanted to ask if he would keep her heart safe, too, but it was way too early to ask or even think that. But as she looked up into his grin and felt the warmth of his touch on hers, Rachel realized she was already falling hard for the firefighter from Atlanta.

They picked their way through the overgrown yard, using the light from Colton's phone as a guide, then he led her up the three stairs of the porch and nudged at the front door. It opened with a lonely creak, into a dark, yawning cavern of a house. A few dots of moonlight speckled the old wood floors.

"Already looks spooky," Colton whispered.

"It does. Really spooky." She gripped his arm. "Maybe I should hold on. In case, you know…the ghost comes out."

"Definitely a good idea," he said and drew her tight against his body.

The scent of his cologne—warm, spicy, dark—filled the space between them. She could feel his heart beneath her palm, imagine the ripples of his muscles under his shirt. She barely noticed the dark or the house or the spooky rooms they explored. She noticed only him, the feel of him and how that made her want Colton more with each passing second.

Her mind kept going back to his kiss. The way he had touched her cheek, made her feel inordinately special. It was exciting and heady and tempting. Maybe too tempting.

They stopped in the kitchen. A shaft of moonlight poured in through the broken kitchen window, illuminating scarred wooden floors and floral wallpaper hanging in sheets. The center of the ceiling bulged above them, as if it were about to open up at any moment.

"This would be a cool house to restore," Colton said. "It would make a cool bed-and-breakfast, too."

She scoffed. "It's way beyond restoration. You're better off tearing it down and building new."

"Maybe so. But then you'd lose the history. And the little quirks that make this house what it is. I like history. Maybe because I only knew half of mine growing up."

"And now you have a chance to know the other half."

"I'm trying," he said. "But my father hasn't been very open to it. Luke thinks it's because it's hard for my father to deal with the stares and gossip."

"That's the downside to living in a small town. I can understand that." How many times had she seen people whisper then shake their heads and look away when she had been a little girl? The rumors about her mother had been constant whispers in the background. She could understand how tough this was for Colton, for Bobby. Stone Gap could wrap around you like a warm blanket, but it could also be a cold, lonely place to live when there were secrets to keep, or people to protect.

Rachel shook her head. Maybe it was the dark rooms, or the fact that Colton still had his arm around her, but she suddenly felt vulnerable and scared.

You'll be safe, he'd said. Did he mean the same thing if she opened up to him, if she told this man—who was, after all, practically a stranger still—all the guilty feelings and regrets that crowded on her shoulders every day? The emotional burdens that kept her rooted firmly in that little hardware store?

"I can understand that because when I was growing up my mom was an alcoholic," she said quietly. "And people talked. They saw her driving when she shouldn't have been behind the wheel or heard her crazy outbursts at a school play, and there'd be talk. And those looks of…pity for me. Because I was her daughter."

Colton turned until she was in his arms, and her gaze had lifted to his. In the moonlight, he seemed taller, stronger, broader. "That's tough," he said. "I can't even imagine how hard that would be. No wonder you're such a tough cookie, Rachel Morris."

His soft words of admiration warmed her. Maybe this man, who was also in that awful club of being the one the townspeople whispered about, could understand her. "It's why I'm so close to my dad. It's like we formed this little team. When my mom was sober, everything was perfect and wonderful. Like a regular family. But other times…" She shrugged.

"I get it. I used to pretend my uncle was my real father. He was just a family friend, as far as I knew, but there were times when he would be over at my house, and I'd pretend that I was his son. I just wanted a father so bad, like the rest of my friends… But whenever he left, it was just me and my mom and my sister. We were a little team, just like you had with your dad, but—"

"It wasn't the same," she cut in, finishing his thought. "I guess we have more in common than just a love of baseball," she said, because right now, she felt too close to him, too close to falling over some crazy edge.

"I think we have more than that in common," he

said, his voice low and dark in the dim space. He shifted closer, then raised his hand to trail along her jaw.

Hot anticipation pooled inside her. It felt like Christmas and her birthday and the first day of spring all rolled together and dipped in chocolate.

Colton leaned in, hovered over her lips for a heartbeat. "I want to kiss you again."

"And I want you to kiss me."

"If we do this," he said, moving closer until his words danced across her mouth, "it might change things. One kiss can be an accident. Two is...more."

She drew in a breath. "Do you want more?"

"I don't know," he said, but his gaze never left hers, those blue eyes looking like dark pools.

"That's okay," she whispered, "because I don't know, either."

She saw the flash of his smile, then he kissed her. This one was faster, harder, more insistent than the first. The kind of kiss that ignited her veins, had her surging into him, made her wonder if there was a floor in this house sturdy enough to make love on. His hands roamed down the silky fabric of her dress, sliding down her back, over the curve of her buttocks, lingering at her waist, then down again.

It was sweet, it was hot, it was one of the best kisses she'd ever had. And she never wanted it to end. But then the wind started up outside, and the house began to creak, and Colton drew back. "I think old Gareth is making his presence known. Maybe we should get out of here."

"There's still some things to see on the tour," she said.

"I can't wait." He grinned, then he took her hand and they darted out of the house just as the walls began to shiver and the wind kicked up, blowing leaves and branches around in the yard.

A wicked storm moved in as they got in the car, canceling the rest of the tour. The rain hit the windshield faster than the wipers could keep up, and Colton drove her back at a snail's pace. It wasn't until they pulled up in front of her building that Rachel glanced at the time.

Nearly eleven. She'd spent four hours with this man, and it had passed as quickly as four minutes. She wanted more, but it would all have to wait.

Turning to say good-night, she suddenly felt shy. "I…I have to go. I have work to do before I go to bed."

He ran a finger along her cheek, and she resisted the almost overpowering urge to lean into his touch. Because she knew if she did, she'd kiss him again, and then she'd never get out of this car. Never get back to the responsibilities she had temporarily ignored. "What are you doing tomorrow night?"

She caught his finger in her palm. "I don't have time in my life for this, Colton."

"Neither do I. So let's just have one more date and then call it quits."

She couldn't help but laugh. "Seriously?"

"One more date, Rachel."

She smirked. "One. No more."

"Nope. Because I'm sure you will figure out after one more date with me that I'm not such a good catch, after all. That I have numerous bad habits…"

"Name one."

He pretended to think it over. "I hate doing the dishes. I'd rather eat out of a take-out container than wash a plate."

She laughed again. When had she laughed this much? With anyone? It was so wonderful, so energizing, so addictive. "That's why God invented dishwashers."

"And I can't dance. What kind of Southern man can't dance?"

"One who lets the girl lead," she said then pressed a quick kiss to his lips and dashed out of the car before she was tempted to stay much, much longer.

Chapter Six

Bobby Barlow stared at his two sons, who were standing in his kitchen with their arms crossed over their chests. They'd shown up at the house late this afternoon, ostensibly to say hello to their mother, but after Della left for bridge with the girls, Luke and Mac had stayed behind and given him the silent treatment staredown. "What?"

"You need to see Colton," Luke said. "He's only in town for a few days."

"I did see Colton." Bobby scowled. "At Jack's wedding, and I ran into him at the Sea Shanty the other night."

Well, ran into him but barely talked to him. He had seen the disappointment on Colton's face, the disapproval on Della's face and still sat there at the table with Jerry and Stella Norton and talked about the Steelers' chances of making it to the Super Bowl. The whole way home, Della had given him The Eye—the one that said she wasn't pleased with what he had done, but wasn't going to say anything. She didn't have to. He'd been married to her for nearly thirty-five years, and he knew when she was mad, and what she was mad about.

This time, it was him. And his struggle with making his fourth son part of the family.

"Family dinner is on Sunday, and I think he's staying in town at least through the weekend," Mac said. "Invite Colton."

"So we can tease him," Luke added. "And so somebody else can do the dishes afterward."

"Great idea," Mac whispered to his brother. "Maybe we'll even tell him it's customary for him to bring dessert."

"And a case of beer." Luke grinned.

Bobby put up his hands. He had to admire his boys for being so stubborn. He wanted to ask where they got that from, but all he had to do was look in the mirror. After all, his mother had always told him to be careful or his kids would turn out just like him. They were—but a better, stronger version of himself. "All right, all right. I'll call him. You two don't have to badger me about it."

"Yeah, we do, Dad." Mac dropped into one of the kitchen chairs. "Listen, we get that it's hard to explain where Colton came from—"

"And the fact that you can't say the stork dropped

him off on the doorstep, because that would have to
be one hell of a big stork," Luke added.

"But he's a good guy," Mac went on. "And he's part
of this family now, so everyone needs to treat him as
such."

Bobby pulled three beers out of the fridge and tossed
two to his sons. He unscrewed the cap, then sent it sail-
ing into the trash. "It's not that easy."

"What's not easy? You say, 'This is Colton, he's my
son,' end of subject." Mac spun the beer between his
palms and kept his gaze on the bottle. "People make
mistakes, Dad. Your friends are going to understand
that. Plus, it was more than thirty years ago."

Bobby shook his head. "That's not it."

"Are you embarrassed by having Colton here?"
Luke said. "Because he's a good guy, Dad, and you
need to get over that."

Bobby could see his other two sons liked their half
brother, and were ready to do whatever it took to include him in the family. They were good kids, he realized, kids that he had helped raise. Though most
of the credit should go to Della, because she was the
one who had kept this family running when he was
busy with the shop or doing the rest of his own growing up—being that Bobby was a man like many other
men, who took their sweet time settling into marriage.
Without his wife, he knew he wouldn't have been half
the man he'd turned out to be, and wouldn't have half
the incredible family he had.

"I'm not embarrassed by Colton's presence," Bobby
said. "I mean, yeah, I have to do some explaining to

folks, but hell, at my age, I don't give a rat's ass if people like me or not. That's not why I'm hesitating."

Luke leaned against the fridge and crossed his arms over his chest. "Then what is it?"

Bobby sighed and ran a hand through his head. One thing about Colton appearing in his life—it was forcing him to open up. For a man who rarely talked about anything more emotional than the crushing defeat of his favorite football team, this stuff was hard. "It's your mother."

"What? Mom is fine with Colton. She's been warmer than you to him, in fact." Mac shook his head. "Don't blame this on her."

"I'm not." Bobby took a swig of the beer but it didn't do anything except delay the next sentence. He wasn't going to tell the boys about how distant Della had been the last few days. How it seemed there was something on her mind, and how he'd avoided asking about it because he was pretty sure the topic would include the words *affair, betrayal, child*. He loved his wife, and if there was one thing he regretted, it was how much all of this had hurt the amazing woman who had stuck by him, even when he was being a total moron. But here she was, paying the price right alongside him. "I'm trying to keep this whole thing with Colton under wraps because I don't want people to look badly at your mother."

"Why would they do that?" Luke asked. Then he thought a second. "Oh…because she stayed with you through all this."

"Yeah." Bobby let out a sigh. He should have dealt

with this years ago, so that it wouldn't have the impact it was having now. Della deserved better than that. She probably deserved better than him, better than how casually he had treated their marriage in the early years. "People in this town love your mother. I don't want anyone to look at her sideways because of a mistake I made."

"They won't, Dad, if you lead by example." Mac put a hand on his father's shoulder. "And Mom is stronger than you think."

"Stronger than me," Bobby said. And maybe it was time he changed that.

Rachel was humming when she walked into her father's house the next morning. She'd hummed that night when she went to bed, and woke up humming. While she got ready for the day, she thought about Colton's kiss. When she drove across town to her father's house, she thought about Colton's smile. And most of all, she thought about seeing Colton again tonight.

She hummed on her way into the house, the light mood lingering, even though she knew she had a huge stack of work to do, and a dying store to try to resurrect. "Good morning, Dad."

There was no answer when she entered the house. She called out again and ducked into the kitchen, expecting to find her father in his customary seat.

But he wasn't there. The song she'd been humming died in her throat. She turned down the hall, worry mushrooming in her chest, and stopped at her father's room. "Dad?"

No answer.

She turned the knob and poked her head inside. Her father was lying in his bed, the shades still drawn. "Dad?"

He cleared his throat. Roused. "Sorry, honey. Not feeling well."

She rushed over and dropped onto the side of the bed. She pressed a hand to his forehead, as if he was the child and she was the parent, but his temples were cool and dry. "What's wrong? Did you take your heart medicine yesterday?"

He thought a minute, his brow furrowed. "I don't remember."

She never should have gone out last night. Never should have left before she was sure her father was okay. "Stay right here. I'll be right back."

Rachel chided herself the whole way into the kitchen. She fixed her father some eggs, a slice of wheat toast, then poured him a glass of orange juice and grabbed his medicine. If she had stayed last night instead of going on that date, she would have made sure her father took his medication. Would have known if he had eaten before he went to bed. She saw no new dirty dishes in the sink, which meant her father had likely gone into his room to watch TV and had fallen asleep on an empty stomach.

This was all her fault. She never should have left him. Damn it.

After her father ate and took his medication, Rachel threw in some laundry and vacuumed while Ernie washed up and got dressed for the day. She tidied the kitchen, assembled a sandwich and some grapes then set the plate in the fridge for lunch. "I'll be back for dinner, Dad," she said, knowing there was no way she was going out with Colton tonight. "How about I fix Mom's meat loaf recipe?"

A soft, sad smile curved across her father's face. "That would be nice, sweetheart. Really nice."

She took off her apron and hung it on the hook inside the pantry. "Do you need anything else before I run over to the shop?"

"I've got coffee and my paper. That's all I need." He smiled at her. "I'm sorry you had to do all this. I don't mean to forget, to lose track. To—" his smile faded "—rely on you so much."

"You don't, Dad. It's fine, really."

"No, it's not." He cupped her cheek, his eyes misty. "Sometimes I just miss her so much it hurts, and I just—"

"I understand, Dad." She leaned in and pressed a kiss to his cheek. "I love you." They held gazes for a moment, then the mood lightened.

"Okay. I'll be back later." She grabbed her purse and headed for the door. Just before she put her hand on the knob, her dad spoke up.

"Did you order the new lures for fall? Folks will be coming in soon, looking for those fancy ones I showed you in the catalog."

It was the first time in a long time that her father had

given her input about the store. "Yes, I ordered them. I only got three dozen. Do you think that's enough?"

Her father thought a second. "Sounds about right. Tell Billy to increase his delivery of fresh bait. Once the kids go back to school, fishing picks up. It's not so hot out there, and all those grandpas who were stuck inside with the grandkids are itching to get out on the water."

"Sounds good, Dad." She smiled, and the urge to hum returned again. "Sounds really good."

Colton told himself he wasn't going to be overly anxious. But after spending the morning at the garage helping Luke change out a transmission, then the afternoon with Mac enjoying a leisurely lunch on the water with him and his fiancée, Savannah, Colton was feeling antsy.

He called his mom and sister back in Atlanta, but changed the subject when they asked when he was coming home. Truth be told, he wasn't sure. He'd come down to Stone Gap sure that he wouldn't stay more than a few days, just long enough to meet his brothers and father. But as one day stretched into two, three, four, the urge to leave lessened. Maybe it had something to do with Rachel.

That's why he wandered down to the hardware store a little after three that afternoon. He could see her car parked out back, and that made his steps quicken, his heart leap. He ducked into the shop, and like the first time, took a second to let his eyes adjust to the dim interior. There was one other customer at the counter, finishing up a transaction for a new tackle box. "Here you go, Mr. Allen," Rachel was saying. "Enjoy. And catch a record-breaker, will you?"

"I'm going to try," the customer said. "But I doubt anyone is ever going to break your dad's record. He's a hell of a fisherman. I sure miss seeing him around here."

"We all do," Rachel said.

The customer, a tall, thin, white-haired man, stowed the tackle box under his arm like a football. "Any idea when he'll be back behind the counter?"

"Soon." But the word had little conviction in it, and even from where he was standing, Colton could tell Rachel didn't believe her own answer.

"Well, if you see him, tell him Paul says hello. And ask him if he wants to partner up on the doubles tournament this winter. I'd sure love some of his expertise."

"I will, Mr. Allen. Thanks again."

The customer turned away and headed for the door, giving Colton a little head nod as he passed. Rachel slid the customer's check into the cash drawer then glanced over and saw Colton. A smile spread across her face, quick and bright, and that sent a little thrill through him.

There was such joy in her face when she saw him, he couldn't help but feel as though he'd hit the lottery.

"Hi," she said. "Here for another fishing pole?"

"Nope. I'm here for purely personal reasons." He closed the distance between them. He loved the way her eyes sparkled, the way her T-shirt hugged her curves. The V-neck made his gaze drop to the slight swell of her breasts. Damn, she was a beautiful woman. "I wanted to see you again. And I couldn't wait until tonight."

Her smile widened, and a faint blush crept into her cheeks. "That's very sweet. But…" She sighed. "I can't go out to dinner tonight. My dad isn't well, and he really needs me to be there, to make sure he eats and takes his medicine."

"Then bring him with us. It might do him good to get out on the town."

"Bring him with us?"

"Sure. We'll go down to the Sea Shanty. As far as I've seen, that's the most casual place this town has to offer. And the food is great. Win all around."

"You're sure you wouldn't mind having my dad along? It's not exactly a date night."

"It is if you're there." God, when did he turn into a sentimental fool? He might as well be a romance novelist, given the lines he was spouting. The worst part? It was all true. He didn't care if the entire Stone Gap High School marching band came along on their date, as long as he got to spend those hours with Rachel.

"That would be nice," she said. "But…maybe another time. I promised my dad I'd make my mother's meat loaf. It's his favorite dinner."

"Okay. I understand." Something a lot like disappointment filled his gut.

"Do you…" She paused. "Do you like meat loaf?"

"I do," Colton said. "Very much."

"Then come over. My dad would love to meet you."

He shouldn't be this excited about being invited

over for meat loaf, but he was. "Sure. Why don't I pick you up at six?"

"My car is here. I can drive myself."

"Or I can pick you up and drive you back to your car after dinner." He grinned. "In case you haven't noticed, I'm trying to grab a little alone time with you, too."

The blush deepened. "You are incorrigible."

"That's what my third grade teacher said. But I turned out okay." He leaned across the counter and placed a soft, sweet kiss on her lips. "See you at six."

And when he walked out the door a moment later, Colton Barlow was humming.

Chapter Seven

Colton was just heading into his room at the Stone Gap Inn to change his clothes when his cell phone rang. Bobby's number appeared on the caller ID, and even though Colton was far past the age where he should get excited about a call from his dad, that didn't stop his heart from doing a little skip in his chest. "Hello?"

"Hey, uh, Colton, this is… Bob—" he cleared his throat "—your dad."

Maybe Bobby was having as much trouble adjusting to the new child in his life as Colton was having adjusting to his new last name. "Yeah, hi. How are you?"

"Fine, fine."

There was a long pause while the two of them scrambled for more small talk to fill the gap in the conversation. Colton didn't know what to say. He knew so little about his father that he wasn't sure how to bridge the conversational gap. "I, uh, had breakfast with Luke and Mac the other day."

"Oh, yeah? That's good. Real good." Bobby paused again. The silence stretched, thick and uncomfortable. "Listen, every Sunday Della cooks this big dinner. Roast beef, or spaghetti, or something good. The whole family comes over. I wanted to…uh, invite you."

Wow. He'd heard about the Sunday meals from his brothers, but he hadn't been sure if Bobby would extend an invite or not. Now that he heard the words, he couldn't wait for the meal. He wondered if it would be like he'd always imagined the father and the siblings he dreamed he had in some other life. Sort of like a modern-day version of the Waltons.

Okay, so maybe he was turning into a sentimental fool. Had to be this small town. "I'd…I'd love to come. Thanks."

"Good. See you Sunday. And, uh, our anniversary party is that night. Just a small thing, over at the community center, with some local friends and you kids. Wanted to invite you to that, too. Assuming…" Bobby let out a breath.

"Assuming what?"

"Nothing, nothing. Just need to talk to Della is all." Bobby's voice sounded troubled, but Colton wasn't sure it was his place to ask his dad what was going on.

"Well, I'll see you Sunday," Colton said. "Thanks for the invites." Again, they'd exhausted their conversational abilities.

There was another uncomfortable pause, long enough

that Colton thought Bobby might have hung up. "Uh, Colton...I'm glad you're staying in town for a while," Bobby said. "And might be staying on for good. I heard Harry offered you a job."

"He did, but I haven't decided yet." Colton needed to talk to Harry first and tell him the whole story about his time in the Atlanta Fire Department. He was sure that Harry would rescind the offer after that. A fire chief wanted someone he could depend upon, and Colton wasn't so sure he was that guy.

He'd missed his job. Missed the camaraderie, the other men, his friends. But a part of him worried that maybe the worry, the doubts, he'd felt since that day would intrude when his team needed him most.

So he'd procrastinated on that conversation with Harry. A psychologist would probably say it was because Colton didn't want to face the ghosts that haunted his every thought. And maybe a little of the fact that Colton was trying to delay on the decision about staying here, investing in his family, or going back to Atlanta and leaving everything and everyone in Stone Gap behind.

"When to move on, or when to start over is a big decision to make," Bobby said. "Not something to take lightly."

It was the closest thing to advice he'd ever received from his father. The words were vague, the meaning even less clear. Was Bobby advising him to take the job or to go back to Atlanta? Maybe a little of both? "I'll keep that in mind."

"Okay, that's good. Well...I'll talk to you later."

Bobby said goodbye, and the connection went dead. Colton tucked the phone away. It wasn't quite the relationship he had come to this town to find, but it was a step in the right direction, and that was enough. For now.

A few minutes later Colton pulled in front of the hardware store just as Rachel was locking up for the night. His heart leaped at the sight of her, with her hair loose around her shoulders, her light blue T-shirt and dark-wash jeans hugging her lithe body. He hopped out of the car and pulled open the passenger-side door. A light rain began to fall, and Rachel ducked under his arm and into the car. "Thank you."

"My pleasure." He lingered a second, his arm on the door, blocking the rain from dropping onto her legs. "In case I forgot to tell you today, you look beautiful."

She laughed. "I'm wearing jeans and a T-shirt."

"And you look amazing in everything." He leaned in and kissed her. The kiss was too short, too little, but it was raining and they were late, and he would have to wait for more. "Absolutely amazing."

"You, my friend, need your vision checked."

He pulled back and gave her a grin. "Is that what we are? Friends?"

"I'm not sure what we are, Colton," she said, the playfulness dropping from her features. "And I'm not sure if I want more."

Neither was he. Hell, he didn't even know if he was staying in town. But more and more, the case for staying in Stone Gap grew stronger. For one, a new start, one far from the Atlanta FD and all the memories he had there, might be the best thing for him. Was he ever going to be able to walk into that station again and not see Willis's and Foster's faces? Would anyone he worked with ever forget? No one blamed him, but the way they talked about *the accident,* as they called it, with that little shake of their heads, made Colton feel he should have reacted faster, should have done more, should have done *something.*

But every time he looked at Rachel's smile, it made him forget for a little while. It made him wonder if maybe beginning again here, in this small town with his brothers and his father, and this intoxicating woman, might just be the solace he'd been seeking.

"I don't know either, Rachel," he said, "but I'm willing to give it some time and try to figure that out."

Then he came around to his side of the car, put the rental in gear and pulled away from the curb. The rain fell heavier now, and the wipers made steady squeaks across the windshield, trying to keep up.

"How was the shop today?" he asked. Because it was easier to change the subject than to circle around the one that didn't have any answers.

She sighed. "Slow. I'm worried I'm going to have to close. Business just hasn't been the same since my dad stopped working there. I mean, I know a lot about fishing, but I'm not him. And a lot of the old-timers came in just to chat with him. He loved that shop. Loved his job."

"And you don't love it."

She pivoted toward him. "What makes you say that?"

"I see it in your eyes. Hear it in your voice. There's nothing wrong with that, Rachel. It's not your passion, and that's okay."

"No, it's not. I told him I'd keep it running, and if I let him down, the shop will die, and then what will he have?" She let out a long breath and turned toward the window. Her breath fogged a circle against the glass. "I have to keep it running."

She sounded so dejected, he wanted to do something. But what? He sure as hell wasn't equipped to run the place for her. His heart had always been in firefighting, in the adventure of it, the puzzle of figuring out the fastest way to tame a blaze. The never knowing what the next call might hold. He was lucky enough to be doing a job that filled his soul, but he could also understand the pain of working a job that left you feeling empty at the end of the day. "Savannah was telling me that you are a wedding planner."

"I *used* to be a wedding planner. Now I'm a hammer and bait seller." She grinned, but the smile fell flat. The rain trailed in long tracks down the windows, puddling in the seals around the door. "My business has been on the back burner for a while."

"And you don't have enough time to do both."

She shook her head. "As it is, I barely have enough time for my dad. And his house…there's always twelve thousand things that need get done. He's just been so sad since my mother died, and I just can't get him to leave the house or do anything. I wish I had the magic words to get him back to his life. Maybe then…" She sighed. "For now I'm where I need to be. If I think too much about the what-ifs, it just makes everything harder."

As if on cue, they pulled into Ernie's driveway. Colton took in the overgrown landscaping, the weedy lawn, the peeling paint on the mailbox. The rain had stopped, leaving the whole scene sparkling with fresh water drops. But that didn't make it look any less... sad, and definitely in need of some serious trimming. He could see how much work there was to do, and could only imagine how heavy that burden weighed on Rachel.

He knew what it was like to be the one everyone depended upon. He couldn't change everything for Rachel, but maybe if he started with one small thing, it would ease the weight on her shoulders. "I know my way around a lawn mower and a Weed Whacker," he said. "If you want, I can take care of the yard while you do what you need to do for your dad or the meat loaf, or whatever magic happens in the kitchen. Trust me, you'd rather have me outside than working the stove."

She blinked at him. "Really? Why would you do that?"

He looked at Rachel, at this amazing woman who was working so hard she barely had time to breathe, and his heart softened. "Because you need someone to."

Tears filled her eyes, but didn't fall. To him, that was yet another mark of how strong she was, how determined. "Thank you, Colton."

"It's no big deal." She kept looking at him as if he was this big hero, saving the day. He wasn't any of those things. He was just a guy who had offered to mow the lawn.

"It's a big deal to me. More than you know. So… thank you. In advance." She gave him a quick, tight smile, then pulled on the handle of the door and got out of the car.

Damn it. She kept looking at him like that. What would happen to that look in Rachel's eyes if he told her about Willis and Foster? He didn't want to find out, didn't want to tell her the truth. So instead of tarnishing that hero image she had in her head, he silently followed Rachel into the house to meet her father.

Rachel's father was sitting at the kitchen table, a crossword puzzle spread out before him. He had the wiry frame of someone who had been active all his life, and short gray hair that smoothed across his head. His glasses perched on the end of his nose, secured to his neck by a dark brown chain. He took them off and let them dangle against his chest when Colton and Rachel came into the kitchen. "You brought company," he said to Rachel.

"I brought someone who actually volunteered to tackle that weedy mess you call a yard, Dad." Rachel leaned in and pressed a kiss to her father's cheek. "Dad, this is Colton Barlow. Colton, this is my father, Ernie."

"The fishing champion," Colton said, extending his hand. "I've heard quite a lot about you from Harry Washington."

Ernie got to his feet and shook hands with Colton. His skin was pale, his grip a little weak, as if he'd spent a lot of time at this kitchen table. Given the state of the yard and the fact that Rachel was running the shop alone, Colton was pretty positive the only place Ernie had visited lately was this one room. "Harry? How is that old bastard?"

"Fine, sir. Just fine."

Ernie slid an amused glance in Rachel's direction. "So this is the one you bought the dress and fancy shoes for?"

Rachel blushed. "Dad!"

Colton grinned. "You bought a new dress for our date?"

"I *needed* a new dress. That was the only reason why."

"Don't let her fool you," Ernie said, leaning in toward Colton. "She was as nervous as a chicken in a doghouse. So, Colton…Barlow? I know the Barlows. How are you related to Bobby?"

Small-town living—obviously everyone who heard Colton's last name was going to ask that same question. "Uh, he's my father. I'm Luke, Jack and Mac's half brother."

"Oh, okay. Well, welcome to Stone Gap." Ernie sat back down at the table and picked up his crossword puzzle. He sat his glasses on his nose again. Apparently, that was all he needed to know.

"Dad, Colton was going to go work on the yard. I'm going to make the meat loaf. Maybe you want to help Colton?"

Her father scowled. "I have the crossword to do."

Rachel started to say something, then instead let

out a long sigh that said she'd been down this road a dozen times. "Okay."

Colton could see the frustration in her eyes. He knew that feeling. There'd been times with his mother when she would sink into a deep depression, and it would be like pulling rope through a needle to get her motivated again. He'd done what he could to take over the care of his little sister, and to cover for their mother, who had often put her children second. He didn't think Rachel's father was like that, but he could certainly relate to the challenges she faced. "Mr. Morris, I don't need your help, but I sure would appreciate you showing me where all the yard tools are."

Ernie dropped his glasses to his chest again. "'Spose I can do that." He got to his feet, tugged a key off the hook by the back door then beckoned to Colton to follow him.

As Colton passed Rachel, she gave him a grateful smile and mouthed, "thank you." For that smile, Colton decided, he would do about anything.

Rachel watched through the window as Colton and her father headed into the shed. She held her breath, sure that in a few minutes, her father would be back in the kitchen, sitting in the same chair, holding the same pen, working on the same crossword puzzle.

But then she saw her father emerge from the shed with the hedge trimmers in one hand. He was talking to Colton as he walked across the yard and gesturing toward the edge of the lawn. Colton nodded then turned back to the lawn mower. A moment later the mower was roaring along the grass, cutting it to a fraction of its overgrown length. Her father was wielding the gas hedge trimmers like a ninja with a sword, taming the wild shrubbery into something resembling its former self.

She smiled and started humming again as she chopped vegetables then mixed up the meat loaf and got it into the oven. While her father and Colton worked on the yard, she whipped up some mashed potatoes and baked a batch of brownies from a mix she found in the cupboard. By the time the men came in, a little sweaty, a little dirty and a lot hungry, dinner was ready and on the table.

"I'm about tuckered out now," Ernie said, swiping at the sweat on his brow. "I think that's the most work I've done in a year."

"The yard should be good for a while now," Colton said. "I'll come by next week and give it another mow."

Next week? Did that mean Colton was thinking of staying?

Rachel handed each of them a glass of ice water. "You guys did a great job. The yard looks amazing."

Ernie put a hand on his daughter's back. "That's a good man you found. I'd keep him around if I were you. I'm going to go wash up for supper. Be right back."

She couldn't have been more shocked at the change in her father if she tried. He had a little color in his cheeks, a little spring in his step. And all because of whatever Colton had said to him that got her father outside and working.

Once her father was out of earshot, Colton turned to Rachel. "Seems I got the paternal vote of approval."

She grinned. "That doesn't mean you move out of the friend category."

Colton leaned in close to her, so close she could feel the heat of his skin, catch the whisper of his cologne. She watched his pulse tick in his neck. "What's a man got to do to impress you, Rachel Morris?"

She swallowed hard and thought it was a good thing they weren't alone in the house. She wanted this man, with his lopsided smile and his easy way with her father, in the worst possible way. In the kind of way that clouded all rational thought and pushed all her pretty little reasons for not having a relationship off a mental cliff. "I think you're already doing it, Colton Barlow."

Colton grinned then pulled away and turned to wash his hands in the sink. "Good to know. Maybe I should do more of whatever it is I'm doing right."

"What did you say to my dad that got him to work with you?"

"My mom would go through these periods of depression." Colton picked up a dish towel, leaned against the counter and dried his hands over and over again. "There were days when neither me nor my sister could get her to eat, never mind get out of bed. A thousand times, I was patient, and took care of Katie, and helped her. But then one day I went in there and asked her if this was how she wanted her kids to remember her, because she was killing herself, one day at a time."

"You said that to my father?"

"Not in that way. I was a little nicer in how I said

it to your dad. I mentioned that he had a really great daughter who wanted to spend some quality time with him. Your dad cursed a couple times then grabbed the hedge trimmers and said he better do them himself because I wouldn't know the way he liked the shrubs to look. But he wasn't mad at me. More...concerned about you."

She laughed. "That sounds like my dad."

"He took it well. And by the time the lawn was finished, we were buddies. With my mom, she got out of bed and never really sank to that same level of depression."

"Thank you." The two words were as thick as paste in her throat. They couldn't come close to expressing her gratitude, how deep that thanks reached inside her. With a simple household chore, Colton had fostered the change that Rachel had been trying to create for over a year.

"It was nothing."

"No, Colton, it was everything." She swiped at her eyes, cursing the tears that sprang there. Colton chuckled softly and stepped forward with the dish towel.

"Don't cry, Rachel. It was only yard work." He dabbed at the tears on her face and then cupped her cheek. "Okay?"

She nodded, and the tears gave way to laughter. "Maybe so, but it was a *lot* of yard work."

"Which means I'm hoping there's a *lot* of dinner as a reward."

She would have made a month's worth of meals

to thank him if she could have. "Oh, there is, Colton, there definitely is."

Her father came into the kitchen. "Watch out, you two lovebirds. Old man coming in the room."

"Dad, we're not—"

"Definitely not," Colton added.

Ernie chuckled. "Whatever you two say. Now, let's eat."

Her father was laughing. Of all the things that had happened in the last couple hours, hearing the sound of her father's laughter filled Rachel's heart with joy. For the first time in a really long time, she had hope. It was still fragile, but it was there. She could see a new road ahead—if her father kept going in the right direction.

Her father sat at the head of the table, with Colton and Rachel on either side of him. He glanced around the dining room, and his eyes grew misty. "We haven't had a meal in this room in a long, long time."

"Too long, I think," she said. It was something she needed to change. Maybe now that her father was coming back to his life, he would step outside that kitchen, in more ways than one.

"Your mom used to do such great Sunday dinners, didn't she? Before she got…sick."

That was the term they all used to describe her mother's alcoholism. The years before she got sick. Maybe that made it easier, Rachel thought, to accept her mother's choices. But it didn't ease her guilty feelings about not being here at the end, not getting that closure and, most of all, leaving her father to deal with it all.

"I thought it would be more comfortable to eat in the dining room," she said. "And maybe a way to kind of include Mom, too."

Ernie's eyes watered. "She'd like that."

Rachel covered her dad's hand with her own. His weathered palm grasped hers, tight and sure. "Thanks, Dad."

Ernie's smile wobbled on his face, then he cleared his throat, dismissing the moment, moving on. Her father wasn't a man given to expressing his emotions much, and it didn't surprise her when he grabbed the bowl of mashed potatoes and started dishing them up. "Let's eat before this all gets cold."

They shared the dishes around, family style, and the conversation gradually turned from the condition of the lawn to the weather to Colton. "So, what do you do for work?" Ernie asked.

"I'm a firefighter, sir. With the Atlanta Fire Department."

"But Harry offered him a job here," Rachel added. A big part of her hoped Colton took the job. She definitely wanted to spend more time with this man who had made her father laugh and brought some sun to his cheeks.

Not to mention that every time she was within a few feet of him, she couldn't help but gravitate closer to Colton. Even sitting at the table with him, Rachel had this awareness of Colton, a constant hum in her body.

Ernie forked up some more meat loaf, already on his second helping. "Harry's a good man. He runs that department like a tight ship, but he's fair and smart. I've known him most all my life."

"I'm thinking about his job offer," Colton said. He toyed with his food. "I haven't decided anything yet."

But he had decided to stay another week, which she took as a good sign.

"Atlanta must be a busy department," Rachel said. "I've only been to the city a few times, but it seemed like it was always hopping."

"It was." Colton shifted in his seat.

"Firefighting's a pretty noble profession," her father said. "My cousin was a firefighter. He lost a leg in a blaze. Got caught under some falling timbers. But the other guys were right there, thank God, and pulled him out. He still gets together with those guys once a week, even though he had to leave the department."

"That would be tough," Colton said. "Can you, uh, pass the potatoes?"

Rachel did as he asked then cut off a bite of meat loaf. "So, what was the biggest fire you ever had to fight?"

Colton's entire demeanor shifted into stone. He dropped the mashed potatoes back into the serving bowl and pushed it to the side. "I, uh, don't really want to talk about my job over dinner and bore you all. I'd much rather hear about Ernie's fishing tips. Since I don't know much about fishing, and if I'm going to keep up with Rachel here, then I should learn some insider secrets."

That got her dad talking for the next twenty minutes about lures and rods and secret fishing holes. The two men conversed like old friends, and by the time the dinner dishes were cleared and the dishwasher was loaded, Rachel could see her father flagging. It had been a lot of activity for one day, after almost a year of nothing.

Ernie stood in the kitchen beside his daughter, sipping a glass of water after taking his heart medication. "This was a good night. A good meal."

"It was, Dad." She leaned into him and gave him a hug. "It was good to see you feeling better."

"Yeah." He started to say something else when a pair of headlights appeared in the driveway. "Huh. Who's here at this time of night?"

Rachel knew, because most nights she was still up, doing the dishes or working on paperwork, and making sure her dad didn't need anything. Ernie Morris was normally in bed before eight at night, claiming he was tired as soon as the evening meal was done. But tonight, between the yard work and the conversation with Colton, eight had stretched into eight thirty, and that meant Daryl was coming by for his usual weekly check-in on her dad.

Rachel got to her feet and opened the door. "Great timing," she said to Daryl. "I made brownies."

"Who are you offering my brownies to?" her father called from behind her. "And why haven't I heard about them until now?"

"I was saving them in case we had company." Rachel opened the door the rest of the way and stepped back. Her father had made great strides this evening. She could only hope the change would continue, courtesy of a little brownie bribery.

Daryl strode in, ducking his head a little under the jamb. He was a tall, lanky man, whose clothes never quite matched the length of his arms and legs. He wore a floppy fisherman's hat everywhere he went, no matter the time of day. He'd grown a beard this year, and the reddish-brown hair on his face made him look a little like a skinny lumberjack. "Ernie. How you doing?" he said, as if no more than an afternoon had passed since he'd last seen his friend.

Rachel tensed. Her father had made it clear over the last year that he didn't want company. Didn't want his friends paying "sympathy visits."

Her father looked at Daryl, then at Rachel, then back at Daryl again. "Well, don't just stand in the doorway. Come on in. Rachel says there's brownies, and we might as well eat them."

"Good thinking on the brownies," Colton whispered to Rachel.

Daryl took a seat at the kitchen table beside Ernie. "It's about damned time you invited me in. You are a pain in the ass, you know that?"

Daryl was probably the only human being in the world that could say that to her father. Ernie grinned. "Hey, we all got to be good at something."

Rachel dished up the brownies and brewed a pot of decaf while her father introduced Colton, and the three of them talked about fishing. It was an ordinary scene, something that could be happening in a million houses across the world at this very moment. And that was what made it perfect. Absolutely, wonderfully perfect.

Chapter Eight

It wasn't just the meat loaf and brownies that had Colton falling for Rachel. It was the way she took care of her father, the way she worried and tended, but didn't hover. She was a woman with a generous heart, and that drew him to her in ways he'd never been drawn to a woman before.

It was that way she had about her that had him thinking about something that lasted a lot longer than tonight. Something that involved dinners around a table and teasing while they stood at the sink, finishing up the dishes.

He reached across the console while he drove her home and took her hand in his. It felt nice. Perfect. Right.

When she'd mentioned she was tired, he offered to

bring her home, instead of back to her car at the shop, because that would also give him an excuse to pick her up again in the morning. He didn't have anything planned for tomorrow, so maybe he could take Rachel to breakfast, drop her off at work then swing by Ernie's again and tackle the leaky sink in the hall bathroom, or do some touch-up painting on the front of the house.

Rachel turned and smiled at him. "Thank you. Again. I haven't seen my father that interested in life in a long, long time. I can't believe he was still talking to Daryl when we left."

"Making plans for fishing trips, too."

"*And* he said he was going to come to the shop tomorrow." Her smile widened. "If my dad gets back to work, then maybe…maybe eventually I can get back to my business."

"Planning all those happily-ever-afters for everyone?"

She laughed. "Exactly."

"And what about you?" He took a right onto Main Street and drove past the dark, closed stores that lined the downtown area.

"What about me?"

"Why hasn't some very smart man married you yet?" Had he just asked that question? It had to be the sugar overload from the brownies. Colton wasn't looking to settle down. Especially not in this little town. But then he thought of the dinner, the laughter, the smile on Rachel's face, the feel of her beside him in the kitchen, in the car. And thought if this was settling down, it wouldn't be so bad. Not at all.

"Maybe I've just been an even smarter woman who hasn't wanted to marry any of those men," she said.

He chuckled. "Touché."

"And what about you? Why haven't you gotten married yet?"

"To be honest, I haven't met anyone who made me want to stay in one place long enough to put a ring on it." Until now. Until this woman with her determination and her caring came along and made him want something more. A lot more.

"This isn't exactly second date conversation," she said with a slight laugh in her voice. "Aren't we still supposed to be talking about our favorite pets or what we were like in fourth grade?"

"My favorite pet was my dog Tommy, a little mixed breed spaniel. I got him when I was six, and he lived until my senior year of high school. Someday, I'll get another dog, but working as a firefighter..." He shrugged. "I can't leave a dog overnight several days a week. And as for fourth grade, let's just say my report card had big words on it like overly enthusiastic and stubbornly energetic."

Rachel laughed. "Stubbornly energetic?"

"My fourth grade teacher was trying to nicely say I was a complete pain in the neck." He grinned.

"Now that, I believe." She sat back against the seat. The golden glow from the streetlights danced highlights in her hair as they drove, and speckled diamonds across her skin. "My favorite pet was a turtle I kept in a tank in my room. I always wanted a dog, but my mom was allergic. So I had a turtle, until I went to college. Then I gave him to my little cousin Sharlene, who promised to take good care of him."

"And did she?"

"He's still alive, last I heard. Sharlene became a veterinary tech, so I think my turtle is in safe hands. And I'd like to think I was part of what drove her into animal care."

"Look at that. A turtle inspiring a life of giving back to the animal kingdom."

"Exactly. As for fourth grade, I was the one getting all As and receiving the perfect-attendance award."

"Teacher's pet?" He pulled to a stop in the parking lot of her apartment building and turned the car off.

"Not exactly. I guess…" She shrugged. "My childhood was kind of chaotic and I guess I thought if I kept everything perfect at school, maybe that would make things better at home. Crazy thinking."

"Not when you're in fourth grade." He unbuckled, then reached across to brush a long blond lock off her forehead. "I know how hard it is to be the one who feels responsible."

And to be the one who had let others down. Who had tried his best, and his best still hadn't been enough. To be the one left behind, with guilt and regret sitting on either shoulder.

She cupped his jaw and met his gaze with her own. "You made everything different today and I…I really appreciate it."

God, she was beautiful. He was drawn to her intensity, the way her gaze seemed to hold him captive. He couldn't have left right now if he tried. "Really, it was nothing. I'm just glad I was there. But you know what I'm even more grateful for?"

Her eyes widened, and a tease lit her face. "What?"

"Meeting you." He leaned closer, fumbling with one hand for the button at her waist. He released the seat belt, and it retracted with a soft whoosh. Colton closed the distance between them and kissed Rachel.

He'd intended a simple, easy good-night kiss. One that would punctuate the thank-yous with one of his own. *Thank you for including me. Thank you for looking at me like I'm someone amazing. Thank you for making my days brighter.*

But she let out a little moan as he kissed her, and all those simple, easy intentions disappeared. He groaned, and the kiss deepened. His hands roamed over her hair, her shoulders, her back, and her touch matched his, sliding down the back of his arms, around to his waist, back again.

The stupid console sat between them like a wall. The bucket seats felt too small, too confined. He briefly considered climbing over the console, but was pretty sure he'd risk serious injury with the gear shift.

"Let's go inside," she whispered against his mouth.

Thank God. "I think that's the best idea I've heard all day." They broke apart just long enough to get out of the car then meet up again on the walkway. His arm went around her waist; his head dipped to kiss her again, the heat building as they walked and kissed, and tried to hurry without running into a wall.

An interminable minute later, they were on the third floor of her building and she was cursing as she tried to jam the key into the lock. Colton closed his hand over hers and the key slid into place, then turned and the lock released. They stumbled into her apartment, and he kicked the door shut then kiss-walked down the hall to her bedroom. Rachel nudged the bedroom door open with her hip. Colton scooped her up, thinking how light and perfect she felt in his arms, then he took a few steps forward and laid her on the bed.

"You look incredible," he said. Even that wasn't the right word for how beautiful she was, in the darkened room, with only the moonlight dancing through the windows, casting her in an ethereal glow.

"And you look...tempting." A slow, seductive smile curved across her face as she rose up on her elbows then reached out and tugged him forward by a belt loop. "Too tempting."

"I could say the same about you." He reached for the hem of her T-shirt and tugged it up and over her head, revealing a lacy white bra beneath. He ran a finger along the scalloped edge then dipped inside the cup and brushed against her nipple. She gasped, and that made him smile. "Very, very tempting."

That blush he loved filled her cheeks. "I wore it because... Well, I didn't know..."

Just the thought that she had worn this for him, on the off chance they'd end up here, flattered Colton. He would have to show her how very much.

He reached for the fly of her jeans. She lifted her hips and he undid the fastener, then the zipper, and tugged the denim off. When he saw the scrap of matching panties, he dropped the jeans on the floor, not even caring where they ended up.

He climbed onto the bed, and Rachel lay down beneath him, her eyes wide, her mouth slightly open, anticipation filling her face. He brushed a kiss across her lips, her cheeks, then down her jaw, along her neck, lingering in the valley of her shoulders. She arched against him, and he splayed his palm, sliding it down her belly, over the mound between her legs, feeling her through the lace. She was wet already, ready for him, but he wasn't about to rush something this incredible.

He kissed every inch of skin between her neck and her breasts. She was warm and sweet, and smelled like vanilla and spice. He peeled down the silky strap of her bra, one side then the other, and her breasts rose above the lacy cups. He nudged back the lace and took one nipple in his mouth. Rachel gasped, and when he put his hand between her legs, she ground against the touch. Her breathing came in faster and faster gasps. Then he slid a finger under the lace of her panties and rubbed at the tender, hard bud between her legs, never taking his attention off her nipple. Rachel bucked up against him and let out a long, long, shuddering breath.

"Oh…oh, my. That…that's never happened before. Not…that easily." Another of those blushes he loved appeared on her cheeks.

"Then we should do it again. And again." He grinned.

"First, I think we should be equally naked." She tugged at his shirt, working her way through the buttons then sliding it over and off his shoulders. Her hands followed the fabric's path down his arms until it lay on the floor and her hands had slid around to his waist. She undid the button fly and shoved his jeans and underwear down in one fell swoop.

He climbed onto the bed beside her and rolled Rachel on top of him, undoing the clasp on the back of her bra, then urging her panties down and off. He reached over the side of the bed, tugged his wallet out of his back pocket and found a condom.

"Let me," she whispered, taking the foil packet from him. She nudged him onto his back then straddled his thighs, and in one deft movement, unfurled the condom and slid it along his erection.

This woman was full of surprises. He'd expected someone who blushed as easily as she did to be shy in bed, but as Rachel raised her hips and slid onto his sheathed penis, he realized she was anything but shy. And he was pretty much done thinking for a while.

She was glorious on top of him, riding him with sure and steady strokes, her breasts full and perfect in the moonlight. He cupped them with his palms, letting his thumbs circle over the nipples. She clutched his hands and moaned, then increased her pace.

She arched back a little, deepening his entry into her, and a second later she was riding him hard and fast, and the gasps were turning into breathless words of nothing, and then she came again, and he damned near lost it.

Instead, he flipped her over and braced himself above her head. "You are amazing. Surprising. Intoxicating."

That blush again, that captivating blush that had

him hooked from the first day. "And you are a serious flatterer."

"Because I'm—" He let out a breath, figured why not say it; where had not saying how he felt gotten him in life? "Falling for you."

"Falling...for me?"

"Falling," he whispered, dancing a finger across her lips, "for you. In a big way."

She smiled, and that sweet smile hit him somewhere deep in his chest. Suddenly, this wasn't sex, it wasn't a moment of relief, it was more. A connection.

And when he slid into her, she reached up to draw him even closer and their strokes quickened, the connection quadrupled, and Colton knew he wasn't just falling for Rachel Morris—he was falling hard.

Chapter Nine

Colton left a little after midnight. As content as Rachel had felt, curled in his arms after some seriously amazing sex, a level of panic began to set in when her mind finally processed the words *I'm falling for you.*

Because she was falling for him, too, and that thought scared the hell out of her. He wasn't staying in town—as far as she knew—and she still had a life too full for a relationship. The old familiar fears, the same ones that had made her keep all her other boyfriends at arm's length, began to creep in. What if she fell for him and made a mistake? Landed in an unhappy marriage, like her parents had?

She'd planned dozens of weddings, watched dozens of couples say I do. And at the end of the year, maybe six out of ten were still as happy as the day they walked down the aisle. She'd seen the giddy, infatuated stage yield to frustration and resentment, and watched those very dreams dissolve for some of the couples she had worked for. It had made her skittish, unwilling to risk her own heart.

Until she met Colton.

And now, in the warm glow of the dark hours after he had left, lying in her bed, with the scent of him still on her sheets and skin, she began to wonder if maybe… just maybe, it was time for her fairy tale, too.

Colton wound his way through the dark streets of Stone Gap, with Rachel's building growing more and more distant in his rearview mirror. He should have stayed in her bed, with her in his arms, but after saying he was falling for her, he'd begun to realize how quickly this had all become so cozy and intimate, and that maybe it would be a good idea to apply the brakes.

Okay, so he was a guy and he thought of that *after* they'd made love.

He'd realized how easy it would be to fall asleep in that bed, to spend a night with her and wake up to her smile—and all the implications that would come with that. Like that he was staying around. That he wanted something permanent here in Stone Gap. When he wasn't sure what he wanted or where he was going.

A storm was beginning to brew, and lightning crackled in the sky, some bolts so close it bathed the car's interior in white, but Colton hardly noticed. His mind was back on Rachel. He missed her already, and had started missing her the second he said goodbye.

Half of him wanted to turn around. The other half said it was a good thing he hadn't stayed.

This town was settling on him, like easing into a comfortable sweater. Tomorrow morning, he decided, he was going to go to Harry Washington and tell him about what had happened in Atlanta. And if Harry still wanted him to be part of the Stone Gap Fire Department, then Colton was going to take the job. Atlanta no longer held the appeal that this tiny town—and one particular woman in this town—did.

As he turned the corner onto Main Street, he saw a flicker of light ahead of him. At first he thought it was a streetlight going bad, but then the flicker showed orange, and he knew, with that pit of dread in his stomach, what the light really meant.

Fire.

He had no gear, he had no hose, no water. He gunned the car and closed the distance between himself and the flickering flames. The fire was licking up the side of the building housing Ernie's Hardware. Colton brought the car to a stop, dug out his phone and dialed 9-1-1.

"There's a fire at the intersection of Main and Berry," he said to the dispatcher. "Small, but not contained, on the exterior wall of the hardware shop."

"Is anyone inside?" the dispatcher asked.

"Not that—" Then Colton saw a shadow pass in front of the window and he let out a curse. "Yes, yes, someone's inside. I'm going in."

"Sir, wait for the fire department. Sir—"

But Colton was already gone, and the dispatcher was talking to the empty interior of his car.

The flames were moving faster now, spreading up the wooden exterior so quickly it seemed the fire was devouring the building like a late-night snack. In minutes it would be inside, and whoever was inside the building—

Colton didn't finish that train of thought. He ran across the street, straight toward the wood-and-glass door of the shop. He tried the handle, but it was locked. He pounded on the door, but there was no response. Had he really seen someone? Or was it his imagination?

He peered into the glass, but the interior was dark. Nothing but shapes, straight edges of shelves and boxes. Then the flames ate through the exterior wall, and orange light danced over the shop. Maybe he'd been mistaken. Maybe he'd seen the reflection of a passing car or something else.

There, on the floor, was the shape of a man. Oh, God. He wasn't moving.

Colton drew back and slammed his shoulder against the door. It refused to yield. He did it again. A third time. The door was thick and locked tight.

Panic drummed in his chest, but he tamped it down. Focus—that was what he needed to do. Focus on what he had been trained to do.

He spun around, looking for something, anything to help him gain entry. The sound of sirens began to rise in the distance, but they were too far away. They'd never make it in time. If he didn't get in there—

No. He wasn't going to think about that. This wasn't Willis and Foster. And there was still time for Colton to find a way in, to save whoever was lying on that floor.

He saw a small wooden bench outside the shop next door. He yanked it up and hurled it through the plate-glass window, straight through the display of tackle boxes and waders and the small sign advertising night crawlers. The closed sign blinked and then went out, as the glass shattered and the window fell apart in a cacophony of sound.

Colton climbed over the sill, careful not to touch the jagged edges. "Where are you?" he called out.

No response.

"I'm coming to get you. Just hold on." He didn't know if he was talking to someone who was still alive, but that didn't stop Colton from moving forward.

The flames were growing on the eastern wall, shivering up the paneled interior like macabre curtains. The smoke was growing thicker, and Colton raised his arm to cover his mouth. His eyes watered, his throat burned and the heat was rising, threatening to burn. But he pushed forward, shoving aside the jumbled mess from the broken window. He rounded the corner, passing the very register where he had first seen Rachel, and there, on the floor, was Ernie.

He wasn't moving. In the dark, Colton wasn't even sure if he was breathing. There was no time to check. There was only hoisting Ernie onto his shoulders and turning for the exit as the flames caught the new inrush of air and spread into the room like a mushroom cloud.

* * *

The phone was ringing.

Rachel clawed her way out of a deep sleep, vaguely aware that this wasn't a dream, and fumbled for her phone on the bedside table. "Hello?"

"Rachel? It's Harry Washington."

The fire chief? Why was he calling her at—she glanced at the clock—two thirty in the morning? After Colton had left, she had spent an hour or so working on a plan that might—just might—allow her to take on Ginny's wedding and work at the shop, before finally going to sleep a little after one. She struggled into a sitting position and pushed the hair out of her eyes. "Okay."

"There's been a fire at the store. Your dad was there, but—"

Fire? Her father? Had she heard Harry right? No, it was impossible. Her father was sitting at the kitchen table talking to Daryl when she left. "Are you sure? Is he okay? Where is he?"

"He's at the hospital," Harry said. "He's…he's had a tough time of it, and I don't know what his condition is right now. But Colton is there with him."

"I'm on my way." She hung up the phone, pulled on the first clothes she could find and ran out the door. She drove through town, taking the turn that would take her past the store.

All this time, she'd been hoping Harry was wrong. That it was some kind of terrible prank call. But the sight of the Stone Gap Fire Department fire trucks parked on Main Street, the firefighters hosing down the last of the embers and the acrid, heavy scent of burned wood and plastic spoke the truth. *Oh, God. Dad.*

Rachel detoured from the chaos in front of the store and concentrated on getting to the hospital. Whatever had happened to the shop—and whether it was salvageable or not—would have to wait. It didn't matter, as long as her father was okay.

A few minutes later she'd arrived at the small local hospital and found her father's room. The hospital was quiet, save for the occasional beep of a machine and the low murmur of voices in other rooms. She ducked into his room, her heart in her throat.

Colton sat in the chair beside her father's bed. He had his head in his hands, his pale blue shirt smudged with soot, his hair and face mussed and dirty. He looked up when she entered and got to his feet.

"How is he?" she whispered. She almost didn't want to ask the question. Didn't want to hear that her father had some fatal injury or that he wasn't going to wake up. She could see his still body beneath the white sheets, looking thin and fragile.

"He's exhausted. Suffered some smoke inhalation, but he's going to be okay." Colton moved in front of her and waited until her gaze met his. "He's going to be fine, Rachel. Just fine."

She peered around Colton. To her, her father looked far from fine. "Are you sure?"

Colton cupped her cheeks and waited for her to look at him again. "Yes, I'm sure."

Only then did relief flood the places that had been

filled with panic. Only then could she focus on Colton for a second, on his sooty clothes and the way he smelled like smoke. "What happened to you? Why are you such a mess?"

"Because that damned fool jumped through the window to save this damned fool," her father muttered from the bed.

Rachel dashed to her father's bedside and sank onto the mattress. She took her father's hand in her own. "Dad. Are you okay?"

Her father's eyes fluttered open and he nodded. He coughed, then cleared his throat, but still his voice remained raspy. "Nothing a little time at home can't solve. Once they let me out of this place. Doctor wants me to stay overnight."

She pressed her cheek to her father's, so happy to have the rough stubble of his unshaven face against hers, to smell the Old Spice cologne he'd worn as long as she could remember. His cologne was mixed with the smell of smoke, but he was here, alive and complaining and exactly the way he'd always been. "What were you doing in the store late at night?"

"Got it in my foolish head that I wanted to check on things. I got all excited by today and talking to Daryl about fishing. Made me miss the place. I couldn't sleep—" he paused to cough "—so I walked down there and thought I'd just see how the old girl was holding up. Lightning hit the building and next thing I know, it's hotter than hell and I can't breathe. They say I passed out, but I don't remember much after the lightning."

She hugged him tight. Later, she would lecture him about going to the shop alone, in the middle of the night, especially with a storm in the air. But for now she had gratitude, and she didn't want to spoil that moment of blessing. "I'm so glad you're okay."

"Thank Colton," her father said. "I can't believe he did such a stupid thing."

"It wasn't stupid, sir. It was my job."

She turned to Colton and reached for his hand, drawing him into the circle of light cast by the lamp over her father's head. How did she get so lucky to have this man drop into her life at exactly the right time? She wanted to thank him, but her heart filled her throat.

"You're welcome," Colton said softly, then his gaze cut away.

Every time she thanked him or praised him, he brushed it off. Because he was humble? Embarrassed? She didn't care. He deserved the praise times a thousand. She squeezed his fingers. "See? I told you that you're a hero."

"No, I'm not, Rachel." His eyes clouded over and his body tensed. "Please stop saying that. I got lucky this time. It might not happen again." He walked to the door, then turned back to meet her confused, hurt gaze. "I'm glad your father is okay."

Then he turned on his heel and left the room. The scent of smoke still lingered in the air, but the danger had already passed.

Chapter Ten

Colton paced his room at the Stone Gap Inn then took a walk and finally returned to his room to pace again for the rest of the night—in the few hours of darkness left—feeling useless. Yes, he'd gotten Ernie out in time, but he hadn't been there soon enough to stop the fire, to stop Ernie from even entering the building in the first place. He should have seen it sooner, should have reacted faster. Maybe then Rachel's father wouldn't be lying in a hospital bed.

He wanted to do *something* but he didn't know what. He couldn't rewind time, couldn't correct yet another time when he had been too late—too damned late.

Damn.

He paced, he thought, he cursed. Then, shortly after dawn broke across Stone Gap and the sun began to fill his room with light, Colton had a plan. He had his phone out and was dialing before he realized how early it was.

Luke's groggy voice came across the phone line. "If you weren't my brother, I would have to kill you for waking me up this early."

Colton chuckled. "I'm sorry. I forgot what time it was."

"Then call me back when the little hand gets past the eight. You know which one is the little hand, right?"

"Don't hang up, Luke. This can't wait."

Luke sighed. There was rustling in the background while Luke got out of bed and let out another tired sigh. "Okay, shoot."

Colton explained about the fire, about what had happened to Ernie, then laid out his plan to his brother. After several days of seeing Luke and Mac, it was easier to think of them as his brothers. As part of his family. "I know Jack is due back from his honeymoon tomorrow morning, so I don't know if we can count on him. And I don't want to wait another day if I can help it."

"He's a Barlow. Of course you can count on him," Luke said. "You can count on all of us."

That sounded good to Colton's ears. Really good. "Thanks, Luke. I appreciate it."

"Did you tell Dad? Back in the day, he was pretty handy. Taught us everything we know." There was the sound of running water then the *glug-glug* of a coffeepot starting up. "And I know he and Ernie go way back."

"I wasn't sure if I should call him or not." Truth be told, Colton was feeling like a teenager who didn't want to be rejected. Yes, his father had invited him to Sunday dinner, but he hadn't talked to Colton otherwise. Colton kept holding off on reaching out. Okay, yeah, he was being a coward.

"You can't know if he'll say yes unless you do," Luke said. "But a word to the wise…"

"Yeah?"

"Wait till after seven." Luke chuckled. "I'll see you down there in about an hour. Okay?"

Colton hung up with Luke then got busy making a list of supplies. He left the inn, walked downtown to grab a cup of coffee at the Good Eatin' Café then drummed his fingers on the table, waiting for the clock to tick past seven. Once it did, Colton dialed his father's number, but got the voice mail. He left a quick, short message then hung up.

"Can I give you a refill?" Viv, the gregarious owner of the Good Eatin' Café, said as she approached his table with a fresh pot of coffee.

"Yes, ma'am. Thank you. That would be great."

"Brownie points for you, young man. You called me *ma'am*." She smiled and patted his shoulder. "I saw you and Rachel Morris here the other night. She's mighty lucky to have you. You two make a wonderful couple."

Colton wasn't so sure Rachel had him, nor was he sure she wanted him to be in her life after last night. Yes, she was grateful he had rescued her dad, but he should have been there sooner, gotten into the building faster. Then maybe Ernie wouldn't be lying in a hospital bed. And once he told Rachel what had happened to Willis and Foster...

That shining light in her eyes that saw him as a hero would definitely dim.

Viv let out a sigh as her gaze went out the window to the smoky, charred remains across the street. "Terrible thing what happened to Ernie's store. That man has been through enough. What with his wife being so needy all those years, then her dying and then poor Rachel trying to fill his shoes. Now this? Goodness, that family has had enough heartbreak to last a lifetime."

"I agree," Colton said. "Ernie's a real nice man. I got to know him pretty well this week."

"He's part of the same quality stock as most folks in this town. You're included in that." Viv pointed a finger at him. "You're a Barlow, through and through."

"Half Barlow."

"The better half," she said with a smile. "And you know, you may have come about being a Barlow in a little bit different way from Luke, Mac and Jack, but folks 'round here, they'll see you as the same. Just give 'em time."

"I'm not worried about what people think about me. I am what I am, and if they don't like it..." He shrugged.

"That is a good attitude to have." She patted his shoulder again. "Harry was right. You're gonna fit in just fine in Stone Gap."

He shouldn't be surprised that the owner of the diner knew just about as much about him as he knew about himself. It was, after all, a very small town, and word spread faster than chicken pox here. "I haven't decided if I'm staying yet."

She glanced at the paper on the table before him, the list he'd bulleted while he was waiting. A smile crossed her face. "Oh, you have already. You just don't know it."

The owner of the café walked away, just as Luke and Mac came in through the door and sat across from him. Viv came back with coffees for both of them and promised hearty breakfasts in a jiffy.

"I think we've got about everything on your list," Luke said. "The rest should be delivered at a *reasonable* hour of the morning."

Mac laughed. "You still complaining about having to wake up before noon? You know, you're about to be a married man, Luke. With a kid, at that. Those bachelor days of sleeping off a hangover are over."

"For your information, I was up late reading to a five-year-old who got scared by the storm." Luke gave Mac a *so-there* glare. "I have reformed my ways and have become a card-carrying family man."

"There is hope for humanity." Mac grinned then let out an *oomph* when Luke slugged him.

"So, did you call Dad?" Luke asked.

"Left him a voice mail." Colton shrugged. "I don't know if he'll show up."

"He'll show." Luke nodded. "Have faith."

That was the one thing Colton had lost a while ago. Faith. Especially in himself. In his future. Every time he thought he might be finding his way again, something like last night happened. A too-close call that reminded him of what he had lost.

The three of them ate breakfast, with Colton getting an extra order of bacon and toast after all, then paid the bill, leaving a generous tip for Viv, and headed across the street. The acrid smell of burned wood still hung in the air, and steam rose from what remained of the still-warm eastern wall of the shop. Half of it had crumbled in the fire, leaving the inside of the store exposed to the elements.

"Okay," Luke said, "let's get this party started." He reached in the back of his truck, pulling out sledgehammers, shovels and crowbars for the three of them. They set to work, dismantling the burned half of the building and stacking the debris to the side. By nine o'clock, the Dumpster had arrived, along with a delivery of fresh lumber, and most of the damaged parts had been pulled away.

A second pickup pulled into the lot and Bobby Barlow got out of the driver's side. He lumbered over, still limping a bit from his knee-replacement surgery a few weeks earlier. Colton found himself smiling, as if he was five years old again and his father had shown up at the father-son baseball game at school.

"Mornin'," Bobby said to his three sons. "Where do you need me?"

Luke waved at Colton. "Colton's in charge, so ask him."

Bobby turned to his oldest son. He looked a little uncomfortable, as if he'd rather ask anyone else on site what to do. But the other three Barlows were staring at Colton expectantly, so he cleared his throat and waved at the shop.

"We got most of the demo done," he said. "Luke and Mac are going to work on reconstructing the exterior wall. I was thinking you and I could rebuild the front counter."

"Sounds good. I've built a few cabinets over the years. Let's get started." Bobby unclipped a tape measure from his belt and walked into the empty store. He turned to Colton as he moved about the space. "You ever build a cabinet before?"

"Nope. Installed them, but never built one."

"It's not tough. Basically a big box. For one this long, though, you need to be sure you have enough interior support for the weight of the countertop. Now, are we making it the same as before?"

"I think that's the easiest option. That way, not too much changes inside the store."

"Ernie would like that. He hasn't changed a thing in this place for thirty years, and I don't expect him to go all crazy now. If it's the same, it's familiar, and that's going to make him more inclined to come back here."

"Then let's keep it the same," Colton said. Bobby called out some measurements, and Colton scribbled them onto a small pad of paper. Then they turned to the pile of fresh lumber sitting in the parking lot. Luke and Mac had set up a table saw on a couple of sawhorses repurposed into a worktable.

"Measure twice, cut once," Bobby said. He lifted one of the boards onto the table and stretched the tape measure along the side, marking where he was going to cut. "You want to cut?"

"Sure."

"Before you start," Bobby said, "make sure you adjust the blade height so the top of the blade is just above the board. It makes it more efficient."

Colton checked the blade, measuring it against the two-by-twelve, then brought down the blade guard. "Check."

"Be sure to keep your fingers far from the guard. I know it's there to protect you, but nothing's infallible. I like to keep my little finger against the fence when cutting something as wide as this. Helps guide the board and keep it all in place."

"Thanks." Colton did as his father instructed, feeding the board through the blade a little at a time. Bobby stood at the other end, helping guide the long piece of wood. They ripped several boards, one after another, working in concert. The plywood backer and top were cut next, then stacked to the side.

From time to time, Luke or Mac would glance over at them, but neither stepped in. The other two Barlows just kept to their own project, leaving Colton and Bobby alone. Other townspeople filtered into the space, lending a helping hand wherever it was needed, whether it was rebuilding the walls, or removing the damaged inventory or cleaning what could be salvaged. Before the little hand got past ten, almost two dozen people had shown up to help. Luke and Mac kept the extra helpers busy while Colton and Bobby worked on the counter.

Once the wood was cut, Colton and Bobby got to work assembling the counter base. "Let's drill the holes for the shelves now," Bobby said. "Easier to do it before assembly than to climb in there afterward. And that gives Ernie an option to move the shelves if he doesn't like the way we do it."

"All right. Let's make a template first," Colton said. "That way, they're all even."

"Good idea." Bobby nodded his approval, and Colton felt like a little kid who just got an A on a paper.

Colton tore off a piece of paper then measured out the right spacing for the holes. He held the paper against the board, and Bobby drilled the holes. When they were done, Bobby routed a groove a few inches above the bottom then held the first shelf steady while Colton screwed it in place.

"This bottom one should be set permanently in place," Bobby said. "Gives the whole cabinet more structural integrity. And by routing a groove for the shelf to fit into, we create an additional layer of support."

Colton helped his father repeat the process with the other side. As they worked together, filling in the center supports and creating the additional shelves, Colton began to anticipate Bobby's requests. They talked less and worked together more, developing a natural rhythm. The work filled the gaps in that awkward space between small talk and conversation.

A little while later Colton handed his father the last screw, and Bobby sank it into the plywood top. The laminate countertop would be delivered later, but for now the counter space was done. The two of them stepped back and assessed their handiwork.

The counter stood in the sun before them, eight feet long and smelling of freshly cut wood, a new beginning for Ernie Morris. But for Colton and Bobby Barlow, those few sheets of plywood were the start of something even more lasting. Something Colton had been searching for all his life, in those Christmases and birthdays and first days of school when he'd desperately wanted a father by his side.

Now he had him. Thirty years late, but that didn't matter anymore.

"Not bad," Bobby said, then reached out an arm and draped it across Colton's shoulders. For a second the embrace felt stiff, awkward, as Colton stood there, unsure of how to read this whole morning, the last few days, Bobby's distance.

"You know," Bobby went on, his arm still on Colton's shoulders, "there are some imperfections in this cabinet. Some would say it's not good enough, because it doesn't live up to the dream. But if you ask me, the knots in the wood and the nicks on the edge give it character. This piece is strong and solid and it's gonna last. It'll be here—" he met Colton's gaze, the mirror image of his own blue eyes "—for as long as you need it to be. You can depend on it."

Colton realized then that *this* was his father's way of bonding. With tools and wood and sawdust. "That's all I ask, Dad," he said. "That's all I need."

Bobby nodded, his eyes watering. "Me, too." A moment passed, Colton's throat tight, his heart full. Then his father gave him a hearty pat on the back. "Okay. Let's build something else…son."

Her father was not cooperating.

"I don't want to go home and rest," Ernie said as they left the hospital and got into Rachel's sedan. It was the same argument her father had given her since she came to pick him up that morning. The doctor had recommended he take it easy for a couple days, and that had set off a litany of protests from Ernie. "I don't want to spend one more damned day sitting in that house."

"But, Dad, you went through a lot last night and you should—"

"I should get back over to the store and see how bad the damage is. That's what I should do." Ernie put up a hand to cut off her objections. "I know I have spent a long time sitting at that kitchen table, having the longest pity party this side of the Mississippi. But I realized last night that I was just dragging you and the store and everyone around me down by doing that. I need to get back to work, Rachel."

"But, Dad, I don't…" She let out a long breath. "I don't think there's a shop to go back to. Harry said the damage was pretty extensive."

She hadn't wanted to tell her father that. She was afraid that if he knew the shop was gone, he would retreat to his cave again, and she'd never get him to leave. Maybe if she could keep him away until the insurance kicked in and everything was rebuilt…

"Then why are you taking the long way home?" her

father asked. "You know we're supposed to go straight down Main."

"I just think it's better if you wait—"

"Rachel Marie Morris, I am old enough to decide if I can handle seeing a little fire damage or not." Her father so rarely used her middle name or got stern that Rachel almost had to laugh. "So don't make my decisions for me, my darling daughter." His voice had softened, tempering the lecture.

"Dad, it's not a little fire damage. Harry said—"

"I heard Harry talking to you in the hall." Ernie reached out and covered her hand with his own. "And I appreciate you trying to keep the truth from me. I know you do it out of love. But isn't it about time this whole family stopped doing that with each other? And just faced the reality head-on?"

She braked at a stop sign and hung her head. Her father was right. For decades, none of them had talked about her mother's alcoholism. None of them had called her out on it. They'd made excuses and swept it under the rug, and when her mother got sick, her mother had played the same game, pretending the cirrhosis didn't exist until it was too late. In the year since, they'd tiptoed around their grief, as if ignoring it would ease the pain. But she was afraid, so afraid, that if she opened that door, the floodgates would burst. She was barely keeping her life under control as it was. "Dad, I can't do that. I can't…"

"Let me down?" His hand tightened on hers. "Because if that's what you think you did, let me tell you right now, you never did that."

She shook her head. Tears welled in her eyes. "I did. For too many years. I left you to take care of Mom and I shouldn't have. I just couldn't…couldn't see her like that."

"First of all, I loved your mother, loved her more than life itself, but she was a stubborn woman, and there wasn't anything you or I or God Himself could do to get her to listen. And second of all, I'm your father. It's my job to take those burdens on my shoulders so you don't have to. I've done a crappy job of it over the last year, and I'm sorry for that. I just got…lost."

"It's okay, Dad."

"If it's okay, then let's go see the store." He squeezed her hand again, and in his grip, she felt strength, determination. "Together."

"All right." She pressed on the gas pedal and made her way down Main Street toward the store. Maybe her father was more ready to see the damage than she expected. He was right; she shouldn't have to keep protecting him. He was a grown man, and one who had handled worse before.

"I really am sorry, Rachel," he said. "I left you to handle all this, and I never should have. And I'm sure as hell not leaving you to handle the rebuilding of the store. It's going to take some time, I know that, but—"

Her father cut off midsentence. Rachel followed his line of sight and gasped. The store, which she was sure would be all in ruins, was a hive of activity. The Barlows were there, building and cleaning, along with several other townspeople who had pitched in to help. There was a full Dumpster of charred lumber, but the new exterior wall was going into place, and she could see Colton and his father working on some repairs inside the store.

There was a lot of work left to be done, for sure, but the transformation was astounding.

She parked the car across the street, then she and her father got out. A table saw whined, punctuated by the pounding of a hammer. There was a low hum of voices, the occasional sprinkle of laughter. The sun was shining and the entire shop, while still half assembled, was taking on an air of a new beginning.

"Who did all this?" Ernie said.

"I don't know." As they crossed into the parking lot, Luke came up to them. His fiancée, Peyton, was beside him, along with a little girl wearing a bandanna and carrying a child-size hammer.

"Hey, Rachel. Ernie." Luke grinned. "Have you met my daughter, Madelyne?"

Rachel bent down to the little girl. "Hello, Madelyne. Are you helping today?"

The little girl nodded. "Uh-huh. Daddy's got me my own hammer. I'm gonna build a store."

Luke ruffled her hair. "Or at least part of one. Anyway, welcome to the madhouse."

"How…" Ernie turned and took in the busy scene. "When? Who…? I don't even know what to ask."

"Well, first of all, you're asking the wrong Barlow. This was all Colton's doing. He's the one who called us all and dragged us out of bed to put us to work." Luke pointed across the lot toward Colton, who was building a set of shelves with his father.

"Luke, why don't you show me what all you guys have been doing," her father said. "And Rachel, you go talk to Colton."

She arched a brow. Her father couldn't have been more obvious if he tried. But he walked off with Luke, leaving her to either tag along or do as he said. As she approached, Bobby wandered off, muttering something about going to get some more wood and nails, leaving her and Colton alone.

He looked so good, standing there in the sun, his face set with concentration as he measured and marked the shelving unit they had started. One of several they were working on, if the pile of cut wood beside him was any indication.

A faint dusting of sawdust covered his skin, powdered his dark hair and caught in the stubble on his cheeks. She thought of being in her bed with him last night, having his warm, long body against hers. It hadn't just been the lovemaking that she had enjoyed—because that had been outstanding—it had been the after, when Colton held her to his chest and pressed soft kisses to her temples. *That* was the man she was falling for—the man who would hold her in the dark then come here the next day and rebuild her father's shop without being asked.

And falling for him was a very dangerous proposition. He wasn't staying, and she wasn't sure where she was going. It was the worst possible time to get involved, to build a connection.

"What are you doing, Colton Barlow?" she asked.

He glanced up at her, and that lopsided smile she

had grown to love filled his face. "Making up for last night."

"Last night? That was…amazing." She blushed. Damn, she was like a schoolgirl.

He put down the tape measure and closed the distance between them. "I'm not talking about that part of last night. And I agree, yes, it was…incredible. I was talking about what happened to the shop. I…I didn't drive by soon enough or I would have seen the lightning strike, gotten your father out sooner. This—" he waved toward the pile of rubble filling the Dumpster "—wouldn't be like this if I had just been here at the right time."

"But you *were* here at the right time." She pressed a hand to his cheek. "You got my dad out safe and sound and got the fire department here fast enough to keep the entire building from going up. Not to mention, the whole block."

He looked away as if he was embarrassed by her praise. "I only did what anyone would have done."

"No, Colton, you did more. Much more." She released him, then looked around at the hive of activity. "I don't know how you got all this arranged and moving so fast. What about the insurance adjuster and paperwork and all that stuff?"

"I called Luke, and he called in a favor. There are some benefits to a small town. Like one insurance agent for everybody. We got Mike Simpson out of bed early this morning. He came over, did his analysis and took his pictures and is submitting the report today. Your dad should have his insurance money very soon."

"But then you did all this..." She waved toward the Dumpster, the wood, the supplies. "Did you pay for this yourself?"

He shrugged. "What's a Home Depot credit card for if you're not using it? Jack donated most of the supplies, and I filled in the gaps."

He'd done too much, Rachel thought, and she didn't know how to undo it. Everything her father had worked for, gone in a single night, until Colton came along and decided to make it right. "Colton, I can't let you do all this."

"Too late. It's done." He grinned. "Now, if you really want to thank me, then hold this end up while I fasten the board to the back."

She did as he asked, watching Colton work the screw gun to connect the shelf to the backer. He had done an incredible thing, and as much as she appreciated it, she was pretty sure there was some part of the story he was leaving out. And as much as her heart yearned to love him, her brain threw up a caution flag. She'd do well to listen.

She knew too well the damage that secrets and lies could do.

Chapter Eleven

There were few things in life that gave Bobby Barlow more joy than working with his sons. Even when they were little, he'd loved having the boys underfoot in the garage, or out in his workshop. Jack and Luke had followed in his footsteps, with Jack turning to wood-working and remodeling and Luke taking over the auto repair business, while Mac tinkered in his free time.

But working with Colton had been an entirely different experience. For one, the two of them didn't have decades of common language to draw from, like Bobby had with the other boys. For another, he was almost starting from scratch with Colton. For the ten thousandth time, regret filled Bobby that he hadn't been there during Colton's childhood. Would things have been different? Would Colton have lived here, been raised like one of the others? Or would they have a distant, difficult relationship, complicated by the miles apart and their different mothers?

He was proud of his sons, each and every one of them. Proud to be their father. But that didn't mean he didn't have a few million regrets about the kind of father he'd been.

And now there was Colton, who didn't seem to be in a hurry to leave town. A part of Bobby was happy— he really wanted to fill in the gaps of the last three decades. But as he talked to one neighbor after another during the rebuilding, and explained how Colton was related to the other boys, Bobby began to wonder if this whole thing was such a good idea. Maybe he shouldn't have come down here to help out. Maybe he shouldn't have drawn so much attention to the biggest mistake he'd ever made.

Della's Taurus pulled up and she got out of the car. They'd been married nearly thirty-five years now— just a few days from that landmark anniversary—but every time he saw her, his heart still leaped. She was curvy in all the right places, and though the red in her hair had dimmed a bit, she remained the sweet, loving, amazing woman he had married. He had been stupid when he'd been young, too scared of the prospect of *forever* to realize what he might have lost when he began that brief affair in Atlanta, but now, he knew he had hit the jackpot when it came to wives.

She was carrying a cloth grocery bag in one hand and a small cooler in the other. Bobby put down the drill he was using and crossed to her. "Here, let me get that," he said.

She giggled—even all these years later, she'd still giggle like a schoolgirl and for a moment he'd feel fifteen again—and gave him a quick kiss on the cheek. "Thank you, my knight in shining armor."

"I'm your knight in sawdust," he said, swiping some of the construction debris off the front of his T-shirt. "I wouldn't recommend getting too close."

"Oh, when has you being messy ever bothered me?" She swatted at some of the sawdust then gave him a second kiss. "I've brought some sandwiches and cookies for everyone. And a bunch of water bottles. It's hot out today."

"Thanks, honey. We can use it." He glanced over at the three boys, their heads together as they collaborated on something they were building. It was a nice sight, one that warmed his heart. Still, he worried about Della, about the ripples that were impacting her, the last woman to deserve this kind of thing. "Do you want to stay? You don't have to. I mean, we have this more or less under control."

"I…" She looked at her sons, gave them a little wave then returned her attention to Bobby. "I don't know what good I'd be. You know me and tools. I'm liable to break something before I fix it."

He saw Harry Washington heading their way. He liked the fire chief, but he could be a long-winded man, and the last thing Bobby wanted was to subject Della to a conversation about Colton. As much as possible, Bobby wanted to shield her from the subject. She'd

done nothing wrong, yet he could see the neighbors
even now, glancing between Colton and Della, whis-
pering about the state of the Barlow marriage. His
wife's reputation was tarnished merely by wearing his
ring, and that wasn't something Bobby liked at all.
"You don't have to stay," he said again.

"Okay." She laid a hand on his arm. "I have something else I need to do, anyway."

This was the third time this week that his wife had
said something vague about where she was going and
what she was doing. Bobby waved off Harry, signal-
ing that he'd be back in a second, then left the food on
the workbench and followed Della to her car. "Where
are you going?"

She shrugged. "I have an appointment."

"With a…divorce lawyer?" He said the words as
a joke, but frankly, ever since the truth had come out
about his affair and the son that relationship had produced, Bobby had been worried Della would leave
him. She'd be justified. What could he possibly say to
make her stay? *Yes, the entire foundation of our marriage is a lie. But I never meant to hurt you. I still love
you. I always have.*

She'd surely stop listening after the first sentence,
and he couldn't blame her. They had barely talked
about this whole thing in the days since she found out
about Colton. Every time Bobby tried to get up the
courage to broach the topic, his resolve faded again.
What if Della said that she was done?

So he pretended the topic didn't exist and made stupid jokes because he was a total idiot six out of seven days a week.

Della didn't answer him until she reached her car. His heart damned near fractured waiting for her to tell him he was being silly. She got to the Taurus, put her back to it and crossed her arms over her chest. "I'm doing something for myself, Robert."

"Okay. Like…a facial or something?"

"No. Something bigger than that. I don't want to say anything until I figure out if this is what I want." She let out a sigh and toyed with her car keys. "This whole thing with Colton really threw me for a loop. Everything I thought I knew about us, about you, was based on a lie."

Bobby wished the ground would just open him up and eat him whole. The last thing he ever wanted to do was cause pain to the only woman he had ever loved. "I don't know how many ways I can say I'm sorry, Della. I was a moron. I didn't realize how good I had it until I almost lost you."

"You best keep that in mind, Robert Barlow." She wagged a finger at him. "Women like me don't come along every day."

"Trust me, I know that." He gave her a grin, hoping it would lighten her mood, but if anything the line in her lips tightened.

"I think…maybe it's time I stopped being Mom and wife and maid and cook. I think it's high time I did something for me."

"Uh…okay." He could feel it in his bones. This wasn't going to end well. His heart was already starting to break, and he readied a thousand pleading sentences in his head. "Della—"

"Stop." She put up a hand. "Just hear me out."

"Okay." He nodded.

"You did a terrible thing years ago. The worst thing you could have ever done. And even though it's more than thirty years in the past, it's only a few days in the past for me. I'm still dealing with it and trying to see my way back to loving you."

Damn it. "Della—"

"Let me finish, *please*." She let out a breath and stared down at the keys in her palm. "I'll get there, Bobby, but it's going to take me some time. As for Colton, he's a wonderful young man, and I welcome him into our family. He did nothing wrong, and it wasn't his fault how he came to be or who he was born to. We can't undo the last thirty years, but we can't pretend they didn't happen, either."

"I know that. I just want to make it easier on you." He ached to reach out to her, but she was holding herself stiff, in that way that told him that touching her would only make it worse.

"By ignoring a son who needs you, even if he's grown?" She shook her head. "No, Bobby. That's not the way to do it. We are going to have this family the same way we always have—out loud. We've never been quiet people, and I'll be damned if I'm going to let some busybodies make me feel like I can't keep my family just the way it is, warts and all."

That sounded good to Bobby. Except for the unspoken *but* he heard in her words. "Okay. We'll make

Colton feel as much a part of the family as the other boys."

"And at the same time, I am going to start carving out my own little corner. I need that, Bobby. My boys are grown, my husband is busy with his own things—"

"Della, don't do this." Dread churned in his stomach. He wanted to rewind the clock three decades, be a better father, a better husband, a better man. "God, please, don't—"

She put up a hand. "After thirty-five years, Robert Barlow, one would think you would have learned not to try to guess what a woman is thinking. Especially this woman."

"You're right, but..." He didn't finish the sentence. He needed to let her say what she was going to say. Putting it off wasn't going to make the words any easier to take. "Go ahead."

"It's time for *me*, Bobby. To figure out what I want and where I'm going to go from here. So my appointment is something to do with that. I don't know how it's going to work out, and I don't want to tell you about it because I want this decision to be entirely my own. Not Della the mother or Della the wife. Just me."

"Will you..." He let out a long breath. "Will you be home tonight?"

A smile crossed her face, and she pressed a hand to his cheek. "Of course. You aren't getting rid of me that easily. Now go back to helping your sons and don't worry so much. We're Barlows. We're going to be just fine."

Then Della got in her car and pulled away. Bobby

watched her go, until the taillights flickered and the car disappeared around a curve. He wasn't sure what Della had just told him. Didn't know whether to be sad or hopeful.

He loped back over to his sons and sat on overturned buckets with them, eating sandwiches and drinking water, and praying for a miracle.

Colton knocked off for the day a little after six, as the sun began to sink in the sky and it got too dark to work safely. They cleaned up, then the three Barlow boys stood back to assess their progress. Bobby had gone home a little while earlier, but Luke and Mac had stayed, waving off Colton's offer to finish up on his own. They were good men, his brothers, and he was proud to be related to them.

"It's coming along nicely," Colton said.

"Yup. Glad Dad was here to make sure we did it right. He knows more than all of us put together." Luke let out a breath then turned to Mac. "Speaking of Dad, do you think he seemed a little...distracted today?"

Mac shrugged. "I don't know. Maybe. Or maybe he was just tired. This was a lot of work for him, and he's still recovering from his knee surgery."

"Yeah." Luke thought about that for a second longer. Didn't seem to come to a conclusion. He turned to his brothers and brightened. "Okay, well, I better get home."

"You do realize you look like a complete fool when you say that, don't you?" Mac said. "All grins and sighs. *Oh, I better get home.*"

"Hey, I have an amazing fiancée and daughter waiting for me. Of course I'm glad to get home. And you're the same way when it comes to Savannah, you big lug, so don't pretend you're any less *in love* than the rest of us."

"Colton's not in love. The only smart one in the family. We're all getting married, and he's still doing his own thing." Mac grinned. "Lucky stiff."

Luke scoffed. "I've seen the way he looks at Rachel Morris. And besides, look at what he did today. That's a man in love, mark my words."

"Hey, guys? I'm right here, you know," Colton said.

"Yeah, and you're a Barlow. Which means sometimes you need a wake-up call to see an amazing woman is right—" Luke pointed across the parking lot "—there."

Colton turned and saw Rachel standing there with a smile on her face. She was wearing jeans that hugged her thighs and outlined her amazing shape, and a pair of spaghetti strap tank tops, pink over white. He could see the pale pink straps of her bra beneath, and for some reason, it struck him as one of the sexiest things he'd ever seen. She had her hair down, loose around her shoulders, and he wanted nothing more than to bury his hands in those golden locks and kiss her senseless.

"See? Look at how he stares at her," Luke whispered to Mac. "How much you want to bet we have a fourth Barlow wedding in the near future?"

Mac thought a second. "Hundred bucks."

Luke laughed. "You must think Colton is made of stronger stuff than you or me."

"Again," Colton said, "I'm right here."

"That's right," Luke said. "You want in on this, too?"

Colton just laughed and shook his head then left his busybody brothers behind as he crossed to Rachel. "Hey," he said, because he didn't seem to have too many words in his head right now.

"Hey yourself." She smiled. Dazzling. Absolutely dazzling. "I managed to get my dad to stay home, but only with the promise that I would stop by and see how things are progressing."

So she'd come to check on the building, not to see him. He shouldn't be disappointed, but he was. "We got a lot done today. Do you want to do a walk-through with me? The power is still off, but it's light enough out to see pretty much everything we did today."

"Okay. Thanks." She followed along with him, stepping through the temporary door they had hung in the entry. It would be replaced with a new glass door tomorrow, but for now an old interior door was doing the trick.

Once they got inside, a wave of nerves choked up his throat. He'd done all this without permission or input, and suddenly Colton worried that he had gone too far. What if neither Rachel nor Ernie liked what Colton had done? What if Ernie wanted an entirely different design? Or what if Ernie wanted things exactly the same, and Colton had mangled the details?

He wanted Rachel to love the renovations. But the only way to find out if she did was to just show her and quit standing here like he'd lost his voice and his brains on the side of a highway.

"My dad and I rebuilt the counter," Colton said.

"The laminate should arrive tomorrow, and then that'll be done. We couldn't get the exact same pattern, but we found one that was close and has a more durable surface." He gestured to the left. "We hung shelves and pegboard behind the register, to give you more options for last-minute purchase items. I thought if people could see the things there while they were paying, they might add on to their order."

Rachel nodded. "That's a great idea. The whole thing is great, Colton."

He liked that she was pleased with the changes. He liked it more than he wanted to admit. Mac and Luke were right—Colton had a thing for Rachel Morris, and he suspected it wasn't a feeling that was going to go away anytime soon. It had started in this very shop, and had been quadrupled by the time they had spent together, that amazing night at her place and now this, watching her reaction to the work he had done on her father's store.

"Did I tell you that the shelves are all adjustable?" Colton went on. "So you can change the height of them to accommodate inventory changes." He stepped over a pile of lumber and put out a hand for her.

She could have gotten over the wood on her own, but she put her hand in his, anyway. "This is all fabulous."

He gestured toward the eastern wall. "We had to tear that entire wall down and rebuild it from scratch. The siding and Sheetrock should go up tomorrow, but for now we have a tarp over it, in case it rains."

"It all looks great. I can't believe how much you got done."

Colton kept moving, but didn't let go of her hand. "We also took the liberty of rebuilding the break room. The way it was set up before—"

"You couldn't open the door without hitting the table." She spun in the new space. It seemed bigger, brighter, even though it was the same square footage, just rearranged. The new design made so much more sense, she didn't know why no one had thought to do this before. "So you moved the door? And relocated the shelving to the far wall? Oh, and the counter is L-shaped now, instead of just one long piece."

"I was worried about changing it. I wasn't sure your dad would approve."

"Actually, my dad has wanted to do that for years. It's like you read his mind." She smiled at him. "Another great job here."

"No problem." He cleared his throat as if the praise embarrassed him. "Anyway, tomorrow we're going to run another waterline so you can have an ice-maker refrigerator."

They stood in the dim interior of the room where Rachel had eaten dozens of sandwiches, or sat beside her father while he drew pictures to keep his little girl occupied on the Saturdays she'd gone to work with him. It was going to be a slightly different, but much more efficient space. She could already see how much better it was going to work out, and how much easier it would make days at the shop. Not to mention the forethought and details Colton had put into the front of the store, with the adjustable shelves, the flexible space behind the counter.

Colton, it seemed, had thought of everything. He'd matched so much of the original store, it was as if he'd been the one working here for the last year. "How did you come up with all of this? I mean, you've only been in the store once. It's like you divined all the issues we've had over the years and fixed them in one fell swoop."

He shrugged. "I didn't sleep last night. I came down here, did a walk-through to assess the damage then went back to my room and drew up some plans. I'm no carpenter, so thankfully my father and brothers helped me fine-tune it. And I'm sorry not everything is here or in place yet. Some things we had to wait on and—"

She rose on her tiptoes and placed a kiss against his lips. "Thank you."

He seemed surprised, but a smile crossed his face and he kissed her back. "Oh, Rachel, you don't have to thank me."

"I do indeed. You went above and beyond, Colton." She curved into his chest and wrapped her arms around his back. He smelled of fresh-cut wood and fall air, and she thought she'd never before known a man to give as much as Colton Barlow had, to people who were essentially strangers. "You really know what matters most to people and just…do it. No wonder you're always saving lives."

He shook his head, as if he disagreed, then wrapped her in his arms, and when his gaze connected with hers, she felt as though she was in a fantasy world where everything was going to be just fine. That all these challenges and problems would pass in a blink. "I just hope with all the changes, and the new start, it's enough to get your dad back to work. So then you can go back to what *you* want to do."

She stepped out of his arms and let out a sigh. There was the real world again, intruding like an unwanted party guest. "I don't know if it's as simple as that."

"Of course it is." Colton gave her a grin. "Besides, I hear there's a girl named Ginny who really wants you to plan her wedding."

"How do you know that?"

"It's a small town, remember? And her fiancé was one of the ones who pitched in today. She came and brought him a soda and went on and on about how this was such bad timing, because she really wanted you to be free to, and I quote, 'plan the pinkest wedding this county has ever seen.'"

Rachel laughed. "That is what Ginny wants. And it would be the kind of big, bold, over-the-top wedding that would make the papers and give my business a nice boost of publicity."

"So...what's stopping you?"

The sun was nearly gone now, and the shop was almost too dark to see inside. It had become a space filled with shadows, instead of the new opportunities she had seen earlier when the sky was still light. "I don't want to leave my father shorthanded."

He snorted. "Is that all it is?"

She spun back toward him. "What do you mean?"

"I think you're afraid."

She scoffed. Colton didn't know anything about her. He couldn't tell her how she was feeling. Even if deep down she knew he was a little—okay, a lot—right. But still she protested, because admitting the truth meant dealing with the truth. "I'm not afraid of anything."

"You should be." He paused a beat. "Because I am."

That surprised her. This powerful man, who could rescue people and save buildings and transform a shell of a store, was scared? "Come on. You? What could you possibly be afraid of?"

He took a step closer, winnowing the space between them to almost nothing. A moment passed, another, and outside the streetlights came on and cast a shaft of gold down the center of the store. "I'm afraid of falling for you and falling for this town and changing my entire life to be here."

He was really falling for her? Those words had been more than just something said in the heat of the moment last night? And he was thinking about staying here?

"That's not so scary." She said those words, but inside her heart was pounding, and her pulse was racing. Because the whole idea scared the hell out of her, too. The very thing she never thought existed—a happy ending for herself—could be standing right before her, in this six-foot-two firefighter who gave more of himself than anyone she'd ever met.

"It is for me." He took her hands in his. "I told myself I was happy with my life in Atlanta. But that was a lie. And admitting that means I need to make a change."

"A change to Stone Gap?" She hoped so. Good Lord, did she hope so.

"Maybe. It depends on…a couple of things."

Once again, she got the sense that there was a wall between herself and Colton, something he wasn't sharing with her. Their relationship was new, barely a week old, but still, after last night… "Well, you've already got a job offer and a reputation as a hero, so—"

He spun away. "That is not what I want people to think of me."

"Why not? That's what you are. Running into a burning building and rescuing my father? That's heroic and amazing. I'm sure you did that dozens of times in Atlanta. Stone Gap would be lucky to have a firefighter like you on the force."

He cursed and kept his back to her. "I'm not what you think I am, Rachel. I'm not even close."

"Come on, no need to be modest. You did a great thing—"

He wheeled around, and even in the dim interior, she could see the flash in his eyes, hear the anger in his voice. "Is it a great thing to be responsible for two of your friends dying? For getting in that building too damned late, then watching the beams come down and seeing the fire follow like an angry, hungry beast, and then hearing the screams of terrified men? Then, the worst part of all, the part that haunts my dreams. Hearing the screams…stop." He shook his head and cursed again. "I'm not a hero. So quit saying that."

He stalked out of the break room. She waited a moment, taking in everything he'd just said, then followed and found him in the front part of the shop, staring out at the quiet street. No wonder Colton hadn't wanted to talk about his career as a firefighter. She couldn't even begin to imagine how painful and difficult something like that had been, to see and hear your friends die and know you were powerless to stop it.

But to her, that made him *more* of a hero, not less. Because he *had* tried, even when the odds were against him. He'd fought for the lives of others. And what's more, he had stayed with the fire department, and kept on running into burning buildings, like her father's store. That was a hero, whether Colton saw the truth or not. Rachel put a hand on his back. Colton tensed, but didn't move away.

"Colton, things like this happen," she said softly. "You can't save everyone."

"I *should* have saved them, Rachel. I could have. If only I'd been faster, faster into my gear, faster off the truck, faster into the building. I only needed a minute, maybe two, and I could have saved them." His voice was thick, the words catching in his throat. "But I wasn't, and they died, and I…I haven't been the same since."

"I'm sorry," she whispered and pressed her cheek to his back. She could feel the pain in his muscles, hear it in his voice. The regrets lay heavy on Colton Barlow, and he couldn't seem to find a way to let go of them.

"I can't work here," he said. "What if it happens again? In a town this small, everyone knows everyone. And if a guy dies because I'm not fast enough—"

"Stop that." She came around in front of him and

met his gaze. "Stop planning for things that you don't know are going to happen. Stop creating situations that may never exist. Accidents happen, whether you work for a fire department or a fast-food place. You can't predict when or where or how. And you can't beat yourself up for simply doing your job."

"If I was doing my job, they would have been alive."

"You *were* doing your job, Colton. And sometimes, that job doesn't turn out the way you want it to."

He shook his head, still not hearing her, not believing her. "Rachel, just stop trying to make me into something I'm not."

"You *are* a hero, Colton, whether you accept it or not. It's *you* that has to stop trying to make yourself into something that you aren't." She cupped his face and met his gaze. His eyes were dark clouds, filled with pain, regret and disbelief in her words, in himself. "You're not a failure. You're a good man who went through a terrible loss."

The wall in his eyes bounced the words away. Whatever demons Colton was facing were not going to be solved with one conversation in a dark, half-constructed shop. "Come on, let's go for a walk," she said.

"A walk?"

"I never did finish the twenty-five-cent tour," she said, taking his hand before he could argue. "And there's something I want you to see."

Chapter Twelve

Colton was tempted to turn around and tell Rachel to forget it, but her hand grasped his firmly and left no room for argument. They started walking down Main Street, just as the moon was rising in the sky and dappling the streets with pale white.

"So, what are we going to see?" he asked, because it was easier to concentrate on the walk they were taking through the darkened streets than on the shadows that dogged him still. It was as if his friends were following him, reminding him with every step that he couldn't escape his past.

"You'll find out when we get there." She shot him a mischievous grin then turned right onto Berry Lane, and then a few minutes later a left onto Mulberry Avenue. It was the neighborhood of berries, apparently, because he saw a Strawberry Drive and a Raspberry Lane on either side of them, and they had passed a Blueberry Drive a second ago.

"You're acting like a woman of mystery tonight," he said. "I like it."

Even in the light from the street lamps, he could see her blush. "One more street," she said, and they turned onto Blackberry Lane.

The houses here were all squat bungalows, with scrappy yards and pastel paint jobs. He could smell the ocean, hear its soft song, just beyond the trees. Sand gritted under his shoes as they walked, mixed with crushed shells that sparkled in the moonlight.

Rachel stopped in front of a sunflower-yellow house with white shutters. A swing sat in the front yard, drifting a bit in the breeze off the water. Somewhere in the distance, a dog barked and a boat motored across the sea.

"Okay, so here's the next part of the tour." She cleared her throat then took a serious stance and tone. "Stone Gap is a town rich in history. It was settled long ago, soon after the Pilgrims colonized New England. It took a while to get its name, but it's always been a special place, filled with its share of legends and stories."

Colton chuckled. "That's part and parcel of living in the South. I think all the Spanish moss inspires people to make up mythical tales."

"I agree. But this particular story is true. I know this, because I went to school with Arnie Teague, who is a direct descendant of the family that used to live in this house."

He looked past her at the bright bungalow. "Cute little house, though a bit yellow for my tastes."

"It wasn't always that color. Back in the day, it was the only house here. The Teagues owned this entire section of Stone Gap, in fact."

"Judging by the street names here, they were big fans of fruit?" He liked Tour Guide Rachel, with her serious stone-and-stern face.

"That's how they made most of their income. Winona Teague grew all kinds of berries here, canned them and offered them for sale, locally and, later, up the coast, sending the orders off with her husband, who was a ship's captain. The berries sold like wildfire, because they were rumored to make people fall in love. A little jam on a sweetheart's toast in the morning, and wham, a proposal would come by the end of the day."

"Clever marketing or truth?"

"Maybe a little of both." Rachel gestured toward a bench a few feet away. They walked down and took a seat, facing the little yellow house. A cat darted out of the shadows and under the bench, then wound its way between their legs. Rachel bent down and patted the cat, a scrawny orange tiger. "Winona's husband, Charles, loved her to death. Would have done anything for her. But he was a sailor, so he was away more often than he was here.

"One winter Charles had to make an unexpected trip. A delivery, I think, for a local merchant who wanted to get his goods up north. The weather was bad, but Charles needed the money, so he set sail. The storm kicked up, and several sailors returned home early. But not Charles."

The cat jumped over Rachel's lap and settled itself between them. Colton scratched the fur ball behind its ears, and it leaned into him with a purr. Colton barely noticed.

"A week passed," Rachel went on. "Another. A third. A month. Winona was inconsolable. As time passed and there was no word or sign of her beloved husband, her precious berries grew overgrown, and either rotted or were consumed by birds. The thing she loved most to do was forgotten, and the canning jars grew dusty. She spent more and more time inside that little house, weeping for a man she would never see again."

"And this story is supposed to make me feel better?"

Rachel smiled then put up a hand. "Just wait. After two months of this, Winona realized her appetite was gone, not because she was grieving, but because she was pregnant. The baby that she and Charles had prayed to have was finally on its way, but Charles wasn't here. Everyone told her to move on, forget her husband and start her life anew. She was a pregnant widow, and she would do well to find another husband. This was decades ago, remember, and women didn't have many options or life insurance plans."

"That had to be tough."

"But Winona was tougher," Rachel said. "She decided to believe that Charles was still alive and that he would come back to her. So she got back to living as if he was. She tended to the berries, canned the jams and jellies, cleaned her house and painted it a bright yellow color, so that he could see it from the ocean. She wanted to be sure that he had a beacon to guide him home."

"And what did the rest of Stone Gap think?"

"They thought she was crazy. They told her she should accept reality and let go of the impossible. Move on and quit believing in what wasn't real." Rachel's voice was quiet, dark, carrying a spell as the tale wove between them. "But she refused to listen. Every day, she'd dress in her prettiest dress, do her hair the way Charles liked it and make a dinner that he would enjoy. In between, she grew her berries and canned, and made enough money to keep up with the property and the taxes."

He was completely hooked on the story. He wanted to know more, to hear how it ended. The cat had fallen asleep, its tail twitching against his back from time to time, but Colton kept on rubbing the cat's head, his attention fixed on Rachel's words. "How long did she do this for?"

"Five months and two weeks. The baby was nearly here, and still Winona refused to let any other men court her or to give up on the dream of Charles coming home. One night there was a terrible storm, more terrible than the one that Charles's ship had disappeared in. Winona went into labor, alone in that little house, so sure she was going to lose her baby. For the first time in the months since her husband disappeared, Winona gave up on ever seeing him again. She was certain that she and her child would die that night, and she accepted that fact, because she knew they would be reunited with Charles. Maybe, she thought, this was what God intended for her and their child."

"This better have a happy ending, Rachel. I'm starting to get depressed." Seriously, thought Colton. He wasn't quite sure how Rachel saw this as a good way to pass the evening, not to mention help him see through the despair plaguing him. He might need to ask for his money back on the twenty-five-cent tour.

Rachel laughed. "Hold your horses, cowboy. The storm raged on, with the wind howling outside and beating up the little yellow house with branches and rain. Lightning flashed as bright as sunshine, over and over. And just as the baby was about to crown, the door burst open, and there, standing in the doorway, soaking wet and with a beard reaching his chest, was Charles."

"No way. Where was he all this time?"

"He'd wrecked on one of the barrier islands off North Carolina. It took him months to build a boat big enough and strong enough to get him back to his beloved Winona. But he'd done it, and just in time to help deliver his son."

It was a story that left even Colton a little choked up, but as touched as he was, no way was he willing to admit he had a couple of tears in his eyes.

"Charles said it was the bright yellow paint that got him back to the right place. As he neared the coast, he could see the house through the lightning, so he set his course and kept on going until he reached home. He knew Winona would never give up on him, so he never gave up on her." Rachel smiled, a soft, sweet look that touched her eyes.

"That and eating all that magic love jam."

She laughed. "Yeah, maybe that, too. But the point of the story, and the reason people still tell it to this day, is that it should remind you that all is never lost. That there's always hope for a new beginning, for a new start."

He knew what she meant. That just because he had watched a tragedy unfold before his eyes, powerless to stop it, didn't mean that he wasn't a good firefighter. Didn't mean he couldn't take this job in Stone Gap and find a new life here. Maybe with Rachel. Maybe in some little yellow house on the water with berries growing in the yard and the ocean breeze drifting in through the windows.

A part of him really wanted that. Could even picture it, seeing Rachel standing in that yard, waiting for him to come home. But then he reminded himself that dreaming of a new future and actually having it were two different things. It was entirely possible that Harry would rescind the job offer once Colton told him about Willis and Foster. Then Colton would have to go back to Atlanta, back to the small brick building where the other men gave him those looks of pity and sympathy, and where every corner held a memory of the friends he had lost.

He could go back there, but where would that leave Rachel? He thought of the little hardware store, and knew she intended to go right back to working behind that counter instead of pursuing her own dreams.

"I'm not the only one who should remember the lessons from Winona and Charles," Colton said.

"What do you mean?"

He sat on the bench, his arm draped on the back, fingers brushing against her shoulder. The cat stirred in its sleep but didn't move, like a furry wall between them. "You have a chance at a new start, Rachel, once the shop reopens and your dad goes back to work, yet you keep dodging the answer of whether you are going to take it."

"I'm not dodging anything. I'm just helping my dad."

"Which is noble and wonderful. And which is what you have been doing for a year now, while the business you started withers away."

"There are only so many hours in the day, Colton." She scowled. "I couldn't keep both going."

"Couldn't? Or chose not to?"

She spun toward him. "What are you talking about?"

"You could have hired someone part-time for the hardware shop. Or worked at night on the wedding planning business."

"Easier said than done." She blew her bangs out of her face. "The shop has been struggling financially. I couldn't afford to hire someone else to work there. I barely took a paycheck myself all year."

This was where it got difficult. Where Colton had to say the things to her that he was pretty sure she already knew, but hadn't acknowledged. Things he was pretty damned sure he should also say to himself, but it was far easier to lecture Rachel than to face the same truths himself. "Don't you think you could have asked any of the dozens of people in this town who showed up throughout the day today to help rebuild, to take a shift or two for free? All I heard from the folks of Stone Gap was what a great guy your dad was and how they were more than willing to do what it took to help him get back on his feet. All you would have had to do was ask, Rachel, and I bet they would have lined up to help."

She shook her head. "It's not that simple."

"Why not?"

"Because it had to be me. Because I owed him." She jerked to her feet, scaring the cat. It jumped from the bench with an angry yowl and disappeared into the woods. "You don't understand, Colton, so stop pretending you do."

"If anyone in this world understands owing people, it's me." Colton crossed to her and took her hands in his. "We're so much alike, Rachel. Both of us trying to make up for mistakes we didn't even make."

She shook her head and tugged her hands out of his, putting distance between them again. The ocean whooshed in and out, like one of those white noise machines playing behind them. But it didn't ease the stress in Rachel's face.

"But *I* did make this mistake." Her voice was soft, broken. "I ran away when I should have stayed. I just couldn't...couldn't handle my mother another day. She drank and she got mean and she was so much to take care of. I was young and selfish and just wanted... space."

He could understand that. There were many days

when he was younger when he'd wanted to just leave town and not be responsible for his mother and sister. He'd wished he didn't have to be the "man" of the house and he could have just been an ordinary kid. "There's nothing wrong with that. We've all had those moments."

"But I left my father to deal with her. And when she got sick, my dad did everything alone, instead of telling me. He wanted me to keep working at my business, to pursue my career. By the time I found out…it was too late." She bit her lip and swiped at the tears welling in her eyes. "The least I could do for him was to run that shop while he grieved for however long it took."

"And put your own life on hold."

"I…I had to." Now the tears in her eyes brimmed and spilled over. Colton reached up and caught them on his thumb, wiping them away.

"How long are you going to let fear run you, Rachel?" he said.

"I'm…I'm not afraid." The words wobbled, and he knew he'd hit a truth.

"Oh, honey, you are. And that's totally okay." He drew her into his arms, not caring that her tears dampened his shirt. Colton was a man used to rescuing people. And once again, he couldn't rescue this one. If Rachel wanted the life she deserved—the life she had walked away from a year ago—she was going to have to be the one to go out there and get it.

There was probably a message in there for him, too, but he was going to have to shelve that for now.

"Take a chance," he whispered against her. "Take that leap."

She held on to him for a long time while the ocean crashed against the shore and the little yellow house stood bright and determined under the moon. "I wish I could, Colton," she said.

Then she walked away. He let her go, because he knew that until he was ready to take his own advice, he was never going to have the right words to convince Rachel to do the same.

Rachel woke up Saturday morning and lay in bed for a long time, staring at the ceiling. She missed Colton. Her hand snaked across the empty space beside her, but found only cold sheets. She'd dreamed about him, a dream so vivid, it seemed as if he should be here.

But he wasn't.

And a lot of that was her fault. He tried to get close to her, and she pushed him away. She kept undermining the very thing she wanted.

He was an incredible man. Considerate, loving, giving. He'd rushed in there and saved her father when another person might have run from the flames. He'd gone and single-handedly spearheaded the rebuilding of her father's store, and for no other reason than to help him. And he had made love to her in a way that had left her breathless and feeling like the most treasured woman on the planet.

All of which terrified her. How many years had she been planning weddings and dreaming of the very same happy ending for herself? Now that she had finally met a man who could fit the image she'd long wished for herself, she was afraid it would all pop, like a balloon.

Either way, she needed to focus on her father for now. Colton Barlow—and all he represented and all the questions he raised in her heart—would have to wait. Okay, so maybe she was making excuses, but she really didn't want to answer the questions that Colton had asked her last night.

She swung her feet over the bed and got up before she was tempted to lie there another second. A few minutes later she had showered, changed into old jeans and a T-shirt and pulled on some sneakers. She swept her hair into a ponytail and grabbed a granola bar and a water bottle on her way out the door. A little past seven, she pulled into her father's driveway and knocked on the door.

To her surprise, her dad opened the door. For almost a year, she'd knocked and gotten no response, and always ended up letting herself in. But there was her dad on the other side of the door, already dressed, his hair combed, his face shaved and a hot cup of coffee in his free hand. "Good morning."

She blinked. "Wow. You're up and ready, Dad?"

"Yup. Figured it was about time I got my act together."

"Are you feeling okay? Shouldn't you be resting—"

He put up a hand to cut off her words. "I feel fine. And I'm going to feel a lot better when I get out of here and over to the store. Sun's been up for thirty minutes already, and time's a-wastin'."

She laughed. This was the father she remembered, the can-do man who would work all day and then take her out in the yard to play catch or build a birdhouse. In her memory, her dad was tireless, a superhero she could always count on. "Okay, but what about breakfast?" She started to brush past him. "I can make some eggs and toast—"

"Already ate. I left you a plate on the stove. But eat fast, will you? I want to get down there as soon as I can."

Rachel turned to her father. "Who are you?"

His gaze softened, and a smile filled his face. "The dad you used to have."

That made Rachel's eyes water. Good Lord, she had cried more in the last few days than in the last year. She drew her father into a tight hug and said a silent prayer of thanks.

He patted her back. "Okay, okay. Enough of this before we turn into weeping willows. Eat your breakfast and we'll go."

She took a seat at the table. The roles had reversed, she realized, when her father put a plate before her and poured her a cup of coffee. Maybe her father was more ready to go back to his life than she thought.

How long are you going to let fear run you?

Was Colton right? Was she avoiding her business because she was afraid? Afraid that it had sat by the wayside for too long and may never recover?

Yet another set of questions she was not going to answer today. Or at least not right now.

Her father sat down across from her and sipped at

his coffee. "Before we leave, I wanted to talk to you about your mother. I know you've been bothered by what happened last year. And I just didn't talk about it, no matter how many times you tried to bring it up."

"It's a painful subject, Dad. It's okay."

"No, it's not okay." He let out a long sigh. "Not talking about the painful subjects is how we got to this place. With me sitting at the kitchen table, working on the same crossword puzzle all damned day. And with your mother, getting to the point where the cirrhosis was irreversible before she told us about it."

Rachel fiddled with her toast. "Maybe because we all perfected that over the years. Not talking about her drinking, not talking about how she had changed."

"Acting like if we pretended it didn't exist, it would stop being a problem?"

Rachel nodded. "Yeah."

"I loved your mother, Rachel. Loved her more than I can even say. But I failed her. I didn't stop her. I couldn't stop her. I tried, Lord knows I tried. Three times, I put her into rehab."

Rachel had never known that. She'd always thought her father had looked the other way, ignoring the truth for years. "You did?"

"When you were away at school. I thought maybe she'd get clean and we could have some semblance of family life. But every time, she'd come home and start again. It was as if she couldn't shake those demons, no matter how hard she tried."

"She was stuck in a rut, too scared to climb out of it." Gee, who did that sound like? Rachel realized she was doing the same thing, only she was using the shop instead of alcohol as a reason not to move forward. Except moving forward was a lot easier to think about than it was to do.

"I guess that's what kept me in this house for a year." Her father sighed. "I always felt like I had let your mother down. If I had tried harder or pushed her more…"

"We both should have, Dad," she said. The sunshine-shaped clock in the kitchen ticked past the hour, as it had for most of Rachel's life. So many things in this kitchen had stayed the same, stuck in a time warp. Her mother hadn't changed anything, not the stoneware pattern or the curtains in the window. Everything the same, day after day. "Honestly, I don't know if anything we could have done would have made a difference. She was the one who had to want a change, and we couldn't force that. Only encourage and support it."

"You're right, but that's a hard truth to accept," he said. "Maybe we all just needed to try harder."

"And maybe I shouldn't have gone away to school or worked so hard and left you to deal with all this." She sighed.

"I don't blame you, honey, for staying at school and working all the time. You saved yourself, and you have to do that."

She covered her father's hand with her own. "I did it at the expense of you. That's not right."

"It's exactly right." He patted the back of her hand and his eyes softened. "What do they tell you on the airplane? Put the oxygen mask on yourself before you put it on someone else. You saved yourself, and got yourself out of this situation so that you could grow up and be happy and healthy. And when you were strong enough, you came back and saved me."

She thought of the last year, of all the time and energy she had given to the man who had scared the monsters out of her childhood closet and taught her how to fish. Hours she would gladly give again and again.

He drew her into his arms. His cheek was smooth, scented with the familiar cologne she'd known all her life. His hug was firm and solid and comforting. "I love you, too. All the way to the moon…"

"And back," she whispered. "All the way back."

Chapter Thirteen

Colton stood in Harry Washington's office on the second floor of the brick building housing the Stone Gap Fire Department at an ungodly early hour on Saturday morning. Harry was eating a glazed donut and sipping from a giant coffee mug.

Harry had called last night and asked him to come by and meet before reconstruction got underway for the day at the hardware store. Harry had said they needed to talk before the sun got too high in the sky and ruined the day for man and beast. He gestured toward the seat opposite his desk and waited for Colton to take a seat. "Coffee?"

"No, sir. I'm good. Thank you."

"I can't start the day without a caffeine drip. My wife keeps trying to sneak decaf into my cup. Says I'm too high-strung," he scoffed. "You know what makes me high-strung? Drinking decaf. Waste of hot water, I say."

Colton chuckled. "I agree."

Harry leaned back in his chair and put his feet up on the desk. "So, you going to start with the department as soon as you can settle your affairs in Atlanta? Because I'm a man short, and you're just the firefighter I need to fill some empty boots."

Colton had thought about Harry's job offer most of the night. He'd tossed and turned, thinking about Willis and Foster, thinking about the mistakes he had made, the moves he wished he could do over and the regrets that hung heavy on his shoulders. Every thought circled back to the same thing—one of the last things Rachel had said to him yesterday.

There's always hope for a new beginning, for a new start.

Hope. An emotion he hadn't allowed himself to have in a very long time. Maybe he needed to start looking forward, instead of wallowing in a past he couldn't change. But first he needed to be honest with Harry Washington, so that if he did come to work at the Stone Gap Fire Department, it was with a clean slate.

"There's something you should know first, sir," Colton said. "And if it changes everything, I understand."

Harry dropped his feet to the floor and leaned forward. "Okay. Shoot."

Colton ran a hand through his hair and let out a breath. Even now, months later, talking about that night was akin to dragging a fish hook up his throat. "About six months ago, I...I lost two of my guys. I was the incident commander, and this was one of my first big fires. We got the call at 1320, rolled out at 1326 and pulled up on scene at 1338." All those details didn't matter, but somehow, delivering the information like an incident report made it easier for Colton to talk. "We secured a water supply, and I assigned Engine 4 to ventilation, keeping Engine 3 on fire attack. The building was almost fully engulfed before we got there. Access was impeded by an adjacent construction site."

Harry just listened, nodding once or twice. Colton went on, the words coming slower now. "I had a lot to assess when I first got on scene, a lot of pieces to set into place, you know?" How could he describe how overwhelmed he felt? Even though he had almost eight years of experience with the department, that first time when it was all on his shoulders—

Colton cleared his throat. "The building was a known location for transients. We had a report of a man trapped inside, and at 1358, I sent two of my most experienced guys in to attempt a rescue. Soon after they entered the building, the winds shifted, which forced the fire into the location where my men had gone. The flames had already leaped to the second floor, and—" Colton paused, forced the words out of his throat "—there was a catastrophic failure of the roof. My men were trapped under the debris. Engine 3 attempted an extraction, but—" He shook his head and let out a curse. He could see it now, the falling timbers, the way the fire chased behind, eager and hungry. The screams, oh, God, the screams. Colton had to struggle to keep his composure, to breathe. To speak. "I'm sorry, sir. The two men were DOS and I—"

"What were their names?" Harry said, his voice quiet.

"Sir?"

"What were the names of the men you lost?"

"David Willis and Richard Foster." He hadn't spoken their full names since the incident. As soon as he did, he could see David's wide grin, hear Richard's deep laughter. He could see them raising a beer at the Pint & Slice after a hard day on the job, hear them teasing him about his terrible cooking skills. As soon as Colton said their names aloud, they were alive again in his head, and that made the loss sting ten times more.

Harry nodded. "You write those names on the inside of your helmet, Barlow. Write David Willis and Richard Foster in big letters so you see their names every time you turn out. You remember them, son, and you remember that you are only human, and try as you might, you won't be able to save them all. You'll save the ones you can and remember the ones you can't."

Colton swallowed hard. "Yes, sir."

Harry leaned forward and crossed his hands on the desk before him. "When I was two years into this job, I lost a man. His name was Joe Dunlap. I've never forgotten that, and never forgotten him. His name is written inside my helmet, inside my coat and inside here." He leaned back and pulled open the center drawer of his desk. "He's my DOS, Barlow, but he's never going to be dead in here." Harry smacked at the space above his heart. "That's what keeps us from getting burned out. From getting to the point where we don't care. It's what gives you heart. And that's the kind of man I want in my department. One with heart."

"Sir, are you sure—"

"I saw you out there, rebuilding Ernie Morris's place with your bare hands. You didn't do it because he was going to give you a lifetime supply of fishing tackle—though if he does, I want in on that action." Harry grinned. "You did it because you have heart. Soul. That's why I don't give a crap about your résumé, Barlow. I don't care what's on a piece of paper or on an incident report. I care about what's inside the man. And what's inside you is exactly what I want to hire." Harry got to his feet and put out a hand. "So... what size uniform should I order?"

There was a definite spring in her dad's step as he headed out to Rachel's car later that morning, as if a weight had been lifted from both of them by finally talking about the subjects they had avoided for years. Maybe there was something to this facing your fears thing that Colton kept urging her to do.

In the car, they chatted about the work Colton had done the day before on the short ride over to the shop. As Rachel turned onto Main Street, she stopped dead. "Oh, my God. There's got to be fifty people there, helping."

Her father's eyes filled as he took in the dozens of parked cars, the multitude of people working on the job site, as busy as bees in a hive. "All these people? Helping me?"

"It looks like that, yes." A lump formed in Rachel's throat. She'd known Stone Gap was filled with good folks, but this many? Being this generous? To her dad? It was overwhelming and touching. And wonderful.

"Well, then, let's get to work," her father said. "Best thing I can do is open up the store as soon as possible, and thank everyone by being ready to help someone catch the biggest fish at this year's derby."

Rachel parked, and the two of them headed toward the store, her dad moving faster and with more eagerness than she had seen in a long time. It was good to see her father so excited about his business again, as if this setback had recharged him, rather than added to his despair. She hurried to keep up with her dad, then slowed her step as she neared the center of the construction site.

Colton stood in the middle of the parking lot, a pad of paper in his hands and a circle of people around him, waiting for him to dispense directions. He was wearing jeans and another button-down shirt, with the sleeves rolled up. The morning breeze ruffled his dark hair.

Dad leaned into Rachel. "That man's a keeper, I'm telling you."

"You might just be right about that, Dad."

"I'm your dad, I'm right about everything." He winked then strode forward and into the crowd. He grabbed Colton, gave him a quick hug and thanked him for his help. "Now, what do you want me to do?"

Colton greeted her father with a clap on the shoulder. "Morning, Ernie. Nice to see you here and glad you want to help. If you could direct people inside, that would be great. We need help restocking the inventory that we saved, and figuring out what needs to be reordered."

"Can do. I know that shop like the back of my hand." He grinned. "Can't wait to get back in there."

Rachel watched her father head off to the shop and marveled at the change in him. She had all but given up hope that he would ever get back to his old self. She felt that lump in her throat again, and thought if she didn't get busy doing something, she was going to turn into a sobbing mess right here in the parking lot.

"You want something to do, don't you?" Colton said.

"How'd you know?"

He just grinned and took her hand. "Come on, help me sand these shelves."

She gave the long boards a dubious look. "I don't know anything about sanding shelves."

"Good thing I do." He handed her a rectangular block of sandpaper. "Go with the grain and keep your strokes even. Nothing too hard and fast, or you'll create a divot, and you don't want that."

"Divots are bad?" She gave him a teasing grin.

His gaze slid over her, hot and slow. "Depends on where they are."

"Yes, indeed. Some divots are very good."

"Maybe later," he murmured against her ear, sending her pulse racing, "we can explore some of the very, very good divots."

"Maybe, Colton. If you're good."

He chuckled. "I'm good. Very good."

That made her mind go down some very dark, very naked paths. "Uh, I should get to work on this before…" Before she did something crazy.

She took up a space at one end of the board, Colton at the other. She tried to concentrate on sanding, but every fiber of her being was aware of him, just a few feet away. Every once in a while, she caught the scent of his cologne, or saw him smile, and her heart did a little flip.

"So, how did you learn how to do all this stuff?" she asked, because if she didn't start making conversation, she was pretty sure she'd start kissing him.

"Actually, I didn't. Not until this week, anyway. I mean, I knew some basic stuff—my uncle Tank showed me how to do things like paint a wall and replace the washer in a faucet. But working with my dad…" He smiled. "It was great. Really great."

"I'm so glad. I'm happy things are going well for you."

"Actually, things are going really well all around." He stopped sanding and turned toward her. "You're looking at the newest member of the Stone Gap Fire Department."

"You took the job? That's great. That means you'll be staying in Stone Gap."

She should have been excited. Overjoyed. Instead, this weird little fissure of fear ran through her. Colton was staying in Stone Gap, which meant there was no excuse not to get involved with him. No excuse not to risk her heart.

Except…risk. Yeah, she wasn't big on that. In any area of her life.

"So I was thinking…" Colton started to say, when a car pulled into the lot, decorated with Just Married in fading chalk paint on the windows. Jack and Meri emerged and were immediately surrounded by townspeople and the Barlow family. "Hey, Jack is back."

"Let's go say hi," Rachel said, because then she could put off the conversation she was having with Colton. The one where he asked her for more, and she had to decide if she wanted to take that risk.

She'd seen happy endings, and she'd seen heartbroken endings. What guarantee did she have that her own would be happy, like Jack and Meri? Or Luke and Peyton? Mac and Savannah?

"Rachel!" Meri broke out of the crowd and came over to Rachel, drawing her into a hug. "Just the person I wanted to see!"

Rachel had known Meri in high school, and had helped Meri over the years with finding gowns for her pageants. That had led Rachel into becoming a wedding planner, because she found she really enjoyed the planning, the shopping, the process of helping someone else create a fantasy. Now Meri was working as a photographer and settling into life in Stone Gap as Jack's wife. "Congratulations again. I hope you had a wonderful honeymoon."

"I definitely did." She smiled, the kind of secret smile that only women in the in-love club had. "If you want to marry a good man, marry a Barlow."

Rachel definitely wasn't thinking about marrying

anyone. Especially not Colton Barlow. Yet her gaze strayed to him, talking to Jack, the two brothers looking so much alike they could be twins. Luke and Mac joined them, the four brothers joking and laughing as if they'd been together all their lives. Colton had fit right in with his family, with this town. With her.

"So, are you still doing the wedding planning?" Meri asked.

"I..." Rachel saw her father, bustling in and out of the store, his arms filled with boxes of supplies. He looked energetic and excited and raring to get back to work. "Yeah. I am."

"That's awesome!" Meri grabbed Rachel's hands. "What do you think about joining forces? I'm trying to get my photography business off the ground, and I'd be glad to give your clients a break on my rate."

That would be a wonderful thing to offer in her wedding packages, and she knew Meri would do a terrific job. "That's awesome, Meri. Yes, definitely. And just in time, because Ginny wants me to plan her wedding."

"Great! I'm surprised I didn't hear about her engagement all the way in the Bahamas, given Ginny's power of publicity," Meri said. "I'd love to help you. It should be a win for both of us."

"I agree." The free advertising with Ginny spreading the word was yet another reason why handling the former debutante's wedding would be great for business. In that moment Rachel decided to take the leap. To call up Ginny, agree to take on the rushed, too-pink, too-loud wedding from hell and recharge her business in a big way. "It'll be awesome to work with you, Meri."

Meri drew Rachel into a one-armed hug and the two of them faced the quartet of Barlow men. "So, when are you going to be planning your own wedding? Don't give me that look. News of you and Colton did, in fact, reach the Bahamas." Meri laughed. "Blame Luke. For a former playboy, that man is a huge romantic."

"Let me just get back to the business of planning other people's happy endings," Rachel said. "And leave my own for...later."

"Uh-huh. If I remember right, I was saying the same thing myself a few months ago." Meri wagged her left hand and the sparkling diamond band sitting there now. "Things can change in a blink of an eye, so be ready."

Rachel let out a little laugh. "I've never felt less ready for change in my life."

Meri looked her in the eye. "If you ask me, that's the best time to fall in love."

Chapter Fourteen

Colton's mother Vanessa took the news poorly. She started to cry on the phone, saying she would never see her son again. Colton assured her he would visit Atlanta often and that Katie would drive down to see him and bring their mother along. His mother never had handled change well, but Colton hoped that without him to rely upon, she might finally be more inspired to take charge of her own life.

Katie, on the other hand, was overjoyed. "So, what's this town like? Lot of single men?"

Colton laughed. "I'm not exactly checking out those particular stats. But...there is one woman I really like."

"Oh, really?" Katie let out a low whistle. "I never thought I'd see the day when you considered settling

down. I thought you said you didn't want to have anyone depending on you ever again."

"Rachel isn't like that. If anything, she's trying her
best not to depend on me for anything at all. She's determined and stubborn and—"

"In love with you? Because you sure sound in love
with her."

"Me? No. No way. We haven't known each other
that long."

Katie laughed. "That is an awful lot of denials, big
brother. I think you fell hard and fast, and I think she's
part of the reason you're staying in that town."

"Maybe…" He wasn't going to give any more of
an affirmative than that. For one, it was too soon, like
he'd said.

On the other hand, he couldn't put Rachel from his
mind. When he was standing right next to her, all he
wanted to do was kiss her. When she was away from
him, she lingered on the fringes of his every thought.
He wondered what she was doing right now. On a Saturday in a town so small, someone could sneeze and
they'd hear it on the other side of the street. Was she
thinking of him? Was she out with friends? Walking
the beach? Curled up in bed with a good book?

"Maybe?" Katie said. "Sounds pretty definite to me.
I'm happy for you, though. Really happy."

"And a wee bit envious?"

"Maybe." His sister sounded a little distant. She
usually kept whatever she was going through to herself, and that made him worry about her.

"Why don't you come down and visit once I get

settled in for real?" Colton suggested. "And check out the single male population for yourself?"

Katie let out a faux gasp. "Are you telling this work-aholic to take a vacation?"

"I am indeed. An entire week would be great. Maybe even give you a minute to catch your breath."

Katie thought for a second. "Okay, I will, but only if you introduce me to this woman who has your head all ajumble."

"'Ajumble'? Is that even a word?"

"It is now." Katie laughed again. "All right, speaking of work, I have to get back to my job. I'll see you soon, big brother. Good luck with the new job."

Colton said goodbye then hung up. The sun had gone down, so work on the hardware store had come to a halt an hour ago. There were a few things to finish up first thing tomorrow, then the rest would wait for the shipment of replacement inventory. All in all, though, Ernie should be able to open up on Monday morning and get right back to work.

Colton should have been pleased with the work he had done, the changes he had brought to this little corner of the world, but something was missing. No, not something. Someone.

Was he really going to wait for her to come to him? Or was he just going to go take the risk, tell Rachel how he felt and then see where it went from there?

A few minutes later he was standing outside Rachel's apartment door. He knocked then waited, as nervous as a seventh grader heading to his first dance. She pulled open the door, looking sexier than he'd ever seen her in a pair of yoga pants and an oversize tee that hid her curves, but left his memory to fill in the blanks. "Sorry for coming by so late, but I really wanted to see you."

"It's fine." She smiled that dazzling smile that nearly took his breath away. "Do you want to come in?"

"I do. Very much." He pulled his hand out from behind his back. "These are for you. They're not as nice as the ones I got from the flower shop, but I picked these myself. I'm hoping they weren't anyone's in particular, or you are going to have a very angry Stone Gap resident on your door in the morning."

"They're beautiful." She took the bouquet of wildflowers, a jumble of pinks and purples and yellows, and brought it to her nose. "Where did you find them?"

"Remember that old, abandoned haunted house you showed me? I had seen them in the back of the house that night, and I thought that if flowers could grow in a place like that, one that had been neglected for so long, that maybe there was hope for anything to grow in this place. Or anyone. Like me." He stepped inside her apartment and nudged the door shut. He decided to just get straight to why he was there. No more delaying—hadn't he put everything on hold long enough? "I've gone a long time with just…standing still. I want more, Rachel."

"More? Like what more?"

"Like a future with you. I know it's too soon, and too fast, and a thousand other things, but I started falling for you hard from the very first day. I mean, how many women does a man meet who are beautiful, talented at fishing and fabulous shortstops?" He grinned. "You're one of a kind, Rachel Morris."

He'd realized on the way over here that he didn't want to lose her. He didn't, in fact, want to spend another day without her. He loved the way she lit his heart when she smiled, the way she asked more out of him and made him expect more of himself, the way she surprised him with things like the tour of the town or a little-known fact about herself. She was everything he'd always been looking for—even if he didn't realize that until he found it.

"A future?" Her eyes were wide, and she was shaking her head. "You're right. This is too soon and too fast and—"

"And what are you afraid of?"

She let out a gust. "There you go again, assuming everything is about me being afraid."

"Fight or flight, isn't that the old adage? Most of us either fight against what we don't want or run from it, but in almost all cases, that comes out of fear." He took her hands in his. "I'm scared as hell that I am going to screw this up with you. That you're going to look at me and think, *What am I doing with this clown?*"

She laughed. "I could never think that. For one, you don't have a red nose."

That made him laugh, too. It eased the tension in the room and all this seriousness of his. "I'm pretty sure I can buy one, if that's your thing."

"I have more of a thing for firefighters." A teasing grin lit her face, her eyes. "Especially ones who know how to fish."

"Whoops. Guess that rules me out." He held tight to her hands and inhaled the sweet scent of her perfume. "Unless you're okay with a slightly damaged firefighter who is eager to learn how to fish?"

She smiled up at him, one of those hundreds of smiles that he could draw in his sleep. "That could work."

"Good." He swept her into his arms and kissed her. A long, sweet kiss that seemed to make time stop. She tasted of vanilla and chocolate, like a candy that he had been long denied. And when she curved against his body, it was as if the missing piece he'd been looking for was fitting right there against his heart. Damn, he was falling, and falling hard for Rachel.

"So, what do you say we start the future simply?" he said. "Come with me to Bobby and Della's anniversary party tomorrow night. It's a casual thing, just close family and friends at the Sea Shanty."

She pulled out of his arms and crossed the room. "Colton, I don't know if we should have a future. I mean, you're right, this is moving fast and I am afraid. Who wouldn't be? We barely know each other. What if it doesn't work out? Do you know how many weddings I've gone to, only to see the divorce announcement in the paper before the year is up?"

"But how many have you gone to and that didn't happen?" he asked. "Rachel, there are no guarantees in life. There's only taking a chance."

"I don't like taking chances. I like to know what is coming tomorrow, and the next day, and the day after that." She let out a breath. "It's why…it's why I stayed at the store instead of keeping my business going. Part of that was for my dad, yes, but part of it was because I was scared that I could fail."

"Me, too, Rachel. I'm just as scared as you. But I'm tired of letting that fear rule all my decisions. Life is short," he said softly. "I don't want to live another minute of it being afraid."

"I know that, and tell myself I feel the same way, but when it comes to actually moving past those fears…" She bit her lip. "Working for yourself means taking a risk every single day. For me, that was like jumping out of a building every day. It scared me, and when I had a chance to stop doing that…I took it. Now I'm looking at being able to go back to my business, and frankly I'm scared as hell."

"Scared of succeeding? Or scared of failure?"

She let out a breath. "Both. And now you want me to take a chance with my heart. That's…even more fragile. And even scarier."

"You can't know, Rachel, if this will work out between us or not, if you don't take that chance." He took her hands again and drew her closer. "So take that chance with me."

Rachel had made up an excuse to avoid answering Colton's question, and to get him out of her apartment. Okay, yeah, it was the coward's way out, but she just needed some room to breathe, to think. She could see everything she'd ever wanted—ever dreamed of—within reach, yet she hesitated on going after it? What the heck was wrong with her?

"You're an idiot," Melissa said later that night, while she wrangled her squirmy baby back into a seated position and tried to give her son a bottle. He batted it away. "And I mean that in the nicest way."

"Gee, thanks." Rachel picked up one of the tiny T-shirts in the basket of clean laundry beside the armchair and folded it. Melissa's house was a comfortable mess, the kind of place that said *home*, with toys on the floor and a box of Cheerios on the counter, and the kids playing a video game on the TV across the room. "What made you say yes when Jason proposed?"

"Between you and me? A really good bottle of Chardonnay. I was just a tad—" she lowered her voice "—*tipsy* when he proposed. The next morning I woke up with a hangover and a total panic attack."

"You did? You never told me that." Rachel kept on folding. There was something cathartic about watching the jumbled laundry become straight, even piles.

"I did, indeed. I was a mess for about twenty-four hours," Melissa said. "I was so sure Jason and I would end up—" she lowered her voice again "—d-i-v-o-r-c-e-d, like my parents. And there was no way I wanted to go through that."

"Then what made you change your mind?"

"A Post-it note." Melissa let out a little laugh. "Jason had left me a note on my car the next morning, on a Post-it note, and he said sometimes the best things came out of what seemed like the biggest mistakes. And he told me to look up the story of those little sticky notes."

"Really?"

Melissa held up a hand. "Cross my heart. So I did

it. And do you know that the guy who invented them was actually trying to mix up a batch of glue, when he failed, or so he thought, and made an adhesive that could be applied and reapplied. It took him a bit, but then he thought of putting that glue on a piece of paper, and voilà, the sticky note was born. He took a risk, and it worked out pretty darn well for him."

"You got married because of that?"

"Well, that and the fact that Jason has a hot body and can—" she glanced at her kids "—uh, make me... happy like it's an Olympic sport." Melissa winked.

Rachel laughed. "I'm pretty sure it's that last one that swayed you the most."

"Honestly? It was the note. I had turned him down when he first proposed, but that man kept coming back. He refused to give up. He told me that we were meant to be, and he was going to spend the rest of his life proving it."

And he had, given how happy Melissa seemed. Yes, they had their stresses with the kids and the mortgage and life in general, but Rachel couldn't remember a day when she hadn't seen Melissa smiling. Every time her friend spoke about her husband, it was with that special little smile, the one that said she'd entered an exclusive club.

"That firefighter is a genuinely nice guy," Melissa said. "And he's worth a hundred sticky notes, if you ask me."

"But is it the right time?" Rachel started folding faster, as if increasing the pile of T-shirts and leggings would make the rest of her worried mind fall into order, too. "I'm debating whether to relaunch my business. I have Ginny's wedding, if I want to take that on, but what if that takes too much of my time or it fails or—"

Melissa put a hand on top of Rachel's, halting the furious folding. "There's always going to be a but and a what-if," she said. "And as much as I love the fact that you are taking care of my laundry tonight, I think you need to quit worrying and start doing. Because I think your biggest problem—and I mean this in the nicest way…"

"What?" Rachel prompted.

"You don't believe in the very thing you are creating." Melissa gave Rachel a wry smile. "You have to believe in happily-ever-after to pull it off successfully. Both for others and for yourself."

"I do believe in…" Rachel paused. "Okay, maybe I don't. I mean, look at my parents. Married for almost thirty years, and I don't know if they were ever truly happy. The Barlows—everyone would call Bobby and Della the happiest couple in this town, yet they went through a period where Bobby had someone else."

"But he came back to Della and has made a wonderful family here. He made a mistake. That's all."

"How many happy couples do we know, Melissa? Even in my business, at least a third of them end up divorced."

"That's not your fault."

"No, but it doesn't exactly make me believe that a ring is any kind of guarantee."

"It isn't." Melissa shrugged. "That's the truth of it. No ring or piece of paper or vow in front of a priest is any guarantee that your life together will be happy or that your marriage will last. All you can do is take that leap, have faith and then work like hell—" she glanced at her kids "—I mean, heck, at keeping it together."

Faith. It was what Rachel had told Colton to have. What she had seen in Winona and Charles's story. And the one thing it seemed she lacked. So she went on folding shirts and leggings and pretending that she wasn't mostly afraid that she was going to miss out on something wonderful if she didn't take that leap.

Chapter Fifteen

Dinner with the Barlow family was, apparently, always an adventure. That was one thing Colton learned pretty quickly. The Sunday meal was held a little earlier than usual, due to the anniversary party scheduled for that evening, but that didn't matter. And with Jack, Luke, Mac *and* Colton all in the same house, the entire event was raucous and loud and really gave Colton a feel for what it must have been like to have grown up in a house with dozens of siblings.

He loved every minute of it. He had seconds of the lasagna, he ate dessert and he joked with his brothers as if they had always been together.

Jack and Colton offered to wash the dishes while Mac and Luke cleaned up the dining room, leaving Bobby and Della to get ready for their party. Meri had left early, along with Luke and Mac's fiancées, to finish decorating the Sea Shanty for the event.

Jack started the water running then glanced over his shoulder to see if his parents had left the room. "Did you think Dad and my mom seemed a little off tonight?"

Bobby had been distracted at dinner, and Della had barely talked to her husband. They'd each talked to the boys, but the easy camaraderie that he'd witnessed before with Bobby and Della wasn't there. "Yeah. But then again, I don't know them well enough to know what normal is."

"Luke and Mac said Dad's been kind of distant lately, and that they've hardly seen Mom." Jack shook his head. "What happened in the week I was gone?"

"Nothing that I know of," Colton said. "Except for… well, except for me showing up in town. I'm sure it's been tough on your mother to have me around, a constant reminder of what happened years ago."

"Yeah, that could be it, but I'm not so sure. I just hope…" Jack let out a breath, and started loading the dishes into the soapy water. "I hope they work it out. They've got more than three decades together."

"You talking about Dad and Mom?" Luke said, as he set a pile of dirty plates on the counter. "Whatever's up, neither one of them is talking about it. But I heard…"

"What?" Jack said when Luke didn't finish.

"I don't know if I should even say anything." Luke let out a long breath.

"If you don't, I'll have to use the sprayer on you." Jack brandished the black nozzle.

Luke feigned fear and put his hands up to protect his hair. "Oh, no, not that. Anything but the sprayer!"

Jack laughed and slid it back into place. "Okay, okay, your hairdo is safe with me, Elvis. What did you hear?"

The tease dropped from Luke's face and his blue eyes filled with worry. "Mom has been talking to George Wilcox, the Realtor. She even went to see a few properties this week."

If Colton could have packed up and left town right that second, he would have. This was all his fault—he never should have come to town and upset the apple cart. Now he'd taken a job in Stone Gap, which meant he'd be a constant reminder to Della of what Bobby had done three decades ago. If their marriage broke up because of his presence—

"Maybe I should skip the party tonight," he said to his brothers.

"No, don't do that," Jack said. "I'm sure whatever this is with my parents will blow over before then. They've had fights before, but they always resolve them."

"I hope you're right," Colton said. He picked up a dish and dried it, then replaced it in the cabinet. He'd come to Stone Gap to make a change in his own life, but it seemed everywhere he turned, he was causing changes in other people's lives. And not necessarily the kind they wanted.

Bobby stood in the Sea Shanty and looked at his friends and his kids and wondered if he shouldn't just send them all home. He was supposed to be celebrating his thirty-fifth wedding anniversary, but it felt more like a funeral of his marriage. Della had barely talked to him all weekend, and when they'd first arrived, she'd gone off to talk to the local Realtor.

Bobby wasn't a smart man, but he was no moron, either. He knew what it meant if Della was looking at real estate. Now he just needed to confront her on it, before this party got too far underway. The last thing he wanted to do was stand around for four hours, letting people congratulate him on a marriage that was over.

He found Della standing on the outdoor deck, looking out at the water. She looked stunning tonight, in a sequined navy blue dress that skimmed her knees. She'd put her hair up and little curls dusted along her neck. She had on a pair of dangly earrings that swayed a bit in the breeze. "You look beautiful, Della," he said when he came up beside her.

She turned and smiled at him. "Why, thank you, Robert. You look dashing yourself. Exactly the same as the day we got married."

"Well, maybe a little more of me than the day we got married." He patted his belly beneath the button-down shirt and tie that felt more like a boa constrictor on his neck. But ties made Della happy, so he'd worn one without complaint.

"That's fine," she said. "There's more of you to love."

"Is there?" He screwed up his courage and let out a breath. "I saw you talking to George. I know you're hiding something from me and if you're leaving me,

Della, then just tell me straight out so we don't go through this sham—"

"I bought a house."

Bobby's heart shattered. He could have driven a samurai sword through his chest and it would have hurt less. "A...a house? When?"

"Yesterday. Don't worry, I didn't use our retirement savings. I used that money my mother left me when she died. I've had it in that CD for years, and it was just enough to buy the Richardson house."

The Richardson house? That dilapidated piece of crap about ready to cave in? "Wait. The one that Gareth guy owned? The one that's supposed to be haunted?"

"The very one." She gave him a grin, as pleased as the Cheshire cat.

"Why would you buy that place?"

"Because nothing does better marketing for a bed-and-breakfast in the South than a haunted house once owned by a suspected murderer. I know the place is a mess, but with Savannah's keen eye for restoration and Jack's amazing building skills we should be able—"

"Wait. Did you say bed-and-breakfast?" Bobby wondered if maybe he should get his hearing checked, because every word that came out of Della's mouth made little sense to him. "Why would you care about a B&B?"

"Because that's what I'm going to do," she said, and her Cheshire cat grin widened. "I'm going to renovate that house and run it as a B&B. I love cooking, I love keeping a house and I absolutely love company."

"And..." He took in a deep breath then pushed it out with the next words. "What about us?"

"What about us?" She looked at him, and then her eyes softened and her smile widened. "Oh, Robert Barlow, you big fool. You don't think you can get rid of me that easily, do you? I've been with you thirty-five years. I've barely got you broken in. I'm not going anywhere. Nowhere at all."

He laughed, a big whoop of a laugh that scared a nearby seagull and seemed to echo across the ocean. Then he took the love of his life into his arms and gave her a long, hot, deep kiss.

"My, my, Robert," Della said, a sweet red flush in her cheeks, "you still do surprise me."

"And you, my dear wife, still surprise me." He brushed a tendril of hair off her forehead then cupped her cheek. "Thank you for the best thirty-five years of my life. I can't wait for the next thirty-five."

She leaned her head against his shoulder and fit into the place where she had always been happiest, right in Bobby's arms. "I can't, either. But I can promise you one thing. They're going to be an adventure."

"They will indeed," Bobby whispered, then kissed his wife again, softly, sweetly and with a whole lot of gratitude in his heart.

The Sea Shanty was filled to the brim by the time Rachel arrived at the party. She was late, but only because she had changed her dress three times, then at the last minute invited her father along for moral support.

"You look beautiful," her father said. He gave his daughter's arm a pat. "Your mother would be so proud."

"Oh, thank you, Dad." Rachel pressed a kiss to her

father's cheek then headed into the dining room. She saw Della and Bobby sitting at the head table set up by the window, flanked by their sons and their wives and fiancées. An empty seat sat to the left of Colton.

When she entered the room, he looked up and smiled at her. Even from here, all the way across the restaurant, a simple smile from him sent a flutter through her heart. She wanted to close that distance and leap into his arms and forget every silly fear she'd ever had.

There was a band on the stage and they launched into a version of "At Last." Bobby got to his feet and put out his hand to his wife. Della blushed then took his hand and went with him to the dance floor.

Rachel watched them, two people still happy together after three and a half decades of marriage, still laughing, still blushing when they flirted. They spun around the dance floor, a testament to taking that leap and making it work.

"Shall we dance?"

Colton's warm voice in her ear slid through her like butter. She could feel a blush filling her own face, and for a brief moment wondered if thirty-five years from now, that would be them in the middle of the dance floor.

"I thought you'd never ask," she said, then slipped into his arms. She fit perfectly against him, and they moved as if they'd been made for dancing together. As they waltzed past Bobby and Della, Della gave Rachel and Colton a smile.

"You two make a wonderful couple," Della said.

"I keep trying to tell her that," Colton said to Della, then he turned back to Rachel. "When are you going to believe me?"

She drew in a deep breath. Either she took this risk or she risked something even bigger—losing this incredible man. "How about tonight?" she said.

"Really?" A wide grin filled his face. "What changed your mind?"

"It was a desk." Rachel swayed with Colton to the right, their movements easy and fluid with the music. She could see the confusion in his face, and that made her happy that he didn't realize how one simple thing had changed everything. "On the way over here, I stopped by the store with my dad to see what you guys had done this morning. He wanted to see if the shop would be ready to open on Monday and it is. We need to wait on some inventory, of course, but there's enough to get started back up again. So thank you for all your hard work and turning that around so fast."

"That was my intention," Colton said. "I know business has been slow and I didn't want him to lose too much business because of being closed down for too long."

Yet another vote in the thoughtful and considerate column for Colton Barlow, she thought.

"Then I go into the break room," Rachel went on, "and I see the ice-maker line and the new refrigerator, and the new doorway all complete, and then I see—" even now, thinking about it made her smile, heck, even choked her up a little "—a desk in the corner. A small one, with a little set of bookshelves above it. And a small sign over the top, carved out of a piece of wood. With my name on it, and the words Wedding Planner after it. You wouldn't know of a certain firefighter responsible for that desk and that sign, would you?"

He shrugged, and she swore she saw a blush in his cheeks. "I know it's going to be hard for you to leave your dad. And that you probably want to take things slow with your business and easing him back into work. So I set up a little space for you in the back of the shop, so you can run your business and be close to him if he needs you."

She had told herself she wouldn't cry today, but tears welled in her eyes all the same. Colton had truly thought of everything, and she knew she could never thank him enough. "How do you know me so well, so quickly, Colton Barlow?"

"I think because we're two of a kind." He stopped dancing with her and reached up to cup her jaw and meet her gaze. "We both are so committed to taking care of the people around us that we forget about ourselves. I wanted you to be able to have everything you wanted, Rachel, whether or not you were with me."

That was the moment when Rachel fell in love with Colton. When she'd seen that desk and realized that he only wanted what was best for her, what would make her happy. Even if he wasn't part of that picture. "You are an incredible man," she said.

"Only because I'm in love with an incredible woman." He traced her lips with his thumb, and she ached to kiss him, to never stop kissing him. "I know it's crazy, Rachel, but I am in love with you. I have loved you since that first day of the twenty-five-cent tour when you showed me that old house and you were so sentimental and sweet and—"

She rose on her toes and kissed him. To heck with the crowd dancing around the two fools standing still in the middle of the floor. "I love you, too," she said. Because she couldn't wait another second to say the words.

The smile on his face beamed as bright as the sun. "You know this is crazy, right?"

"It is, indeed. It's like the kind of fairy tales I create for my brides. But sometimes," she said softly, "sometimes, those fairy tales end in happily-ever-after."

Colton looked over at Della and Bobby, dancing to celebrate more than three decades of marriage. They were joined by Jack and Meri, then Luke and Peyton and finally Mac and Savannah. The dance floor was filled with people in love, people who had taken that risk and found something worth having on the other side.

"They do, indeed," he said, then he took Rachel into his arms and together, they joined the dance.

* * * * *

MILLS & BOON
MEDICAL
Pulse-Racing Passion

Set your pulse racing with dedicated, delectable doctors in the high-pressure world of medicine, where emotions run high and passion, comfort and love are the best medicine.

Eight Medical stories published every month, find them a

millsandboon.co.uk

LET'S TALK
Romance

For exclusive extracts, competitions
and special offers, find us online: